T0366191

ENTER, KNIGHT ⚔ HEL'S STORM

A Duology by

K.A.Keith

HEL'S STORM

K. A. KEITH

iUniverse

HEL'S STORM

iUniverse books may be ordered through booksellers or by contacting:

iUniverse
1663 Liberty Drive
Bloomington, IN 47403
www.iuniverse.com
1-800-Authors (1-800-288-4677)

ISBN: 978-1-4917-8129-6 (sc)
ISBN: 978-1-4917-8130-2 (e)

Library of Congress Control Number: 2016910802

Print information available on the last page.

iUniverse rev. date: 9/26/2016

Author's Page

What has defined the hero? What defines the epic?

Hero sagas from the cradle of civilization transmuted themselves in scene and setting, yet their essence endures. One might hear in any heroic adventure the echoes of Gilgamesh, Odysseus and Beowulf, Roland, Orlando and Siegfried.

Joseph Campbell defines the epic protagonist as one who departs the safety of his or her own village to enter the mystic, becoming hero through personal evolution and successful return to one's countrymen with the sacred fire. Certainly Tolkien's extended works and L'Amour's *Walking Drum* speak to this. Zelazny's *Nine Princes in Amber* and Wolfe's *Wizard Knight* are yearly rereads for me, each as pleasurable as the last.

As to inspiration in terms of style; *Enter, Knight* and *Hel's Storm* would not be the stories they are without Robert E. Howard of Texas, who spun many more yarns than *Conan* in his brief life. Fantasy, to me, is an unlimited palette for those traits worthy of the pen: nobility and sacrifice; lust and hatred and love; the pathos of the human condition; and our ultimate naked departure from this world.

And finally, *What is an adventure tale without you, seeker of the divine fire?* I am humble in your presence. My eternal gratitude for those of you who have read *Enter, Knight* and now continue our tale to its conclusion in *Hel's Storm*.

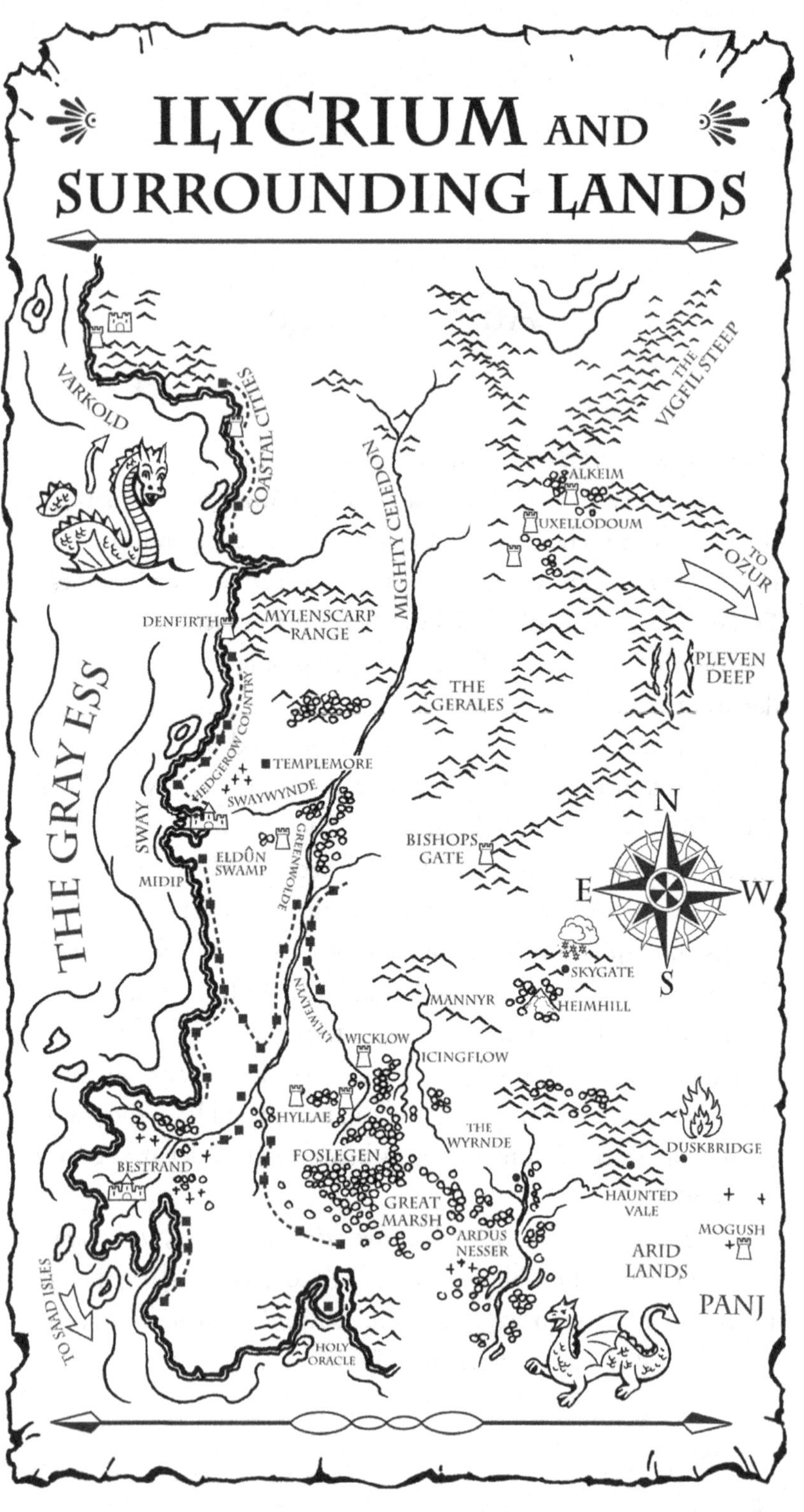
ILYCRIUM AND SURROUNDING LANDS
VARKOLD
COASTAL CITIES
MIGHTY CELEDON
THE VIGFIL STEEP
ALKEIM
UXELLODOUM
TO OZUR
DENFIRTH
MYLENSCARP RANGE
PLEVEN DEEP
THE GERALES
THE GRAY ESS
HEDGEROW COUNTRY
TEMPLEMORE
SWAYWYNDE
SWAY
GREENWOLDE
BISHOPS GATE
N
E
W
S
ELDÛN SWAMP
MIDIP
SKYGATE
LYLWELYAN
MANNYR
HEIMHILL
WICKLOW
ICINGFLOW
HYLLAE
THE WYRNDE
FOSLEGEN
DUSKBRIDGE
BESTRAND
GREAT MARSH
HAUNTED VALE
ARDUS NESSER
MOGUSH
ARID LANDS
TO SMAD ISLES
PANJ
HOLY ORACLE

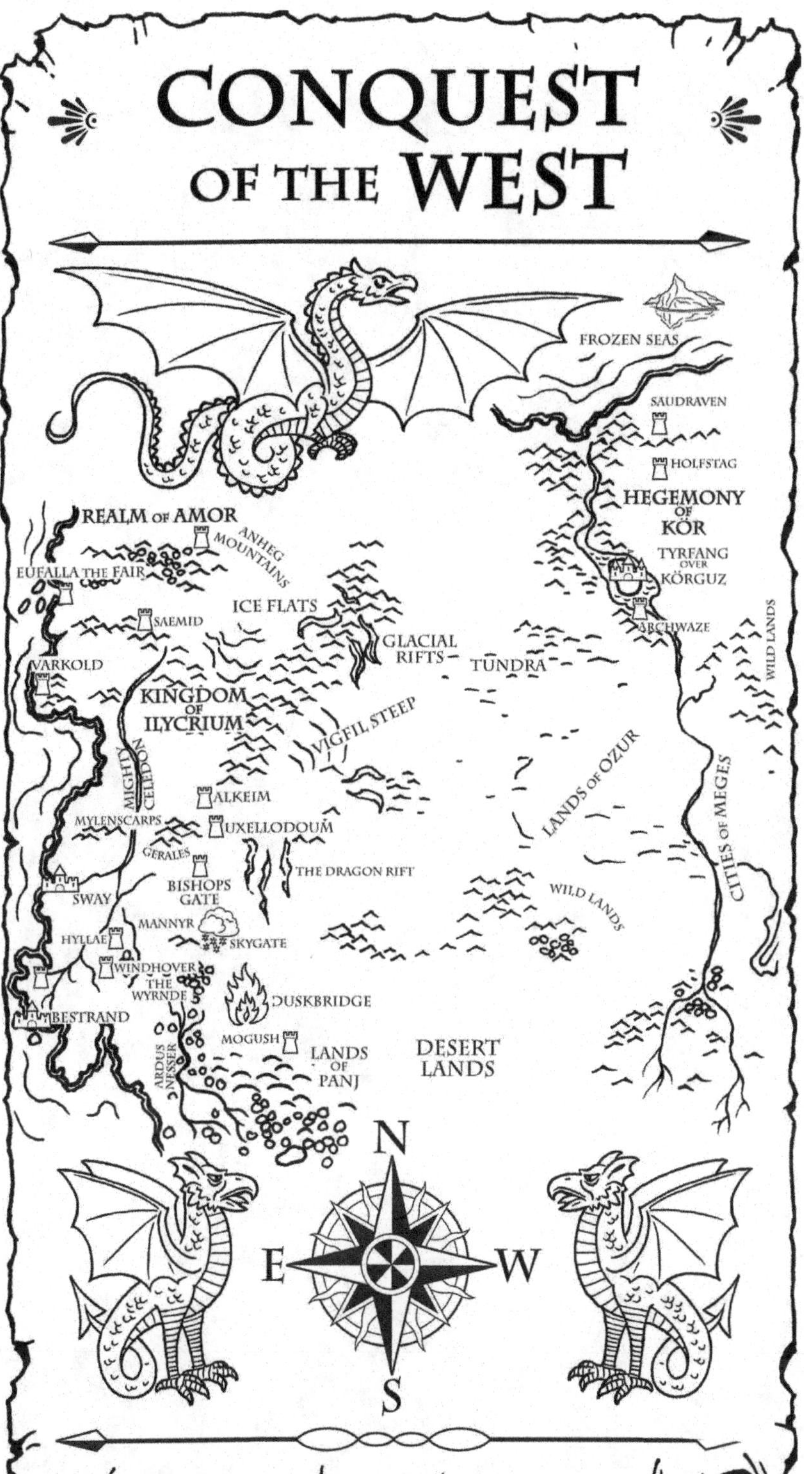

CONQUEST OF THE WEST
FROZEN SEAS
SAUDRAVEN
HOLFSTAG
HEGEMONY OF KÖR
TYRFANG OVER KÖRGUZ
ARCHWAZE
WILD LANDS
REALM OF AMOR
ANHEG MOUNTAINS
EUFALLA THE FAIR
ICE FLATS
SAEMID
GLACIAL RIFTS
TUNDRA
VARKOLD
KINGDOM OF ILYCRIUM
VIGFIL STEEP
MIGHTY CELEDON
LANDS OF OZUR
CITIES OF MEGES
ALKEIM
MYLENSCARPS
UXELLODOUM
GERALES
THE DRAGON RIFT
BISHOPS GATE
SWAY
WILD LANDS
MANNYR
HYLLAE
SKYGATE
WINDHOVER
THE WYRNDE
DUSKBRIDGE
BESTRAND
ARDUS NESSER
MOGUSH
LANDS OF PANJ
DESERT LANDS
N
E
W
S

Dramatis Personae

Adestes Malgrim, known as **Malesh**. He shares the Star Burn with Apieron.

Apieron Farsinger, son of Xistus, is a veteran, husband, and father of three small children. He is also the secret vessel of the Star Burn.

Eirec is jarl of Amber Hall; no lowlander is his better.

Gault Candor is eighteen when his father, King Belagund of Ilycrium, is slain by a flying imp of Kör.

Gilead Galdarion, a gold elf warrior-mage. He awaits Kör's Malgrind.

Henlee, the black dwarf, is Apieron's childhood guardian. He wields a fearsome maul and rides the irascible **Bump**.

Isolde, warrior-priestess of Gray-Eyed Wisdom. She is betrothed to Xephard.

Rudolph Mellor, who is called Jamello, a rakish troubadour of sunny Bestrand.

Tallux, the emerald-eyed archer, has kin amongst the wood elves of the Greenwolde. His war dog is **Sut**.

Xephard Brighthelm is Wisdom's perfect warrior.

To Callie

She Who Listened

Farsinger: "Whither have you gone, proud son of the morning? Thee I did love."
Brighthelm: "How can I have slain the demon when I hath already died? You shall see …"

Book I

It being the thirtieth year of the second century since Betelgeuse Candor was reckoned overlord of the Wgend Race, the ninety-third year since Baemond first marked white horses amongst the marsh green, Ilycrium's coast on the gray Ess.

And the song of mighty kings was writ upon the earth, whilst 'neath the slumbering crust, Leviathan stirred.

Chapter 1

Windhover

Duner could not sleep. How hot and oppressive the night was! No breeze stirred the window hangings of his room. With a groan for his creaking joints, he swung onto the floor, pausing there to enjoy the feel of the cool planks on the soles of his feet, then flung wide the shutters. From the aperture, he could see a goodly portion of the bailey and its sentries at the wall and before the keep. All was quiet.

A hunter's moon was newly risen over Foslegen. Orange and huge behind forest mists, it cast a fitful light upon the uppermost floor of the tower where his mistress and the children slept. In the gibbous illumination, the flat face of the donjon, with its blackened windows and arched doorway, possessed the aspect of a yellowed skull, empty and leering.

Muttering a curse for the sleepless habits of old men, Duner drew on tunic and jerkin, reflexively fastening belt and scabbard. He strode across the nighted yard to find the door wardens alert. They saluted crisply as he pushed his way into the main hall. The fires of the great hearth were banked low, yielding the barest flicker of winking coals in ashes. His lord, Apieron, had accumulated much in his travels; the dressed stone walls and cold flags of Windhover were graced with many bright hangings and strewn rugs. And Melónie, Apieron's wife and gentle soul, had not been idle these six years. Rainbow-plumed pheasants and peacocks strutted in verdant tapestried landscapes where lithe Eastern warriors leapt proud stallions over azure streams to war or hunt. Apieron's trophies kept station amongst silks and weavings, silver-chased mail and well-forged weapons proclaiming the noble traditions of the West. Ilycrium's white horse over mountain and sea was there, as was a shield bossed with the horse and field vert of the King's Scouts. Above all hung the speaker's stave on field of blue, the heraldry of Apieron's ancestral house. Duner, castellan of Windhover, knew it all without looking, nor did he take up torch or lamp, for he could find his way to every room of castle Windhover with eyes closed.

Bypassing passageways that led to kitchens and servants' mess, Duner came to a landing with steps leading up and down. He merely glanced at the flags leading to cooler depths and instead took his way around two bends of the ascending stairwell onto the second floor, acknowledging the quietude of the landing with an appreciative grunt as he approached the man who stood warden at the base of the final flight to Apieron's private apartments. The presence of a guard in this place was a new post, initiated by Duner himself on the eve of his lord's departure. The man's face was visible in the moonlight of a narrow loophole. Duner felt some of the tension melt from him at the reassuring sight of a trusted man.

"Well, Gurden, how like you your duty?"

The man spoke seriously, "It agrees with me, Commander. Ever my father advised me to seek a job close by food, drink, and women."

Duner's weathered face cracked into a smile. The man Gurden was a known teetotaler. Duner nodded, took his way upward, and tried to walk on his toes, thus quieting his progress. This was in order not to startle his mistress or the children, he told himself, although his hand grasped the hilt of his sword. Was that a shuffling step he heard? Unmistakably, there came the low laugh of a woman.

Gaining the final landing, Duner peered around a corner into the hallway that led to Melónie's apartments and the children's bower. A woman of lustrous midnight hair and a sliding gait entered the children's room. He breathed a sigh of relief, for it was merely the refugee girl, placed under the protection of Windhover by the graces of Melónie. Sooth, but two days past, gate sentries had bowed low to the beauty, so similar in stature and coloring to the lady Melónie was she they thought her some close kindred of their mistress come to visit.

Perhaps the woman had escaped from reavers on the long road, for her garments were threadbare and she, a highborn woman, alone on the wild roads. Generous welcome Melónie had given her when hopeful words of her lord's return were spoken. Men cheered loud at the mention of Apieron's name, banging spears on shields until Duner busked them forth so that his lady might receive her guest with good grace, and learn in private aught she could of her lord's state.

But what did she *here*? Gurden had not indicated that any had passed on his watch, and Melónie had nursemaids enough. Of long custom, Duner would not think to interfere with a woman's attendance on the children, yet something about her sleek stride struck him wrong. Similar in stature to his lady perhaps, but not of countenance. The wondrous, guileless visage of his lady—no living woman could match. Chastening himself for being a meddlesome old gam, he crept behind in stealth. Squinting in the darkness outside the children's suite, he heard only the gentle, noisy breathing that sleeping children make. He could smell them, clean in bedclothes that smelled faintly of lavender. A stray shaft of light broke from a casement to illuminate all. The woman was there, leaning over the cribs, her lust-filled face leering, and from her sharp-toothed mouth protruded a vermillion tongue.

With a shout, Duner bounded into the room, drawing his sword. She wheeled instantly, talons outstretched as she hissed, her hair writhing like living snakes.

"She witch!" he bellowed.

The babes woke and filled the air with a thin wailing. Behind him, from the end of the hallway, resounded a crash. Mistress Melónie! The succubus laughed, marking well the indecision on his face.

In that instant, Duner made the choice that would haunt him to his mortal end. With an inarticulate cry, he launched his blade sideways at her. She slid back, easily avoiding the blow. He bull rushed, scattering the cribs to interpose himself between the terrified children and the demoness. She proved the quicker. With a lightning-like swipe, she laid open his chest, rending as naught his jerkin of boiled hide. Duner winced against the searing pain as her second hand found his face, shredding the cheek and the skin about his eye. Inhumanly fast, she struck blows he could not follow.

A torrent of blood closed his eye as he thrust wildly and pushed through her blows. Squinting and blinking, Duner saw her give back to the wall against a wooden frame where she mouthed a spell with her full, crimson lips. The sound of it made his muscles itch and crawl. Duner realized he must act decisively or the children were lost, yet she had proved she could evade him long enough to complete whatever devilry she planned.

He made as if to swipe again, but shifted to an underhand grip at the peak of momentum and loosed his blade. It sailed like a javelin and pierced her midriff, pinning her to the lattice. A mindless shriek shattered the air, stealing every other sound. Duner stood horrified to see the werewoman melt to nothingness, leaving only an acrid stench. Of his blade, there was no evidence.

"Bitch of hell!"

Duner staggered, then swept aside a spray of sweat and blood to bind a strip of bed linen around his tattered face. He soothed the children in hushed tones and gathered them to his breast. Stepping cautiously into the corridor, he was greeted by silence. Gurden was there, neck broken. An unnatural chill wafted from Apieron and Melónie's suites, but he hastened from it, stifling his frustrated rage. He tore open the door of a service stairwell to the basement. Stumbling in darkness, he clutched his precious burdens before finding the lowest level. He set the children gently aside and, after drawing out the steel crossbar, placed his key in a rusted lock. The metal door protested loudly and stuck at a mere foot's aperture. Retrieving the children, he pushed past festooning vines. Above him rose startled yells and the clash of gathering conflict from the bailey.

Duner gripped the children, crouching beneath a stone shoulder to enter Melónie's garden, hot tears mingling with oozing blood from his eye as he made for the sheltering darkness of a stream bank grove and the hidden culvert beyond to Foslegen. He prayed that none of the marauders mark him. Hunching over his burdens, he shuffled with all the speed he dared beyond the outer ramparts. Thoughts of leading his force at arms against the attackers were now fled before weightier concerns in his arms. When he could spare the breath, he attempted gruff soothings for the puling infants and passed into nighted woods, the sound of the raid growing faint behind him, and still he pressed hard into forest deeps where the trees grew wild and hung the moon on moss-crooked branches. This was the place.

Duner set the children down and took a steadying breath. "So," he said, facing the shadowed figure who loomed over him. "I only half-believed the rumors that you were real, and I more than most."

It rumbled, that voice deep as a well. "Then, come."

Adestes Malgrim faced the Gorgon of Hel. "Black Mouth, who art thou?"

The sepulchral answer rang hollow, "I am nothing."

"What is thy desire?"

"To feed."

Adestes grew impatient; the dark angel had fed enough. He waved the starfall blade, and the dragon in his ring shimmered down its length. "Thou hast consumed a world in thy time."

The Gorgon's shadow diminished. By the power of the ring Fafnir, Adestes could see Ulfelion's features whensoever he wished, and the vampire's mien was not pleased. It raised a pallid hand. Adestes tensed. A pack of hounds, residents of Windhover, tore into a shaggy wereman not ten paces from the twain. The combatants went down in a snapping flurry. Ulfelion's hand waved, and they fell into death's still.

A third figure materialized. It was a woman, a cross-hilted sword protruding from her breast. She fell to Ulfelion's feet. "Dread Master, remove this steel. It pains me!"

The seductress's face would have melted ice. Ulfelion did not stir. "Knowest thou, fair fool, what magic might had been wrought from the lives of the infants?"

The woman's stricken face twisted into an agonized plea. Adestes spoke, "No time now to dally with sucklings."

"There is the mother," moaned the woman.

"Her body I will take as trophy," added Adestes.

"That were dangerous … twice the fool," spake Ulfelion. "Weak slaves are the dead; thy rash blade hast cost me much."

She wheedled, "Mayhap a hunt for the children?"

"Silence, bitch!" Ulfelion's voice sounded scarcely above a

whisper, yet the force of it blew her wraps and hair in a frigid gust. She recoiled, clutching the impaling sword. The lich mage turned from her to front Adestes, but a faint dawn glow blurred the man's features, and Adestes' ring cast a painful, aureate pattern onto the starfall blade, which crawled with anticipation. As usual, the man's mind was closed to intrusion.

"Idiots," hissed Ulfelion, and was gone.

Adestes regarded Aetterne. As soon as the necromancer departed, her countenance flowed. Those tresses that remained burned and cropped grew long and indigo. Her features darkened as the last of her garments ripped free, her frame expanding to near the size of the man, buxom of chest and swollen at the hips. Her talons ripped forth the sword and hurled it aside. "By Aurgelmir, I hated wearing that pathetic form." Her voice was maddingly feminine yet rang with power and suppressed violence. "How I longed to plunge my claws into that insipid ranger, whose desme this was, yet I deem we have dealt him the greater wound. Why do you smile, Malesh?"

Adestes replied harshly, but his voice held no threat. "Do not speak such names in this place."

"Do not blunt my question, mortal man! Why dost thou smile when your schemes rob Ulfelion of many magics?"

"That one has powers enough." Adestes extended a gauntleted hand to her. "My dear Sin, gather for me our trophy."

Aetterne pressed her rounded form against his cuirass. The rainbow-hewed helstones felt cool on her hot skin, and her red tongue licked greedily as talons caressed the muscled relief in the mold of his chest and belly plate. "And when, most noble Malesh, are you going to reveal some of *your* power?"

"Perhaps later," laughed Adestes. "First, your chores …"

The fighting was mostly subsided. Coarse laughing shouts of the raiders were on occasion punctuated by sounds of sporadic conflict. Nine parts Windhover's garrison had died in the first devastating rush, yet here and there an enraged parent or brave youth would take up mattock, hunting spear or shovel to defend kin and hearth with lonely valor against the bestial raiders, then the attackers would make sport and bait their victims with great cruelty, to an inevitable outcome.

Buthard sat his horse in silence. Half a hundred men, his personal guard, were ranked behind him. The breath of their horses misted on the cool predawn. Some stirred, eager to cut into the raiders, though their company was but a tenth the number of attackers. However, the majority of the armsmen waited stolidly, wise to their lord's will.

"And if his little leman lives?"

"My good Dolon, we are come upon a great tragedy for Ser Apieron. I am quite certain that none of his family will be discovered alive."

"And this?" The lieutenant proffered a parchment, its elaborate tracery and official wax-stamped ribbons making legal the revocation of Windhover from Apieron Farsinger.

Buthard took it. It was heavy in his hand. Beyond a shallow fosse stood Windhover on high ground. The fight was over, and strange figures loped off to seek the murks of Foslegen, and onto whatever destiny Hel dealt them. Only the burning remained to play like a fiery beast amidst white stones.

Buthard let fall the scroll. "It has been delivered."

Chapter 2

Lampus at Hyllae, Valley of Wisdom

Rudolph Mellor sat on a carved bench outside the chamber where Apieron lay. For the thousandth time, he drew forth one of his new daggers to study its edge and feel its balance, slowly resheathing it, then ripping it free to toss it spinning near the ceiling, only to deftly catch and replace the weapon. He moved to the next.

That a temple of priest-warriors housed a fine armory had not surprised him. That Isander led him to a hidden stair and bade him enter a wide vault had elicited a cocked eyebrow. Jamello had followed Isander's outstretched hand, an expression of bored amusement on his face, hoping at best to find a studded belt or perhaps a small buckler to suit him. Isander laughed aloud when the jaded thief gaped, astonishment writ on the handsome, roguish face. Weapons and armor of every type that he knew, and many he did not, lined the walls in wooden brackets or sat on tables for display.

Colored ceramic breastplates stood next to jointed suits of finest steel. Nearly every sort of weapon that might be borne in combat was represented, all quite serviceable. The faintly sweet odor of preserving oils filled the room. Even thus, none of these finely crafted items elicited true greed in the worldly thief's eyes, until they lit on a leathern bracer of ten throwing daggers.

Tiny griffins amongst flowering trees and pegasi soaring through sun-rayed clouds were cut onto the ebony surface of the bracer. After a smug nod from Isander, Jamello grasped a silver-wired grip beneath a pommel capstone that appeared to be a beryl of sea-tint green. Jamello held his breath as he drew the blade, expecting a disappointing tarnish or poor balance to mar his find; instead, the steel glided from its sheath like a sinuous serpent, deadly and beautiful.

Isander pointed with sword tip to an iron cap such as worn by the infantry of Kör. Of thick metal, the bowl was flanged on all sides and slung low as sallet to cover most of the wearer's ears and upper neck. A silver streak marked the dagger's path from Jamello's hand as it screeched into its target. Paladin and thief blinked. The dagger was embedded to the hilt, the heavy helm scorched and cracked.

Isander laughed and tossed the helmet to Jamello who caught it and drew forth the blade. Its seven inches of gleaming perfection revealed not the slightest burr whilst the fifteen-pound helm looked as if it was struck by a wizard's bolt.

"Keep the daggers, thief, lest the Matron punish you tomorrow for returning to steal them in the night." With a booming laugh, the warrior-priest had stomped off, leaving Jamello to carefully shut the door behind him. There was no lock.

""What do you here?" accused Isolde. She approached Jamello on his bench before the cell wherein lay Apieron, her eyes narrowing with suspicion as she regarded the thief and a rather familiar brace of daggers. To her irritation, he did not rise as would a proper gentleman.

"Where else have I to go?"

A light of understanding came into her eyes. She nodded to the darkened entry. "You watch over him. Well done. I will see to him now."

Isolde found her way barred. The thief stood. Similar in height and stature, they regarded each other eye to eye. "He needs his rest," said Jamello firmly.

"Who then better to tend him than a priestess of Wisdom? You may leave."

Jamello faced her a long moment, and at length performed a bow so elaborate that it fairly dripped with polite discourtesy. Not used to such effrontery, Isolde pushed past through beaded hangings into the cell beyond. From a single embrasure, a square of light revealed the man on the cot; a sheet was drawn to his chest. The room's other furnishing was a stand that bore a pitcher of water and a single clay cup. Isolde squatted beside the low bed.

She studied Apieron closely. No longer pale with malnutrition and loss of blood, nonetheless his face was cut with lines of age and weariness of spirit, so different from the gentle man of song she had known.

Apieron's lids snapped open, full alert. Her blue eyes sought his, which remained fixed on the ceiling, as if in waking, the sights he beheld were no different than those of his dreams. With a trembling hand she touched his bandaged chest and shoulder, and bearded face to fall away. He did not blink.

"How did he die?" she whispered.

Apieron continued to stare upward. What strange vistas he beheld Isolde tried to imagine. Were she possessed of a higher knowledge, she would attempt to walk within the mind of the man before her, so desperate was she to know what had befallen her love.

Xephard. Bright Helm! To see what he had seen, to feel what he had felt. Gladly would she know any anguish, even unto death. If only it was *his* anguish.

Isolde made to speak, but her voice crumpled in on itself under the weight of grief she carried, and from nowhere, tears filled her eyes. Her hair brushed Apieron's swathing and bared breast, and a sob escaped her lips.

With his wounded arm, Apieron gathered her. Isolde felt the strength leave her limbs. Surrendering, she curled into him and laid her head upon his bosom. The steady rhythm of his heart comforted her. "Forgive me … not much of a warrior-priestess."

"He died," said Apieron, "defending us."

Isolde burst into tears anew. Spasms of anguish racked her frame, and Apieron's brown arm held her until she was through. By the time she gathered herself, he was asleep. She remained where she was.

"Goddess, see how I am weak! And take from the man I sought to heal."

For an hour, she remained thus. At times, Apieron's breath would falter, and his face twist in pain. She rose, made a gentle motion of her hands over Apieron's broad chest, and touched his brow, evoking a tiny sip from the wellspring of the goddess.

Apieron's breathing eased, and his long frame relaxed deep into the bed. Isolde searched his careworn face one last time. She departed in silence.

Days passed. Cynthia lied, "You look well."

Apieron's face was dimly lit in the patterned light of a bronze censer, yet he appeared nigh ten years older than when the five companions had departed Hyllae that fair spring morning a mere half-year gone. "I've drawn the poisons of the Hel plane from your body as well as those of your companions." Apieron's only response was a nod of acknowledgment.

"The dwarf is nearly fit, and growls like a caged badger when my acolytes seek to tend his wounds. Tough as a mountain root is that one, and as flexible of mind." Cynthia chuckled. "And the elf possesses the evergreen vitality of his people; soon he and the dwarf will depart, perhaps with Rudolph Mellor. They seek word of their peoples."

Apieron's posture revealed nothing as he sat facing the Donna, chair to chair. To her, he seemed a brooding force, veiled in shadows. The sun had passed the westward wall of the compound, leaving Apieron's cell cool and quiescent, seemingly isolated from the ordinary bustle of the Lampus. Thus she had commanded the high-back chairs brought and the lamp kindled here, away from the ears and eyes that always seemed to orbit her personal suites.

"On second thought, your young friend, Jamello of Bestrand, will certainly join them, so soon he tires of my hospitality." Her laugh was dry as lake reeds rustling in winter. "No doubt whatever fate befalls him were better than the ignoble life he led in the sewers of Bestrand. His wounds were least, his scars he bears lightly. Too lightly, I fear."

Again the deliberate nod. "For the cure of my friends, I thank you, Perpetua."

The lines of humor fled her eyes, which glinted like those of a hunting falcon, missing little. "And what of you, quickest of body to mend, if one accounts the hurts you bore. Who are you, Apieron Farsinger?"

"Donna?"

The old woman's gaze narrowed as if trying to pierce the shell of his body into the spirit within. She held this pose a long moment, then visibly relaxed. "Whilst you lay in the fever of your wounds, something befell. I took upon myself the task of your healing, for the shoulder had suparated into your very chest. Its poison whelming the defenses of thy body while the loss of blood (and hope!) took you to the very door of the nether realm. As I searched deep for an untainted scrap to receive the power of the goddess, something recoiled at my touch … then, as if a vessel were broached, it surged outward, repairing thy form as it went. Bright it was! Verily the noonday sun descended into the wards of healing. It burned me."

Blinking, Cynthia passed a trembling hand before her eyes, and she motioned to him. Apieron filled the clay cup and passed it to her. When she had drunk the water within, she continued, "Indeed, had I not been in this, my place, warded by the powers of the goddess, and seconded by those of the faithful, I doubt we could have contained it. What might have befallen, I cannot say."

Flights of emotion flickered across Apieron's face as if the flipped pages of a book. Well the Donna read them, discerning much of the nature of a man whose secret, seemingly a blessing, now seemed a curse. To live when those who loved him died, and worse, because of that same love.

Cynthia handed the cup back to Apieron. He gathered it clumsily in two hands. She changed tack. "Here we have won a small victory. Some five hundreds brigands and despoiling creatures were destroyed, yet we have not fighting strength to defend our own vale should but one of Kör's Snakes wend hither. Our mounted company remained to await the return of Xephard. Thus, when the wild men came—possibly many of the same who reaved Windhover, they found our reception most bitter." Apieron's hands shook on his knees, and a grim twist took the corner of his lip, but his silence held. "Since your arrival, I have pondered muchly where to send them. How they chafe for war!

They rail against me in their thoughts but speak them not." She chuckled again.

Apieron again nodded. Cynthia was pleased his interest held. "And why not? What good to keep order in one remote valley when the kingdom itself reels before the onslaught of the Dream Throne? Yet a lack of knowing stays my hand. What if other forces align against us? Each night, the earth groans in torment, and the Oracle at Land's End has fallen silent, or hast fled." Cynthia stared intensely at him, seeking to plumb the depths of his thinking. In yellows and reds, the fenestrated light of the censer glinted on the mirror-gray surface of his eyes.

"Tell me now, young Apieron, what you alone can say. What power rouses to our doom from beyond the Duskbridge?"

The sound that came from Apieron's lips astonished even Perpetua, confident in her ancient wisdom. He laughed long and low. "You who dispatched us to the land of death, question what waits therein?" Shadows played across his face, alternating dark and light, and the perfumes of the censer became the stench of sulfur. "Aye, mistress, a death was there, one for Xephard and one for traitorous Turpin. Giliad fell there. And one found noble Sarc, who stood alone whilst we fled." The old woman's hands clenched her chair bloodlessly, her lips pressed thin.

"Yea, noble Donna, onto me a death also came in the black land, whispering without cease. It knew the very secrets of my soul." The cup shattered in his hands, its shards clattering to the floor. The scrape of a booted foot sounded in the hallway beyond the hangings. Cynthia's brow furrowed a moment in thought. The noise receded.

"Then Donna, it sent 'gainst us a warrior. Tall and fey he was, one that but for happenstance and garb, was me." Apieron touched his breast. "Is me," he corrected. "He it was and a phantom of unlife that slew us."

Cynthia shook her head. "Nay, Apieron—"

"When he saw we contrived to escape, it was again he who came to Windhover. What knew or cared he for their names? Melónie dark-eyed, Setie and Ilacus, and Sujita, my Jilly," Apieron's voice choked. "They were a defenseless part of me, like an exposed leg whose greave has fallen free."

Apieron's left arm fell lifeless to his side. It twitched slowly, involuntarily remembering the wound it had borne. The light of the lamp burned low, while outside, evening deepened and grew overcast. Through the window, Cynthia could see a crimson smear where the dog star rose to cast the land in its fell light. To her surprise, Apieron spoke again, his low voice seeming to resonate from the stones beneath her feet.

"Priestess of Wisdom, a death lurks for you as well—and many more who dwell in this land. The mind of darkness has a purpose greater than destruction. As my adversary knows much of my thoughts, so I have dreamed a portion of his. A way is prepared for She you have named Tiamat. My dark twin shall be Her herald when She bursts onto the world, awakening Her sons and calling to Her side the mightiest of Her servants: Iblis, prince of Kör."

With the speaking, Apieron's voice gained in power until it filled the cell with its resonance. "Many times, you spaketh of hope and will, Donna. They are not the same. No gift of hope—or any other—can you offer me."

"And of the will?" queried Cynthia softly, but Apieron had again fallen silent.

Chapter 3

Lampus

The day of the companion's departure from the Vale, word came from Windhover. Following their arrival at temple, a loaded wagon had departed thither bearing much dry goods and food, and it was accompanied by six stout acolytes skilled at both weapons and husbandry. Now it returned, lighter than before, yet with a cargo more precious. Thirteen orphans there were and one adult, each ensconced in a medley of castoff garments and blankets. The youngest was a mere two months of age and accompanied by a wet nurse, herself heavy with child. Only two of the temple servants who had departed with the wain returned, their brethren choosing to remain at Windhover and aid in the tedious work of salvage and reconstruction in preparation for a winter with no hope of commerce from the interior.

Apieron was first to the wagon. From the way the acolytes nervously avoided his gaze, the only query he had for them was useless to ask. He lifted the woman and the bairn she clutched from the wagon into the hands of the senior healer of the temple. The children waited patiently, their solemn eyes upon him. No outcry did they make, nor did they make shift to leave the huddled sanctuary of the wain. A surge of tender emotion filled Apieron, and the power of the fey stirred in him. One by one, he searched their faces and named them, gathering each to himself before passing his burden to the willing arms who awaited.

Apieron turned to his companions, who were geared for travel. and stood waiting, reins in hand. They hoped to find the Meoelstede, the gathering of the army of Ilycrium. The mounted knights of the temple, one hundred forty in all, watched them go where many wished to follow. There was no fanfare and little speech; only Jamello fidgeted, adjusting minor details of his attire, which included a new pair of riding boots, if anything more flamboyant than the first. He bore sword and kindjal of the Wyrnde crypt, and its heavy shield, muchly dented, had been repaired. Yet time and again his hand returned to the brace of daggers slung at his waist as if to reassure himself that the magnificent weapons were no mere artifice, a cruel jest by his betters.

"Can you not see, thief?" called Isander, "The Donna favors you."

Apieron clasped the shoulders of Tallux and Jamello, sharing with each a look too poignant for speech.

Tallux smiled and leapt upon his mount.

Jamello muttered something inaudible and mimicked the elf, adjusting the harness and stirruped saddle provided by the lancers. Apieron stroked Bump's nose and turned to Henlee.

"Soon," the dwarf said.

When then they were gone, Apieron stared after them as the warmth inspired by the children fled. The first winds of winter felt chill indeed as he trod in quietude back to the temple and his dark cell.

RAT'S LAIR

"That's disgusting!" The unkempt dwarf pushed back from the board. Soot hung in the vault, and the cloying smell of charred meat mixing with odors of decay and rodent dung conspired to turn the outcast's stomach.

"What?" Bizaz indicated the source of the smell. A roasted corpse lay supine, split from sternal notch to groin. "Health food! Biceps for strength, brain for wisdom, and heart for stamina," the half orc winked and popped a glistening oval into his file-toothed mouth. "And you know what these are for."

Deuce spat. "Why don't you use your vaunted powers? Pray to that rat deity of yours to cure me."

Bizaz appraised the battered dwarf. The face was swollen with bruises, his beard bitten away in red patches. "You do look a mess, but"—his yellow-nailed finger wagged—"a caution to you. He listens, always listens."

"Faugh. You look worse, one eye."

The shaman's swart features cinched with rage as he leapt up, wiping greasy hands on his hunting leathers. "Tempt me not." His finger pointed. "Who spoiled the attack? Bested by an ass!"

"Bastard." Deuce drew his short sword, much notched and rusted.

"Pardon the interruption, gentlemen."

Bizaz's remaining eye bulged. With flying words, he whipped an incantation of death at the man. Torches guttered, and the dungeon grew chill. Deuce screamed and fled noisily up echoing steps. The man's response was a laugh, menacingly soft. A Helstone flared on his cuirass.

Moments later, he spoke a word, and his dark brand immolated, cleaning itself of the half-orc's blood. A trail of the same substance dragged across the floor and into the furthest crypt where guttural sobs and curses were answered by an animal grunting so base in timbre, it seemed to emanate from the very stones of the nighted vault. "Lucky for you the ambush failed," called Malesh, "or even yon abomination could not shield you."

His glance fell on the half-eaten corpse. "Impressive!" A nonchalant whistling followed him out.

THE GEHULGOG OF KÖR

""So it is true," mused Pilaster. "There is *some* life left in him."

The skin of the Faquir of Kör flickered vermillion to purple like a flowing curtain before returning to gray against the stone. He turned to instruct the Drudge. Set deep within the malformed face, soulless black eyes returned his gaze. "Not yet shall he die. For now, I gift him a *dream* ..."

Thir did not bow. There was no need. Ever had Drudges been slaves of Kör, and none of his race had left Gehulgog, the prison mines of Kör, nor imagined it. As Pilaster turned to go in the glooming, the deeper shadow of his pinioned wings stalked across the moldered wall.

The prisoner saw them—shorter in stature than common men and taller than dwarves, he guessed perhaps they were some race of man evolved in this lightless place. He had seen their pale bodies endure freezing extremes and scalding blasts, disease and mutilation without pause. And when they died, they died silently. The mines of Kör were a dangerous place, wherein a life was of less value than a handful of silvered rock or a piece of bread. Like he, the Drudges existed on befouled food and water, the very air heavy with poisons from the deepening earth.

There was the clatter and thrum of some mighty engine. It

ceased. From somewhere echoed a wailing like a shriven soul. To and fro, it faded but did not die entirely. The prisoner was weak from Pilaster's dream. Irresistible, it came at random intervals. He had ceased to resist, and each horrific death was inevitable. Futile. His home was here forever, stranger to the shrinking world above and out, that far green-and-blue place beyond torment and ceaseless labor. Mountains and snow, forest and river—that fictitious land, but a whimsy for the mind insane.

Chapter 4

Hyllae

Apieron stopped. His lungs labored, and the shoulder ached deep within his chest. He felt better than he imagined he might. Normally a pleasant stroll for an experienced woodsman, the journey to the Falls of Voices was a challenge this eve, and Apieron had yet to ascend the last rise before the chasm in which lay the enchanted stream. Having left hours after darkfall, none at temple marked his going. Summer lingered in warmer lands, borne on a southern wind to dry the sweat that beaded Apieron's brow. He collected himself and pressed forward. No sword hung at his belt; instead, his right hand bore a wooden stave. Already, it had saved him a nasty fall or two. He clenched and unclenched his left fist. It remained weak.

Apieron surmounted the last slope and sat on an outcrop to gaze down. Only a shimmer of pearl on water was revealed, and for a long moment, he did nothing but breathe. Why did this little journey mean so much to him? And yet the exertion of the climb and the notion of a hopeful omen were welcome relief from the lassitude of past weeks.

For a moment, the voice of the falls tinkled in high pitch. Apieron thought of solemn-faced Setie, and curious Ilacus, who touched everything at least once, three times when told no, and of the baby whose owl eyes took in everything around her with equal consideration. Apieron had always desired to know what a person of but a few months' age thought of anything. He remembered Melónie suckling the babe while snapping her brown fingers at the other two children and conversing with her ladies all at once.

"By the frowning gods of heaven and hell, I miss you."

The wind gusted, blowing Apieron's hair as the voice of the falls began to murmur. Moonlight flickered across the water's surface. Apieron resumed his internal discourse, knowing that the spirit of the enchanted waters would reveal itself first to the ear, unaware of self. He remembered Xephard standing erect, cloud-blue eyes regarding all with open-faced wisdom. There had been no dim paths for the paladin; each moral choice weighed on one effortless scale. How Apieron envied him this! When he laid Leitus on the old Donna's knees, he had seen the small death in her soul.

"By the Archer and Gray-Eyed Wisdom, what has brought us to this?"

The wind surged, the force of it blowing grasses about his feet into bent submission. His cloak fluttering, Apieron gazed at the waters. The fickle moon was partially obscured by high-flying clouds, casting the river into running shadows. The sound of the falls coursed and ebbed like some undying engine, waxing and waning but with steady increase as the voice within Auroch evolved from the water's rush. To Apieron's waking mind came whispers, seditious plotting against the land he loved, his own name cursed, and the ancestral line of his house damned. The voices of many men he heard—most recognized, others vaguely familiar. Some he had thought friends, or at least neutrally disposed toward him. Courtiers and officers, royal servants and landed neighbors alike spoke evils small and large—from deceits of law for personal gain to traitorous alliances, yet each shared the black fruit of corruption.

The wind died. Fell voices drifted the night airs. Apieron had heard such before, monstrous utterings issued from throats never meant for human speech. Undulant chants in the sybilitic tongue of Kör were discernible in the background like some unholy rite. This was punctuated by shouts of human men, thus the more loathsome for their joyful exaltation, openly worshipful of the gathering darkness. The mist rising from the stream's chasm became chokingly oppressive, as if the air itself longed to smother him.

Apieron did not stir. He listened, enraptured. There! Rising amongst the calls of anger and violence, and mightier than they, he discerned the voice he knew would come. One like unto his own but unrestrained, overweening in its swaggering confidence. To hear it was to see again the face of his wife's murderer. Apieron leapt up, grasping his walking stick. He struck forth blindly, pursued by a cacophony from the falls that chased him from the slope like a pack of vengeful hounds. Now he knew what Xephard had known: in the world, there was only good and evil. Apieron cursed himself, staggering forward at swift pace despite the night. Always cautious, ever circumspect, too fair to judge had he ever been. Faugh. Folly on, the fool! Youngest son, politically sensitive. Compromiser! Intermediary between those more passionate than he.

"No more," Apieron growled. Spurning the stones of the slope that dropped away, he fixed his sight on the lone vigil lamp that marked the Lampus some seven miles below. His pace was near a run; he would be there soon.

Behind, on the escarpment he quitted, the wind returned to scatter clinging mists that held the last echoes of the tormenting stream. It chased away rags of cloudwrack over the Ravine of the Auroch. There was no one to witness the wreathed bow of the Archer God, cast in argent brilliance. Thrice it flickered into view, upheld by the rippling bosom of the stream, then faded into night's gloaming.

The sound of children crying drew Apieron to the nursery where slept the orphans of Windhover. They stood in a circle around a pallet where lay a girl-child of ten summers. A healer placed a gentle hand on the small forehead above the pale, immotile face. The cleric turned to Apieron and shook her head.

"Triath," said Apieron as he bent to cradle the body. He found Cynthia taking breakfast where the morning sun graced her hemicyclium. Many plants and singing birds were there. Her acolyte gasped as Apieron lay the small body at her feet.

"Her name was Triath."

For a space, the Matron closed her eyes, then released. "Her soul has ascended; it is pure and without blight. A happy day for her, if not for us."

"I think it was not thus for Xephard," said Apieron.

"Respect!" cried the acolyte, a short but broad lad of perhaps twenty years.

Apieron spared no glance for the man, even as the temple servant started forward.

Cynthia dismissed the monk with a wave. His shoulders were set in angry silence as he gathered up her food and retreated, leaving the two in the little garden with the body of the orphan child.

"Xephard's virtue," began the matron, "was not skill at arms, although in this, he had no peer. It was rather his humility before the will of the goddess; his every breath and deed exalted Her."

Cynthia's hair was white in the risen sun, her face seamed with countless wrinkles. "Countless times, She cast him into the very pit of sorrow, always to raise him up in glory. As to his soul—" She shrugged helplessly, her voice dropping, "Those who fell in the raid beyond Duskbridge, I cannot scry."

"In the gray lands, we found no glory," said Apieron flatly. "To live a life of righteousness, is that not enough?"

"Not for Xephard Bright Helm," declared the Donna, "and not for the house of Farsinger."

"Fickle goddess who must needs be amused by the life's blood struggles of mere mortals." Apieron thundered his fist upon a rosewood hand table, shattering its subtle patterns of many hues into scattered fragments on the pave.

The old woman's gaze did not waver. "To contemplate such is without value. Attend, the spirit of the goddess fills the warhorse, and he neighs his challenge before the charge. At that moment, his fear and bravery and strength consume his being without thought." She raised her finger to prevent any response. "The Goddess of War is as simple as the edge of a sword yet more complex than the hand, heart, and mind that wield it. A profundity unfathomable by mortal man." Her eyes flashed in the streaming sunlight, bright as gems.

"Then why, Mother, should I take for myself such a terrible patroness? Many are the gods and goddesses who are worshipped in this land, and no stranger am I to the fields of war. Of honor and wealth, enough have I for any man. My father—"

"Your father would scoff to hear you speak of choosing a god as one puts on this robe or that before the dance." The Perpetua pointed her rheum-bent finger at Apieron's breast. "Xistus Farsinger worshipped the Shining God before he could name Him in the common tongue of men. Of all the gods of wood, sky, or sea, that was his god. He could no more have altered this than he could change his mortal essence." Cynthia dropped her knobbed hand. "As with Xephard Bright Helm, my favorite son, so are you a child of the Goddess Who Loves War."

Apieron's eyes fell to where he shifted the table's colored shards with his boot's toe. "Nay, nay, the paths of my life have led to no such truths. A cruel blow hast fate dealt me. Xephard True Heart, the trust of Windhover, and my family are no more."

For a moment the enclosure was quiet—save for birds rustling in the vines. Apieron gazed at the unmoving child at his feet. He pulled forth a strip of cloth, muchly burned, woven with threads of blue and yellow that Melónie put there. He saw her smiling face. "I found this … wrapped around the foot pillar of our bed. That I should be the death of she who was innocent is worse than mine own could ever be." Apieron wept dry tears. "Dearest wife, is this how I guard and protect thee?" Apieron's hand sought to grip his sword's hilt. It was not at his belt. He bowed under the full measure of grief that filled him entirely.

Apieron's head lifted, for a moment his gray eyes met the Matron's own bird-keen glance, and then he raised his voice to the pale patch of sky above the hanging vines. "Stone-Hearted Goddess, is this the measure of my worth in your eyes? Did the smoke of my house seem more sweet to thee than the fatty kine and fragrances burned for you on my altars? Did the orisons of happy feast and worship sound less pleasing than the screams of my wife?" Apieron's eyes flashed, his jaw working. "Better for me I had never learned thy name!"

Cynthia leapt to her feet, the sun's light played on her head and shoulders, erect and noble. "Terrible, Apieron? Yea, we are all so." Her words boomed, and her arms flung out wide. "Terrible and glorious!"

The force of this last seemed to shake the very columns of the hemicyclium, although each was wide as a tall man might encircle with his arms. Apieron was pressed back into his chair. "The question remains for thou before goddess and god, king and ancestors. What will you do?"

Apieron leapt up and caught her, guiding her shaking frame to her chair as her breath shuddered in her withered breast. She was bent and frail again. "I do not know. How can I heed the Sybil when my Melónie perhaps remains among the living and captive?"

"Search your heart, and you will know."

Apieron's voice faltered. "I know little of anything these days."

The Donna sighed and grasped her shawl tight against her, gathering enough strength for words. "I've spent hours searching the ether for your mate. Her spirit has passed beyond my reach, to the lap of the gods. This could not be if she were alive, either here or beyond the Dark Gates."

"How can I be certain?" Apieron shook his head. "Only the unfeeling gods know."

The Donna gasped weakly. "This I say unto you, Apieron of Ilycrium. It was to you the god of the Oracle called, not to Xephard, or any other. Your paths to friend and kin are sundered. Go now! I am tired and evil forebodings trouble me."

The acolyte returned, drawing Cynthia to her feet. With a stern glance for Apieron, he drew her into a corridor beyond the prayer garden.

Apieron sat for a time, then stooped to recover the orphan girl. He bore her beyond the temple to a raised altar where already funeral had been set by the priests and servants who had grown to love her. Isolde made to take her, but Apieron stepped past to set the small body on the oil-soaked wood.

"What, Priestess? No games today as for Xephard?"

"What matter?" she rejoined quickly. "Your idleness did him no honor."

"For once your admonitions come too late." Apieron laughed grimly. "Isander has already chided me, yet he was nothing loath to take for himself the prizes for running, boxing, and swordplay."

"I loved Xephard as well as you. He was my betrothed." Isolde touched Apieron's sleeve. "If he were here, he would ask what you intend."

Apieron smoothed Triath's brow, framing the child's face with her mouse-brown hair. "I intend this last sacrifice. After that, I have given enough."

Isolde's gaze was hard. "You speak of sacrifice. It has been spoken that Windhover was reclaimed by clan Farsinger without proper ritual to the gods, and that is why it came to be destroyed."

Apieron took a steadying breath, restraint taut in every muscle. "Say you that Melónie was that sacrifice?"

"Nay," she said, grasping his arm with a small shake. "Know you not your friends? And the question remains: what will you do?"

"Perpetua has coached you well, She-Warrior, but heed my words. Your leader lies dead on the Plane of Sorrow. Your sybil's voice is lost; even your gods retreat before the Hel-rising."

"Fire," Apieron commanded. A brand was brought to him. He thrust it against the wood where it raced with a blowing crackle. "Child of Windhover: I, thy lord, have failed thee and pray thy forgiveness. May the gods have at least strength enough to guide thy spirit to eternal joy."

Apieron turned to Isolde. "My time here is done."

Chapter 5

Ilycrium: The Army

There was a stirring in the camp of the army of Ilycrium after far-flung watchers spied a large company of men who approached under a flag of parley. Scouts hastened to the tent of the Prince, where he sat in conclave with Trakhner and Renault, to give report that half a thousand Northern barbarians hied westward along the trade road, accompanied by three hundred dwarves. Gault and his advisors made ready to parley while Renault shouted together an honor guard. "For who could predict the behavior of men from the free tribes?' Unlike their Western, hill-dwelling kin, these Northrons were fair skinned and tall, betimes as wild as wolverines.

Henlee, Tallux, and Jamello waited before a small throng to the side of a low platform, upon which stood the pavilion of the Prince, as two long columns of dwarves marched in orderly fashion at the fore of the approaching companies. They turned with precision, their steel caps and mail hauberks bright in the afternoon sun. As the dwarves neared the receiving area, the companions saw that fully half bore wounds or marched with a limp, yet they held their heads erect with eyes firmly fixed ahead.

Next came a score of men on horseback, their mounts tall

and heavy, thick muscled cold-bloods of the sort best suited to the heavy labors and freezing climes of the high mountain passes. Many of their trappings were coarse-weave cloths or skins that yet bore fur.

Jamello nudged Henlee. "So, Eirec of Amber Hall lives."

An enormous chestnut stallion bore the leader of the Northmen. His great arms were bare, a coat of close-set links covered his mighty torso, a greatsword depended on his left, and a battle axe slung from his saddle. The hide of a bear was thrown casually atop his shoulders, and his head was bald. A bushy, black beard jutted defiantly from his chin.

Jamello and Tallux stepped forward whilst Henlee moved to take news from the dwarves. Tallux took the reins of the stallion and smiled up at the chieftain. "It has been long since you traveled the roads of Ilycrium. Glad are your friends this day."

Eirec clasped the hand of the elf, then addressed Jamello. "We meet again, thief." His glance strayed, eyeing with suspicion the gathering around the prince. The dwarves drew up before the raised platform, clicked heels, and bowed to disperse into small groups. The wounded sought their rest, while Henlee was pulled to dwarven captains who spoke excitedly to him in their gravelly language.

As Eirec swung from his mount, Jamello leaned forward. "We arrived only today. The fleet of mouth say the Prince will soon be king." To Eirec's questioning scowl, he said simply, "Assassin."

"The high officer to the right of the Prince is Trakhner. The mageling Erasmus, known as Black Merlin, was understudy to Tertullion who was slain in the hills of Ulard by a sky drake, he and many others." Eirec grunted appreciatively, but Jamello nudged him and pointed with his head. "The highborn to Candor's left is Renault. Watch him!"

Eirec studied again the nobles, marking the many fineries

of the proud knights whose number spilled over the platform to either side. Eirec patted Jamello's arm in thanks, yet growled deep within his chest. "That one, your strutting Renault, I remember." Eirec's housecarles dismounted and strode with him to stand before the dais as the walking companies assembled.

Henlee and the dwarven captains finished their discourse, and he joined Jamello and Tallux. After brief conclave, the three came forward to flank the barbarian lord.

There was a long pause as each party regarded the other intensely. Gault's auburn locks fell to a collar of sable, and the steel of his corselet was bright and worked with the ensign of Ilycrium, although his hand lay easily on the worn, wooden heft of a two-handed axe. The filigreed scabbard of the king's sword was at his belt, but it was empty.

Eirec stood, legs spread defiantly. His skirted mail and leggings were stained from battle and the road. The men behind him shifted whilst nervous fingers played across weapons.

"Well met, Eirec of White Throat. In days past, at request of my father, I traveled the breadth of this land to hold meet with sundry landholders and officials, but never have I beheld the face of Eirec the Brave, nor had he sent us word by courier or passing merchant."

The mien of the Prince was stern, yet his hazel eyes twinkled with private amusement. "Indeed, I came to believe our Lord Apieron's tales of his robust companion were mere invention."

"My lord?" protested Renault. "This warrior, this rogue knight, is not merely delinquent in his duties (and his taxes!) but here is most uncouth." The royal champion turned to Eirec. "Kneel man, before your liege."

"I see no king," replied Eirec. "We of Amber Hall pledge fealty only to our betters, and no lowlander is my better." Henlee's gauntleted hand grasped Eirec's shoulder in restraint while the

Northman chewed his moustache and glared fiercely at the indignant Renault.

"My lord," interjected Tallux, "Eirec comes to you from the Vigfil Steep, where the legions of Kör came boiling through the passes. He brings with him scarce a quarter part of those who name him leader."

"And the rest?" queried Renault with a disdainful glance for the elf.

"Slain," replied Tallux evenly, "and his holding of Amber Hall razed."

"And the Steeps?" burst in Trakhner as the gathering muttered at the dire words. "Do we now lay open to the army of Kör?"

"They will not quickly recover from the losses we inflicted upon them." Eirec's deep voice was grim. "The pass will have to be cleared, for it is filled with the bodies of the slaves of Kör, steppesmen and orc alike. Also, there were dwarven sappers among us who caused to fall an avalanche of stone and ice; many men of my tribe, but more Körlings, are there entombed. There let them lay until the Final Horn summons them home."

A squire, a man of the prince, proffered a flagon of water to the barbarian chief.

Eirec imbibed deeply, nodded to the man and Prince. He continued, "A rune-etcher has drawn a map on our way from the battlefield." Eirec's gaze focused a moment on the distance, then snapped back to the men before him. "Brave was our defense, but so great were the numbers 'gainst us that a second army breasted the steep and made descent into the high vales whilst the first carried the assault to us."

The hand Renault pointed at Eirec bore a glove of richly worked red leather. "Say you an entire army of mongrel men and goblin kind were left free of scathe? To ravage the tillage of the kingdom?"

"Not so," growled Henlee. "That army pillaged dwarf lands. Even now, it besieges the fastness of Uxellodoum; the Field Marshal of Kör is too wise to leave the forces of Redhand at his rear."

Trakhner ran a calloused hand over the close-cropped stubble on his head, more gray than the yellow of three months past. "Your words, Dwarf Lord, are wise. I also deem the demon generals of Kör must conjoin both armies to root out the dwarves from their mountain. We must pray your kin endure, for with such numbers, the Kör prince can match us loss for loss and yet fly his standard in Sway by spring." Henlee grunted in acquiescence, the dwarf obviously soothed by the blunt, honest nature of Trakhner, whose red weather-lined features and plain mannerisms struck a chord in him.

"Sire," spoke Tallux, his hand on Eirec's fur cape, "this brave knight comes to you not only in search of succor; he brings with him a strong company of blooded veterans. When he and I served your father under Apieron, son of Xistus Farsinger, none was more doughty than Eirec the Brave."

"Careful, Sir Elf," spake Renault, a wry smile on his lips. "Do not so incriminate the man before he has been judged."

"What I did not come for," Eirec said thickly, "is to trade jibes with a womanly courtier whose ignorance is nearly as long as his mouth is wide."

"Sire!" protested Renault. "I demand the right of duel; this man has affronted my honor."

Gault's expression was bland as he regarded his champion. "I accept," snapped Eirec, who began to unsling his broad sword.

"And I will act as your second," added Tallux. The half-elf's emerald eyes darted over the ranks of the royal household, scanning for danger. Sut growled.

"Not now, fools!" said Trakhner. "Can you not see there is a war on?"

"What's one more death in a war?" replied Eirec evenly. "I promise to make this one short, and unlike the slaves of Kör, I do not feed on my prey when the killing is done."

Eirec shook free his great sword, holding its man-sized length before him, its edge notched but honed to a razor's edge despite the dint and wear it had seen. The knights behind Gault hastened to draw arms as five hundred tall Northrons pushed to the fore, while Renault's eyes were glued to the spectacle of the two-hander held lightly in the barbarian's great paw. "I do not name myself vassal, Sir Prince. The holding of Amber Hall has ever been free, paying no tithe. Neither have we ever sought aid against the wild men of the hills or the monsters of Kör. For generations, the men of my tribe vied with such, and the caravan roads and scout trails of White Throat were kept open to the added wealth of your kingdom, and we demand little toll."

"Though I once served your father, I neither asked nor acknowledge any ties of fief or fealty to the Candor kings. But if you help me get my land back, I'll fight for you."

Renault was outraged. "The kingdom of Ilycrium extends to the crest of the Vigfil. Anything in it belongs to the Crown save by royal decree."

"Actually, the prince of Kör now holds it," interjected Erasmus smoothly. "Shouldn't we argue over its stewardship when we have it back?"

The haughty champion ignored these words and pointed his hand at Eirec. "This man would bargain with our prince as if he were a common merchant." In Renault's other hand now depended a long mace of blackened steel, fretted with gold. The accusatory hand was lowered by Gault himself, who stepped down to stand inches from the menacing tip of Eirec's greatsword.

"We are in a war for the very existence of Ilycrium, Sir Eirec. Too long have we slept, the fate of your home may well become that of this entire land."

The strong lines of Gault's face were set in earnest. His rangy frame had filled out in the preceding months and was not diminutive before the girth of the Northman. "We need not more allies and separate pacts. We need knights of the kingdom with exceptional valor. Will you not reclaim your title?"

The barbarian chief looked hard at Gault, seeing no fear in the noble features. He noted the thick wrists and calloused hands of a swordsman, and the easy grace of Gault's stance—an athlete at rest, yet with wit and energy of mind and bearing. To the surprise of all, Eirec dropped to one knee, proffering his sword in two hands.

Gault placed one hand on the weapon and one on Eirec's bald head. He raised his voice. "Let all here witness this man's vassalage, and name him Peer of Ilycrium. I grant to him and his heirs forever the land of the White Throat that I name Axe Grind, for the great hardship from which he comes."

A mighty yell erupted from the men of Eirec's band and Henlee clumped him so hard on the back he nearly pitched forward. The dwarf whispered in his ear, "More than you deserve, hill humper."

Eirec regained his feet, slinging his sword and bowing to the prince all at once. He winked at Renault.

Trakhner nodded his approval, and Erasmus spoke quietly, "Tertullion would have wished to witness this. He foretold the Prince would someday wake and realize he was king."

"Then it is settled," said Gault. "Gentlemen, seek your repair. Tonight I would hear your counsel, and we shall look at Sir Eirec's map over a cup. I would fain learn more of this dwarven avalanche."

Trakhner gave Erasmus a thoughtful look. "May men long remember the words you said today, Lord Mage. I shall speak them to many."

Erasmus' eyes widened when the old warrior presented him a formal salute, then turned to join the retreating prince.

Wiglaf found Cusk shrugging into a chain shirt the foot soldier had acquired from the kit of a knight felled by the mist dragon. Dunstan sought to cinch out the slack with leathern ties. Its previous owner had been a large man, and apparently a wealthy one. Its links glistened without blemish in the afternoon sun. Many men milled about after the arrival of the dwarves and barbarian refugees.

Dunstan shrugged and spat. "Tried to talk him out of it, Sarge, but he wasn't havin' any o' it."

Cusk nodded angrily at the pavilion where the heraldry of many knights fluttered under ensign of the Prince. "I heard what 'e said 'bout Apieron and t' other brave ones who've fallen. Eirec canna fight 'im, or he'd break the peace. But I can."

Wiglaf rubbed his grizzled chin and turned to Dunstan, who spat again. "Apieron and his troop once saved Cusk's mother's sister an' their family by killin' a demon cat that was poachin' their farm."

The gangly youth's hands trembled as he hooked a scramasax into his waist belt. It was an oak-leafed blade as long as his forearm. "I owe the lord Apieron a debt, and I'm figurin' that Renault is 'bout to pay."

Wiglaf had heard enough and grabbed a fistful of the chain shirt. "He's a born noble, lad. You think to challenge the likes o' him?"

"So!"

"So?" Wiglaf buffeted Cusk's iron cap from his head, the blond hair shaking free in disarray. "If'n you don't use this thing, ye'll lose it."

"He ain't so great!" retorted Cusk. "'E's no better'n you or I."

"That may be, boy. But his lordship's been reared to do but three things: drink, fight, an' you know t'other! Stab'im while e's in his cups, maybe. Or better, while e's on top o' the scullery maid, but gods help ye on an even field."

Cusk's jutting jaw softened a bit when he looked around to see the stare of other soldiers. Dunstan picked up the iron cap, the even tones of his slow, farmer's drawl were quietly reassuring, "Come, lad, let's find us a quiet spot and work on that link blouse o' yers. I don't want you clankin' and flappin' such when I'm around." Dunstan winked at Wiglaf. "A drunken goblin might spear me by mistake."

Jamello reconnoitered the encampment of the army of Ilycrium. He lingered in the vicinity of a young peasant soldier who looked as if he intended to rush the raised platform and slash off the head from one of the knight lords in attendance on the Prince. Jamello tsked when the soldiers' fellows tackled him and made to buffet a modicum of sense into the man. The betting would have been good. Soon the sharp-eared thief found what he sought in a gathering of men from Bestrand. Dark skinned and lean, these were accoutered as might be a seafaring people; trident and net, dirk and cutlass were slung over fighting leathers or swordsman's blouse and trousers. Jamello made to cry out a greeting, but it caught in his throat. A lighthearted people by nature, these citizens of Bestrand sat with heads in hands to weep or meandered without purpose.

Trembling, Jamello hovered on the fringes and listened. His olive face grew pallid, and he shivered although a southern breeze played under the sun of the camp. He hastened to find Tallux and Henlee and bade them sit. The news was dire. Bestrand, chief maritime ally of Ilycrium, was fallen.

Henlee's pipe nearly fell from his mouth. "The defenses—"

"Oh, I know," said Jamello. "None better than I, who was born there. The bastions of the seawall are mounted by tall derricks whose cunning mechanisms (dwarf-crafted of course) might grapple and capsize any unfriendly ship foolish enough to venture near." Jamello waved his arms in circles while Henlee and Tallux shared a concerned look. The thief continued his exposition. "More fearsome are cleverly angled cannons of bronze, charged with a liquid fire that defies any attempt to quench it with water."

Henlee nodded. "Those derricks cost many a talent of gold, and are well worth it. What's more, fifty or so years ago, Redhand sent there a train of heavy catapults and ballistae large enough to shoot a ship's spear half a mile."

Jamello's tone sank. "Dwarven toys availed my brothers little. Have you ever seen roaches or rats that swarm from a sewer like a running shadow? Sadôk! Thousands came from the cisterns that underlie all the city. Bestrand is old and always sinking; each new building is builded over the old. Men do not go beneath because of the water and filth." Jamello shuddered. "I have, and seen Sadôk in the tens and hundreds. But who knew there were so many? I guess the townsfolk fled to the countryside or to Sway. Sadôk are fast, and they swing and shriek like apes when they hunt."

Jamello sat heavily, and his voice trailed off. Henlee and Tallux waited. "How many people in a city can defend themselves, truly fight back? One in a hundred? A thousand?" At length, the thief spoke again. "Ill news for this army. Bestrand's entire fleet was destroyed, save those privateers and merchants already at sea, an' those I'm sure are scattered to the winds."

"And the city herself?" asked Tallux earnestly. "Does she stand?"

"Bestrand cannot easily be burned or leveled," answered Jamello. "She is interlaced with more canals than there are tents in this camp."

"And the men who name that town home?" asked Henlee. "Will they stay to fight?"

"I have no family," said Jamello slowly. "Those that do, I can only imagine." He pulled the cowl of his cloak over his face and stared at his feet. The graceful hand of a wood elf touched his shoulder. Jamello nodded in recognition, then started when he felt the hard hand of the dwarf on his other.

"We know, lad," came Henlee's graveled voice. "We know."

THE GEHULGOG

Thir pushed back a furl of lanky hair that he might see with two eyes. He had followed them. Masters had taken the prisoner.

"You're to be considered truly fortunate … to be offered a death of honor." Luchenzeril nodded to his companion, an Azgod as broad as he was tall. Azgod, the denizens of Kör. When the captive had first been cast into the prison mines of Kör, the place called Gehulgog in the tongues of men, and yet possessed the strength to ponder such, he had deemed them some accursed mating of demons with humankind.

Ugrup's back flexed into straining cords, and the captive was stretched immotile, face down over a bloodslick timber. The prisoner's mane fell over the block. "Have you something, wretch? A coin or other? That my stroke be clean?" From the prostrate figure came no response. Naked and abused, the captive yet gleamed in the perfection of his form.

The convex surface of the executioner's glaive traced from the back of the prisoner's neck to buttock, and a lock of hair fell to the fouled stone as blood welled along the path of the steel's caress. Luchenzeril laughed and signaled again to Ugrup. Strange muscles bunched under the executioner's leathern skin, and the prone figure was stretched tight. Luchenzeril's booted foot struck under the hollow of the arm, and again. Ribs snapped, breathing ceased, then shuddered forth to resume its slow rhythm. The blade was withdrawn. It whistled overhead, whirled and descended with a mighty thunk, deep into the timber. There was silence in the execution chamber of Gehulgog.

Luchenzeril's laugh was high and hideous. His claw waved, the gesture heavy with disinterest. "Remove this from my sight!"

Drudges hastened to obey. Thir bent to retrieve an object from the damp, it was a silken tress. A soft and fragile thing in his clutching hand, its gold hue flickered in the gloom.

LAND'S END

The man strolled from the grotto, and breathed deep the chill mountain air laced with salt tang from the slated sea below. The stench, unique to burning blood and hair, was tolerable out in the breeze. He wiped his blade clean on one of the rags he had torn from the Sybil's body.

Adestes Malgrim shook his head to clear it of the fumes. Foul witch brought it on herself! If only she had died with the merest shred of dignity, instead of screeching and cursing in some archaic gibberish. How else to silence her lying tongue, than to cut off her head and shove it onto her brazier?

Adestes picked his way down the rocky slope to the bordering stream. A man lay face down across its icy waters, his misshapen form somehow more grotesque in death. "Just where I left him," grinned Kör's Malesh. "I like you better now."

Blood oozed sluggishly from the crumpled form, flowing in water that nudged wolf's head and skin of python. Adestes bunched his powerful legs, and leapt onto the man's back, and sprang onward to the far bank, thus avoiding a frigid bath himself. He turned one last time to regard the place he had seen oft in dreaming, this time never to return. The black slope of the precipice seemed to touch the lowering sky.

"Oracle indeed," he sniffed. "What passes for gods in this land would barely make jest for the average stripling of Körguz." The herald of Hel focused inward and found the dark presence within. It twisted at his touch and harkened to his mind's sending.

"That was for *you*," spoke Adestes Malgrim. "Now, one for me."

Chapter 6

Ilycrium: The Army

Evening came early to the encampment. Slanting runners of wet laden clouds got up from the south and marched overhead to cover the high plain with a gray pall. Night descended and with it came the rains of autumn. Despite invitation from the Prince, Henlee and the dwarven captains did not attend the royal board. Some urgent business known only to them kept Henlee sequestered among the secretive dwarves the night entire, nor was their absence missed by any save Jamello, and no one asked his opinion from his position on a low stool in the lean-to that served as scullery to the pavilion of the Prince. Here he pretended to munch bread and flirt with serving women whilst he kept an ear and a half on the proceedings within.

Gault set at table with advisors and certain of his household knights. Conversation was brief as attention was paid to spits of pork and stone bowls heaped high with squash and onions roasted on the fringes of a low fire. General doings of the camp were bandied with the jests of men wearied after a long day of drill. The need for respite and healing after the disaster of the dragon assault provided occasion to weld the sundry forces who marched under the banners of Ilycrium. Outside, mountain tribesman bantered with citizen levies of Sway and the larger burgs, as household troops of rural barons compared gear and tactics with the professional soldiery of the Crown.

The entry flap of the tent was thrust open, admitting a wet gust. The helmeted head of a sentry glinted wetly. He nodded toward Gault and stepped aside to admit the imposing figure of Eirec of Amber Hall, who shook water from his fur cloak.

"Sit and be welcome, Sir Eirec," beckoned Gault warmly.

The tall barbarian bowed. "I cannot, Liege. Many men of my steading bear grave wounds. Some will not see the dawn, although I thank the lord for the aid of his chirurgeon. We have not such as they in the White Throat."

"We have you to thank," said Gault, rising, and as he did, so followed all. He indicated a leathern map stretched on a frame. It was skillfully worked with colored pigments such as the women of the Northrons made. "This is of greater aid to me than the advice of eldritch sages."

"I know not of such," said Eirec. "I came to say this. The men of my following, your steading, Prince, have voted to stay and fight for you. Yet I wonder where are the other free peoples of your kingdom? Some of our Western cousins I have seen outside and beyond, and yet none of the forest-ranging soldiers of the wood elf king. Dwarves are here, and their kindred do battle under Uxellodoum as we speak, but what of the Baron Wulfstane of Wicklow and his son? I have heard they covet the lands of Apieron of Windhover. Is this true?"

"A traitor to the Crown!" rejoined Renault. He received a stern look from Gault who, with the others, retook their seats. "Well, a deserter in the least."

Eirec's face grew florid. His beard fairly bristled, but his speech was low and intense. "The son of Farsinger has many allies, of which I am proud to be one. Why, this very day I've heard of marvelous swamp elves that fly—"

"Swamp demons and moonshine," laughed Renault with derision. Armor doffed for the meal, Renault's padded jupon was scarlet like his gloves and worked with a silken griffin enface, the heraldic symbol of his ancestry. A verdigris sword descended easily from his baldric.

"Someone should still thy tongue, Sir Knight," said Eirec quietly.

"You will not be the first to try."

"No, but I will be the last."

"Gentlemen," coughed Trakhner, clearing his throat in distaste, "your antics task my patience and that of our Prince."

Eirec's ham-like hand released the hilts of his broadsword. "Men of the North do not make idle speech, Prince. When I say my clansmen will stay, that means they will fight without retreat, unto death."

"More cannot be asked of any soldier," added Trakhner.

Renault resumed his seat, his sharp glance never leaving Eirec's broad front. "Then it is so," said Eirec. He took a long-legged stride to Gault and stooped to one knee, whispering a moment, then kissed his hand before rising with a swirl of his bear skin to depart into the night and the rain.

Trakhner ambled to the map. The runescribe had depicted wolves' heads to mark the position and number of the invaders. Each was inked on the hide in crimson and indicated one thousand foemen, afoot or mounted. Through the passes and ringed around the fastness of the dwarves, there were more than fifty such heads.

Trakhner's sword-worn hand swept down the line of red. "If even our hopes prove true and yon dwarves endure, these swartings that serve the serpent king of Kör are light horsemen unequalled in speed of advance. Their foragers may bring sword and torch to the lowlands before we can present ourselves for battle."

"Then we must haste eastward!" cried Renault.

"Aye, an' behind us the land will groan," answered Trakhner, "but it is not to be helped. And I like me these Northrons of Eirec's clan; they sing and laugh around their cooking fires, hopeful to strike a blow at their enemy. Without delay of our march, we will gather like others amongst the tribals as we can. Methinks country barons will be loath to bar their gates to such an army, especially surmounted by the ensign of the royal house." The general concluded with a throaty growl.

"No man doubts it," said Gault. "Yet I feel guilt for the woe that will come to the people in our absence. See how quickly Bestrand is fallen; who does not grieve for our Southern neighbors? What of Sway? I fear her governor-general, old Hardel, will soon have his hands full."

Trakhner grasped a fistful of small scrolls such as might be borne by pigeons. "Aye, reports trickle in. With the coming of another crop blight, a black rust that sticks to kernels of wheat and corn, beggar armies roam the countryside. And here is another: students and peacemakers have overrun and blockaded the chancery."

Renault laughed. "Small strategy in that. Seek they to terrorize a scribe or two?"

"Their claptrap is the same as ever," continued Trakhner. "They blame their fathers, and us, for the unrest in their souls." Trakhner laughed without mirth and let fall the tiny parchments. "They demand to treat with officials of Kör."

"Are those not your friends, Mage?" inquired Renault of Erasmus.

The darkly handsome spellcaster stood and smoothed his robes. "Tertullion once told me that when evil wakens, fell things that were hid arise in many places. Perhaps the young and rustics have sensitivities most easily affected."

"I had not thought to hear you speak of religion," said Trakhner.

"Remember you not the attack of the dragons of mist?" replied Erasmus.

"Careful, mageling," cautioned Renault. "Many brave knights left we in the Ulard."

"None perhaps more dear to you than Tertullion to me!" The ebon skin of the mageling's face became infused with the passion of his speech. "Dark entities seek a pinpoint of light to escape nameless prisons. That pinpoint is Ilycrium."

A knight stood, his black hair spilling onto a coif of chain about his neck. "And the church of the capital? Where are their prelates, so officious and outspoken before we departed?"

Gault thought of the missive he had received from Tallux, whom he had but glimpsed briefly that morn. How he wished he could have conversed with the doughty scout. "They are silent, as are our friends from the cloister at Lampus." Heads turned to regard the Prince. Flagons were half raised, forgotten in hand. Gault continued, "Tragedies have come to them. The master of Sky's temple at Sway did not return from the dark quest undertaken by Apieron of Windhover." Gault's voice fell, "Nor did Xephard, knight captain of Templars."

There followed a silence broken only by the slap of wind and rain against the tent and the soft sizzle of meat over coals. Renault scraped back his chair. "How true now soundeth the words Exeter spake at council. Golden elves of Amor by the Sea, cowering wood elves of Ilycrium, and now winged elves of the wild nigh to the estate of Windhover. Mark how Eirec, chieftain of savages, complains of the war that has befallen that one."

Trakhner's thick fingers drummed impatiently. "Eirec himself is not without loss."

"And by the generosity of our prince has he not thereby gained more?" No self-doubt softened the lines of the knight champion's face.

Erasmus spoke. "Who has lost more than our prince?"

"I do not know," replied Candor in barely audible tones, "but I think Apieron Farsinger has lost much." No more was said, and the meal was completed, each with a thought to his own home and family.

Jamello exited the camp kitchen. None marked his going, save one. Green eyes flashed in the darkness. "You heard?"

"I did."

"What will you do?"

"Go to my king. In the Malave, our Greenwolde, I was not born of a high house. I am not even a true elf, only half so. My mother was human. What rank I hold was earned. Even so, those closest to my liege thought it best I serve as ambassador of sorts to the Candors. Much blood have I spilt for them, and will do so again." Tallux touched his war dog, a large pale shadow in darkness. Sut's eyes gleamed yellow.

"And no noble am I! Think of yourself," Jamello urged. "Go where you will; Apieron has lost himself."

"Then why do you stay?" Tallux chuckled softly. "The companionship of a dwarf?" Jamello's face glinted in angles while the ruddy light of a cooking fire played on his gleaming black boots and belt and on the wire of his sword's pommel. For once, he had no reply.

Tallux laughed again, gently. "Nay, say it not, Rudolph Mellor. I feel your mind. You love the ranger of Windhover, as do I. Tarry here three days, whatever the schemes of the dwarf! In that time,

I will return—alone or with such a company of knights of the wood as to make even Renault's small heart soar."

With that, the elvin scout and war dog departed without a whisper to mark their passage. Rain pattered on Jamello's new cap as a wind tugged gently at the tents of the army. He hitched his trousers and bethought himself of somewhere dry to sleep.

Henlee found Jamello early the next morning. In the night, a high breeze had pushed aside the heavier clouds, and the sky paled in the east, awaiting the sun. The dwarf's booming voice roused the thief to a painful start. "I see you got yourself another weasel hat and fancy shirt. Back to your old tricks, eh?"

Jamello stood, smoothing his garments. "I would have you know, these I purchased … who is that?" He looked suspiciously on a second dwarf, nearly as broad shouldered as Henlee, but older and of a height more appropriate for dwarven kind. His forearms were as thick as Jamello's legs, and his front was covered by a leather apron.

"This be Bagwart. He is an ironsmith, the best ironsmith. He's been showing the farriers of the man-king a thing or three." Bagwart only grunted.

"Prince," corrected Jamello, feigning disinterest.

"He was at Windhover." This brought Jamello fully awake. "And no news!" snapped Henlee to the unspoken question. "Found his way hither on the wings of war, so to speak. He's got a mission," said the black dwarf with a smirk. "He'll take my Bump back to Windhover whilst we go onward."

"I'm not going anywhere without breakfast," said Jamello. "Besides, I made promise to Tallux I would tarry here three days. He goes to his king."

Henlee pulled at his beard, which had regained its brown luster, already seeming half again its normal length after the fires of Hel. "You promised an elf?"

"A half-elf, and a noble one."

Henlee pursed his lips in thought. "Agreed. I have things to work on anyway."

"Go where?" called Jamello to the retreating dwarves.

"Just be ready!" tossed back Henlee.

"What of Eirec? And the army?"

Henlee paused a moment, then resumed his stomping gait while calling back, "That one and I also have unfinished business."

THE GEHULGOG

Thir shuffled into the cell, silent on padded feet. He saw that the huddled creature yet breathed. It uncoiled and raised its head to regard him with uncanny eyes, clear as diamonds that glittered by torchlight, the stone that was cherished in the mines, for there would be meat and cessation of labor for a time. Thir ran his pale tongue over thin lips, a gesture of uncertainty. That angered Thir. He raised a flail and lashed down. Again and again fell the remorseless strokes, yet never did those eyes leave his own. The savage beating ended when Thir was certain the captive was unconscious. He stood a long while over the bloody form, grunted once, and left.

KÖRGUZ

Like a forest of dark spruce atop snow-garbed mountains, ice glittered on the innumerable towers of Körguz, city of the demon king of Kör. Her northern face was a waterway, salty and deep. Commands were given, and flags raised. Men shouted and strained at rime-bright cordage, and eighty proud ships, striped black and gray for war, pushed into frigid waters. Turning west by north, twenty thousand marines of the Dream Throne went on errand for their master.

"What hast thou wrought, Magnus?"

"A small thing, a mighty thing." Pilaster shrugged. "A promise from Galor of Amor. 'That no person, or force of Amor, make war on us.'" Pilaster's skin rippled like falling colors, red and black again.

"Ah. I did not know that archmage yet lived in this world. And the exchange?"

"A life, that a prisoner, taken by your slave Malesh, be spared the headsman's axe—"

"Amor's navy!" hissed Iblis.

Pilaster bowed his ram's head in triumph. "And Her navy."

"Indeed," rumbled the tyrant of Kör. His bulk relaxed, one massive hand supporting his head in repose. "You have done well, Faquir. Here your prisoner will suffer the long centuries, surety against our future needs."

SAEMID

Jamello climbed a rocky outcrop on the fringe of Ilycrium's bivouac, which was in uproar. Tents were rolled and tossed onto wagons as drovers yelled and brandished whips at obstructing soldiers who ignored them. Mules bawled, donkeys bucked, and oxen chewed their breakfast with placid eyes. Every man grumbled upon leaving the first comfortable quarters since departing home.

Jamello was dressed for travel. The last of the rains had blown away north, and his boots gleamed with ebon luster. He turned to his comrade. "Of what do dwarves speak in such earnest yet become silent as standing stones when any other draws near?"

"You mean when you draw near," corrected Henlee with a chuckle. "Maybe they just don't like you."

Jamello tapped his foot, obviously in consideration of a grand retort. The black dwarf laughed with open pleasure. "You are a thief, a master thief, it is said. Why ask you me what they say?"

"I speak a smattering of common dwarf," admitted Jamello, "but none of the jaw-breaking, triple-secret, hidden trap-and-treasure dialect of your mountain kin."

"Do you wish to know where we are going?" beamed Henlee.

"What? Where?"

"Meet Ohm!" Henlee stepped aside.

A strange dwarf fronted Jamello. Hundreds of wrinkles creased his face, and his beard was white and long, but the eyes were black as jet and shined like polished stones. What drew Jamello's gaze most was a great mantle encircling the dwarf's shoulders and chest. It was the color of gray rock and contained patterns of bright minerals and metallic veins that shifted and flowed down its length. The dwarf bowed slightly. Jamello returned the gesture, his eyes never leaving the mantle of living stone.

"Ohm shall guide us on our journey." Henlee's beard winked and flashed as many gems caught the fresh light of the day. Jamello wondered anew.

"Where are we going?"

"To a secret place. My place."

"Why? What of—?"

"Tallux?" asked a voice. "He is here!" The wood elf ascended the ledge. He bowed to Henlee and embraced Jamello. A green cloak of elfin make and his leather jerkin showed the strain of recent travel, yet his bearing was strong and vigorous. He bore Strumfyr, his mighty bow, as well as short sword, hunting dagger, sling, and knives.

"Where's Sut?" asked Jamello.

"Sent on with Bump and Bagwart and the others to

Windhover," interjected Henlee. "The beasts cannot go as do we today."

"And the king of wood elves?"

Tallux's face grew grim under his mahogany locks. "They have withdrawn to their inner fastness. The gate is shut. Men were right; they will not come."

Ohm faced Jamello and Tallux. "Do as I say—and you will enjoy a short passage that saves a season's journey."

"An' heed well my instructions! Do not release the mantle, even if we must needs fight." As he spoke, the dark-eyed shaman unwound the ends of his rippling garment and placed an edge into the hands of the others. Jamello started, for it felt like liquid rock that shifted beneath his grip, its undulant patterns out of focus to his eyes.

Ohm stood erect and spoke a resonant intonation that sounded like falling rock, the echoes of which cascaded down the scarp like tumbling drums. The ground gave way under Jamello's feet. He jerked involuntarily yet held tight while noticing that his companions also descended rapidly into the stone. With a dizzying pace, they sped four abreast through the earth. Jamello fought the urge to flinch and dodge as they rushed past deposits of oily shale and sharp-edged granite. Bastions of colored salts and underground lakes whirled by like an enormous kaleidoscope.

"You may breathe!"

Ohm's voice sounded as if from beyond a hollow place. Jamello realized his mouth was clamped shut. He gasped and shouted, half-expecting some metallic nugget to break his teeth. He found instead hot, close air. How long they so traveled he did not know, yet what the shaman had meant by fighting conjured a sudden fear of any creature that might endure such a place.

Afraid of losing his grip on the mantle, Jamello looked to his benumbed hands, but found them obscured by a blurred veil of stone. Eventually their rushing pace seemed to slow and angle upward, then they passed through tubes of magma that pierced basalt like roots of a tree. A dull reddish glow grew up, and they shot into a great cavern of black-frothed lava, but there was no blast of heat, only a dull chill as they ascended past the faces and shapes of what appeared to be fiery dwarves who leered and stared. Finally, the companions traversed into gray stone, and they were out! Jamello felt wind on his face. He inhaled gulping lungfuls of cold and rubbed his eyes. It was night, and many stars dotted the sky. The four stood on a leveled place.

Gathering Tallux, who bore an intense look as he studied the sky, Jamello fell in behind Ohm and Henlee as they walked. "I feel we have journeyed long," said the thief, "yet was not aware we had done so all day and the better part of a night. I am famished!"

Ohm nodded and sprouted more wrinkles as he smiled. "It is often thus the earth traveler is hungered by his efforts, but you are mistaken about time. Dawn has not yet come to the day we departed. Bifrost brought us northwest at great speed, outdistancing fat and lazy sun." The ancient dwarf laughed aloud.

Stopping before doors of bivalved stone, Jamello saw they stood a crag over a steep valley bounded by imposing, frost-lit peaks on which conifers wore blankets of snow. A thin road wound its way around the mountain many feet below. Henlee addressed Tallux and Jamello, "You're standing on Ul Osse, Sky Window—my back door."

"A redoubt?" asked Tallux.

"Far west from Uxelludoum and only a short jaunt to Amor." winked Henlee. "If only they knew."

"The Golden Bower. Galor. That is why we have come!" exclaimed Jamello. The stone valves opened at a word from Henlee, and they pushed into a torch-lit passage, straight and smooth. Silent guards regarded them from shadowed niches and pulled the doors closed behind them.

Jamello plucked at Ohm's sleeve. "What is Bifrost?"

"The name of my casting, of course."

"Why do you call it that?"

"Because that is what it is called."

Jamello persisted. "But why was it named so? Did you name it?"

"The path to wisdom is long and arduous, some never attain it. Come, let us haste, it seems the lord Henlee is eager to feast as well."

Jamello and Tallux lengthened their strides and followed. The corridor passed many side passages, some broad and well lit, until they came to a postern at which stood an armed sentinel, his features obscured by a boar-crest helm and steel mask that hung low over his beard.

They entered without stooping and came into a meeting chamber furnished with skins and small tables and chairs of dark, well-worn wood. Food was brought, hearty but not extravagant. As they ate, dwarves would enter, invariably salute Henlee, then address he and Ohm in their mountain tongue. Some were armored, others wore robes or work tunics. All were bearded, and Jamello guessed that the intricacy of pleats and knots, as well as interwoven ornaments, were badges of station. Henlee's once more swung heavy with a king's ransom of gems. *And not a poor one*, mused the thief.

At last, Henlee put aside trencher and cup. "Our repast is over, and we must be off today. I regret our pressing errand; otherwise, I might share the hospitality of my house, this Saemid, with you as long as you would stay."

"Amor and Galor?" asked Jamello.

"Only by the power of the golden elf can we continue our quest," said Tallux, "and he is a close friend to Apieron."

"Or was," said Henlee. "That was long ago as men reckon it. Anyways, we will try. Packs have been prepared. Refresh yourselves for a time. I will meet you after attending Darla of the brown locks."

After Henlee departed, the old one pulled close to Tallux and Jamello. "He trusts you well, wood elf and man of the city. Dwarves speak not of their women folk."

"We are, er, honored," replied Jamello.

Ohm's fingers were like stone on their arms, and his black eyes like depthless wells in his seamed face. He smiled again. "Aye, Ohm, servant of the keepers of stone, deems that you may deserve more honors than dwarves can bestow, if you live." The mantle writhed silently as the ancient cleric followed Henlee's path beyond the sentinel.

Fatigue overwhelmed Jamello, and he pulled a short bench against his chair. Cloak for a pillow, his eyes closed and he pondered time, and the naming of beautiful chariot-riding Helios, god of his friend Apieron, fat and lazy.

ILYCRIUM: THE ARMY

> *Salutations to His August Highness, Gault Candor. Most Noble Prince, please accept this missive for what it is, a burden and a gift. I have heard it said that you are wise and patient, although young and sore beset. I deem this writing a burden for it is but the scribbling of one unworthy to steal the briefest moment of thy time.*
>
> *I am a thief, and former resident of sun-kissed Bestrand. Who would think to remember her muddy byways with fondness? I do. All the more for the tale*

of her fall. Mine are the reminiscences of one who has at times been thy guest, though I was welcomed only by jailers and sergeants. If you will but read further, you will know why I consider this letter a gift.

Your soldiers say you have lost a father and a throne to sit on. I have learned that a man may lose much and yet be undiminished in any way that matters. Such a one is my lord Apieron. Great men deem him unpure of descent, a born rebel. Yesterday a camp wench said her paramour, a high officer, put the name of traitor on my lord as have others. What I know of royalty would not fill a thimble, but my eyes do see. This is what they beheld two fortnights ago:

Apieron Farsinger, Lord of Windhover, led six stalwarts to the land all men fear. Four did not return. Apieron drove us into the Helstorm to protect your kingdom, and the home's hearth he left behind, this and for the fool's notion of honor that affects men such as he.

Forgive my pitiful script. My hand falters at the memories I relive that I might impart them to you; there were lights of chaos that revealed roiling smokes shot with rays of darkness. Should one stray across you, they leave you pale and staggered, but one must heave up and flee hulking shapes of monstrous bulk sinewed with strength beyond what is known in breathing lands. Loathsome faces they bore, vile and twisted into mocking profanities and deadly curses. And I cursed Apieron in turn, and cared not what accident of birth or affliction of his twin gods drove him there … and we to follow!

So we trod amongst treacherous spicules of rock, sheared like daggers, or upon burning sands of strange colors that writhed in the radiant heat. Lo! Up comes ventings of red flame, or a torch of blue-white incandescence, or yellow foul and sulfurous with gases that make the lungs bleed. Or worse, a shower of molten rock paste that would kill the unwary in a trifle. Perhaps a boulder greater than a horse is flung into the wrack above, maybe ne'er to return, or mayhap to burst into a hundred killing missiles of razor-edged stone.

Once I beheld my Lord Apieron stop to clean the Heldust from a small token on his breast fashioned in the shape of a white horse over blue and green. This he did before wiping the smoking grit from his eyes and mouth. He bade us forward, else we had all been lost. Now his woman and sucklings are slain and ne'er once has a word contrary to you passed the gate of his lips. Perhaps we go again to challenge the Evernight. An' his will not be broken entire, for I left him bearing grave hurts.

If this letter finds you in good fortune, or at least good health, say a king's prayer to the gods, for ours have gone unheeded. An' surely they have turned their faces from us.

In this Year of the Dragon,
Rudolph Mellor

““What is that?” asked Gault, his finger tracing the final symbol.

"Mark of the thieves' guild," replied Erasmus. "Only a master may place it thus."

"Ah," said Gault, his eyes growing distant. Erasmus took his leave, but his prince did not notice.

HYLLAE

Cynthia's eyes blinked against the wind, and the chill of it stung her face. She squinted the direction from whence it came. Northeast, where so much hurt had come. Almost could she feel the hate that flowed from the passes of White Throat and the high steppes of Kör.

Away east had passed her mighty champions, Xephard Bright Helm and Apieron of the noble heart. One never to return, the other perhaps forever maimed in spirit. In the north were fought great battles. A young prince, faithful to the ways of the twin gods, received her benedictions for strength and wisdom although he knew her not. And now to the bitter east walked the last of her cherished, adopted children—Isolde, once again heiress to the mantle of Perpetua, should she return to claim it.

Had two decades passed so swiftly? Well Cynthia remembered the day she welcomed a gangly Northron girl, tough as a thorn root inside and out. *Was this how a birth mother felt when her only daughter left?* The Donna, accounted the wisest servant of Wisdom, did not know. Embracing the pain that clenched her breast too tight for words, she turned to gaze upon Isolde, who was girt for war.

Isolde held her matron's eyes a lingering minute. She was grateful the Donna did not approach for some last-minute remonstration. Isolde was in her prime, and the righteous strength of an aggrieved goddess flowed powerfully within her. It spoke to the cumulative wisdom of the generations of women who had served the holy office beyond the dim mists of a gray past, unremembered even by they, the record keepers of their age.

Isolde turned away and adjusted her pack. It bulged with provision for the three-day walk to Windhover—her first stop. She would lend her strength to the people of that stricken place. As the pack's contents settled on her shoulder, she perceived the faint clank of metal, it was a heavy spear point and weighted grounding spike. After Windhover, she would see.

Isolde glanced at her companion, tall and somber beside her. "If you are ready, let us be gone. All my life, I never wished to leave this vale. Now my feet yearn for the freedom of the road."

"I am ready," came the deep-voiced reply.

Chapter 7

The Gehulgog

For the ten thousandth time, the prisoner regarded the nail-scoured stone. Many had died here before he, yet when it became apparent that he would survive his many wounds, the jailers of the Gehulgog that Azgod called Archwaze, had pinioned him to this rock. He closed his eyes. Behind them, he again beheld Luchenzeril and Ugrup pull forth with tines the liver of a living captive. There was the snapping of bones, the boiling of skin, and black blood-spattered feral eyes.

Ears pounded by the eternal cacophony, the prisoner shrank from an endless, whispering despair. He opened his eyes. "Thir not b'leve t'ings what you say."

"Is that your name?"

"It not matter you hear Thir's name. Soon you die."

"Then let me show you." One manacled wrist stretched to the limit of its chain. Fingers touched Thir's face behind the eye, and a burst of light touched off in the Drudge's mind.

Thir stood stock still, staring into nothing. He saw the great skylight that man-slaves named Helios before they died. It climbed over mountains fair and proud, where snow-draped peaks glistened above indigo-washed shoulders that gave onto rolling hills, bright as a peridot he had once held. Flights of birds wheeled gracefully over verdant uplands cut here and there by rushing streams. The aura allowed him to hear and smell. The bubbling chatter of invisible rills and subtle calls of a forest flowed over Thir, and smells like nothing he had ever imagined. So clean and open! For the first time in his life of uncounted days, he inhaled a great draught of air for pleasure's sake. The vision narrowed to a tree.

Before this, he had seen only the dark and twisted tendrils of mountain giants that, over untold centuries, thrust their roots into the Gehulgog. The tree he now beheld was beyond any naming in his words, its upswept limbs clothed in a garment of rich bark, endlessly complex of texture and colored tones, and surmounted by a vibrant canopy. Thir could see and hear the myriad small creatures that dwelt therein. Gently asway like a world unto itself, the tree awed him as would a god. In one hurtling moment, both marvelous and tragic, Thir realized this one event held more beauty than the cumulative sum of all he had ever known.

A melodious voice called his name, and the Drudge blinked to see the prisoner withdraw its hand. Whether it had touched him once or once again, he could not say. He met the crystalline eyes and saw how they resembled the sky of the vision. He held the prisoner's gaze a long moment, then looked away. None of the Drudge had been able to meet those eyes for long.

"Now you know," whispered the prisoner. "I am sorry." Thir said nothing but turned away to a hole in the chamber, like so many tunnels and chambers, all the same.

The prisoner slumped back against rough stone, for even the minor magic he had summoned taxed him sore. Trembling, he sagged fully onto the chains. Eventually any creature that went on two legs would be broken by the wall bolt. He could see dank strands of his hair blanched white. How long had he hung thus?

He sank into meditative calm, ignoring the scream of ligaments wrenched beyond abuse.

The prisoner's gaze chanced down to something that lay in the mould of the cell floor, a jug-like vase of cheap glass, marred by burn and scratch. Its green circuit was interrupted by a jagged, fist-sized hole at the flute. With his feet and by twisting leverage, often failing, the prisoner at last held it before him, firmly, so that the shake of his hands not drop it. He knew it as Thir's most cherished possession. He brushed its pitted surface.

"Thank you," he spoke to the darkness.

SAEMID

Almost immediately (or so it seemed) a youngish, armored dwarf with a square red beard shook Jamello awake and beckoned Tallux to follow. They trailed their silent escort back to the mountain porch to find morning's thin light upon a small assembly gathered around a table laden with cold meats and ale. On it was set an enormous map that detailed the east-west mountain chain and surrounding environs.

Henlee looked up from a cluster of advisors. "You rightly surmised that a few hours sleep is better than a tour of my humble cave." Jamello noticed the fanciful beasts and filigree of precious metals on the steel hauberks and gauntlets of the assembled dwarves.

"Come, eat and advise us on the best path to Amor," said Henlee. He seemed to be in fine cheer. "Rel, here, thinks only in terms of marching armies and not three travelers in need of some secrecy and more haste."

Man and elf glanced at the map, then out at the splendid view offered by the lookout post. Glittering snowcaps of the Anheg chain stretched away eastward beyond the ripened dawn, and in the north, dark tundra defied the risen sun. To the west, the mountains arched northward in descending heights. Although impossible, Jamello fancied he decried a hazy line beyond the horizon that gave hint to the flat expanse of the gray Ess.

"Our destination," murmured Tallux, "the fastness of Amor, the Golden Bower."

Rel's stubby fingers stabbed down at the map. "When you leave the road past the last frontier town, follow Cutthroat Gorge around to the South Gate, a journey of ten days, I reckon."

Tallux pointed to a small notch on the map beyond the little town. "Does this mark not indicate a high pass by which we might shortcut the southward loop, coming direct from our descent to East Gate?"

"It is a very high pass," said Rel, favoring Henlee with a toothy grin, "a cold and no doubt treacherous one between snow melt and first frost." The dwarven war master began a contagious chuckle.

"Two days march if we are lucky," said Tallux. "Though no footing for a pack animal."

"Forty-eight hours from Saemid to the gates of Amor." Rel laughed. "If'n the golden lords only knew!"

Henlee sighed with gusto. "Well, I deserve it, leaving the decision to an elf scout, a forest-runner no less."

"At your service," Tallux bowed and smiled beneath his dark locks.

"Why hurry?" protested Jamello.

"Kör marches under banner of the Queen of the Abyss," replied Tallux, his smile gone. "When stir the dragons of earth, thus tumble the thrones of kings."

Heavy packs rigged for climbing were brought forth. Henlee and Tallux shrugged into theirs as dwarves adjusted their fit. Jamello eyed his own, seemingly larger than the others. "Why us?"

Henlee paused his preparations and faced the small assembly. When he spoke, his words filled the carved dell and rolled off Saemid's outcrop with the authority of a lord in his own hall, strong in arms and rich in wisdom. "Xistus Farsinger came from lonely wilds. I knew him. The strength of his arm and his persuasion of men was very great; easy would have been for him to ally with the barons and chiefs of fell peoples who had robbed the land for years. Instead, he supported the old king's father, who was just—the Old Marshal, Baemund Candor.

"Xistus brought tokens to dwarves for parley, where before there had been only mistrust. Rich in minerals were we, yet lived often in hunger. Gifts were exchanged, Baemund gaining gold for his armies as our own people's lives were muchly improved. These things we do not forget, for dwarven oaths are stronger than the clay of our bodies or the metal of our forges. Dwarves will not allow Apieron, son of Xistus, to tread the fires alone."

"Oh," said Jamello.

Henlee cleared his throat. "There, I've said enough to last till Amor. We go." Without further word, he stomped off, followed by the easy-striding wood elf.

Jamello watched their retreating forms. He felt whelmed by a wave of events that seemed to submerge his will, drowning his identity and pulling him into a cascade that would probably end his life. Unable to take the first step after his friends, he hoped the remaining dwarves would mistake the trembling of his legs for a result of the cold.

Ohm gripped Jamello's arm. The latter hoped his face revealed no sign of the inward wince he felt at the strength of the dwarf's hand, hard as horn. He wondered what would happen if the elder dwarf truly squeezed. The white-locked shaman pulled Jamello's gaze into his own dark orbs. Jamello gasped and beheld a pillar of black fire that churned across a nighted landscape. Jamello gasped, then nodded his head in acquiescence. He knew that the companions' escape from Duskbridge had been but a dream, that they truly remained in the land beyond hope.

"You have seen the fires of Nightfall, the hell of despair writ by She Who Devours," spake Ohm. The grasp was released.

Jamello blinked. "As has he," Jamello jerked his chin toward Henlee, who was picking his way past a middle sentry, already well below.

"He will not speak of it for perhaps a hundred years; the mantle of defeat fits him poorly."

"Not me," shivered Jamello.

Ohm laughed like falling stones, and the dwarf's locks blew weirdly on the frigid wind. "Remember, manling, only within the hottest furnace—and by the heaviest hammer—is true steel born."

Saying nothing, Jamello turned and strode to catch up his companions ahead on the path that walked the western spine of Henlee's redoubt. Rank upon rank of mountains marched into a haze of gold and blue in the distance wherein it was said dwelt the golden lords of Amor.

PLEVEN DEEP: THE DRAGON RIFT

"What of the other? The one you hold captive at Llund?"

"He titles himself defender of the Temple of Wisdom."

"Thy lich hast read his intent?"

"Day by day, the substance of his mind is shaved. Soon his soul will be naked in the Night."

"It seemeth he chooses far and remote places from which to defend his sacred vale."

A clawed hand, jewel bedecked, appeared in the murk of the conjuration. Although more than four hundred leagues distant, Adestes Malgrim felt the unpleasant caress of Iblis' thought. "Let me enlighten you: This same Xephard of Ilycrium has slain more of my spies and servants over the past decade than any. A scourge to us as long as he draws breath. Prisoner or no, kill him."

Adestes pondered a moment, then inclined his head, saying flatly, "He will die."

"Did you find that amusing, priest?"

The monk bowed. His hair braid brushed the floor, and when he rose, the emblem of a dragon, blazoned in flawless platinum, gleamed on his white robes. He appeared to bear but a single weapon; although with this one, Adestes knew any appearance was carefully crafted. A naked dagger depended from a cord at his waist. It was long and of tapered gold. Adestes had seen it before. It was a weapon for piercing—a priest's tool, useful in the sacrifice. Blodig was one of its many names.

A wide grin was writ on the monk's pallid features. "Well, we know you, Dark Star. Did not we of the Dragon March imbue you with the skills of warrior, adept, and assassin?"

Malesh's dark blade licked out and returned to its sheath—a wing's flap of death's raven. "Idiot, I don't need you any more." Stooping, he turned the head to face the nighted chasm beside him where came the merest vibration of sound. "Neither does he."

Adestes Malgrim, Kör's Malesh, squatted. "Now where might I find a scrap of skin to sheath this fine poniard?" Whistling a happy tune, he began to work.

THE GEHULGOG

The captive remembered it was time again to touch the stone. Already chill as a tomb-dwelling wight, he nonetheless pressed his palm flat against its cold surface. In muted tones, he sang to it.

Proud mountains, once new and shear, now slept after countless suns as rounded scarps tickled by split of root and ice. He sang to the slow, seeping life of secret waters and buried lakes of oil. He beheld man-carved dolmens, raised when earth was young to bear lonesome witness to unraveling millennia, and times afore, when dwarf and elf named and shaped each offering of the awakened planet, summoning them to their perfection under the glory of newborn skies.

"Obey me, sleeper in dreams of yore. Obey, stone to flesh, clay to my hand!" Again the prisoner felt the tiniest quickening under his fingers. As with the nightmares of Pilaster, he gathered each sending to himself, and like dust blown under the rim of a door, soon it would be enough.

GLORIOUS AMOR

"Whom the gods intend to slay, at times are first driven to madness." So said the elvin champion. His flaxen hair was parted over broad shoulders, and on his argent surcoat gleamed the heraldry of Amor. Tower beside ocean, stream beneath tree.

Jamello turned and scowled. "Shh, she approaches." The woman seemed ephemeral, clad in gossamer threads. A flitting shadow of her green bower, she stepped light as falling petals and sang sweetly.

"Hold there, young Rudolpho!" Henlee and Tallux made haste to catch up the thief who had dashed ahead of their escort and stood under the trees.

A strong hand grasped Jamello's arm. Quick as ever, he broke grip and twisted away, his hand seeking the hilts of the crypt blade.

Drust, champion of Amor, grew wroth. "Ignorant son of an uncouth race, when thou suckled watery milk, I stood the shores of Avalon and gazed on the Dragons of Morning." The heavy steel of the crypt blade flashed in the sun as fast as Jamello had ever drawn small sword, for he had grown strong. A brand likewise found the elf's hand, and it glowed like blue lightning. "Mushrooms of the mould grow by night, only to wither by midday. So shall your short life end, for it were deadly peril to gaze on Dorclai Translucia, the Gray Lady." The unearthly blade's tip pointed at Jamello's heart.

"Not a fair fight!" shouted Henlee, huffing toward the pair. Tallux came first, and his leather-clad arms embraced Jamello whilst his emerald eyes bore stern reproach onto the golden elf.

Jamello struggled wildly. "Leave me be, damned elves!"

"I like your fire, boy," said the black dwarf, half-bowing to the enraged paladin, "but p'raps another time."

"Peace, friends," called a voice melodious as birdsong. A slender hand was laid upon the tabard of the knight. "Lord of Waters, Drust, stay thy sword's arm. This one's destiny lays elsewither."

The hand touched Jamello's eyes. A woman! No, an elf lady she was, clad in a queen's raiment. He blinked against a yellow haze as if the sun favored her with special light. Finally he understood what had been seen and said, indeed, he would not forget until his dying day.

The companions noted another elf, clad in golden armor. He seemed as great a knight as the other, although youthful and merry where the champion seemed worldwise and stern. The youthful elf accompanied the elf queen from the forest, then sat upon a bench of stone. The woman smiled and gave warm greeting to the trio.

"Great Lady," stammered Jamello as he fell to one knee. "I knew not—"

Laughing, she bore him up. "I know your heart, son of fair Bestrand. I gazed on thee from afar when Perpetua made her magic at Lampus."

"You know me as well," interjected Henlee. Drust had sheathed weapon and stepped back, but the dwarf kept half an eye on him as he spoke. "Long have we toiled and bitterly suffered. A knight of your cup, Giliad the warrior mage, fell in the Evernight."

"For this late news, I thank you." She glanced at Drust and the seated elf. "Some would say the pride of Amor was thusly pricked. Not I, who have cautioned elsewise daily since these ill tidings came to us."

The dwarf's ire was not mollified. "What of the fine promises of Amor? Fair face and fairer words arose in the Fire Mirror. Were they false?"

"You misspeak, son of clay," growled Drust. The uncanny blade again quivered, held upright before the elf's breast. He now stood between the dwarf and his queen.

Dorclai's voice rang clear as bells of crystal. "The valiant sons of my body shall not be spent on this ill-fated errantry." She glanced again to the seated elf. Dark hair hid his bowed face, yet his hands were clasped before him as if against great effort.

Henlee's frown deepened. The frustration and grief of the last months boiled up in him. He thought of Apieron, broken of body and spirit. Ignoring the glowing blade, Henlee shouldered Drust aside to front the elf queen. The seated elf did not stir as the dwarf's face worked with wroth. Astonished, Drust bellowed and leapt forward.

Dorclai's hand rose imperiously, stilling both dwarf and champion. "By my own eyes, you are a mighty warrior, no doubt a bulwark to your people, Henlee Dwarf Lord. I know your path from many shadows. Doom accompanies you!" Again she silenced the dwarf's protests. "Stay thy ready tongue."

"Although my heart fears it, and he does so against my bidding," a flickering grief came to her face, "my husband himself, Galor Galdarion, shall guide you." The elf queen shuddered slightly and gave back. She smiled wanly, as if afraid to speak for tears. Silver and gleaming, she stepped into the solemn gloom of trees and was lost to them.

Chapter 8

Foslegen

Jamello laughed and jumped from the rainbow. Behind him sprang Tallux, never missing a stride. Henlee rubbed his eyes and pursued on wobbly legs, wishing to gain as much distance as he might from the spell creation. The wreckage of Windhover loomed uncomfortably as the keep remained as the fire had left it, yet many small shelters had been erected against the retaining wall, apparently with salvage of the palisade.

"Who is that?" asked Jamello. "Ah, the comely temple priestess, and at her side, a pilgrim."

Isolde's blue eyes held no warmth for the thief. Her companion was tall, and his hand bore a walking stave. A traveler's mantle draped his shoulders. His beard jutted at a medium length, brown like his hair and touched with gray.

"Welcome to my home," said Apieron.

The dwarf spoke as he worked. "Black sand, slag o' broken blades, red paint rock, yellow boggy ore, or gnomish iron pigs—all the same to me. With a little this or added that, come out good, like makin' a cake."

"And twenty or so of Redhand's forgers and clerics, and a crucible as big as a dragon."

"That's what I said!" snapped Bagwart, "then take it here and work it good." The short, broad dwarf shook his head. "I forgot. Not any more, not since that bit o' wodensteel you sneaked me." He held up a three-pound sledge, bent at a useless angle. "Stuff's harder than abomination."

"Just one shield and one mask, Bagwart," encouraged Henlee.

"Would that be a shield an' mask ye ordered, such as never been made afore?"

Henlee waved about him, indicating the half-subterranean forge at Windhover. "Hardly touched in the raid, and you have plenty of help."

"Help's not enough."

"Then what?" cried Henlee.

Bagwart's forge-tempered face crinkled in mirth. He let forth a piercing whistle from his bearded lips. Shortly there was the pounding of mighty hooves and the slab oak door of the foundry was kicked open with ease. "Special help."

"Oh, no." Henlee clapped hand to face.

A long-haired centaur stood grinning in the doorway, and the two-quart jug on a leathern thong around his neck seemed diminutive above the mighty chest. Behind him, two other centaurs stomped and flexed. "Like I said," chortled Bagwart in triumph. "Special help."

"They're drunk!" accused Henlee. "And you must be."

Bagwart placed a stubby finger to his lips. "They're my secret. Now leave me be."

Apieron sat huddled before a little fire that slowly fed on the side of a felled willow. He made camp in Melónie's garden, although the stream flowed no longer, and the vines were withered. He fingered the scrap of cloth he wore next to his breast; it was his family's weave of muted blues and creams in the style of Melónie's shuttle. It spoke to him while the fire's shuddering flame danced on the surface of his eyes ...

It was the first time they had met. Xephard was there, also a small delegation of tradesmen and a young squire named Thadius. They had come to the wide lands of her father through thickets of pink-flowering laurel. Fragrances of orange and myrtle filled the air as lowering shafts of sunlight lit the arbor, turning dun branches to a suffused glowing emerald, with recesses of dappling gold where there were many doves. Like all their kind, they warbled when startled, but not overly loud for they knew, in this place, no harm would come to them.

A gentle music arose as the forest gave onto a greensward where handsome ladies offered smiles to gallants who displayed their finery like strutting peacocks. A midday meal was set, and the gathering had the quality of a fete, yet Apieron's eyes found those of only one. He strode boldly forward while ladies tittered and young warriors frowned, but held their places when Xephard grinned broadly at them.

Melónie turned to face Apieron and offer welcome to the tall, bearded ranger, but when she beheld the purpose in his gray orbs, words left her, and a morsel fell from her hand.

To Apieron then, as always thereafter, she was a woman who seemed more tall than she was, and lithe and fleet of step. Entangled tresses framed an innocent, sensuous smile. Her eyes were fawn, observant yet also shadowed with the secrets of her gloaming. "Fawn," he named her in his native tongue and sang to her, and she was his.

Curved waist daggers were fingered as darkling looks followed the newcomers. Melónie's father, being wise, declared games to welcome the Northern knights. Apieron won easily at javelin and running and poetry, and after Xephard boxed and wrestled, there was no more talk of fighting.

… Apieron held the cloth to his nose. Remote, ever remote, her scent lingered. He pictured her, singing sweet charms into the threads, quick brown fingers dancing gracefully over her creation. A woman happy in her love.

Apieron hung his head, his dark locks hiding his face from the flamelight. There was something, and he looked up, "How long have you stood thus?"

Galor Galdarion beamed a smile of friendship, and the darkness lifted a little. The elf put out his hand, receiving the scrap from Apieron, and sifted the silken weaving. "Your friends mourn her."

"It is *he* who holds the power to go freely between the Hel land and our green earth." Apieron's hands sought his sword. Not finding it, he waved at the gloom-drenched destruction of Windhover. "It was he, and a phantom of unlife, who did this."

The golden elf pondered in silence. "Ah," he breathed at last, "a dweomer remains in the cloth. Strong spells of keeping and love lie therein. Keep this near you always; it is very potent."

Apieron retrieved it. "I thought I imagined the spell charms. Thank you." Galor left him to his solitude.

The night was at its midpoint, and the ground was chill. Sleep seemed a distant and foreign thing, nor could Apieron escape the thoughts that cluttered his mind like webs strewn by a hanging spider, heavy and malignant. He remembered the curse of the vampire. How true it had become! The witch of the Oracle had once said he was fated. That she was dead, he had no doubt. Of the instrument of her doom, he knew this as well. His searching hand tightened to a ligament-straining grip on his stave as he drew its familiar length across his lap.

"The folk of the temple have built houses of stone. Do as have we and find one for a last bed before our journey. Surely any family hereabouts would welcome their lord."

"Why? They have suffered enough my ill fate."

"My memory is better than yours," said Isolde. "You did not wish for the task appointed you."

Apieron's gray eyes softened. "Maiden, you are more close to me than the daughters of my father. Better for you and I had Xephard never come from Northhome."

Isolde burst into tears. She stood outside the warmth of the fire, shivering in the night chill. "I loved him more than life." Her voice became a halting whisper. "More than even the goddess."

Apieron leaned forward, and his hand touched her face, lingering on the wetness. "You are gentle," said he. "Stay here with thy monks and tend the village. By decree, it is no longer mine to protect."

Isolde pulled away. "I cannot. As much as you, I cannot."

Apieron nodded slowly. "Then be warned. Henceforth, all shall name me Avenger—for this only do I live." Apieron did not stir from his seat, but to her, his shape loomed in the shadow.

Isolde lifted her chin and met his gaze directly. She stood again as warrior maiden, supple and strong. "I am resolute. My parents gifted me with power of mind and spirit, the order of the temple adding skill at arms. With these, any woman can forge what destiny she wills."

"So be it."

A slight quaver crept back into Isolde's voice. "Think you the others will seek to keep me from this?"

"They cannot. Be at ease, sister."

Isolde's honeyed hair swept his forearm. Once again the vulnerable woman, she kissed his hands once, and then whirled into the darkness. Apieron lay his head against the smitten willow. A bone-damp mist clung to Melónie's stream garden, now a broken culvert. He saw a few other fires, neglected by villagers who had long since sought shelter indoors. The yellow light of the scattered burnings glowing drearily in the outworn night. A fog was rising, but there was another mist, another time …

Apieron thanked the morning's vapor for softening his step on the carpet of pine needles and sparse forest grasses, and he paused often, looking and listening. Most hunts were so, with more time spent waiting than walking. Above him was an old and hoary spruce, its wagon-spoke boughs perpendicular to a single towering trunk from ground to sky-searching top, twenty man-lengths above Apieron's head. Those branches below lay dead and tangled as witches' hair, whilst those above were lifted upward, their verdant leaf spikes glinting blue in the sun and laden with thumb-sized cones as dense as clusters of grapes on a vine.

Next to the elder tree was a true giant, over two hundred feet, but it had died years ago. Pale lichens covered its naked, drooping limbs, and orange mushroom caps marched its height like miniature cupolas on the tower of the Candor kings, but mightier in scale than any device of man. Countless boreholes pockmarked its surface, powdered with yellow sawdust where woodpeckers found fat grubs that ate the forest giant from within.

Nearby were a dozen aspen, clustered like grass, their bone-white trunks barren and straight below nets of green-and-yellow leaves that flickered in the warming sun. Today was Apieron's day to hunt for the squadron of the king's scouts he led on high trails before winter's snows rendered them impassable. Not all his troop were hunters, yet with each man sharing the rotation to provide a day's provender, soon all would be. Apieron chuckled silently; it was one thing to fail to fill one's own belly, quite another to explain to twelve labor-famished men that it would be biltong and hardtack again for supper.

Apieron resumed his course along an ice-cold stream, steep in descent from the mountain's flank. He had seen much deer scat, and once a boulder that a scavenging bear had pushed aside for swarming ants and their larvae. Apieron's javelin, held high, quivered in his ready hand. The breeze was in his face, and the rush of the water would mask his approach until the last moment. In the tall grass at the river's edge, he might flush any beast, fearful hart, or yellow-tusked boar as they fed ravenously on waterlogged root or sweet clover in a late-season glut before winter's fast.

Apieron smelled blood. The grass parted before him, and the grizzled head of a cinnamon bear turned on its haunch and snarled in low-throated menace. The carcass of a dappled fawn lay at its feet. The old boar's snout was bathed crimson to the eyes; its piggish glare fixed on Apieron as it swung to a rushing attack. Apieron's dart flashed true behind the beast's muscled shoulder, transfixing the barrel chest between counterweight and steel heavy barb. The bear roared and leapt, and Apieron dashed sidelong and behind, his sword upraised, although it was a needless gesture. The ursine galloped only a dozen paces before dashing itself senseless against a tree. The breaths of the dying beast were ragged as each shuddering gasp spewed frothy drops of pink lung onto the forest mould. Apieron stood a respectful distance and breathed a prayer of relief to the Virgin Goddess Who Hunts, and to the spirit of the animal that would provide of itself for his men.

"My lord, you have returned," came the voice, melodious and full of love.

Apieron rushed to the bear's side where its face lay hid. "Why do you hurt me so?"

With trembling hands, Apieron pulled free a shielding claw and beheld a face framed with midnight hair—olive-complected—with soul-deep eyes. "Melónie!" he screamed as the world wheeled. Apieron slid back ...

It was hours after last light. The armorer of Windhover had completed every task assigned by Henlee. Bagwart knew he must be tired. Iron-hard muscles had cramped and recramped during the heat-drenched toil, yet his mind felt fresh and a cool wind flowed through the smithy doors, open to the night.

Bagwart held a dusky coal in his scarred hand and blew gray dust from its surface, and again as it transformed to a glede, glinting orange. This, as always, rendered the master forger much pleasure. He tossed it into the blow furnace where fresh fuel waited and nodded to his assistants. He liked them. These three had taken him in when their leader and most of their kind fled Foslegen and the coming war. Nigh seven thousand pounds of muscle raised and lowered a bellow's pole as great as a tree trunk.

"Criticize me, will he? Holed up with the centaurs, I did!" The massive shoulders shrugged in response to the memory of a glowering Henlee. "What 're you expect? They make strange an' powerful ales. Kick enough to make drunk a horse!"

Bagwart chortled at his own jest and wiped a sooty arm across an equally sooty brow. Tired indeed. One last task remained. Bagwart shook out the contents of a leathern bag. A resplendent spear tip and butt spike clattered to the stone floor. The forge master whistled in his beard.

From a shelf he lifted an ingot of wodensteel—the last of Henlee's Hel trove. Bagwart eyed it carefully, then the pieces at his feet. He gathered them up, holding each before his face in turn and feeling their weight. He tasted them, laid them reverently on a ledge, and emitted a low whistle. "Don't know which is better."

Bagwart flexed his knotted arms a few times to loosen them up. For weeks, he had slept in the forge, but the flawless steels before him banished all weariness. "Faster boys," he urged the three centaurs. "This is going to be a good one!"

Morning did not dispel the mists of night. A fog crawled from every shallow, lending the shell of Windhover a haunted aspect. The forest was obscured, and voices fell flat. Jamello regarded the others. Gone was Apieron's traveler's mantle, in its place was a knee-length cotehardie of sturdy linen and leather. Its colors were done in green and gray. Jamello knew Apieron's gift of woodland stealth, plus the garment, would render him nigh invisible. He bore Sarc's twisted bow and his stave, as well as a sizeable pack. From its brace protruded two unusual lengths that the sharp-eyed thief could only surmise to be some type of javelin.

Tallux held converse with Isolde. Both wore jerkins: his sleeveless over a buckskin shirt, hers of brown suede with yellow inserts. Most remarkable was the spear Isolde held easily as if she had her life entire. Its shaft was three cubits length of ash, reinforced with wodensteel twined as vine along the shaft with filigreed beasts and heraldry of war. Its point glistened in the wet. Of the other forgings of Bagwart, there was no evidence. The dwarven smith had departed with some others of Windhover before dawn, grumbling with every step whilst waving aside Henlee's admonishments.

Lastly, the thief analyzed Galor. He knew the elf mage might appear different to each who beheld him, yet seemed clad in shouldered robes of gray-blue silk shot with cloth of silver. As always, the gold elf seemed to glide rather than stride, his finery never kissing the soil. Jamello shrugged away the foibles of such and tested the draw of each of his ten daggers, which were slung across his flank in the magnificent ebon bracer. Others had he secreted about his person, as well as many other devices. He grinned and slapped at his new knee boots and leathern breeches. The crypt blade arched cockily from a double-wrapped swordsman's belt, and he adjusted his weasel cap at a jaunty angle. He felt quite dashing, but his companions were perhaps too preoccupied to pay him proper compliment. "What now, Apieron? First a swamp, then a desert, then a burning. I can't wait."

Galor stared at him with eyes like the morning star. Jamello cringed inwardly a little; he remembered such glances.

Apieron cleared his throat as if unused to open speech. "A quick hike east by north will take us to a high mountain step, an ancient gate of planes."

"That is more like it," encouraged Henlee, rubbing his hands together. He stamped his injured foot, testing its strength in his steel-shod boot.

"Serving monks have laid out warm clothing and kit for each of us." Isolde indicated six bundles.

Jamello eyed their apparent weight dubiously. "We number six where before seven have failed."

"One a traitor," growled Henlee.

"This … task is voluntary," said Apieron. "You are a faithful friend, Rudolpho, and have my gratitude as long as I may live. From here, you can strike north and seek again the army—or go wherever you will."

"Army? Me? Nay, I prefer it here."

"Surely the Kör king can now breathe a sigh of relief," smirked Henlee, his beard winking with more gems than ever before, even by the fog-blanched light.

"The actions of that one are no matter for jest," said Galor. The elf mage's presence grew large, his voice majestic. "This Abomination he worships and would bring into the light shall break all that is fair. She will remake the world as She would in the beginning of things. Seas of chaos shall vie with earth-torn mountains under naked space. Endless wars will rage for Her delight. Nay, goddess though She be, we must confront Her in Her own lair, lest all we know perish."

In answer, there came a dog's deep-throated growl joined by the braying of an enormous burro. Two boys, garbed as temple squires, stepped back hurriedly as Bump nipped at their knees. "Bump and Sut must stay," said Galor. "They cannot go as do we."

"This is not to my liking," said Tallux. His dark hair was bound with a thong of leather, and his fair elfin face bore a frown. "I vowed not to part from Sut again."

"Nor I from ol' Bump," added Henlee. He shot a dark-eyed glance at Galor while roughly caressing the donkey's bristly mane. Henlee looked to Apieron for support, but the latter shook his head in the negative.

Tallux wrapped his arms around Sut's gray neck. "Already I am much saddened, and the first steps have not been taken. I will not say I break oath to you, for I go now beyond the margins of this world to walk the Everdark with my brother, Apieron Spear Runner."

Sut placed his head atop the elf's, his yellow eyes alight. "Look after the dwarf's good steed," instructed Tallux. "I deem you have become friends."

Henlee snorted. "Bump puts up with your pup, and like as not, he'll have to save his butt a few more times 'ere we get back."

"How cold is this high mountain, Apieron?" asked Jamello. "The fens weren't altogether bad."

Isolde smiled for the first time. "You'll have to eat big, little man. You're apt to freeze, like a brown popsicle."

Jamello pulled his goatee. "Droll," muttered he, "big and pretty, and droll."

Less than an hour's walk found them a good step into Foslegen. Apieron was no longer its patron; nonetheless, he knew every rise and crease as a townsman knows his front step. Into the weak sunrise, they struck a sure trail that appeared well beaten although no sign remained of recent travel. A gentle declivity took them to a fog-bound stream where the path was flanked by shade-loving ironwood, gray-barked with muscular limbs that flexed above knobby elbows. The trail crossed the brook into a copse of swamp hickories whose shaggy bark lent them the appearance of beggars in cast-off clothing. One locust was there that had mistaken fall for spring, and its slender limbs bore hanging blooms that suffused the air with thick perfume.

"Here is a remarkable thing," said Tallux who had seen many woods and many trees.

By some trick of sound, they heard it, a bell tolling mournfully from the direction of Windhover. Faint but discernible came a keening wail fading to and fro, the noise lilting eerily through rock cuts and mossy tree trunks. It crept through their bellies like the death groan of an animal. Questioning faces were trained on Apieron.

"A man has died," answered he. "He was sick in the night."

Galor let fall a blossomed stem. He waved Tallux forward, and the wood elf led off in solemn march upslope, their path true to their desired course. Throughout the morning and past midday, they oft heard hoofbeats, southward where the forest was dense, yet they saw nothing. A haze lingered in the trees, and sounds were muffled. "Shall I set trick or trap for our shadows?" asked Jamello.

"Those are not the sound of men on horses," answered Tallux. "I wonder of the legends told by men, of centaurs and sileni." His green eyes sought Apieron's. The ranger walked stolidly onward.

Henlee turned rapidly to avoid the gaze of the elf and nearly collided with Jamello. The thief was flipping a long dagger of unusual make. Deep and wide crosscuts marked its length on one side from cross hilt to tip. "What in tarnation is that?" cried the dwarf—obviously aghast that any forge man would so defile good steel.

"Main gauche," grinned Jamello triumphantly. "Blade Breaker. Bagwart made it for me."

Henlee clapped hand to head. "Drunken ironsmith and loony thief, what have I done?"

Jamello favored Isolde with a wink. She sniffed in derision. The trail turned left and joined a wagon road that marked the northernmost boundary of the fief of Windhover. Tallux drew Strumfyr, nocking a clothyard shaft. Henlee's experienced eye caught the sheen of wodensteel on the barb. "Bagwart's been busy," he mumbled.

Three horsemen stood the road. "Name yourselves, friends," shouted Henlee's basso voice. They were clearly of Ilycrium, and armed as knights, they wore yellow tabards over brigandines and link shirts. Their mounts shifted at the dwarf's challenge, but the men made no reply. Isolde stared at Apieron, whose stave quivered with the force of his grip.

"What news of Kör?" called Galor. His robes of gray and blue seemed to float, yet there was no wind. As one, the horses turned and spurred away.

"What manner of man cannot tell friend from foe?" asked Isolde.

"Those were not friends," replied Tallux, who lowered his famous bow only when the armsmen were gone from his long sight. "Their tabards proclaim the bristled boar of Buthard and his sire, Wulfstane of Wicklow."

"This is his road," said Galor. "Even so, I do not think he will come to greet us."

"Perhaps we might then pay him a visit," growled Henlee.

"No," stated Apieron, stirring at last from immobility. He began to walk. "We go."

"You lead, Apieron, but mark me." The dwarf's dark glaive found his hand. "I have a weighty query for Buthard when next we meet."

The road bore them uneventfully into more open country. They hurried past a leftward branch that led to Buthard's thick-walled keep and further, to the sprawling estates of his father, Wulfstane. A strong march with infrequent rest saw their track narrow again to footpath on a rise where sparse pines lorded over grasses that rattled the season's demise against knees and thighs. The toilsome day had broken in boots and feet for the long journey ahead. Dusk shadows fell toward the companions from a tumble of granite ahead and west off the trail where it caught the lingering sun.

Tallux sniffed. "I smell wood smoke."

"And cooking meat," added Henlee. "A camp!" The dwarf poked about the rock pile. It was thrice his own height, jutting from a spur that rolled athwart their way and into the darkening east.

"Advance no more!" came a gruff voice.

"Who are you that speaks from the stones?" demanded Henlee.

"What does it matter? I have no fear that you will come closer to discover, he who is always first to table and last to battle." The dwarf shook with rage yet the voice continued, "You act the toughling, Henlee of the heavy axe, but that did not save you a bottling like an ugly pickle by the red wind sprites."

Henlee staggered back and fumbled for Maul, then gave up and shouted in anger, "You—"

"Never was your mind quick! You are vain and easily distracted, like a milking girl who sees her reflection in a pail and stares in a trance, her long braids hanging down."

Henlee bellowed. From his pack, he whipped free his black horn of iron and leapt to the side of the pile, thrusting it into a crack to sound a blast with all his might.

The top of the tumulus blew free in a shower of pebbles and grit. A man emerged, his black beard and bearskin cloak covered with rock dust. His brow furrowed, and his bald pate wrinkled in stern disapproval of the dwarf, whom he fixed with a menacing glare. He thrust his thumbs truculently into a broad belt, which caused his enormous arms to bulge even more. "My sire was a mountain king—"

"A hill-climbing ruffian," countered Henlee.

"Eirec!" shouted Jamello with glee.

The Northman growled, "Who else?"

SWAYMEET

Hardel, governor general of Sway, tossed the sheaf of papers aside, instead turning his gaze to a desk model of the capital he had discovered and restored. He fiddled with a tiny wood and linen ballista, frowning when it did not fire its dart.

Dexius cleared his throat. "The requisitions, sir."

"Ah, yes. That's all good, Dexius, but I never had an ear for such."

"Sir?"

"Would you be so good as to mull over those drafts and do what's right?" Hardel paused in his manipulations of the miniature Sway. "You do think we shall have enough provender and equipment if we are laid siege to?"

"Yes, sir."

"The old king slain in his very chair! And the boy-prince runs off without leaving me a proper staff or even a decent adjutant. He's got enough trouble, gods aid him."

Dexius remained silent. Hardel scrutinized him for the first time. The man's slender physique, well-cut dress, and pale, intelligent bearing seemed the norm for the bland functionaries of the capital. "You never served, did you?"

"Regrettably not, my lord."

"That's as is. If the old king counted on you, then you are surely worthy."

"Thank you, sir."

"Never an academy appointment?" Hardel shook his head solemnly. "Well, then, of what noble house are you?"

"None, sir."

"Oh, I see." Hardel recovered quickly. "I'm off to inspect my mighty legion." He chuckled from deep within his belly. "Scarcely a battalion, you say?"

The general squared his shoulders to gaze into a tin mirror against the wall, his line of sight never falling below his yet broad chest. "An' I still fill out the old uniform nicely, eh, Dexius?"

As the old warrior exited, Dexius allowed himself a faint smile. The hopeless fool was perfect. "And, General, I am my own house."

Chapter 9

Foslegen

The companions retired to Eirec's camp on the rock shelf. It was clean and well laid out. "Arvak and All Swift have drawn Sun Maiden to her bower, now it is time for counsel and feast." The Northman indicated a small keg and a goodly amount of supplies.

"How came you here?" demanded Isolde.

The only member of the troop he had never met, Eirec strained to hide his discomfiture with her direct mannerisms. He pulled his moustaches for a moment's reflection. "I knew you intended towards Amor to find the grand elf. Although a dweomer caster, he is wise and well born."

"In other words, he got our message," added Henlee.

"And so," agreed Eirec, "a few comforts wheedled at great price from that robber Buthard—and I am here."

Apieron shifted uncomfortably. "My friend, know you we hie to darkness and misery, perhaps never to return?"

The big man was slow to respond. When he did, his words were deliberate, "Maybe I understand little of such things, but I know somewhat of misery, and have fought against the whelming darkness these long months." The others regarded him. His mighty frame was, as ever, rendered more imposing by the bearskin. His arms were scarred and burned, and his legs were knotted with muscle below pleated leathern kilts above elk-skin boots. A shirt of close-linked chain widened to a skirt below a broad belt that housed knife and axe. Above his head loomed the four fist-length hilts of his great sword. Eirec's eyes found Isolde's. "Xephard was the bright star of this land. Famous in war … he was my friend. Where you go, so go I, if there is chance for his return."

"I thank you," whispered she.

"We are back to lucky seven," drawled Jamello.

Eirec pulled forth his mighty blade as he stepped to their center. It made a thick noise as it sliced the air overhead. "This is Waelwolf. When feast is served at the tables of Hel, who will be the last to enter?"

Jamello paused in midswallow when the great sword was thrust slightly in his direction. Henlee stepped before the Northman, as wide as the other, although the great blade overtopped him by a foot. He tugged his beard. "You ought to 'ave showed up sooner; Bagwart could have reworked that pigsticker."

Eirec laughed and whirled his slaughter wolf in a sweeping arc of watered steel that arrested mere inches above the dwarf's head.

"And I'm telling you, where we go, it'll probably break."

The moon passed to silver overhead, and the day's haze departed the upper airs, leaving the night bright and crisp. "I am glad you have come," said Eirec. He took a deep pull from his wooden cup. "Welcome!"

"We too are glad," answered Galor. "You journeyed far on short notice."

"I, for one, would hear of your Northland home," added Isolde.

Eirec drew himself up, seated on a length of long-dead pine he had felled. "In my land, there are mountains cut like a pudding with a knife, not like these pebbles you call hills, and the sky is clear, unlike this lowland murk. By the white thighs of Sister Moon, it is like trying to peer through milk."

The needle-boughed trees above them creaked slightly as Eirec's cup rose and fell. "And the trees, mighty trees. Rock pines, shaggy like an old man's beard, and white-barked aspens whose leaves are yellow when the snows come. When I was but a brat, my grandam told me the aspens are wise because they have many eyes to see, yet no mouth to speak."

"Bah!" said Henlee.

"Thus they see much and talk not at all. Surely then they are the wisest things on earth."

"Firwood," snorted Henlee, foam on his beard.

"Like yer head!" said Eirec, rising to stare hard at the dwarf who sat unconcernedly, gazing into his beer.

Eirec reseated himself with a huff. "Two hundred feet straight as a mast pole they are, and wider 'round than a man can reach. There are spruce as well, with branches like wagon spokes and blue as yon wench's eyes. In the summer, the vales be covered with flowers of every color, and many birds nest there."

Again the cup was emptied and refilled. "My people are tall because they live where mountains and trees are tall, and sturdy, because the land is hard as flint, like your mountain dwarf." Henlee was snoring lightly, yet his hand had not relinquished his tin cup. "Lowlanders say we be a large folk because our forefathers mated with giants, but that is a lie they speak because they fear us. Giants live only in the lonely places and are shunned by all men." Eirec paused. "I reck this has changed, some say giants have come again … that the foul lord of Kör has many slaves of that breed."

"I am not a wench," said Isolde. "Tell me now, what will become of your people?"

"The Prince said he will reclaim my home, and though many

of my people doubt it, I believe him. Not so different we are, he and I." A mockingbird pierced the early night with a song, mimicking many birds of day and eve, thicket and treetop.

"Tell us, Eirec, how you came hither?" urged Tallux. "You have shared Buthard's meat and bread with us. Will you not tell your tale?"

"And so," drawled Eirec, obviously not at all displeased with the prospect, "because you ask, I'll unlock my wordhoard." The others leaned in, none having heard the tale told in full, and Isolde, Apieron, and Galor not at all.

"Life on the White Throat is hard, and the men we breed there are tough as anywhere. So when battle thanes were called, mighty carles whetted their axes, and nigh a thousand free men stood spears like a thicket of steel. Thus we did not fear what Kör had to send. By Gul's dragging bullocks, we even struck collar from every thrall fit enough to swing a blade, and there were many of those."

Henlee roused at the content of Eirec's speech, his brown eyes glinting prisms of orange in the light of the dying fire.

"Our far scouts did not sleep, and when the enemy's outriders came, they found our pickets ready and were soon put to flight, for even the black prince of Kör cannot bring great numbers of horses over the Vigfil of a sudden, and those that survive the ice wastes best are only mountain ponies, good enough for patrol and to shoot a dart or two, but useless in the charge.

"Our far-dwellers lit relay fires before retreating to the burg, as I said. So we had been forewarned when the bulk of Kör's force came on. We taunted them with words, and a few flung shafts and rocks, but they did not take time to parlay or make defense. Nor would they send forth a champion, they simply kept formation and ran right into our lines. Kör must value the lives of his rabble not at all. Gods below! We slew them in droves. Halfmen and goblin types and wild hill folk—more ape than man—screamed like rabid beasts, and the folk sang our song of slaughter as each wave after bloody wave we thrust back. My thanes and chiefs fought well. Nary a man shirked, and when one fell, his brothers closed ranks, for if we let those bastards into our rear, we were done. Of course that what's happened. But later."

An odd look found Eirec's face and his dark beard jutted defiantly over his chin, yet he shrugged and continued. "Anyway, my thanes crushed orc skulls and lopped off their filthy limbs until our arms grew tired and our blades notched from the butchery. I tell you, I'd be amazed if the din was not heard down in dwarven mines. And the stink! The carrion birds circled thick as swarmy bees, and still Kör's army came on." Eirec wrinkled his nose and took a great draught of beer as if to cleanse away a foul taste.

"Then what happened?" cried Henlee.

"Even a Northman tires of slaying, that's when the demon general, Iz'd Yar they call him, set his Mgesh on us. These seem a folk of the grass plains, brown skinned, p'raps thus from the cloudless lands they hie from. He must keep them in great numbers, the Kör king, an' they are doughty warriors, neither asking nor giving quarter. They thrust the orcs aside and foamed 'gainst our dike like a flooding river. Ye gods! the bodies were piled high enough for a man to simply walk over the wall. These men chant in an uncouth tongue and they smell as bad as any goblin, but their curved blades are of fine make, and the swertings kill without mercy." Eirec stared at nothing, then gave a gusty sigh. "Eventually their numbers whelmed us, and a break was made into the compound. We rallied and drove them back. Women and boys who lingered came out to fight. Night was come, and it was cold, but the steppesmen were led by helions who do not need light to see.

"Again they breached the walls, man and goblin together, and fire was set within. This worked in our stead, for a space, an' we could see as well as they. Again we slew a number equal to our own force standing in as many minutes as it takes to tell, but they did not relent. A dying orc will entangle a man's hands or feet as he falls, so that another might cleave him. All was chaos, and only my housecarles kept formation; together we were driven from the crag."

"I wish I had been there," enthused Henlee. "Maul grows thirsty at your tale."

"What a fight!" nodded Eirec. "There was not a man among us who escaped scathe. Many brave thanes fell there, and the women and children who did not leave after the warmoot were slain." Eirec read their thought. "Few would be taken, you see. No Northwoman would suffer herself or her children capture by a foreign enemy." His tankard nodded toward Isolde. "The lady knows whereof I speak. I see the blood of the Norting in her, as was in Xephard Bright Helm."

A fitful breeze teased sparks from the campfire. "South we came and gathered such of the scattered kerns and freeman that found us and could march swiftly. By dawn in two days, my score of bloodied thanes had grown to a half a thousand angry men. We joined three hundred dwarves who bore similar tale. We were not a mighty force, and wounded at that, yet enough to discourage any that would think to oppose our march. No patrol or scout of Kör who found us ever lived to report to his demon general." Eirec grinned fondly at some grim memory.

"Your precious barons made fast their gates. They watched us with frowns from their high walls, so we paid them in kind by helping ourselves to a beeve or two, and what grain and fruit there was. A strong man can make a long day's march on a handful of your southern wheat!"

"And you, Eirec, have you married since last we met?" queried Tallux softly.

"Ach, you know me. I need not some wife to chide me."

Jamello laughed aloud. "No wife would have him."

"True enough, trickster, but I've kept a leman these last few years. Her name is Cani. It's amazing how time passes."

"Did she leave with the others … before the attack?" asked Isolde.

"Nope."

"Alas, my friend, I did not know," said Tallux, his face filled with empathy.

"Not to worry. I'm sure she's fine," replied Eirec cheerfully.

"What?" cried Isolde. "I thought you said no woman of your tribe would allow herself to be taken?"

Eirec slapped his knee with glee. "She's no Northwoman, but a sloe-eyed beauty I acquired in trade from a Seod reaver. He could not master her and was afraid she'd make him a castrotto. By Uline's frozen teats, that woman's a fighter! Hair brown as an acorn, and she's formed like Love herself, and meaner than a snow leopard."

The party shared looks of amazement except Apieron, whose face was in shadow.

"Fear not for Cani. One of her beauty will not be given to some vermin-infested goblin. An' the gods help any horse-humper who thinks to take her on; she'll be frying his cockles for breakfast. Besides, I need a break from that woman's lashing tongue. Any plan Apieron has will seem a vacation after her."

Eirec met the gaze of Tallux and Isolde. "What?"

The tales and speech of his friends warmed Apieron. He had cut boughs of juniper for his bed. It was soft and fragrant, yet he did not sleep.

"Hey Apieron," called Henlee. "Know you a stream nearby? Tomorrow we must find water."

"Water!" scoffed Eirec. "I had thought better of you."

"You'll learn. Aye, where we are going, you'll learn."

Apieron listened to the voices of dwarf and Northman. They volunteered first watch, they had much to discuss and ale to drink. Apieron let a last pull from his waterskin drain slowly down his throat. He remembered the Falls of Voices. Oft he had slept nearby, the sound of its water rushing always seemed greater at night. This night, theirs would be a dry camp, with water only for drinking and that from skins. So much the better for he named the spirit of the Falls unfriend, and would go there no more.

KÖR: LAND OF THE MGESH

Cani raised the hide flap and peered at the many yurts around her. It was an hour before dawn, and the eastern sky was already alight on the grassy sweeps of the Mgesh nomads. She had been sent hither in a caged wain with other select captives taken in Kör's raids against the Northmen of Ilycrium. Her great beauty and quarrelsome spirit prompted war chiefs to send her with other booty and the riding wounded, three hundred leagues to their homeland of Ozur, a gift for the khan who rode not to war.

Ghar had called the grand feast, his scarred, swart features splitting into a black-toothed grin when he beheld his new prize. Cani's hair was tawny, and her brown eyes cupped scintillant fires within their depths. Beneath womanly curves, her walnut-skinned, voluptuous body belied the strength and stamina of an athlete.

Ghar gorged on charred meat and guzzled fermented milk until he spilled more of the foul-smelling spirit down his rawhide vest and dangling moustaches than into his gullet. Thus he had roared for his guards and serving wenches to absent themselves from his yurt, which was more like a moveable palace, so that now he might sport with his new plaything.

Cani's quick eyes noted movement in the Mgesh encampment. A war camp was never truly still, and the Mgesh knew no other condition. The whole affair could be up and riding to the attack or retreat within minutes. By law, it was death for a Mgesh warrior to be found asleep without at least a horseman's lance by his side. She could hear the Khan's guard shifting in the false dawn as vigilant men do, and a few still mumbled in their stringy beards, chortling at the Khan's boasts of prowess he would prove on the new wench. They had placed more than a few bets of their own.

The interior of the yurt was silent and dark, for she had let its oil lamps smoke out, the better to conceal her position, and the Khan would not need light again. After the last of his war chiefs staggered off, he slashed her bonds in his frenzy of lust. Cani had allowed his drunken pawings until the last revelers sought their beds. How Ghar's eyes widened as his own magnificently jeweled dagger crossed his throat! She thrust the curved blade into a sash. This went over leather trousers and concealed beneath a horsehide vest she pilfered from the yurt's great stores. Food and water she now had aplenty, as well as a length of rope and various and sundry small items that caught her fancy—payment against his drunken jests and ineffective fondlings. Indeed, she felt she took more hurt of his breath than his hands.

As dawn's mists uncoiled, Cani finally spied what she sought; the small steed of a scout was left tethered close by. The Khan's own stock was inaccessible, guarded more so than his person. She slipped from the tent and wended her way to the horse picket, her felt slippers making not a sound on the hard-packed earth. Keeping her eyes down, she followed a course that kept her within night's lingering shadows.

There! A smallish, box-headed pony already tacked to ride as she had hoped. The beast eyed her peevishly until she swatted its ugly snout and settled swiftly into the thin saddle on his back. He snorted but swung obediently to the darkling west after she jerked his head in the desired course. Cani cursed the tribesmen again, for they rode without stirrup or steel bit. Cluck-clucking the little horse along, she soon found a well-trampled trail; behind her, the tempo of the camp was unchanged.

Some thirty minutes later, she allowed a little smile as she looked upon open plains. A tall form on rearing stallion hove in front of her. The pony pulled up as if poleaxed, then stood truculently before the intruder. Somehow Cani managed to keep her seat, and the Khan's curved dagger flashed free as the horse warrior approached. Broad of shoulder with razor-sharp features and a fierce bearded moustache that conjoined vibrant black hair, he loomed over her like some mounted god of war.

Cani was motionless. As he approached, she noted the tattoos of many victories on his face and the rich workings of his garb. Here was no sentry, but a mighty chief! Perhaps a son of the Khan himself. She moved not a muscle, not daring to inhale as he urged his steed around her with subtle commands she could not discern. Although he displayed no weapon, menace was writ in his every gesture.

He completed his circuit and brought his charger nose to nose with her little mount. He was doubtless aware of her identity, so great had been the fanfare of her arrival with the news of victory and first of the booty obtained from the men of the West. With a jerking nod, he held out a sword-calloused hand for the dagger. She met his black, unblinking stare, as alert as that of a raptor, yet neither did her own brown gaze falter. Slowly she handed the hilts of the magnificent jambiya over.

He gazed at it, surely there could be only one such weapon.

She was astonished when he handed it back with a wide grin more terrifying than his scowl. He drew his lance so swiftly she could scarce follow, and before she could react, he saluted her with a flourish, then laughed aloud his delight when he saw she did not flinch. He reared his stallion before her and walked it back on two legs to turn and plunge at once into a graceful gallop directly en route to the city of tents. She had no doubt that the tall warrior would become the new khan in Ozur, mightiest land of the Mgesh.

As Cani turned again westward, it did not concern her that her own deed set in motion events that would shake the standards of the grasslands, and would darken the eyes of Iblis, Prince of Kör. She knew only that the horse warrior's strange actions meant that she was free. She would proceed warily as always, yet somehow felt her way would not be hindered. The little horse seemed glad at the open expanses that lay before them. Tough and wiry, the ugly pony was perfect for the lengthy journey and could subsist indefinitely on food and drink that would leave its Western brethren rolling in the dust.

It never occurred to Cani that she might stay with the Mgesh. Although swift and savage, she knew their morays to be no worse than those of many "civilized" men she had encountered. It never crossed her mind to stay, and in time, wield the power of a queen over these proud peoples. She had one Eirec of Amber Hall to repay for abandoning her when the Steeps were reaved. Aye, she knew well the way. Every painful jolt and jounce of the prisoner wane had been bruised into her memory.

Cani rode west by north, where lay the wild hills of Kör under the high pass at White Throat. Beyond was the land of the Northmen of Ilycrium, and somewhere south of there, she would, no doubt, find the mighty jarl, Eirec of Amber Hall, skulking and chewing his moustaches and mouthing excuses. It would help fill the hours of the tedious journey to prepare her scornful responses to any ditherings he might summon when he beheld her again. For the first time in months, Cani was happy, and she heeled the ugly pony to a quicker gait.

Chapter 10

Foslegen

The seven companions paused for a rest. Eirec hummed a stave that Apieron seemed not to hear. Soon the ranger resumed point and moved off, the stony ridge of Eirec's camp left far behind. The day was clear and temperate, perfect for walking, although the long legs of their leader had Jamello and Henlee at nigh a trot. Isolde enjoyed the exercise, glad to fill her days with doing after crawling months of waiting for a man who did not return.

It was the ninth month, and autumn touched the countryside. Gentle declivities oft housed dry streambeds where canopies of cottonwood and sycamore appeared sifting facets of gold and green. "How lovely your hair is in this light," quoth Jamello to Isolde. Her flaxen locks had grown somewhat since his temple sojourn, and the leaf-filtered light burnished her bound tresses copper and honey.

"Be silent and walk," said she.

"And why?" said Jamello to no one and all. "Why must we toil like sunbaked beetles when our spell-master might whisk us wither we wish with a word?" Apieron revealed no reaction, yet he was forced to pause as did the others. Isolde glowered at the thief.

"I might," replied Galor at last. "With ease could I take us to the Hel door we seek, albeit who knows what we shall find there? Best perhaps to arrive in stealth."

Eirec tossed aside the last remnant of Buthard's yearling calf and wiped his fingers on his shirt. "Why not spell-walk a short distance from yonder portal?"

"Are you as dense as the popinjay?" asked Isolde. "Mayhap the winters of Alkeim have frozen the sap of your mind."

Eirec fixed her with his best beard-bristling scowl. Isolde impatiently tapped her spear butt on the ground as if addressing naughtily ignorant temple squires. "Though it seems not so, the savants of the enemy search the ether for us as we speak. By the powers of the goddess and the shieldings of Lord Galor alone are we hidden."

"Good," agreed Henlee. "I prefer to walk."

"And so, woman?" huffed Eirec. "Let them come."

"Not here. Not now," said Apieron, his voice low but intense. "Only in the heart of darkness will we find She that waits, and he who serves Her." Apieron wheeled and struck in his stave.

The shifting sea of Galor's eyes fell on Jamello and Eirec. "For now, walk faster, talk less!"

The way chosen by Apieron shelved downward as the day aged. Underbrush grew proportionally more dense, slowing their march, and for hours, tangleroot and thorny vines snagged boot and pack with no clearing for rest and air. Even Tallux suffered scratch of skin and rent of garment, albeit the wood elf did not slap and curse the offending creepers as did man and dwarf.

Ever they descended, following a murmur dimly perceived through bole and bramble until at last the ceaseless chuckle of water running was unimpeded. The forest opened up, and a grove of river elm brought them to its bank. The companions slowed to breathe mist-cooled air as innumerable saw-toothed leaves weaved their dance in amber. Camp was made on a graveled beach, clean and breezy. Echoing bluffs lined the farther side of the river whose green water was nearly clear, save in small shoals where the water streamed over moss-slick stones, yielding countless iridescent eddies. A gray crane flapped ahead of them, only to light on a submerged branch and turn to regard them as if expecting the companions to follow.

"A beautiful stream you have found us," enthused Jamello as he readied his nets. They could see tapered, golden bass that darted from blue-green pools, and near the shore, an orange fish nipped and struck at anything animate within the sphere of its suzerainty.

"You are first," promised Jamello with a chuckle to the orange fish.

"Hold," commanded Isolde. "This is Lylwelvyn, is it not?" Apieron nodded. "Then I will make commune. This stream gathers many waters and touches many lands north to south." Isolde began to disrobe.

Jamello edged to peer around Henlee's broad back, yet saw only a dwarfen scowl. "Gather firewood!"

After a time, Isolde rose from the water. Apieron held her shawl in outspread arms. She shook water from her hair, and laughed when cold drops spattered Apieron's front, then bound her hair in a rag of blue. "You may fish now, thief. The daughters of Lylwelvyn will allow it."

"What news, lady?" called Galor softly.

"The war goes hard for the prince of men; Kör pursues the army of the West." Isolde faltered. "Lylwelvyn's daughters say the knights … soon the knights of the Temple will ride their last."

Tallux and Jamello were crestfallen. They busied themselves, mechanically ordering the camp. Apieron escorted Isolde aside.

Eirec scowled and turned to the others. "My mood has grown

foul." His large hand pointed. "And that one! The lass is comely enough, but no woman should walk the battle way."

Isolde donned her travel garments, pants tucked into leathers over a swordsman's blouse. She retrieved her spear and swirled it about so rapidly that its steel appeared a flashing circuit.

Tallux seemed cheered and grinned at Eirec. "You tell her."

From the stream bank, Jamello stifled a laugh.

The Northman rubbed his bald pate and tugged his beard but was otherwise immobilized. Henlee stood behind Jamello, hands on hips. He chewed his moustache and sucked his teeth, noting that the orange fish deftly evaded every trick and device of the thief. "And who told her that?" he demanded at last.

The outburst startled Jamello whose cast fell wide. The fish struck angrily at the net and eyed Jamello with defiance. "Who told her what?"

"News from the Northlands," snapped Henlee. "Who told her, a talking fish?"

"Nay, nay, yet I once knew of an oyster who was quite intelligent and gave rather good advice, save his master never listened."

"And why was that?" offered the dwarf suspiciously.

"Because, my dear simple dwarf, everyone knows that oysters are notorious liars. How can one take them seriously?"

"I know how to take them," pronounced Henlee, patting his stomach. "That's baked, with a dozen mullet on the side."

"What's an oyster?" demanded Eirec.

Henlee whirled on him. "You can't live your whole life on deer liver and seal fat."

"Exactly," agreed Eirec. "Catch fish, thief."

Jamello shot Eirec a withering look. "You've spooked them, oaf. Maybe you should thresh them out like a bear."

Henlee rubbed his hands. "A bet, thief against bear?"

River daughters murmured their ceaseless song throughout the night. By dawn, the companions walked the river mist, enjoying Lylwelvyn's pebble strand although eventually her long arcs swerved away eastward, and the travelers were obliged to cross the friendly stream. Before their feet, fingerlings flashed like silver coins in their thousands across a shallow ford where the green water ran swift. A hand-pulling climb up a fold in the far bank discovered a hardwood forest that carpeted steplike rises mounting to a high flat, which was the planned course of Apieron and Galor. For three days they traveled thus.

Fox squirrels scolded the intruders in shaded ravines whilst their gray cousins scampered the rises with quick crunching sounds across bracken at the companions' approach, agile as acrobats. Once safely ensconced in their leafy homes of hilltop hickory, they barked and chided in anger. Deer scrapes marked many a game trail and bucks grunted amorous songs by dawn and twilight, soon the day entire.

Farstriker felled a hind, small but grown fat on beech and honeysuckle. Its meat lasted only two days amongst hungry travelers, yet Tallux wasted neither skin or sinew that the woodsmaster put to various uses. Once they glimpsed flocking turkeys, the large birds walking a skirmish line through the trees, clucking softly and foraging red-berried dogwood and wax myrtle. Ungainly though they seemed, the uncanny fowl soon disappeared without seeming to hurry. Apieron did not alter stride.

On the eve of the sixth day from Windhover, they encamped below an isolated hilltop, the first of a chain that Apieron named Mannyr, and Henlee simply Giant Hedge. It was there that the salty-chinned ancestor of squirrels singled out Eirec for abuse. "Limb rat," pronounced he with disgust as a rain of woody debris and odour pelted the big man, flecking his beard and back.

"Come, Sir Elf," pleaded the barbarian. "Feather this white devil with that pretty bow of yours."

Tallux eyed the chattering squirrel and then the man. "I do not kill for sport." A smile ghosted his lips. "Besides, Grandfather Squirrel asked me the same favor of you."

Eirec snorted in disbelief as the wood elf retired to the warmth of his bedroll, his form nigh invisible against the ground. "What of you, thief?" demanded Eirec.

"Alas," answered Jamello, "I must beg off. It seems my throwing wrist has gone lame this eve."

"You are ambidextrous," accused Isolde.

"He's useless; I told you," said Henlee to Eirec.

"Fine allies you have chosen, young Apieron!" snorted Eirec. When no response was forthcoming, the Northman flung himself down under another tree and rolled into the furry mantle that also served him as ground cloth.

Jamello's olive face gleamed warm in the last light. "And you, dear lady, tell me of Lylwelvyn's daughters. How did they appear? Were they comely?"

Isolde stared as if deep in thought, then raised to regard the thief with a little smile, flipping a blond wisp from her face as the troubadour fidgeted with impatience.

"Naked, sir."

"Naked?"

"Naked." She faced away from him, wrapped in her blanket.

Jamello sputtered, fully awake and quivering, then stomped off to assume first watch, cursing the duplicity of clerics and women—in particular the deviousness of female clerics. The camp grew quiet, save the patter of a squirrel's offerings begun anew above the locale where Eirec lay. A soft, wheezing chuckle was heard that sounded much like that of a dwarf …

"Tell me, my friend, do you believe in ultimate justice?"

Xephard was a long time in answering, so long that Apieron feared he had fallen asleep, as was his habit when with friends in comfort. The Falls of Voices churned a peaceful resonance behind them. "Yes, I do. My Northern fathers said those who live and die with honor gain seat at the eternal feast. I believe this to be a hero's reward at the right hand of the Goddess Who Loves War."

"I meant resolution for all who suffer, warriors or no. Children, women, men of any sort, the maimed, the helpless. Those without hope"—a restless angst stirred again in Apieron, something undone—"a time when the world will be mended."

Xephard looked to the sky. It was blue and perfect, dotted with dragon's breath clouds. "I do."

"I am glad."

"But there is something—"

"Yes?"

The famous knight fixed Apieron with his unshadowed eyes. "If we two are here to believe in the ever-peace, it must be there are those who strive for endless war."

Apieron beheld a vision. It was a man, formed much as himself in mind and will, who wore a sculpted hauberk over chain of adamantine, his plate adorned with helstones that shimmered with dark enchantments. The man's hand held a sword of destruction, and on his left was the shield of a hero—a mighty circuit of gods and champions borne by Apieron's friend for a decade and a half. A golden serpent crawled the man's finger.

Apieron turned to Xephard, who sat placidly in sunlight. A mist from the falls caught the light behind him. Xephard ran his knotted arm in unceasing rhythm with a rag along Leitus's shining length, then grinned to see his friend regard him so. "What is wrong?"

"You."

Xephard smiled placidly. "Me?"

"You are dead …"

Apieron woke. Leitus had found his hands. Unsheathed, she suffused the camp with a bluish glow. Galor stared at him, and the elf's eyes reflected the azure light. Apieron nodded, resheathed Xephard's sword, and lay down to sleep, perchance to find again his friend. He did not.

The companions rose to a chill morning. Below the hillside's knees where they made camp, a steading was revealed, its cabin rotting back into the earth from which it had risen in happier times. A dawn fog lay over fields and woodcuts like feathery serpents, and the rising light caught on yellow- and russet-leafed maple and burnished red sorrel into dayglow. Autumn was full on the land, and the travelers traversed the weed-grown cot in hopes of finding fence grapes or a neglected plum tree, but there were none. They abandoned the garth for the forest beyond, and their feet found a fold where poplar and larch grew. It gave onto the rim of a small lake, shallow where emerald grasstops dotted its surface. Shoreline willows arched over the water in quest of sunlight, while clusters of birch stood in low places and held shagbarked conclave. Teal bobbed, silent and dark in the mere's center.

The companions left them for a climbing fosse that shadowed the long limbs of a green hillock. From there was another cleft and a greater rise such that all the day, down and up, the travelers passed beyond lesser downs to the feet of a higher country. Jamello practiced, "I love thee … thee I love." Each time he spoke, he changed inflections or added an eloquent flourish.

"How utterly revolting you are," said Isolde between leaf-crunching steps.

"Repetition is the key to success, milady."

Jamello broke into song. "Who shall be my lover tonight? Flirtsome Belamunde, or the almond-eyed beauty of Seifu?"

The day was nearly done. Fireweed and buttercup and many clovers covered an upslope dotted with spruce. Lagging behind,

Eirec happily added yellow parsley and bittercress to a wicker creel he lightly bore that already contained the last (and most potent) of his beer, as well as a mound of potato and rhubarb he managed to forage.

"Instead of wasting your time and money wenching, knave, you should seek a woman of character to be true to."

Jamello sniffed and pulled his moustache. "The ladies I accompany are true. They allow a man to be a man." The thief touched his embroidered doublet. "In return, I provide for them, and they need not fear the streets. For their part, my comforts are seen to and my bed warmed."

Isolde shook her head fiercely. "A true woman is happy in herself—she need not seek the measure of her worth in the eyes of any man. Nor, thief, does a true man need continuous reassurance of his dominance." An accusing finger pointed at Jamello's breast. "He is strong enough to respect strength in his partner."

Jamello stared upward, as if thinking mighty thoughts. "So, who wants a partner?"

Isolde's face colored. "You are impossible! The voice of Wisdom is lost on you." She increased the pace of her steps.

"Being wise does not sound like any fun," called he.

The fair sound of elfsong rose and fell against the rock face. It was accompanied by the rush of frigid water over stones—a southern distributary of Icingflow, a glacier river. Man and dwarf did not recognize the words, yet toasted them silently as echoes of things that grow and die were stirred in their memories. When he had finished, Tallux helped himself to Eirec's stew, although not the last of the ale whose weight had been carried many miles. Eirec tossed off the contents of his wooden cup and moved to fill another. "I have no ear for flowery ballads. I have known men, some strong warriors, stir and cry out during the skald's song, yet they would sleep through life. Such men are but empty shells, a fruit that has hung too long in the sun; its skin is perhaps pleasing, but the meat inside is worthless."

Above them, the cliff's face was pockmarked and the nesting place of many swallows. Small and swift, they arched from the overhang to swoop after invisible prey or to chase rivals and lovers on backswept wings. Down the edge and over the stream they soared before cutting and fading back to their craggy homes. To Jamello, they looped in the air like glide-fish in water. "How I miss fish."

To Henlee, they resembled doves that resembled squab, which were almost fat game hens that are (of course) almost as tasty as pen-raised goose. The dwarf rapped a biscuit on his tin plate; it sounded like a rock. "Those birds are a trifle small, I reckon. Might not a master thief rig a net and snare a dozen or three to make a pie?"

"Swallow pie?" Isolde's nose wrinkled.

"A master thief," quoth Jamello, "does not knit nets for dwarves."

Apieron looked up, a rare smile creasing his careworn face. "Master or no, those swallows are quick as falcons and brainier than city-born thieves."

"Do I detect a wager?" challenged Jamello archly. Henlee smiled broadly, as much to see Apieron relax a trifle as at the jest. He began to dig for his cooking pot.

Eirec snorted. "The appetites of dwarves … and badgers."

The pot clanked back into its bag. "You, Eirec, seem happy enough to sit by the fire and drink a stoop whether the skald sings or no."

Eirec laughed heartily. "I was thirsty." He stood and drained his flagon in one draught to the dismay of the dwarf.

Tallux's finger wagged chidingly. "As the bird is born to fly, one might be thus moved to sing. P'raps others are thereby inclined to listen."

Eirec waved his hands disparagingly. "Pretty words, Sir Elf. I smell your smoke, but where's your fire?" For emphasis, the big man tossed an arm's length of pinion onto their little blaze. Its light reflected orange off the rock. Eirec puffed out his chest, awaiting approval for his cleverness.

"Braggart." Henlee stood before the tall human, hands on hips. Eirec's face flushed and returned the scowl. "To repeat the words of an ancient dwarven saying: Have another!" Henlee slapped the Northman on the shoulder.

Apieron and Tallux moved to sit nigh Eirec. His bearded face was red in the firelight, and his eyes shined. "Do you wish to know the ultimate ballad? It is the battle song … when men make the dance of steel. Ha! The song of steel." He slid down the log and fell instantly asleep.

"I deem the people of his kindred hear the battle song all their waking days," said Tallux.

One corner of Apieron's lip lifted slightly, and he pointed his beard at the snoring Eirec. "Only when they are awake?"

"Indeed a fell people. I do not understand why their short lives are spent entire in pursuit of war."

"My father told me once," said Apieron, "nothing is more fearsome than the sight of an elvin host come to battle. He guessed the flames of anger come rarely in their long days, yet when they are kindled, the fire is hot."

"True enough, and happily not often." Tallux produced a small tool knife and meticulously inspected each arrow of his quiver.

Isolde tried to regain the presence of the divinity. Late in the final watch, a light mantle kept her from the false dawn's chill. She could feel his eyes upon her. On her knees, Isolde pretended to adjust an ankle wrap and scanned his position. Rudolph Mellor was there, squatting on a tall stone and fiddling with a quirt. He whistled softly an absurd ditty. He nodded to her and grinned, his pointed moustache only accentuating his roguishness.

Isolde yielded no sign of recognition, and by the chill in her glance, he might have been a stump or crawling worm. She tried to recall her holy thoughts; for twenty years, she had risen before Sun raced his golden chariot, to pray and meditate with the priestesses, first so as a child pupil, then the prodigy who soon led the praises. Alone or in travel, she never failed to find a moment of cleansing before each day's challenge.

Jamello's tune rose a pitch, the thief now interposing the words of some lewd sailor's ballad.

Isolde squeezed shut her eyes and pictured the blessed temple, its fine white columns overlooking olive-studded hills and rows of grape far to the valley's edge. In her head, a skinny drunken seaman hid under the skirts of his captain's wife, as her blustering husband searched high and low for the missing deckhand.

"Stop that inane noise, thief! It is not clever, you know … only base and stupid."

"Lady, whatever—"

"I do not ken why Lord Apieron and Henlee ever chose you to accompany us."

"I must—"

"All you do is eat and swill and brag. Even if you have stolen anything of significance, which I doubt, I don't see how a mere cutpurse might aid us anyhow."

"Please, madame," Jamello pushed back the air with his hands. "If you permit me, I will relate the true tale of how I did steal something despite grave peril; it was of great value."

"I do not doubt this to be another absurdity of a bantling, most likely grown magnificent in a thousand barside retellings."

Jamello shrugged and resumed his humming and dart tossing.

Henlee sat up and shook free sheets of dew like a shaggy dog. Apieron stood, checking the draw of his sword before anything. "So much like Xephard," muttered Isolde.

"Very well, rogue. You may speak, but mind your tongue. Or I shall place an unlucky hex on you."

"Assuredly, milady. I would do nothing to risk your reproach." Jamello dropped from his perch and sprang lightly to her side.

"Now listen while I relate a tale of such renown and daring that most travelers have heard of it, and those fortunates weep tears of joy as their noble hearts swell with pride." Oblivious to Isolde's scowl, the troubadour continued, "After countless leagues of trackless wastes, one comes to the inland sea of Noissap. Although it is surrounded on four sides by land, it is an ocean with salt and tides, but is unique amongst all the waters of the world, for it is hot and thick like syrup from a cauldron. If a man be bold and hearty enough to venture across pitiless lands, scale red heights, and cross the viscous sea, he will find an isle of enchantment: the garden palace of Queen Anigav."

"Indeed, sir. Were you such a man?"

"'Tis true, Your Worship." Jamello touched his fanciful doublet humbly. "And accompanied by none other than Lord Apieron and the peerless Xephard. It was there, in the beautiful despot's secret and magical grotto, that I stole her famous jewel, her most valuable possession." Isolde scowl softened. She disliked her proximity to the young scoundrel, yet she felt safe enough. Admittedly her curiosity was piqued by the sensuous young queen and the mysterious gem.

"Would you like me to continue, milady?"

Isolde nodded.

"Very well," said Jamello with a wink. "It was from the very bower of the royal lady that I found her treasure. Perfumed were the hanging silks that adorned the inner sanctum, songbirds wooed sweetly, and a perfect breeze caressed my skin. Ever mindful of my peril, nonetheless I thrust forward. Many daring noblemen had attempted passage only to be lost forever, so fearful the grotto's barriers."

Jamello sipped a little water. "Boldly I groped toward the famous yet never seen holdfast … here 'twas dark … the air close, and hot! There in murky shades, I—alone of all men—purloined her hidden jewel."

Jamello appeared quite pleased. Isolde opened her mouth to query him further when the dwarf bellowed from ten paces away. "Thief, cease that yammering and fetch us some good water."

"But, Master," protested Jamello, "we filled our skins last night from yonder brook." He pointed to the chill stream, shaded under ferns and mossy banks.

"And I, Master Jongleur, prefer the taste of the spring we encountered last eve, the one half a mile back our trail."

Jamello's mouth opened, but the dwarf's bristling, gem-bright beard and fierce, wrinkled brows gave him pause. "I agree. That lovely rill does indeed possess a fresh taste. I will gladly be off to fetch water for breakfast." Jamello bowed apologetically to Isolde and scooped up their water johns.

"And hurry!" Without meeting the cleric's eye, Henlee returned to shaking his bedding dry.

Isolde looked up. The men of the rock-face camp seemed to

concentrate with unusual diligence on the pack up. She placed her hand on Apieron's shoulder plate to stare up at the tall ranger.

"Did you really—"

Apieron bowed, his brown hair partially hiding an odd twist to his mouth. "One must subtract somewhat from the tales of a thief."

"As to your question, popinjay, Amber Hall is what it is called because of the amber, of course. 'Twas my father's best treasure, a log of amber, big as an ogre's head and pure, like frozen honey." Eirec smoothed his paw-like hand over his bald head, then stroked his black beard. "'Tis all gone now—melted or stolen I'm guessing." He cleared his throat. "Now for my question, Apieron. What of the woman?"

The ground had grown soft, and footfalls deadened as the companions walked an upland forest. Shadows crawled beneath dense stands of noble fir and narrow spruce. There was little undergrowth here save star moss, and sphagnum, and orange rubbery fungi that climbed sullen hemlocks and age-contoured pines.

"The value of the priestess lays not in her strength of arm," said Apieron. "She is a focus for the power of the goddess, like a tall tree that draws lightning. Or a mirror that holds reflection of the sun."

Eirec scowled, and his eyes tracked Isolde who was some distance apart. Galor was nigh. They halted, and the mage poured out the contents of a small bag upon a scrap of cloth. Eirec ran a hand over the hilts of his great sword as if to reassure himself. "Yon golden magnus said that where we go there is no sun. Instead of a focus for your goddess's powers, she is like to be a lodestone that draws the wrath of the accursed."

"You speak truth." Galor looked up from a small pile of glittering dust that he traced with a white stick. "However," he twirled the wood to make his point, "it is given to the handmaidens of her goddess to see much that many do not." Eirec snorted, but Galor was unperturbed. "More like to the Eldar children they are."

He gestured to Tallux who sat listening. A breeze had gotten up and sifted in the wood elf's dark hair. "They see beyond outer forms of natural and builded things, to the spirit that moves within." Where fell Galor's uncanny gaze, the others shifted uneasily.

"And more so than the Eldar children is their perception of ghosts and the occult artifices of man. Whether this be from insight gleaned from their human nature or absence of concern on the part of the elves, I do not know, yet such is not to be scorned or neglected."

"You are the mightiest of your people in battle, my friend," added Apieron. His eyes were level with Eirec's. "To know where and when to strike the blow is as important as the sinew of the arm that guides it."

Eirec looked hard at Isolde, his brow furrowed in contemplation. Beyond her, Jamello glided into view from the netlike patterns of the sun through trees. Henlee whistled when Jamello performed the most eloquent and courtly bow that any had ever seen and smiled widely at Isolde. "Methinks this forest is haunted, how sad the wind is."

"You are nothing but a thief."

"A thief? Do you know what it is to go hungry, milady?"

Rudolph Mellor's face gathered a distant memory. In a second, it was gone, yet Jamello's half smile was shadowed by the thing that had fled. "The rich man welcomes the first awakenings of his body's hunger as with pleasant diversion he contemplates the feast. The poor man dreads it for he knows its rumblings will pang and grow, a poker through his middle when not assuaged."

"Do not confuse the issue." Isolde grasped her spear as if for reassurance. "One might be a thief and wealthy, or poor as we of the temple, yet noble. Do you realize Messir, the devotees of our Goddess of Wisdom, take vows of poverty?"

"You baffle me again, lady. Who would seek to be poor by choice? I knew in my heart that the clerics of the Lampus were insane." Jamello touched his breast apologetically. "And here am I, more foolish than they."

Eirec shook his head as if to clear it of their distracting notions. "Who is the most powerful sorcerer, Master Elf? You?"

"Why, it must be Jamello." Apieron emitted a wry laugh. "Have you forgotten his magnificent dice tricks last eve? A twenty winning streak could be nothing less than magical."

"Aye, dangerous magic," agreed Henlee, fixing Jamello with a scowl. The dwarf's hand involuntarily sought a small but heavy pouch at his belt. Jamello stood transfixed, his argument forgotten. With the group's attention entirely on him, he smoothed his breeches and leaned casually against a smooth-barked trunk while he endeavored not to meet the fierce glare of the dwarf whose treble-stitched coin pouch seemed unnaturally light in Henlee's protective grasp.

"I mean not that," persisted Eirec. "Jugglers and cutthroats are niederlings to me."

"Cutthroats?" echoed Jamello.

A sound buffeted the party. It was a cat.

Jamello caromed into Eirec and fell forward onto his knees. The animal's unnatural roar shook trees and sloughed bark as an angry wind snapped green boughs and blew pine dust into airborne wheels. Over ten feet in length, the beast crouched its mighty bulk in preparation for a spring. Behind it, a man strode through a door of pulsing light, a taint of demon leering from his face. At his side were soldiers bearing the ensign of Kör.

Apieron leapt to the fore, javelins of white and black in either hand. The witch-man spoke. "You, Child of the Starfall, I shall slay and earn favor of She Who Stirs." The panther's teeth were steely daggers, its eyes, green fire. With his little stick, Galor slashed the air. The demon mage was sundered into two parts, and the resulting explosion blew his trailing cohort into receding oblivion. The companions staggered to their knees and blinked through swirling forest bracken.

Henlee spurred the unmoving cat with his boot, but it was dead before he arrived. Two javelins were fixed at neck and lung. "Metal mouth!" He lowered Maul. Apieron wrenched his javelins from the beast, and its blood hissed as it burned free, the stink of it fading on the wind.

"Nice toadstickers the old spaedam gifted you," enthused the dwarf.

"Our blessed Donna," corrected Isolde.

"No disrespect." Henlee's brown eyes fixed Apieron's gray. "She loves thee well." The javelins returned to their hiding place.

A crystal cut goblet found Galor's hand, and a maroon wine appeared within the faceted glass. He imbibed deeply. Eirec and Henlee, Tallux and Jamello and Isolde simply stared. "I needed that." The staring continued. "What? I am not a stone!"

"By Njard's frozen teats," chuckled Eirec. Henlee sniggered, and soon a welling laughter overtook them. Isolde shared in the mirth. Galor scowled but held forth his hand as the burgundy elixir reappeared and was drained again.

Galor turned, and the goblet vanished. Apieron had not

shared the jest. His gaze remained on the fixed snarl of the cat, baleful even in death.

Galor drew near and spoke words only for him. "Even stalwarts such as our friends need levity; they are not automatons." He touched Apieron's breast. "As you are not."

"My heart is cold, Lord."

Apieron fingered a cloth scrap of blue-and-brown patchwork. "Against this—" he nodded to the mighty beast, "she had no chance."

Chapter 11

Sway

The men of Sway fortified the lookout posts placed in bygone days upon their harbor's sister hills, now making them strong. Great stores of wood for signal fires by night and colored smokes by day were set thereon. Cranes were builded with iron dropweights that could hull a ship in a splintering second. Ballistae and mangonels were placed on every level surface to cover the harbor approaches with threat of slung stones and mighty javelins, and flaming vessels of oily naptha, which was the terror of any seagoing vessel.

Thus, the sisters were given names anew. Broad and steadfast Haskald became Scyld, the shield maiden; her taller sibling was dubbed Iphus, Lady of Victory.

From under his prominent forehead and thinning blondish hair, Dexius's dull blue eyes studied Hardel. The old soldier was stuffing himself with baked hen whilst conversing with one Brockhorst, prefect of the city guard. Sweat stained the tunics of both men as evidence of their morning rounds under a sun that remembered summer and raised steam from cobblestones and the plastered flanks of buildings. Dexius fingered his collar of fox, gratefully inhaling the perfume placed therein. That the Prince had chosen the aging military bureaucrat over one of his own excellence was no surprise. Because he was not born of their ranks, he hated the nobility, and hated commoners no less, for the fact that they were common.

The men discussed the disposition of what little troops remained, and those were mostly harbor police and guards of the watch. Rural conscripts tardy to arrive had been sent to join the army and face chastening by Trakhner's heavy hand. Dexius scoffed. Dolts! The abandonment of the capital was a master stroke by Kör. He thought of the gallant princeling. Young fool. Sway *was* Ilycrium, and soon she would have a new master. The Strategos of Kör, concerned with affairs north and east, would surely be reliant on the benign but firm hand of a ruling prime minister. Dexius smoothed the front of his brocaded robes.

"Are you well, sirrah?"

Dexius startled to find the bland face of Hardel and the policeman's dissecting gaze directed at him. He sketched a hurried bow. "Thank you, Lord. Concerns of office."

"An' we shall leave you to them! We've an inspection or three before sup." Hardel heaved his girth from his seat. "Brockhorst seeks to make me a lesser man, methinks he schemes with my surgeon." Both men laughed; Dexius spared a polite chuckle.

"And why not, General?" added Brockhorst. "It seems every other man in the city hides some plot."

The soldiers departed noisily, their steps marked by Dexius who stroked his collar. "Fox indeed." Although he found every aspect of their persons distasteful, he inhaled their passing as rather a wolf that marks the scent of prey.

THE GEHULGOG

""What?" shrieked Luchenzeril, warden of Archwaze.

Singing echoed from the blackest reaches in the mines of Kör. He ducked into the cell in which hung the pallid captive, and

Luchenzeril's bloodshot eyes bulged, for the prisoner stood. His manacled limbs bore their chains, but the long pins had somehow been fractured from the stone.

"Silence, naked rat!"

The coping above opened like the jaws of some mighty beast, and the Azgod was snatched and drawn up into its depths. There came a single crunch. The prisoner strode free, and into shadowed passageways, he walked without fear. Well he knew the way; it was etched in his mind, told by the very stone. Thralls ceased their labors and gave back in pause. He came to a domed crossroads lit with flambeaus.

With a rushing bellow, Urgup squeezed his bulk into the clear. He nodded to a tall human at his side—a favorite assassin. Without hesitation, the man-creature sprang to the attack. Grasping a bandolier of five wicked daggers, he pumped his hands in rapid succession, his motions a blur. Against a normal opponent, the prisoner would parry and dodge the blades, but against one such as this, he knew the knives would come at cunning angles meant to target different vital areas. The assassin would anticipate speed of defense, and perhaps the first three attacks merely set up a fourth or fifth critical blow. The prisoner's manacled wrist swirled from the side, drawing its chain in serpentine coil. The daggers clove to its trailing surface, somehow magnetized to the steel.

The prisoner flicked missiles of his own. Prepared to dodge, the man watched them approach. Bits of greenish glass they appeared, and off target. He laughed his derision as they spiraled overhead, to his sides and at his feet. The prisoner snapped his fingers. Each shard exploded, and there was a smell as of burning sand.

Urgup unslung his heavy glaive. Borne by his mighty limbs, it whooshed lightly through the turbid air like a farmer's scythe in the guttering light. Urgup felt mildly disconcerted when he met the crystalline gaze of the captive. Enraged, he roared and charged. There was a quick cut. A cry rang out.

The Azgod towered over the pale figure who took a short, unsteady step back. Urgup took a step to follow. He toppled. The prisoner tossed away the executioner's glaive. Drudges rushed to strike the irons from his limbs.

"Thank you."

Thir rushed into the prisoner's cell. So it was true. The bolt stone was empty and oddly twisted. Thir ran his heavy paw over its undulant surface, then bent to retrieve something from the floor.

It was his jar, strangely altered. Where before had been aged glass, stained and broken, precious aquamarine and green peridot flashed in the gloom. Its surface now cut in a thousand perfect facets as it glowed like a glacial lake in the cup of his hands, star-flecked on the black surface of his eyes.

ILYCRIUM: THE ARMY

As it went, Ilycrium's army gained speed and cohesion. Slow ox-driven wains were exchanged for mule carts. Foot gear, the life of marching infantry, was redistributed based on need, irrespective of rank or coin. Protests aimed at Trakhner's stiff back sunk to barest murmur when Seamus hulked into view.

For the greater part, the levies of Ilycrium were men born to simple toil or trade, never had they thought to partake in strife with the masters of Kör, by their reckoning a land of immortal demonkind populated with strange monsters that no doubt overmatched the muscle and wit of ordinary men. Rumors of Xephard's demise filtered through the ranks. The Temple Peers were folk heroes throughout the lands now; good wives and elderlings of thorp and burg shook their heads with doom in their hearts and muttered rumors of the fall of the paladin captain.

To lift flagging spirits, an occasional gallant would show his colors and break free of the toiling columns to gallop ahead, then pace his destrier with knightly grace. Many cheered the displays whilst catcalls and boos erupted from the ranks of any rival house. Better yet was the stolid example set by marching dwarves who strode with grim purpose, eager to strike a blow in vengeance for their fallen king, and also by Northmen of Eirec's household who sang as they went, glad to follow an axe-wielding prince who kept troth, guiding his army ever northward and east to reclaim their ravaged lands.

Craftwise dwarves aided greatly the repair and remaking of many weapons, as foresters and scouts oversaw construction of many thousands arrow shafts for horn-tipped bows of bois d'arc and yew. With slings, camp boys downed egrets and lake gulls for feathers. They twisted hemp and linen into strings for the man-high bows whilst shaggy hillmen set aside horse bows to finger finely wrought arrow tips and share hungry grins.

Renault scooped a red-gloved handful of arrow points, then let them fall with steel music back to their bucket. "I wonder, Master Bagwart, if these tribesman think to sink your pretty bodkins into Kör-men, or rather their cousins once home."

Bagwart paused at his labor. "I care not, Sir Knight. As long as they kill Körlings first." The dwarf spat, taking up a file to strip burrs from an infantry lance twice his own length. Renault laughed and saluted before exiting, but the master smith paid no notice. The journey from Windhover had been swift and uncomfortable. Ohm was not disposed to stonewalk mere smiths, such were for his betters. "An' leave it to them!" he growled. The corded muscles of his forearm drove rasp across steel. Once.

Twice. Done. He grasped another pike. Aye, there was work here enough.

"Careful with that oil, boy!" Bagwart sighed. *Hard to find good help in an army of mankind.* He wondered where and how his special friends fared. He had bade them good-bye beyond the encampment and wished them well. Bagwart grasped another pike, he would work harder.

Two miles from the camp of the army of Ilycrium, where a portion of the King's Road bisected a sunny field of hay grass, Erasmus rushed forward to embrace another. He was a young man, tall and fair—garbed as if for a walk in the country and fashionably awkward in his finery. On the road and in the grass stood a dozen comely youths around a riding wagon. Its drover was a surly faced serving man who wore a scowl around his short, fat pipe.

Erasmus pulled back. "Henred, what do you here? Come with me to the camp of the Prince. Know you not there is a war on?"

"That is why we have come," replied the other, whose features were cordial but stern. "My father supports your prince with monies and men-at-arms, but this is *my* country as well, and I choose to defy the bloodstained house of your upstart kingling, and also his warmongering bootlickers! So have we all." He gestured to the pale students behind him. These conversed eagerly, occasionally sharing an attenuated laugh at some new subtlety.

To Erasmus, away from the confines of Sway for long weeks, they stank of perfume and pipe smoke. Behind their casual demeanors, he perceived nervous shiftings and glances at the open country around them. The tail of the Anhegs loomed gray and hard, short leagues to the north. "Please, Henred, you are my friend. Come to the camp for a meal and a cup. I shall introduce you to Gault. Most of the captains are true and even pleasant; we can jibe the others!"

"And I say, come with us, Black Merlin. Those others accept you only because of Tertullion."

Erasmus's dark face suffused to deeper color. "He died in the hills of Ulard, slain by a son of perdition." Erasmus gathered himself for one last effort. "It is dangerous here. Do these others ken a very legion of Kör is nigh?"

"Poor Erasmus," answered Henred with a thin laugh. "I said that is *why* we have come." He drew himself up and smoothed his houppelande as if giving a well-rehearsed speech. "The generation of our fathers was great in industry and war, but it is up to we of enlightenment to make the peace."

He gestured at the wagon whose drover was alternatively kicking a wheel and glowering at Erasmus, who was no doubt the chief culprit of their delay. "We who are the true patriots of Ilycrium, we shall be the ambassadors of goodwill to the kingdom of Kör. When the new order is forged, will you stand with your friends? Or your brainwashed princeling, himself not pure of blood?"

Erasmus bowed. "I wish you well." His face was sad, and he turned to go, then paused. "If you, or any, change your mind, you may shelter with us."

"They will not, Black Merlin," replied Henred archly. "But I too wish you well."

THE STEPPES

The escapee stood on the dirt floor of the room they had given him. Its walls were of clay and animal blood, baked by wind and sun. It was winter, and a fireplace set in the wall warmed the entire structure. The whitewash lime of last spring showed in places. "*Ase*" the peasants called this place.

The tiny steppe town had been hard beset by war, although indirectly as the great armies bypassed the region for there were no important roads or great resources nearby, even so, raiders had come. Gatherings of the stunted forest and thin crops were hidden as might be, yet the pillagers had amongst them those who had a knack for showing when a hog was butchered or root cellar broached.

After the stranger's offering of gold, a fire was lit and winter ales found, and he had blessed the marriage of two youths who celebrated nuptials by light of the feast. Later, when trusting peasants slept their first sated repose in many months, the visitor sat watch. As he knew they would, robbers came—slinking like weasels in the dark of night.

The figure reached into somewhere and pulled forth a shimmering blade. Graceful fingers stroked again its familiar hilts. It knew him, glad he had become himself, and more … the being, recently the prized prisoner within the Gehulgog, prison mine of Iblis prince of Kör, turned eyes cold as the depthless sea upon the despoilers.

TIAMAT'S PALACE

"Greetings, leman!"

Adestes crossed the threshold to his suites. Dark opulence welcomed him from every surface, suitable quarters for one high of station in the Court of the Eternal Queen, Goddess of Old Night. The woman ran with mincing steps to fall prostrate before him, knees drawn in, backed arched, and shining hair spilt onto his boots. Her gestures were sultry, a trifle defiant, just as he recalled.

"Rise, wench."

Adestes quickly but methodically scanned his surroundings

as was his wont, whether the room be new or familiar. Always cautious—and living.

"Yes, wary even of one such as you." He grasped her petite jaw into his sword-hardened hand, then drew her face to his. Her palms roamed over the stone-set breastplate of black steel, hammered in the likeness of his torso with muscular swells over the chest and rippled abdomen.

"A sharpened tooth, perhaps? Or venomed kiss? Think not I will hesitate to bind thee with serpents, nor deny myself pleasure in your dying."

Her dark orbs returned his gaze unwaveringly. Though a slave, little more than a girl, she remained unshaken. "I can see your stay in the Tyrfang did you little harm. Did Iblis' foul son caress you?"

The girl's breasts heaved, her eyes liquid. Without further speech, Malesh crushed her lips to his, drawing her soft form to his steel.

HELHEIM: FASTNESS OF LLUND

"Behold, the Lion of Ilycrium."

"What? Him? He is nearly dead!"

The man lay quiescent, pale on the cinder. The scars of many battles adorned him head to toe, and a garish wound on his chest weeped serum and blood as his chest rose fitfully with each faltering breath.

Astypylus bent to peel back one eyelid. "Why should we bid on this one? Only a human, unfit to live." A canine-sharp smile split Astypylus's long yellow face, and his proboscis wagged. "Ahh, apologies to you, Dark Star."

Adestes scowled at the mockery, as behind Astypylus, a dozen others snickered. Adestes Malgrim, Kör's Malesh, fingered his heavy ring of serpentine gold but did not reach for a weapon. Instead, he kicked Xephard's wound.

The paladin surged up. Naked and mazed, he grasped the nearest target, dismantling the creature with vengeful hands. Astypylus chittered as he died. Adestes' ring awoke, and a snake of fog encoiled the man, suffocating him into oblivion. The bestial audience applauded, keen brains already factoring the death of their colleague into their black calculus, the politics of Hel.

"Enough amusement," intoned Ulfelion. "The prisoner remains here." Tusks grated in champing jaws, and pinioned wings flexed, yet none gainsaid the countenance of Death.

"""Speak," commanded Malesh.

The man's lips moved, his eyelids fluttered. "May the Gray-Eyed Goddess strengthen my right hand so that I might visit ruin on the wicked! I behold a noble iris, shining white on a field purpure. Lances kiss with honor—"

"Heresy!" The man jerked at the wracking dweomer of Ulfelion's words. "What do you see!"

"The winged elf, gallant Sarc, dies by your hand." Xephard's breast heaved. "The priest of the highest god, he named Turpin, a traitor to his kin. And Apieron," Xephard's words faltered, his corded belly arched with agony, "wounded, he lays in a dark cell, ready for death."

"Melónie!" Xephard cast off the vampire's spell and sat upright. His eyes promised destruction.

Malesh laughed as adamant chains rattled from the paladin's four limbs. "Not so foolish are we, Xephard Bright Helm."

Ulfelion's ghastly visage filled Xephard's vision. "Mayhap I will shrivel the last flesh from thy bones." Xephard simply stared. Ulfelion bent his entire will, the evil wisdom of centuries gone to dust, upon the man.

Xephard lifted his chin. "There are fates worse than death, bloodsucker."

A gale of unlife deluged the man. "Those fates are to be yours!" roared Ulfelion. "I will bide the moment of your life's end, then sunder mind from soul—an insane, mumbling thing to wander naked the timeless halls of mourning."

Xephard fell, receding. Like a frowning titan, Adestes hove into view and the whip fell, and again, a machine of pain. The blows fell like a hammer. Xephard prayed it was his body that suffered, that the wight had not made good its promise to prison his very soul in some eternal hell.

Xephard ceased to feel the lashing, although he felt its weight in his ears, and the smell, the sweet stench of blood on burning metal. He thought of the harvests of his youth, the lifting of grain sheaves taller than he. How hard that had seemed. Always the most arduous tasks had been allotted him, the cutting and hoisting of logs and boulders, the endless hauling of water yokes, each as heavy as a man.

"That's enough." Adestes discarded his whip. It writhed its anger, deprived of the sweet blood of the man. "Stay your spell, dwimmer-lich. He must live that the other hie to us. You heard again the name. *Apieron*."

When the sepulchral voice answered, it sounded more unto a moan than speech. "I heard yet there is some life left in this other one, Dark Star. Dangerous life. Soon I shall feast on his heart's blood."

"Soon, but not yet!" Malesh drew back his head to laugh, the sound bellowing from the blocks of Llund. The sky rained fire, and he gathered again his flail.

Chapter 12

Ilycrium: The Army

Dawn crept into the mountains, yet above the trailing Anhegs, lingering stars winked serenely on their indigo swath, their silvery light seemed somehow more pure, as if blown into life by the cleansing cool of the night. Finishing her evening's hunt, a lone bat flitted overhead, and the rush of water beneath the high place was unchanged, tirelessly foam-chasing down the mountain's spine where it found repose in an alpine lake. And far below, the heraldry of the sun came in ochre, fading to blue above.

Westward, upper peaks nudged one another for shoulder space, their tops bald above the tree line and their steep slopes textured with standing ranks of conifers. Cloud mists hung damp as sodden blankets, although in the eastern vales, Gault could see it would be clear and bright for whatever the day would bring. From the knoll by the bowl lake where the army encamped, it seemed he might simply step from the descending slopes and, with a few stretching strides, be among croft and cottage of the gray-swaled vale below. Sounds of the waking army began to murmur. Only a few lingering fires dotted the steeps above the lake, as Trakhner had commanded that only one in five the norm be made. "Impossible to conceal our movements completely, even with the wizardry that Erasmus promised," he had growled, "but I'll be a new-frocked cadet if we give away our numbers entire to the crawling spies of Kör."

The mere was still now, holding in tranquil reflection bole and bough of rimming trees. It had not been so the night prior, Gault chuckled at the memory. The levies from Bestrand discovered walleye and trout in the waters and soon enjoyed a welcome change from army sausage and iron rations. The inlanders put up such a ruckus that finally the men of the distant port town constructed a woven sieve and ran it shore to shore, yielding an amazing bounty of fish. "Would you deem it unmanly of me if I express a concern that we have stricken the last of the fish from the lake?" had queried Gault of one Cistus, captain of Bestrand.

"Not so, yer Highness. See yon stream spillin' down the shoreline an' out the far side? Soon she'll bring many a fingerling to this lil' dab o' water. They'll feed an' grow without their cousins tha' we've et to et them!" Cistus's cragged face grimaced with rugged laughter. He bowed and moved off to rejoin his men.

Erasmus, overhearing the discourse, had taken a wiggling trout from a basket despite protests from sailors, suddenly halfhearted upon discerning the robe of a spellweaver. "A female," said he to Gault, "in her dwells the seed of eggs to be."

Its iridescent scales of pink and blue flashed in his brown hand. Erasmus said a word and touched the belly of the trout before returning it to the mere. "There will be many fish come spring." He grinned, teeth and eyes white in his dark face. Gault smiled again at the recollection.

The risen sun now burnished western peaks a coppery hue. It had been a good camp. There occurred a small something he had never seen. A striped chipmunk perched and swaying upon a tall thistle, balanced like a dragonfly to feed industriously on seeds beneath white tufts. Gault remembered Apieron, who had taught him much of the world men called wilderness. He wondered, at that moment, what new things Apieron beheld.

SKYGATE

""By the Unholy Scepter of Argnosh, what are you doing, woman?" A wisp of smoke drifted from Jamello's thin pipe.

Isolde busied herself. She set out fur-lined breeks, an oiled jerkin, and heavy gloves. She added to the stack an ivory cowl of lambswool before favoring Jamello with a frown. She batted away a smoke streamer that always seemed to find her face.

"Indolent ne'er-do-well, the lord Galor said it would be bitter cold come morning."

"Perhaps I *am* lazy. After our fight with kitty and his friends, I'm inclined to laze." Jamello waved to the arbor overhead. A quick march had distanced them from the site of the skirmish, and they had set an early camp. The fading sun lit fall leaves of oak and beech with a warm glow. No wind stirred, and Henlee tended a cozy fire.

"Cold for an elf, maybe," said the dwarf. "I like it nippy at night—helps me sleep."

"Indeed," drawled Jamello in rare agreement. "This day ended mild as a silky Bestrandian night. I think tomorrow will be warmer yet."

Tallux flipped an acorn at Jamello's head. Without looking, Jamello snatched it in two fingers, expending no effort in the rest of his frame. Tallux jutted his chin toward the reclining thief. "When the master of boundaryless Amor speaks of weather, it were best a city lad of less than thirty-some winters pay heed."

"And I, Sir Elf, believe what my eyes see and my nose smells." Three puffs of smoke wended insolently toward the wood elf.

"Useless," muttered Isolde.

"What of you, Apieron? Eirec?" called Jamello. Apieron's back was to the others on the camp's edge, facing east. Eirec was already mumbling to himself and beginning to snore. Neither responded as the sun gave her parting gift to the sky and sank to her westbower.

The others were resting. Without a sound, Apieron gathered the acorn Jamello had let fall. He examined it by feel in the darkness. Many such as this he had planted in happier times at Windhover. "Never shall you grow," he whispered.

He felt the textured cap and the smooth shell of the nut. He moved to toss it onto the dying flame, but inexplicably placed it in his pouch. He patted it once as if to assure himself of its placement, then resumed the night watch.

Jamello woke to find his clothing frozen to his body. Cross-legged, Isolde sat facing him. She poked with a stick and laughed when a rind of ice popped free from his side. "I believe what my eyes see and my nose smells!" She rose, tossing the twig atop him.

When the thief extricated himself from his icy papoose and donned new clothes, he joined the others. They stared, for the mountains had grown close in the night, their sheer faces catching the first rays of the risen sun. They wore their mantles of snow proudly in the roseate glow. Behind the companions, a fir-clad valley was a spiculed monochrome of gray. A river wended dark in its mist.

"I have advanced our progress," stated Galor. "The war goes ill for our friends."

Tallux looked alarmed. Apieron also stirred but said nothing.

"Events are forward beyond the ambuscade yesterday,"

continued Galor, "beyond even the imaginings of the adepts of Kör who yet seek us. We must haste."

The companions moved off, and soon their journey carried them beyond the receding forest. Whether it was the same forest they entered the day before, Jamello doubted. Winter was upon the land, and an upslope of tundra lay before them. Grasses bowed, brown and brittle before a gusting wind, and trees were black under a cold blue sky. Jamello felt he might see forever in the clear air. A white-breasted hawk sat high on a barren branch, its neck feathers rustling when the wind blew. Jamello wondered what the hawk could see. If the bird cared aught for their presence, it disdained to reveal it.

Apieron set a quick pace that led high onto the knees of the mountain they sought. *Heimhill*, Henlee had named it. The sun grew watery under low clouds. It began to snow.

Jamello sat with a groan after Apieron called a midday halt under three mountain junipers. A jackdaw shook out its inky plumage and cackled ugly things to the thief. Jamello's hand went to a quirt, although did not free the dart when Tallux's emerald gaze found his. The bird hopped and fixed the thief with its malevolent eyes, first one, then the other.

"I hope you freeze!"

"Come deep winter, no birds nest here, save ravens and eagles," said Apieron. He waved his crooked bow. The bird fled, its two brown consorts in swift tow.

By late afternoon, the seven travelers pierced snow-heavy clouds, ever upward to find the mountain stark and foreboding. Skunk spruce, tall and spindly, were white laden such that their sweeping limbs strained. Occasionally one would snap with a report that echoed in the narrow places. Jamello remembered the demon guns of Pankaspe.

Although temperatures remained freezing, the sun was here unhindered as their marching feet crunched through a brittle glaze atop the snowpack, and its light was painfully reflected from the crystalline expanse.

Eventually Apieron called a halt and bound their eyes with torn cloths so that they peered through shaded slits, and still they climbed. Behind and below, Jamello looked with envy upon the warm lands they had quitted. High on the western face, the sun lingered until late. Man and woman, elf and dwarf toiled until no light remained. When they halted, a gibbous moon rose to dominate the sky. It loomed, dependent from its black cradle like a drop of molten silver. Shadows played in its depths, and its lurid glow cast a sickly green nimbus over the mountain.

"The moon makes evil magic tonight," said Eirec. The wind moaned, accentuating his words.

"Look, the Dog Star returns!" Tallux's pointing finger indicated a crimson smudge that rounded the near shoulder of the mountain. It lifted clear of the pall to glower over the world.

Apieron's deep voice was disembodied in the near dark. "It is *She* who puts the stars of blight to their dark orbits, thus bringing woe to men."

"Foul mate for harlot moon," growled Eirec. "See how they dance! They mock us."

"Nothing else dares such a sky," added Tallux.

Indeed, no other stars were visible as the wind quickened and grew fierce. Soon gales of ice lagger pelted the camp, the sky was veiled, and their fire became fitful and provided little warmth. The company huddled together. Isolde pulled close her mantle such that she resembled a formless stone. "I do not know which I prefer less—the evil star or the frost!"

Henlee chuckled darkly. "Aye, lass. There is a casting in the heavens, or p'raps from yonder Helgate. I have not felt so weary since the Year of Horn an' 't will be worse tomorrow."

Tallux looked up. "You speak of the Peaks of Bitter Ice?"

"Aye, the windswept barrens of Skywall. Only then have I felt such an ague as now." The dwarf let forth a sigh.

Jamello looked at Eirec, an unspoken question on his face. The big man nodded his black beard. "Skywall's peaks touch many lands, a border betwixt wild and wild, but they are not empty. The Sons of Scotti claim them."

"This interests me," said Tallux. "Some say the Sons of Scotti are cruel spirits, oreads who take the shape of men—warriors of ultimate power. Others tell they are men who have dwelt for ages where no other tribe can dwell, become at last so fierce that none may withstand them, as they are beyond the ken of ordinary peoples. Which do you believe, Galor?"

The golden elf had been listening. "The latter, although there is a ring of truth to the former, as there be oft a kernel of truth to old tales."

Jamello sniffed. "Enigmatic answers as always, but that is expected from an overlearned sage. What say you, noble dwarf? What are the Sons of Scotti? You have walked many high places; have you had dealings with them? Are they man or spirit?"

Henlee mumbled something in his beard and stared down at his hands. He rubbed them slowly before the fire. The mountains were shadowy sentinels behind him, and the words he spoke were in old dwarvish, sounding low in their ears and indecipherable.

It was Isolde who spoke from the huddled shadows of her swathing. "In my blood also are songs of the Nordic. It is not written that the Sons of Scotti have ever known defeat, yet we have heard tale that once, in the Year of Horn, did they suffer one to pass."

"He, and one other," said Galor softly.

Henlee left the blowing circle of light to walk the perimeter. Apieron was also absent. "I know something of the dwarven tongue," added the golden elf. "The words meant: Let the dead lay."

"You should be resting, lass. By nightfall tomorrow, we walk the Helroad."

"Why do you watch him so closely?"

Henlee tensed. "It is my watch. When you have the watch, you watch."

Isolde started into the dwarf's dark eyes.

"Watchers watch!"

"You know what I mean, Uncle. You watch Apieron."

Henlee shrugged in the darkness. "Old habits die hard. His father—"

"Yes, I know," Isolde recited. "The redoubtable Xistus entrusted Apieron's training to you when it became apparent that he was too honest for the intrigues of the Court in the Clouds. But that was long ago, many times has my beloved recounted tales of Apieron's prowess."

"All you say is true." Henlee fingered his beard, unconsciously counting the wealth therein. "Young Apieron is a veteran many times over, mayhap the mightiest soldier of the Western Kingdom, and then he would not deny the incompleteness in him. Born into fame and wealth, he rejected all not of his own making." Henlee's hand waved, searching for a phrase. "—An unpolished statue. He has not vanquished his perfect foe. Live or die, Apieron awaits his moment of truth. Dwarves have a word for this. I will not say it, but it speaks to the Way of the Warrior." Henlee's hand fell. "So here I sit and watch. Best you should sleep now too, lass. Don't you know that if you listen overlong to an old dwarf's harangue, you'll grow whiskers?"

Isolde's smile flashed in the thin light, and she pressed her hand briefly to Henlee's, then scampered to her bedroll. As she wiggled deep into the fur and fabric, she made out the shadowy silhouette of the dwarf's hunched shoulders against the ghostly radiance of cloud-veiled moon on snow. She felt secure knowing that Henlee would watch well over the travelers this night. Isolde closed her eyes and let her thoughts drift, as always to Xephard. It seemed he whispered the night entire, long and low … of the Way of the Warrior.

The black dwarf stared at his rough hands where the vibrant girl-cleric pressed hers so soft against his. He sighed and thought of these young ones, so confident and happy in the prime of their strength. Faces flashed before his dark eyes, Apieron and Xephard, Isolde, and even the thief. "It would be fortune's miracle if most of them were not lost in the red wastes."

In the deep hours of the night, the Dog Star was again revealed, and by its casting, Henlee could see his companions had come far up the mountain. Before morning grew old, they would pass the last stragglers of trees. Barring mishap, day's end would find them the Skygate. If any were doomed to die, then it must be, and yet such a death would not come cheap! Aye, the manbot would be costly, even by the standards of the lords of Hel.

Henlee raised Maul in his hand. Its black mass obscured the omen star. Not many men could have hefted steadily the weapon even with two hands and legs braced. The wereguild would be high indeed.

Eirec stamped his feet and drew the bearskin close about his neck. Of all the party, he was perhaps most inured to cold and the hardships of high places. Eirec gazed upon Jamello, son of the sun-kissed South. The thief's lips were blue, and his teeth chattered as his thin frame hardly impeded the swirling ice that skirled across the ascent.

"Just like home, eh, Eirec?" Henlee drew near. The dwarf's beard was swathed in hoarfrost, and diamonds gleamed icily therein. About his shoulder was a cape of elk, its leather backing intricately embossed with tooled runework.

"I am cold," admitted the Northman, "but I think yon thief suffers greatly."

"Bah, he's all right. I've seen him take worse and come back grinning. Besides," Henlee added with a wink, "you can't kill a cockroach." At this juncture, Apieron approached to check their guide ropes, an indication that their short respite was over.

"Re … remind me again, Apieron," stammered Jamello. "Why are we doing this?"

Apieron squared off and addressed the thief, his stern features unaffected by the wintry blast. "Because I am the single one cursed with a mystic energy that, at the proper time, I will attempt to release that we might slay the Dragon Mother. *She* who seeks to destroy our world." The words were delivered forcefully, enough for all to hear, yet devoid of passion.

Eirec shook his head, then laughed gustily. "The son of Farsinger minces no words."

Jamello's brown eyes looked down from Apieron's face. "Oh," he said quietly. A hand was laid on Jamello's shoulder, and a golden warmth infused him, quieting the quaking of his muscles and easing their cramps no less than if suspended in a warm bath. He glimpsed the sky blue and cloth d'or of Galor's mantle, who spoke in answer to Apieron.

"There is one other."

Surprising all, a flicker of rage lit Apieron's eyes as he met those of Galor. Then was his mien again impassive. "Then he too will I slay."

They were in the clear, and their destination reared dizzyingly—nigh a thousand feet its face lifted sheer above the mountain spine they traversed, its top broken into jagged teeth and crested sails of rock. Among them, stark against an aurora sky, were ominous profiles. Carved at random by wind and rain or by spell, none of the seven could guess, but thereon were faces of glowering titans and leering giants. The wind howled with such force that to relax would to be thrown backward.

"Ware your step," shouted Tallux to Jamello and Isolde. "Beneath this crust, the snow is rotten. 'Tis a tumble we do not wish to take."

Each frozen breath bit painfully into straining lungs as the sun grew dazzling bright in the thin air, yet in all directions, the horizon was of deepest indigo, as if theirs was the only place in the world revealed by sun's golden chariot. Lines of luminescence danced in the blue.

As one, the party paused to regard the final, looming ascent. Its grade in places was near vertical, and jutting edges of rock, limned with a layer of glittering ice, offered the only possibilities for traction by hand, foot, or rope. Between rows of stone lay slopes of crystalline snow whose outer layers had melted many times under the midday sun, only to refreeze each evening, leaving the surface slick as oil. Superimposed upon this were knives of jagged ice, a full hundred feet in height. In close, the titans of stone were no longer visible.

Jamello mumbled that the escarpment looked like the grotesquely magnified interior of a shark's mouth he had once seen hauled thrashing and biting from the fishing waters of sunny Bestrand. "I would rather face the shark. Can this truly be the way to the place of fire?"

Henlee peered closely at the thief. Jamello's sun-browned face was gray in the frosty light, and his shivering lips mumbled. "Does seem a bit odd," reckoned the dwarf. "What say you, Apieron?" No answer was forthcoming from the ranger, whose snow-laden eyebrows were furrowed in thought.

"An inhospitable place," agreed Tallux. He unslung his pack and dumped out several lengths of elfin rope spun in the Greenwolde. They fell onto the snow in liquid coils.

"Two files of three and four," commanded Galor. "Apieron and Tallux shall lead because they are the nimblest and more experienced on the ice." The golden elf's tone brooked no dissent despite Eirec's rumbling protests at the perceived slight. "Jamello shall follow Tallux, myself, and Isolde behind Apieron, for we are the lightest. Last shall come Eirec, behind me, and Henlee behind Jamello—for they are strongest. Our anchors shall they be."

The two human warriors, wood elf, and mountain dwarf nodded their assent. All took Jamello's silent quaking as consent enough.

Isolde appeared distracted. She stared with intensity at the impasse, as her cerulean eyes flashed like frozen waters of the glacier rifts whence came her ancestors. "There waits a great evil above. Whether it marks us or no, I cannot discern. It fairly stinks on the wind!"

Apieron woke from his reverie. "I felt it from the moment we set foot to this slope." His gray eyes fell upon her, unguessed passions swirling in their depths. "Keep you back, woman, when the fighting starts. Mine shall be the first blow."

Her welling argument was stilled by a gesture from Galor. "Keep back, child. We shall need the abilities of a high priestess in the Hel place."

Against the aged wisdom of the elf lord and Apieron's burning intensity, Isolde gave up her umbrage and nodded meekly. Without signal, they began the final push. No slip of foot or sway of body shook dwarf or barbarian whose deep-thrust thews were anchored deep in the snow and gravel. Again and again, they held firm the rope when the others might have slid into white oblivion. Warning shouts were slapped away by ice-heavy scuthers as the gale rose to a steady shriek. Step followed heavy step as faces, hands, and feet first burned, then lost all sensation.

"How beautiful," said Jamello.

"We are here," agreed Apieron.

ILYCRIUM: THE ARMY

Near a southern remnant of the Anheg, the army of Ilycrium poured into the lake vale like a silvery flood in moonlight. Berich gazed outward from his high place. He marked some eight thousand footmen and half again their number of archers, upland skirmishers on rugged mountain ponies, and mounted knights.

"How festive," he crooned.

His companion's chalk-white features split into a wide grin. "Indeed," returned Astorath.

"You really are a handsome devil."

"And you, brother." Astorath laughed long and low, that jest never grew old.

"Shall we report to father?"

"And quickly. Here is news to please him."

The twin demon spawn turned to wend their way back to Iz'd Yar, general of Kör.

Chael was bored. He climbed another rock-bosomed hill. Grasping a handful of wire-stemmed gorse, he hoisted up with a grunt to spy the broadening coomb beyond. With a gasp, the young scout beheld the army of Kör, laid out like a carpet of steel.

"Merciful gods!" he breathed, counting off hundreds of orc standards, each heraldry marking the position of a tribe entire. Oxtails and bloodied whips of the Mgesh were there as well. Under their lee, thronged horse regiments of the fierce nomads, each warrior bloodied in the ceaseless battles of their homeland. A smoky pall lurked over the far end of a river valley where Chael could but dimly guess at monstrous shapes that moved in shadow. The river must be mighty Celadon, and yet the vast numbers beside it made it seem a creek.

Rooted with morbid fascination, Ilycrium's scout realized this place would soon witness the coming battle. He gazed long and cursed himself with a start when the thought occurred that to enjoy such a view, he must be beyond the outguards of Kör. Without stirring a pebble, Chael backed slowly from the overlook and turned to skid silently back the way he had come. Too late.

A noose of braided leather jerked the young scout headlong back to the hill's crest. He choked, grasping it with one hand whilst his second sought his dagger to sever the strangling cord. Aqchec the Mgesh laughed and crushed the dagger hand with his boot. His companion squatted to set his feet astride Chael's shoulders and pulled mightily. The neck bones gave with a loud crack, and the scout of Ilycrium jerked once, then lay still.

Aqchec read the question on his companion's wizened face as he drew a gleaming kindjal. "A fine young scalp," he said and bent to work.

Chapter 13

The Army: Banks of Celadon

Gault was accompanied by the ever-present Seamus as well as Renault, Trakhner, Erasmus, and various officers. They rode the periphery of the army, liking well its order. When the royal cavalcade passed, Wiglaf cleared his throat but not the gravel from his voice. "That, boys, is every inch a king, though he don't say as much. Now, stand to an' put yer jaws back on yer faces! Ne'er did I see such a bunch of milk-sucking, snuffle-nosed …"

Before the battle, there was a pause. Cusk found it hard to breathe, and the fear that had been crawling all morning in his stomach moved to his chest.

"Jes' stick close to Wiglaf and me"—Dunstan patted him—"we'll look after ye."

"In my granfar's days—" Cusk gulped something back down where it belonged. "Then was wars wi' Kör too. Those were ugly times, they say, but I ne'er heard o' no commoners fightin'. Jes' the highfolk gallopin' by wi' their painted shields an' iron toys."

He touched the glistening mail over his breast. "Now look at me," he pleaded, "pretendin' to be what I ain't."

Wiglaf's face momentarily softened. "Nor do I know what

has happened, lad. Streams turned yellow, lambs born with two heads, burnin' rains, and kids gone sick. Neighbors murdered ..."

From the east, a swelling murmur drifted on the wind, a strange chant, low and ominous. "Mayhap the gods 'ave left us," whispered Cusk.

"I remember one time," said Dunstan in his slow, farmer's voice. "Jes' before the war. I was leavin', an' me wife—she begged me not ta' go. She was cryin'." Wiglaf and Cusk crowded closer. Soldiers were ordering their ranks. Wiglaf glanced about; they had more time.

"'Twas then ..." Dunstan wiped a strand of black hair from eyes that squinted against the rising sun. "'Twas then I said the best thing I e'er did." Dunstan stared into the golden haze, beneath which the legions of Kör awaited. "She said, 'Do you care more fer yer country than yer lovin' wife an' helpless babes?'"

Dunstan regarded his friends, his eyes bright in the dawn. "I said, 'Dearest Byrinae, love o' my life.'" He swept his arm in an inclusive gesture. "'You *are* my country.'" Cusk stared and swallowed past the lump in his throat. Wiglaf clapped him hard on the back. Cusk squared his shoulders and found his new chain hung like he had borne it his life entire.

"Dunstan, no man coulda said it better, prince or pauper—"

The veteran sergeant's words were lost in the bray of trumpets over the waters. Events were forward in the ranks of Kör.

"Trouble, m'lord," remarked Trakhner. "And I see here many ensigns of orc clans not recorded by the scribes of your father or grandsire."

"What is that?" Gault pointed.

Celadon's waters churned slowly in the sunlight. Beyond its

bank, a coffle of youths, garbed in white, were led to the fore of the Mgesh formation. Scattered cries of surprise and astonished dismay sounded at random places within the Western host, for many faces were recognized amongst the pale-faced captives.

"The kidnappers," muttered Gault. "Brockhorst suspected some such perfidy."

At that moment a lilting command rose from the rear of the enemy rank, and a detail of swart horse-warriors stepped forward. Without delay or flourish, knives flashed and the line of captives fell as one, their faces upturned to the new day. Wolfmen and bestial goblins crawled forth to lap the blood.

With a blast of horns and primal screams, Ilycrium's rural knights and peasant levies flailed across the river to charge straight for the Mgesh center. Made mighty by their wrath, they trampled outlying skirmishers and wild archers who fired one panicked volley before turning to flee. Armor-cased dwarves and tawny-haired barbarians of the Gefylla trotted behind the surge, but at an upraised hand and barked command from a dwarf captain named Fuggo, they held up before the river, for their commander's dark eyes liked not its swirling depths. Generations of fighting men of Amber Hall had learned the long wisdom of their dwarven neighbors; therefore, these also halted but unslung their iron-bossed shields of linden wood.

Trakhner cursed. "Only the Northrons keep their wits. There's nothing for it!"

A flag was raised and lowered, a signal for Renault. The red glove waved, and the peers of Candor's household walked their horses forward, and advancing at their sides were lines of sturdy frontiersmen bearing man-high bows. "Come, gentlemen," urged Gault, "we must surrender the high ground to support our friends." A din of shouts and clashing metal and thrumming hooves filled the airs over the water. Uglich, a woad-faced chieftain of the Seod, also put heels to his pony once he beheld the Prince's banner in motion.

Beyond the river, the main body of Mgesh awaited the first charge of the enraged Westrons. Recurve bows put shaft after whistling shaft into destriers and men, pinning thigh to horse, or finding armor gaps at shoulder and neck. Then struck the Ilycrium's knights. Pinioned lances cleaved lacquered shield and enameled hauberk alike, bowling over Mgesh and steed. Pike-wielding orcs thrust over mantelets designed to support their horse-archer allies. Ilycrium's enraged footmen, bearing glaive and hammer, axe and mace, dismembered these in minutes. Lancers followed and smashed Kör's pickets into red ruin as Mgesh fled north or south, showing the white rumps of their steeds. Goblins were slain outright.

Into the unraveling rear of the orc companies smote the men of Ilycrium while images of blight and loss of home, and the helpless youths murdered before their eyes burned in their brains. Horses plunged screaming while swords rose and fell in bloody harvest. Grizzly orc banners were trampled under, and braying wildmen were hewn from behind as they fled, but the men of the West had pressed too far.

Frantic calls and horn notes from beyond the Celadon went unheeded in the tumult. Hearts pounding and muscles sweat weary, knights and infantry labored to crest a low ridge. Once atop it, they beheld the main of Iz'd Yar's legions. Tall half-demons in resplendent mail swaggered forward. Bellowing Ascapundi, lumbering with speed, fixed piggish eyes that glinted with hate upon the men of Ilycrium. To their flanks, dust arose as the horse-riding squadrons of Mgesh wheeled, their feint completed. Surrounded on three sides and soon to be cut off by fast-riding lines of mounted bowmen, Ilycrium's knights reined lathered horses whilst infantry turned panicked glances in all directions. The shuddering cries of wolfmen rose in joyous anticipation.

Iz'd Yar's trap was sprung. He sauntered forward, drawing his benighted blade. At his side, Berich and Astorath shared wide grins. The slaughter began.

Just as a flock of starlings ups suddenly from a grassy lay to wheel in formation, so did the Mgesh horsemasters close the square. Long arching streams of arrows found Ilycrium's beleaguered ranks. Each three-foot shaft was barbed with a wicked steel point, ground smooth and heavy to pierce shield and armor alike. With no strong front to present the enemy, knight and footman alike suffered. The deluge struck with all the din of hail on tin, yet no ice ever fell with the ferocity of the Mgesh's unerring weaponry. Man and beast groaned under that deadly storm as helm and breastplate were pierced, arm was pinned to shield and foot to earth. Heavy caparisoned and armored destriers went mad, spreading havoc and plunging wildly in pain and fear.

Renault and Trakhner bellowed orders. Royal companies halted straining chargers at the river's edge. As scattered clumps of their comrades sought to recross the waters, the foresters of Ilycrium and tribal bowmen shot desperately into the squadrons of pursuing Mgesh, but too few in number, they could not stay the onslaught. In response, the volleys of Kör darkened the sun. At Gault's side, Seamus was struck from his mount, an arrow sprouting from his eye socket.

Straggling survivors of the initial charge, gasping wet and stained with river muck, found safety amongst the steadfast Northmen and dwarves who remained in formation above the water's edge. Axe and mattock feasted on the blood of any enemy that crossed the Celadon into their lines. Singly or in groups, Renault's chevaliers made daring sorties into the missile-peppered waters to shelter, floundering troopers with horse and shield or simply hoist them to safety across saddle bows. Then came the Ascapundi. Wielding great ranseurs, they plunged unhindered across the river as looping blows of their polearms swept riders from horses and clove footmen in twain. With no pause in momentum, the bellowing giants charged the western bank and plunged amongst the defenders.

Dwarves and nordics gave back but did not break, laying several of the red-skinned monsters low as axemen might fell a tree. On their flanks, however, Ascapundi broke through in triumph, and the banner of the Prince was swept aside. Waves of goblins gave vent to joyous shrieks and sprinted forward. Wolfmen and Mgesh were sent to harry the battle's edge, the bulk of their task complete, for the vanguard of Iz'd Yar had arrived. They bore a mighty standard of the abyss. Without visible device, it rippled above the fray—a void in the airs. Many that beheld it were struck mad or cast aside targe and weapon to flee like harried beasts.

Erasmus stood unheeded on the bank. Arms uplifted, he called a burning steam from the river's belly. Orcs shrieked, blinded and stricken. Scalded Ascapundi hopped in either direction from the deadly waters, swatting aside friend and foe, yet Erasmus's victory was short-lived.

Vodrab's thought probed the vapors for the brain of he who made the river boil. There! The mind was skillfully shielded and narrowly channeled with the intensity of its casting. Yet Vodrab was aged even by the nigh-immortal life span of the demon-lords of Kör, and his time had not been idle. With a snarl, the necromancer launched an eyebite, sharp as any pointed spear, into the thought of his human adversary. He felt it punch through the outer crust of defense into the soft will beneath. Vodrab turned to Iz'd Yar.

"The way, my lord, is clear."

Celadon ceased its frothing. Erasmus's brown eyes rolled as

he pitched from the edge. The battle's contour was now fractured into multitudinous, isolated conflicts. Such had been Trakhner's fear, for the advantage of numbers lay heavily with Kör. Gault plied his grandsire's axe amongst a ring of leering creatures that appeared an unholy blend of orc and wolf. The splinter-toothed beasts bit and clawed but were no match for his thirsty war tool as it cleaved odorous pelts, trailing gore and crimson streamers.

Just as the cubs of the leopard bathe their muzzles in the kill, so was Gault bespattered with the stigmata of battle. At his side, Seamus cursed and slew and bled in a frantic effort to protect his liege. Renault was not with him, for time and again, he and his surviving champions charged the van of advancing demonkind, only to be foiled by the Heraldry of Chaos.

Limbs heavy, Gault grounded his axe. He looked up and his belly turned to ice. "Blessed Lady, save us."

Roaring like a mastodon, an Ascapundi chieftain ensconced in brazen armor hurtled through the ring of rabid beasts. Its onslaught was an avalanche of red hide and pounding muscle as it thrust at Gault's throat with the point of a twenty-foot ranseur.

Panic nerved Gault's limbs, and gathering himself, he unwound like a spring as his upthrust axe sliced, catching the polearm for an instant on the razored edge of his axe blade, severing the ranseur's shaft. Gault's momentum brought him before the giant with his weapon held high, two-handed. The twin-headed axe drew the Ascapundi's eyes wide behind the cheek plate of its helm. Raising its mighty shield, the giant meant to block the manling's blow, then drive the shield's arm-length spike through Gault's brain case.

Quick as a scorpion's sting, Gault crouched, then sprang forward and drove his own axe spike under the upraised shield. The stiff hauberk popped as the wicked point found the solar plexus of the behemoth. The mighty Ascapundi sank with a groan, its hands buffeting Gault who twisted frantically to free his weapon, for heavy steps pounded behind.

Abandoning his axe, Gault grasped the splintered ranseur and wheeled. A second Ascapundi was nearly upon him. He grounded the butt like a pike and angled the splintered tip to pierce the groin of the charging giantkin. It sank to its knees, clutching its shattered pubis. Gault staggered aside to lever forth his axe. He glimpsed Seamus. The man had a wolfling bent double over his knee, his rended eye streaming blood as his mighty hands choked the life from the slavering creature. Its maw mangled his hand before its eyes bulged weirdly and the spine splintered like greenwood.

Iz'd Yar was there. The remaining wolflings yelped and fled whilst his pale-skinned sons laughed through pointed teeth. Kör's general raised his blade level to Gault's face. Waves of black energy shimmered down its length.

Gault struggled to stand upright. He averted his gaze from the dark banner born by a naked dervish, yet the invisible design tugged at his brain like a reeling madness glimpsed in the eyes of a murderer. Vodrab stepped forward, face twisted with elemental hatred. He clapped his bony hands twice, and a wave of dissolution struck Gault. His axe was riven as he was hurled to his knees, and the dust of burning metal smoked on his surcoat.

Shrieking with fury, Iz'd Yar slapped Vodrab sprawling. With lambent eyes, he regarded the mazed prince. "I had not wanted it thus, Manking. Yet shall you die." He advanced, motioning his sons toward Seamus.

Pressed by thousands, mere hundreds of dwarf and Northrons were thrust back. Even so, growing piles of corpses at their feet gave pause to their pursuers, and their orderly retreat lent succor to the men of Ilycrium, who formed ranks behind them. Thus, a second route was averted.

Weaponless, Gault faced the advancing demon-lord. That was when it began, first a vibration underfoot, then escalating to a pounding from leg to spine. A wave of sound like rending metal struck them as the entire front of Kör's host buckled. Bestial wails of dismay were met with the deep-throated cheers of dwarf, barbarian, and man. Silver trumpets rang in chorus. Vodrab screeched at his lord.

Seamus gathered up his benumbed prince. "The riders of the Temple," he gasped. "The Goddess Who Loves War!"

To the fore of an irresistible wedge of armored horse, one peerless knight drove all before him. Undaunted by the magic of insanity, Isander lowered his white lance to charge the party of the demon-lord.

Vodrab whirled, blurring in his motion. Iz'd Yar and his escort grew thin, fading from sight. A new battle was joined. Heedless of life, the Templars plunged headlong into the mist of Kör's monsters that hacked any stalled cavalier, stabbing man and horse alike. Thunderous Ascapundi led unfought companies of orcs across the river en masse, and Mgesh plied again their deadly rain. In response, Ilycrium's bowmen and bow-wielding hillsmen fired their last shafts in futile effort to stay the surge.

The knights of the Temple dismounted, forming a new line of defense at the river's edge. Wave after wave of Kör's host struck them. Not a step—not an inch—did they retreat, thereby giving life to their countrymen. At long last, darkness found the flats of Celadon's shores. Wolf cries shuddered into the night, and from the gentle waters arose a mist to cover the unmoving dead. The battle was over. Kör was victorious.

SKYGATE

While the others geared for battle, Henlee produced a cloth-wrapped object carried under his pack from Windhover. Unwrapped, it was a kite shield of blackened wodensteel. On one knee, he presented it.

Apieron bowed, then bound it to his arm. "No heraldry for a houseless knight?"

"Ah, well, it shows only in the proper light."

Apieron smiled thinly, yet the fondness of a lifelong friendship shined a moment in his gray eyes. "My thanks."

"Arm yourselves, while I speak," said Galor. "In this place flows continuous magic. Thousands more beings live herein than you will see, each avidly tastes the flux that signals prey or danger, and many thereby scour the plane to great distances."

"Also, the abyss radiates its own shifting spectrum of magic. A conjuration might be accentuated in one area, or nullified, or worse, cast to rebound effect in another. I will endeavor to blend our emissions into the background. If I sense a probe, I will deflect it elsewhere into the vortex, rather than openly counter. Hopefully the multitudinous number of castings into the weave shall also serve to shield us."

"Mark me! Even I can grow tired. Stay alert! Heed well my words and those of our cleric. For if we should fail, many tribes of men, elves, and dwarves will cease to be."

An ice bowl lay before them. Lit from below, dark shapes drifted its depths. Frozen stalagmites towered around the perimeter, and on the far side hunched a windowed mass of stone. A flying bridge bisected it to surmount the farther rim whilst colonnaded balconies capped five buttresses, every surface glittering with a pearly rind until lost in shadows under and into the cliff.

"Himinbjorg," whispered Eirec.

"Hardly!" replied Henlee. "What think you, Apieron?" The ranger had donned supple armor of fine steel borne from the stores of the Lampus. At his side, he girt Leitus. His javelins, one ivory with a sigil of black, one of ebony that bore an ensign of white, were slung with the crooked bow on his back.

Henlee approached Isolde. She smiled, then laughed, her words billowing into the cold. "Just the thing, the perfect gift!" She placed helm and mask together over her face. Features exquisitely set in the wodensteel were stern of brow and chin, and bearded! With a spear flourish, she saluted the dwarf, who bowed deeply.

"No skulking in this glare," said Apieron. He stepped forward and led them directly across the bowl. The bastion loomed, yet no challenge was issued until they were nearly up the ramp.

"Disgusting," spat Henlee. His spittle froze in flight and broke on the stone. A standard floated at the apex of the way, suspended by neither lashing or pole. At fifty arm-lengths in width, it was a shadow against the ghost light, and within its depths, twisted a beast.

"We have seen such a device before." Apieron's voice was cold as the shimmering air. He drew Leitus.

"Ha, I know you!" the voice boomed. He was red as a boiled pig, and his dark wings arched the entire width of the walkway. "Stay that hand-axe, hairy oaf."

Eirec paused. "Why? When death beckons, we who dare tread here perhaps greet it no sooner than thou."

"Fool, I am immortal."

"Maybe not," growled Henlee. He stood near Eirec and Apieron, abreast the fore of the party.

A strange sound occurred, the mighty hands clapped in

mockery. Even Apieron held his advance. "I wonder," drawled the voice, "whose mind was quicker, yours or that cave bear you wear, baldie?" The mocking gaze cast over Henlee. "How delicious ... a bearded runt, and black!" Henlee emitted a strangled cry and raised Maul for a cast upslope.

"Liesmith!" bellowed Eirec. His hand-axe dropped to the pave as his patterned great sword flashed forth. The demon yawned nonchalantly. At his side appeared two rotund and slightly smaller versions of himself, although mottled in color. They bore bronze tubes five feet in length. Wide openings pointed at the party, and sparks flashed to their rear.

"Silence, noisome mud grubber! And thou, bald knave," chortled the guardian. A black tongue licked his lips lasciviously as his predatory eyes fell on Isolde. "And a slut wench, knee-worshipper of the trull goddess who bears a spear. Oh, act not so alarmed, I mark thee well, as I do all in my domain. A god here am I, the Eternal Watcher. Ah-h-h, a fungus of a wood elf! And a cave-chested, ne'er-do-well camp boy, perfumed?"

The crimson face broke into a vast leer, "Is it not Galor Galdarion? And this other—" The ears drooped, as did the mouth, into a frown as the long nose sniffed. "A ranger, tainted of blood. I like thee not! Give us this one, and you others may pass."

"One might consider an easier bargain," replied Galor calmly. The elf's open hand displayed a gleaming wealth of jewels. "God or no, who can see the future?"

Henlee looked to his friends and back to the blunderbusses leveled at them. "Aye," he said, his voice slow with wrath as his hand touched his gemmed and plaited beard, "we bear much wealth."

"My name is Gargantuel." The red-jowled chin jerked in signal and, in summons, strange shapes swam upward under the ice and within the structure itself. Growing alarmingly large, their movements quickened. "Treat with you? Why don't I kindle your beard for you? Ugly little shit!"

Apieron's right hand now bore his ebon javelin. It hummed with eagerness as its ivory design cast a pattern that played on the eyes of the fiends, who cowered whensoever it touched their faces. "Best you reconsider."

The demon's fat arm swept out in congenial embrace. "I am not an unreasonable being. Of course I am moved to pity by your plight, and will entertain your offer for twice the elf's sum, plus half the beard trove of the black dwarf."

One of the gun-wielding devils roared in protest. "It is not given you to deal so! She who waits—"

His words were truncated as a horny elbow-spike flashed into the juncture of neck and chest. Gargantuel snatched its gun and leveled it alternatingly at Apieron, Eirec, and Henlee. The objecting demon rolled from the ledge to fall heavily onto the ice-slick stone below. Gargantuel shared a look with the other monster, who sneered and nodded. "A negative attitude never solved any problem."

Galor smiled and made a blowing motion. His offering flew into the waiting grasp of the Watcher. The elfin hand waved, and their counterparts unraveled themselves from Henlee's beard to follow in an undulant stream of floating diamond-glow.

"Who … what?" exclaimed the dwarf.

"Nicely done!" pronounced Jamello.

The guardian studied the jewels a tedious moment before secreting them away. "Very nice, worth more than your miserable lives. I really must someday visit Dwarvenhome."

"Fat toad—" began Henlee.

"And kindly remove that light from my face." The fiend frowned again at Apieron.

"When you have gone."

"So be it!" A trumpeting fart echoed foully in the air and, with a flourish, Hel's sentry departed.

"My Goddess!" exclaimed Isolde as she frantically fanned the air.

"Oh, there's worse to follow," chuckled Henlee, then his hands involuntarily pawed his beard.

"Come," said Apieron, grasping Henlee's elbow as the others followed. Together they came to the wall's height to behold the fate that awaited them.

Epilogue

After the river battle of Celadon, in a field of uncut grass where the blackened ribs of a burned-out garth jutted skyward, two Mgesh outriders found the delegation of students from Sway. Many such skirmishers rode in wide-flung wings that swooped upon Ilycrium's heartland like an enormous bird of prey, and under the smokes of many burnings commenced the rape and ruin of the mightiest country of the West.

Henred and one other strode in delegation with heads high and hands outstretched, their winningest smiles and best garments flashing in the pall. The scouts simply slew them. The shrieking drover they bound beneath his mule cart, and cackled in their guttural tongue when the jolts of the road shattered the old man's bones.

Chapter 14

Sway

Goz spurned the young human from him with a kick. He gazed out to where the last of the wretched beggars were being slaughtered on the river plain before the gates. Diplomats and polished negotiators had issued from the capital city, bearing tokens of peace, gold and food, although the messengers themselves had worn the gaunt, quick-eyed faces of the hungry. Goz laughed and stroked his leathery belly at the memory. Half Ascapundi and half Azgod, he did not feed on olives and bread.

He tossed his mace to a subaltern. "Clean that, dog. You scout, what do you see?"

A Mgesh called down from the top of a willow whose feet bathed in the Swaywynde. "Little moves, General. Canals bear blocking chains. Streets are barricaded but lightly manned."

"Tell me something I do not know or you'll die in that tree!" bellowed Goz.

"Many houses are deserted, some looted." The scout raised his head and squinted against the lowering sun with a shielding hand. "The harbor is very far, yet … nigh a hundred gray ships crowd her mouth."

Goz grunted and began to tug at the limbs of the youth he had slain. "We camp here. Signal the attack for dawn."

Ascapundi and weremen grumbled in their tusks but not openly. The cool night would have been better for the assault, but Goz awaited his human allies, the marines of Kör, and *something* else. He would bide. Better that than openly affront their canny field marshal, Iz'd Yar, whose missive had been precise, and whose notions of discipline rivaled the elite torturers of Körguz.

GLORIOUS AMOR

Drust, champion of Amor, regarded the white-haired stranger. "As instructed, the stave has been retrieved from forest daughters."

"And its dweomer?"

Broad shoulders shrugged. "Impossible to tell. The stave has ever bound itself to a sole wielder with which it feels kindred, augmenting as it chooses the bearer's powers. It speaks not to me! Will you not take instead the mage staff Galor offered? A potent weapon."

"Nay, only Bone Slayer."

Drust unwrapped a stained and age-worn skin over the yellowed stave. Etch work might have been visible along its length, but was dulled by the slow erosion of time. The visitor took the staff, turning it over in his hands. Drust backstepped in amazement as the object transformed itself. Secret words were breathed onto the device, then shouted aloud as the rod was swung overhead to strike the ground. A tremendous furrow shot from the point of impact like branching lightning, piling up mounds and splitting trees.

Drust gasped, "Such power."

The grim stranger allowed a thin smile, and waved the stave tip in an almost dismissive manner. The rents were healed, and trees waved gently in the unseen breeze, whole and undisturbed.

"You must stay," stammered Drust, "our lady Dorclai will declare a fete —"

"No person or force of Amor may war on Kör." The white-haired elf bowed. "I take my leave."

SWAY

Hardel woke with a start. His window casement swung back and forth, a toy of the night wind. The sounds of conflict carried to him, and the screams of alarm and pain from the men of Sway. His men! Although no voice of those they faced. Then he smelled it, a charnel-house reek that filled the room, an odor conjoined with the taint of sea rot. Too late had he roused.

Hardel struggled to sit up; when had he gotten so fat? Too late for so many things. When had the instincts of a warrior left him? Cold fingers found his throat. Too late to scream, Hardel could only behold pinpoint lights of hate in the recessed orbs of the wight that crushed his windpipe.

Sunrise revealed a sight that caused the commandant of the black navy to grind his teeth until they bled. His wave-cutting squadrons had suffered horribly in the assault on Sway's port. By signal, Goz had denied his request to disembark his marines into the soft flanks of the city. Thus Scyld and Iphus had winnowed his vessels like a thresher with a stick, while shore batteries had catapulted shot of stone and pig iron, crucibles of burning pitch and weighted slice-nets.

Sisteros surveyed the town that now lay open before him. The wharf was a blackened ruin, and fires crept inward with a landward breeze. Thirty ships capsized! Each bearing three hundred of his soldiers, perhaps only half of each vessel's compliment surviving the churning chaos of the harbor battle. Curse of the Dreaming Serpent upon that fat pig, Goz! Sisteros observed his sailors and marines hauling mooring lines and sifting the detritus of the battle. That the beleaguered armsmen of Sway had resisted at all was itself an astonishment. The commandant recalled an odd name. *Uggirat.* That one so distant might affect a seaborne invasion was a mystery he would never understand. The walk of the dead from the ocean's floor in the night had sent screams echoing across the waters to the waiting fleet, yet fight the men of Sway had! When Sisteros's ships finally breeched the Sisters, his marines had shown no mercy. Troughs and tubes were lowered and liquid fire was sprayed thrice over the dockside, cooking defenders in their armor, while those manning derrick and grapnel had been charred until nothing remained as his marines avenged their fallen.

Then came the rain of bolts, a deluge from the gray ships such that, for six hundred steps inland, every surface sprouted the bitter harvest. "Orders, sir?" asked an ensign, an indigo crest nodding on his helm.

"Set pickets but no encampment; we shall sleep on board. Leave the city to the ghouls!"

""What is that?" asked Goz.

"A shrine, Lord," answered Feirefiz, lieutenant to the general of Kör's army in the West.

"It is small, yet famous," said Feirefiz. "The manlings believing that as long as the flame lives, so shall their goddess embrace the spirit of the city." At their feet was a slanted walk lined with low stones. In a ring at its center burned a flume whose source found the surface through natural vents discovered when the first houses of the city were built.

Goz's foot crushed the fiery crack into powdered ruin. He regarded the quiescent stone suspiciously, then spat. The flame had been extinguished. "You see, Feirefiz," he laughed, "the tale was overblown, as everything else with these puling Westrons. At least the Northrons and dwarves defended well their high passes before they were killed."

"Sisteros reports a third of his drommonds lie on the bottom of the harbor."

"His precious marines dead, you say?" chortled Goz. "Mayhap now the strutting peacock will be a bit more tractable."

Feirefiz gathered himself with apprehension. He bore the liniments of a tall man, save that he was scaled and had vestigal wings. Often he boasted kinship to the demon masters of Kör, albeit muchly diluted with human stock. "City defenders slew the greater portion of your foragers in the dark, wolfmen and mongrel men alike. However, the wights of the black druid broke them. Strange, none now are to be seen."

Goz tugged his red jowls. "Save your tongue for news of import. Show me the palace!"

XAMBOL THE STONEFIST

When first light found Xambol the Stonefist, living eyes opened on a head that lay against a runestone. No beast or crawling thing had marred it in the weeks following the assault of the dragon wraith and the Black Druid's summons of the dead to walk on Sway. The head of Tertullion, archmage of Ilycrium, regarded the barow fells of Ulard, as the lonesome hilltops softened to blue then green under the wintry sun.

"Your mummery is done, Uggirat. I call walking souls back to earth. Thou shades, be at peace."

SWAY

"My Lord General, I gift you the city of Sway."

"That is good, Dexius." The half-giant turned to Feirefiz. "Your wolves will not completely destroy the town, as per agreement with our future governor."

Dexius bowed deeply, relief penetrating his habitual mask of composure. "The palace has been preserved for your pleasure, Great One."

"Show me."

The council room of Sway had been barren for months. The ancient warriors of darkened bronze and stone, ancestors of the Candor kings, now glowered over a throng of conquerors that pushed into the room of state. "Great General," said Dexius, "there are yet a few, er, organized defenders remaining."

Goz's deep-socketed eyes lit suspiciously on the rogue minister. Dexius continued, "These are students, young civilians, barricaded in the chancery. They aided us greatly in preventing any organized resistance to your legions. Now they ask for terms."

"Crucify them," replied Goz flatly. "And, Minister, has this place been searched thoroughly for spies and assassins?"

"Of course," choked Dexius, his pale skin acquiring a gray hue.

"Very good, for if I so much as stub a toe, you'll dangle with those others."

Dexius bowed again, his forehead nearly touching the hard flags of the floor. "And when you leave, slave, send to me a comely woman of the city."

Dexius shot a horrified look to Feirefiz, who merely returned a yellow-faced grin.

Goz's guffaws echoed from the stern likenesses along the wall. "To eat, fool. They are soft."

"Never question the general!" screamed Feirefiz, but he lowered his whip at a flick of Goz's paw.

"Go, slave."

THE BANKS OF CELADON

Wiglaf hoisted a final stone. Turning towards his companion, he maintained a crouch that lowered his silhouette behind a rank of screening alder. "All clear, Cusk?"

"Yup, them hellions 'ave set camp up where the Prince 'ad 'is banner yestereve." A black stench wafted skyward. "They 'a throwin' their dead onto a burnin' by the river."

"At least Dunstan will not sleep with the bones of such as they," growled Wiglaf. "Come, lad, we go."

Iz'd Yar surveyed the battlefield. The dead lay strewn from the Celadon to the heights. Like cockroaches on meat, orcs pillaged enemy and ally alike, cackling gleefully as grizzly trophies were brandished, later to be borne in triumph to clans as testaments of bravery or as ingredients for their muddy rituals. The hillock on which the Western prince had stood now bore Kör's mighty standard, a serpent of gold on black, and crimson was the star clasped between its fangs. The heraldry of madness was now hid.

On the plain, wolfmen raised gore-smeared faces to howl their delight, then resumed their dark work. These were interrupted only by carrion birds, too clever to squabble within snapping distance of the deadly maws.

One Gommish, a high chieftain of the Mgesh, stood nigh to the Kör general, albeit beyond arm's reach of Berich and Astorath. The man chewed his spindly moustache with teeth blackened from an unvarying diet of horse jerky and mare's milk. Iz'd Yar could smell him from where he stood.

"Your horse-archers were decimated by the Westernlings."

Gommish spat something. "Messengers have been sent, many thousands more dog-brothers ride to you from our land of tall grass."

Iz'd Yar's eyes narrowed. "You mean to say the lands of my cousin, Prince Iblis of the Dream Throne, your overlord!" The Mgesh shrugged his rolling shoulders. "And what of the horse-king, your brother?"

"Fell to the Silver Knights, with many others. They have dead too, their silver in Mgesh tents. Gommish king now."

"What think you, Skegga?"

A wide leer was written on a looming Ascapundi's red face. "A mighty victory, Lord. The manlings are broken. We hunt what few remain."

"Think you so, my sons?" The pallid features of the twin incubi broke into toothy grimaces. "And you, Magnus?" Vodrab's deep shadowed eyes revealed nothing.

"Ahh, there is at least one here who is not totally bereft of wit!" Yellow eyes aglitter, Iz'd Yar pointed an accusing claw at those around him. A dozen orc chieftains fell to their faces and groveled. The claw indicated one who had been slow to his knees. Vodrab hissed a word, and the goblin began to burn.

When the screaming subsided, Iz'd Yar continued, "Where is the Western prince? I see his hide not amongst those bloody rags at your waist, Skegga." The accusing hand swung to Gommish. "Your dung-lappers ride down peasants and camp boys! Where are the heads of Northmen and dwarves who simply marched away? Victory? Vodrab, draw us a map."

The sorcerer bowed to kiss the earth at the demon-lord's feet. Vodrab straightened, and his bejeweled nails inscribed a series of lines in the air that took on substance in glowing red.

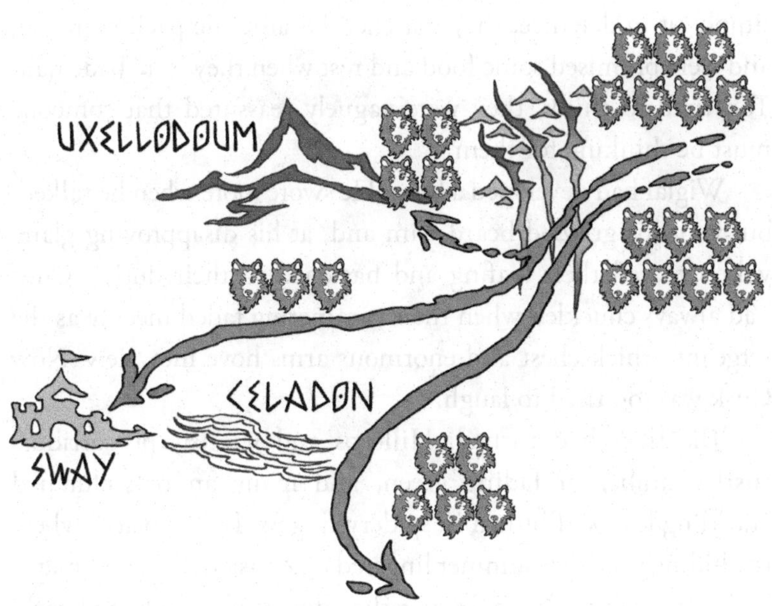

"Two armies. Twelve and two Snakes have I brought hence," instructed Iz'd Yar. "One army is thusly divided. Its first portion roots dwarves from their holes; the remainder I have sent to the Ess. Sway and Bestrand have fallen, there will be no homecoming for the rabble who oppose us. My legions here shall claw the soft belly of this country. When we have found our enemy, it will be the end."

"And if again he flees?" queried Skegga. The giant king's face bore no disrespect. Iz'd Yar allowed him to live.

Vodrab turned, and his construct dissolved. "We are the anvil. A third army will issue from the Matog that men name Duskbridge. From Hel's very abyss comes the hammer of doom."

ILYCRIUM: THE ARMY

Cusk walked in their midst, slogging lines of bedraggled farm boys done up in soldier's garb. Too tired to turn and run, or to simply sit in defiance, they marched because the pack marched, and were promised some food and rest when they were bade halt. Too tired to think, they were vaguely reassured that someone must be thinking for them.

Wiglaf had developed a limp. He swore more when he talked, but kept his grizzled beard trim and, at his disapproving glare, yokels ceased their loafing and hastened to their duties. Cusk had always chuckled when their yammering faded meekly as the sergeant's thick chest and enormous arms hove into view. Now Cusk was too tired to laugh.

The trees had turned. Hilltops and windswept corridors rustled amber or fading green, and many an oak clutched crackling leaves of brown in spidery fingers. In low places where the hiding was best, summer lingered amongst archways of maple and splay-trunked birch. Men gathered nuts of walnut and beech, and tart persimmons. Squirrels and rabbits slow to flee found their destinies in cooking pots; wild mint was plucked for tea, watercress for chewing.

At times, a column would chance upon entire glades ruined by the passage of the enemy, ancient trees recklessly hewn and cast astride polluted streams where a miasma of decay would live in the air. Men breathed through scarves and hurried past the contagion.

Erasmus covered his ears against the wailing of wood-bound nymphs, invisible to others, and he wept as he walked. Often monstrous creatures lurked in such places, and soldiers would rush forward to find a wolfling crouching above a comrade. Transfixed by many arrows, the eyes glowered their hate until dimmed by death. Foresters and scouts, much depleted in battle, took to flanking the march, bows strung at the ready.

On the third day from the river defeat, a halt was called, Kör's foragers notwithstanding, for the wounded could travel no more. Many of the enemy's hurled javelin or sky-arching arrows had been poisoned. Poultices of sphagnum and hairy burdock proved futile as the red blossom of sepsis took root.

Seamus grunted at the sight before them. Involuntarily he touched his mauled left hand to the brow over his empty socket. Two of his fingers had stayed in the jaws of the wolf-orc.

"The backbone of this land is broken," breathed Gault. "By the gods, what is that?"

Erasmus covered his eyes.

Guardsmen picked forlornly about the periphery of a dale. A great burning had occurred therein. Lowborn and lord alike held up in morbid fascination. It was a pile, six man-lengths high and forty across. The bodies of kine and deer, man and horse, and countless varied animals of field and forest were intermingled in obscene jigsaw. Nothing moved. Bone tips gleamed white in the sun upon a base of black char left by the fire. Camp was set where the death hill could not be seen. The army halted like a man exhausted who falls with no plan for rising.

Trakhner ordered construction of a hospital. Surgeons were few and some had died in the fighting, yet those who remained labored like heroes. In time, woodland priests and peasant goodwives found the army, bearing baskets of boneset, black willow for fever, and motherwort for sleep. Patrols were sent to distant villages; some returned with fighting men and trailing swine, others not at all. Wandering fields of fallow oatgrass and neglected wheat were gleaned and milled with eagerness. It was never enough.

Gault tossed a pinyon wedge onto the fire. It flared to yellow life and lit the legs of the men reclined in the circle of its warmth. The boots of Seamus and Trakhner were caked with mud. Renault's glimmered where silver chasing was tooled into the leather, yet these were less magnificent than those of Exeter. The Hawk had arrived at dusk with twelve hundred men. Many bore wounds earned in skirmishes with outriders of the Kör horde.

"It was said at Court," mused Gault, "that my mother's womb grew barren by contrivance once my father wed her."

Trakhner's leathers rasped as he shifted uncomfortably.

In a voice just audible, Gault continued. "He once told me I was adopted heir long before they stopped trying. How I hoped for a brother!"

"He was a noble man," stated Trakhner, "and awarded my own commission with his very hand."

"But ill fated," added Exeter, "to die as he did."

"No man may choose the nature of his passing," quoth Renault. "Thus he must practice knightly virtue all his waking hours."

"I thank your gentle speech," answered Gault. When he moved to add more kindling, the hollows of his eyes were shadowed with sorrow. "And yet I would agree with those who tell the planets of my birth were evil." He looked upward, relieved that the red star did not peer upon them. "Fair Ilycrium is dying. Of our allies, Bestrand lays prostrate, the Saad Isles silent, and the king of wood elves shuts his doors, thus repaying our many slights." Gault tossed the shattered handle of his grandfather's axe onto the little fire. The men watched as it began to smoke.

"Battles twice lost. Gallant Templars slain to a man, and many others." Gault's voice faded to a whisper. "Who shall sing the song of passing for Conrad and Tertullion, and Xephard Bright Helm? Or for my father?"

Trakhner cleared his throat. "What news of Wulfstane and Buthard, Exeter? Will you cheer our prince with news of reinforcements come up from the south? Or perhaps they have been sent westward to ease the sufferings of the capital?"

Exeter leaned forward, his sharp face made more narrow by the fire's planes of light and dark. "The only news from Southlands and the ineffable East are blasphemies that blacken the tongues of chanting monks from the Dragon Fells. Many die on their accursed altars." Exeter stroked his pointed chin. "Buthard sends this: 'Sway's troubles are her own to fix or mend as may be.'"

"Traitor," breathed Renault, and their stew-pot fire hissed its agreement.

PLEVEN DEEP: THE DRAGON RIFT

Tizil crouched in darkness beside the prisoned head of his master. For weeks, it had been thus, after Grazmesnil's dream wraith was vanquished by the boy-king of Ilycrium, and the subsequent sending from the awful Other. How he had groveled, mewling in terror and biting the adamant stone.

Though quiescent in form, the mind of Grazmesnil was not in repose, and at long last, Tizil rose. His head was cocked as if listening, although there was no sound. Even the drip of water on stone had been stilled by Grazmesnil's rage. At last, a fleeting touch of his master's will caressed Tizil. A task! A mission!

With a screech of malign delight, the demonling hastened its flapping way through the nightfall crevasse. The airs over the Pleven Deep were frigid under the red star that lit the broken terrain like a bloodstained mouth. Tizil turned into the wind, north and west would he fly. A mighty battle had been fought and there was death on the wind. He perceived the suffering of many who lived, helpless and weak.

Tizil strained with eagerness.

Chapter 15

Helheim

The companions stood on the edge. Revealed was a world of jarring colors and mixed horizons, where far seemed near and balances tilted. A melting, brown sky rotated at times below a flat expanse of crystalline white, and the heat smote them like a furnace of giants. Isolde looked concernedly to Galor.

Henlee chuckled grimly. "It's like that. By that one's casting, we shall at least not be incinerated."

"Warming up a little, thief?" growled Eirec. The big man's face was florid, and sweat trickled into his bushy beard.

Jamello looked from Apieron's supple mail to Isolde's dwarf-wrought mask and corslet of linked plate. Eirec had donned a hauberk after the fashion of his people, and scales of some iridescent metal gleamed whenever Galor's mantle flowed aside. With envy, the thief regarded Tallux, who had also clad himself in armor of sorts, leather of burnished jet adorned the breast and legs of the stocky elf—though it did not hinder his motions, ever efficient and graceful. Next to the ebon collar, Tallux's hair, cropped above the shoulders, was revealed to be of deep mahogany rather than true black. "By the everlasting forest," gasped he, "where have we come?"

"Follow," said Apieron. He led them down to the base of the cliff, then doused each in turn with a fistful of powder from the Hel plain. "A poor camouflage is better than none."

Jamello touched the morion atop his head. It was heavy, and hot, as was the round shield of the crypt. "Strip off your doublet," commanded Galor. Jamello felt its weight, then shrugged. The finely tooled garment quickened into blowing ash before it struck the hardpan.

"Is this iron?" the elf mage indicated a drift of red-and-black dust.

Henlee scooped up a handful, tasted, then nodded and grinned. Galor bore it to the thief and tossed it aloft where it swirled before coalescing on the thief's blouse and breeches like a layer of glistening rust. "My white shirt—"

"Is now armored as well as can be," stated Galor. "Now to business." From his shifting robes, the elf mage withdrew a second hoard of gems. By some trick of the abnormal light, or a property of the stones themselves, they radiated a shimmering aura beyond that of any natural jewel. "These are the true essence of the treasure given fat Gargantuel."

Jamello and Henlee gasped when the elf's hand clenched, reducing them to powder. "Shall I do the same for your own, Master Dwarf?"

Henlee ran a forlorn hand across his beard. "Nay, nay, though I hate yon pig-demon, I cannot bear to see any gems so ruined. Dwarves do not harvest earth's guerdons heedlessly, as do the slave miners of men." The black dwarf hoisted his fearsome weapon. "Let the devil keep the stones! I'll kill three of his kind for each of my losses."

"I think you shall have your wish," exclaimed Tallux. "Look."

Jamello quickly bent to a folded piece of metal. As he worked, he murmured, "Thank Bagwart, many a long mile I've carried you, now you are home!" As he stood, the thief hoisted a metallic crossbow, oil-slick and gleaming. He strapped a bandolier of iron quarrels above his brace of blue-pommeled daggers. "Which one do I shoot first?"

Apieron held up his hand, a sign to stay both the thief and Tallux, who was sighting along Strumfyr with deadly intent.

Galor pondered, "Of their officers, some I recognize—known fiends of long repute. These others, never have I seen their like."

"We have, Mage," growled Henlee. Many tall men there were, with cruel faces and mighty of stature. Each was clad as a prince, and marched as a column betwixt decurions of Hel, who dared not ply the long whips at their sides.

"The Army of Brass," breathed Apieron, "they make for Duskbridge."

"Much evil will they bring to the lands of men," said Galor.

Apieron's gray eyes studied the winding column as he might a maggoty nest of flies before turning away. "We must hurry."

Although she had steeled herself against the trials of their descent, Isolde felt helpless before a welling anguish. The flinty stench they breathed, and cutting stones upon which they trod made her gag and wince despite the clever wards spun by Galor Galdarion. Fool was she to attempt to deceive the illimitable plane. Under smokes like running water, the travelers crept. Above these loomed thunderheads wherein the lord Galor said dwelt evil spirits in palaces of cloud, and when lightnings flared, the whole was suffused with unnatural blue.

"Less than insects we be," murmured the young priestess through cracked lips.

Isolde knew she and her six comrades but awaited the inevitable and final attack promised by the pervading menace. Three flying horrors had already sprung from a particularly dense fume, knocking Jamello flat. Four of Tallux's arrows had peppered one in an eye's blink. One wing flailing, it had charged the half-elf scout, threatening to transfix him with its long pike. Henlee had hooked its dangling feet with Maul as Apieron skewered the flapping creature with his javelin. The others were disintegrated into a plume of orange skin and bilious entrails when the elf mage raised his hand. A minor moment of levity occurred when a foot-wide swath of demon skin slapped Henlee across the face and stuck, and poor Jamello was fairly inundated with slime. Both glared at Galor.

The band was little heartened by the easy victory. They expected worse, for had not Galor warned that any use of his powers drew the Helspawn like moths to a taper? Isolde spared a furtive glance, afraid she voiced aloud her doubts. Rudolph Mellor was closest. Normally she might have preferred otherwise, yet here their to-and-fro seemed petty and of a dim past, and the thief appeared in no mood to converse. His face bore a mien of poorly concealed pain, and he held his posture rigidly erect, as if all his energy was spent on marching straight … not to flee or collapse in a panic. If this were true, Isolde knew well how he felt.

Tallux's stoic demeanor hinted at much the same. Eirec cursed and grumbled from his position at the rear, apparently yet seething for having not struck a blow in the demon encounter. The Northman had insisted on wearing his bearskin despite the heat. Indeed, with his black beard and a covering of soot, he reminded Isolde of a hulking bear, save for the specks of coal and wisping flame that dotted his cloak and beard.

To Isolde's fore, Galor moved with ease, apparently unencumbered by their surroundings. The oven wind in their faces seemed to slow him little, although his mantle played out behind him. Whenever a particularly nasty gust struck, Isolde and Jamello would stagger, then willed their abused joints to regain momentum, and ever was the wood elf near to lend a boost or helpful word.

A stride or three behind Apieron marched Henlee, who muttered and chewed his weaved beard as he had done since passing the helgate. It had been decided that the dwarf would lead with Apieron, but none could outpace the lord of Windhover. Isolde's blue eyes narrowed. For her life entire, Apieron's presence eased her mind, now his dour mood was supplanted by the driving obsession that had only grown since the temple sojourn. With open hostility, Apieron rounded on any one or thing that threatened to delay his vengeance. Above, in the light of the familiar sun, Isolde had felt their mission one of rescue. She cursed her naiveté. Worse, what was her role to be? There came an insidious whisper … if ever Xephard could be found … would her life be spent for his?

Isolde swallowed, and a tear found her eye, drying instantly. It burned. She saw Xephard's face, strong without need for aggrandizement. Always victorious, ever glorious. Xephard Bright Helm, favorite of the Goddess Who Wars. Who would make the blood offering to elevate Her hero from the pit? Would he then go blithely to greater glories? To eventually be given another puppet female? Isolde touched her dwarven mask, and her hand caressed the armor over her breast. Trappings of a fool! All that she had lived and breathed a lie. She looked again to the others.

How did the eldritch mage not hear the shouting of her mind?

Then her eyes saw. Six men there were, locked in their own internal struggles. Isolde tightened her grasp on the spear, she had forgot she bore it at all. Tall and strong, its fearsome point was forged in the forgotten past to deadly purpose, by the very armorer of the gods. It shined like a beacon to things unspoilt, unbreakable, and undimmed in the Hel glow, like the spirit of the noble and selfless man she sought. So must she be.

Faith, for her love, so would she be!

FASTNESS OF LLUND

Xephard was content. With one ear, he heeded the darkness beyond the camp; with his other, he enjoyed the banter of his friends. Of Apieron's quest, Isander had been wrong. Xephard did not sulk to lead Templars with horns blowing and pennants waving. Nay, it was a good camp, and as a soldier, he accepted the best of every moment, for could not the next be his last? Something roused Xephard. He stood to peer over Jamello's shoulder. The thief was musing; in his hand were several sheets of sheep vellum, inscribed obviously by a woman's hand.

"What is that?"

"Oh, this," said Jamello nonchalantly, fanning himself with the pages.

"It is a note from the Lady Cle of Cudora. She is a tad older but beautiful in her way, and very rich."

"What does it say?" asked Xephard, obviously impressed by the artistically penned characters. "There seems to be a great many things recorded, it must be important indeed."

"Oh, not really. 'Tis a letter of affection," replied Jamello casually. "A pleasing diversion."

"Aye, I know of love. My lady awaits my return, so that we may be fully joined in the pledge of marriage. Your lady must regard you well to craft such beautiful symbols for you."

"Well, maybe. You may peruse it if you will."

"I could not," objected Xephard.

"It's none too private." Jamello thrust his hand forward. "Come,

return it when you will." He glanced at Xephard's face, and a gleam of understanding lit the thief's eyes. "Ahh. You cannot read, can you?"

With indignance, Xephard drew himself up. Apieron and Henlee wandered over in idle curiosity. Seeing them, the paladin's face colored. Henlee chortled, and Apieron made inventive noises while attempting to suppress his laughter. He gave up, guffawing whilst slapping his thighs as tears streamed down his face.

Xephard regained his composure and spread his scarred hands, "In truth, I cannot. My people know many runes and symbols for food or danger. They say that is all a warrior need know," Xephard touched his breast, "but I have learned that is not so."

Jamello stood up. Henlee jogged Apieron's side; with certainty, the witty cutpurse would deliver a scathing jab to the vulnerable chevalier. To the surprise of all, Jamello yielded Xephard a courteous bow and folded the letter into its waxed skin and presented it. "Examine it all you will. You are the only one I trust to hold it."

Xephard silently accepted the proffered wallet. Jamello stalked past Apieron and Henlee with a disdainful air. Ignoring the twain, Xephard returned to his place and removed the note with extraordinary care, the delicate papers unwrinkled in his big, war-hardened hands. He studied the flowing words with rapt attention.

Henlee harrumphed, "How d'ya like that?"

"Rudolph Mellor is full of surprises," answered Apieron.

"That one will come to a bad end, to be sure," concluded the dwarf.

Ulfelion nodded, and Aetterne bent over the paladin, moaning her pleasure. By the hair, Adestes jerked back her head. Her smiling fangs dripped blood, and breasts swaying, she stroked her swollen belly. Well sated, Aetterne sauntered off into the shadows of Llund.

HELHEIM

The girl danced. In the light of a copper lamp, her skin flashed bronze as she increased the tempo of her swaying hips. What scarce cloth adorned her figure floated free, excepting a long piece of gauze. The music's rhythm heightened, and she began to twirl, a perfect arch on one slender leg. As she did so, the filmy veil trailed from nimble fingers to enclose her in a swirling circle which the dancer temptingly raised and lowered as her audience craned necks to see. Timbrels and drums rose in pitch to a barbaric frenzy, and beads of sweat shined where light was cast on her belly, arms, and thighs. The music stopped, and with a wailing cry, she collapsed to worn planks—the gauze now binding wrists and wound into her hair. Men stood, shouting and clapping as more than one loudly offered to pay heavy gold for her.

Isolde's slender, booted foot dug into Jamello's ribs. He woke with a groan to peel his eyelids open like a rusty grate. "So how's the weather?"

"The sky is on fire."

"I hate it when that happens."

"Rouse yourself, thief. Our rest is done."

A halt had been called in the lee of three yellow boulders that reeked of sulfur. Eirec stood nigh. He stared and shifted uncomfortably while the others held converse in low tones.

"Let me tell you something, Priestess." Jamello sat up. "My skin feels like a trank that one has pulled from the fire then smeared liberally with grease, and the inside of my mouth reminds me of a monkey's … never mind."

Isolde scowled. Eirec hoisted Jamello to his feet without taking his eyes from the roiling distance. "What rune-teller could know that Hel be hot, not the frozen wastes of folklore?"

Galor turned. "Your skaalds do not lie. This place is only one amongst many, a dream world quickened by the will of She who was prisoned in another time. We must not name Her here!"

A fog had got up, and its sooty belly loomed low overhead. Jamello jumped up and tried to pierce it with the point of his crypt blade.

Apieron favored him with an odd look.

Like a sudden blast of sound, a molten finger burst up a short distance from them. Its mantle billowed soot, its heart aureate fire. Then, it was gone, although its glowing filled the fog cap for miles around, and yet another scar marked the place of its upsurge on the harrowing plain.

"Let us shelter from the storm," said Tallux.

"Nay," answered Apieron. "We move while this good weather holds."

Henlee smiled at Eirec and Tallux.

As they marched, Apieron's apparition returned, for what the others perceived as half-heard taunts and shrieks on the unfriendly wind, or a wrathful murmur under foot, Apieron beheld with his waking eyes—a form of shadow that writhed on vision's edge. "Well I remember thee," mouthed the ranger of Windhover. Ever it grew as the party advanced. Apieron did not need Leitus's mirror to know what form would be revealed. "I am coming, as you wished, Bitch of Hel!"

"Yeah!" echoed Henlee, unsure exactly what was said.

As if in response to his challenge, sibilant fingers teased at something deep within Apieron's breast. Something that twisted in recoil. Apieron staggered, catching his breath as an insidious laugh lingered in his ear. The others paid no heed, their eyes were fixed on Galor Galdarion.

"See now," proclaimed the arch-mage, "we have come to the water's of Iron Lake."

Swells and falls lifted in expanse before them. The rock they traversed narrowed, continuing into the unquiet sea of flowing stone. As they drew close, portions of the molten surface to either side glowed incandescent and painful to look upon, and in these strange, crystalline meres, beings resembling dark tadpoles swam and rose, then burst into flocks that wheeled before taking flight into the lowering reek. Eirec cursed with passion.

"Is this truly our path?" asked Tallux, dismay lighting his pale face.

"Not a good place to receive an ambush," agreed Henlee. The dwarf scowled darkly at the thin isthmus before them.

Eirec swirled his great sword away from the flux where he had dipped a bit of its length. A dollop of orange cooling glass surmounted its tip. "Like a spit turnip," murmured he before clanging the two-hander clean.

"Do not tarry," called Galor. "The way is straight."

"It is our path," answered Apieron. "I feel it." The furnace of the wind stank of burning metal, and nodules of ball lightning fell onto crested waves of bubbling glass. They walked quick as may, yet none wished to chance a stumble into the cauldron of the lake.

"The woods elf was right about the stone path," exclaimed Henlee. "Look there!" Before the travelers, the rock bridge widened again into the pitiless and blasted expanse of Hel's floor, yet blocking their ingress was pillar of fire, and dimly discerned at its dancing apex was a man clad in shining robes. He advanced.

"Bows!" shouted Apieron, as he ran to a flanking angle while bringing his living longbow to bear. Tallux and Jamello did the same. The man laughed and threw down a glowing crystal. It broke into glass spheres on the scorched stone.

"Ha!" yelled Henlee, who charged with Eirec.

"Down!" called Galor.

The crystalline orbs rebounded high into the air, and the figure clapped. Crimson lightning arched between the nodes to encompass the companions in electrical agony. Jamello and Tallux pitched forward, fingers fumbling, as Henlee and Eirec were riven still, weapons frozen in grasping tetany, beards jutting and eyes bulging. Apieron rose from one knee and resumed his charge.

Isolde's thrown spear arched through the glare, and the figure recoiled but her weapon passed harmlessly overhead to disappear into the slag lake. He laughed.

Galor strode forward and their enemy drew himself erect. His high, intelligent forehead furrowed in concentration. His vestment seemed cast of living diamond. A hand axe struck him in the knee, another smote his side, and dwarf and barbarian shouted with anger when both weapons clattered harmlessly aside to be lost in lava flow.

The dweamorcaster withdrew his hands from his robe. They appeared transformed into pure energy. Grasping fingers expanded with crackling glee at a thought. One encompassed Apieron, and sparks shrieked from the splayed digits, each as thick as a man's arm, as Leitus scored their lengths.

The second sentient hand rushed greedily toward the elvin mage, but Galor had not been idle. A peculiar sound drifted from a thin whistle of carved ivory, and from the water's orange glow surged an enormous bulk of gold and blue. Its flukes thrust, and sheets of liquid fire cascaded down its airborne bulk.

"A whale, a narwhal!" exclaimed Tallux. A horn of twisted jet, twelve cubits long, took the spellcaster in the chest, and the flames of his pillar dissipated into the swirling heat of the air.

Isolde stood unmoving on the lake's edge. She tilted back mask and helm to free the sweat-plastered hair from her neck. A power arose in her, and she lifted her arms in invocation. The magma of the lake bubbled, and there emerged head and torso of the enemy wizard, a thing now of skin blackened tight over cheekbones and skull, and the fires of Hel burned in cavernous sockets. He bore up an imperishable spear. Taking the weapon, Isolde nodded. The figure submerged soundlessly.

"Er, Priestess?" stammered Henlee. "Don't suppose you might do the same for my hand axe?" Eirec also looked hopeful. Without a word, she turned away.

ILYCRIUM: THE ARMY

Gault sat at table. It consisted of an empty rations box and a plank. He cut away molded portions from his allotment of bread and cheese. His poniard lifted what remained to his mouth.

"And our apprentice mageling?" queried Trakhner.

"Gone," said Gault, still chewing. "To Sway, he was muchly shamed that the field hospital was stricken despite his wardings." Candor's hand cast about purposelessly. "He knew about the attack on Sway, of course." Gault looked to Trakhner. "The man somehow reads my spy gatherings before I have seen them."

The crop-haired warrior nodded solemnly, a parchment sealed with broken wax dropped onto the table. "It ne'er left my person, only I have perused it."

"And I have said it often enough," said Exeter, fondling his creamy doublet. "Spell mummers sprout like mushrooms after a mist, yet rarely they endure the sun endings of a week."

"And prone to demonstrations and duels, those exploits grandiose," added Renault.

"Indeed, how unlike my chevaliers," replied Gault dryly.

Trakhner laid his thick fingers on the parchment and cleared his throat. "Sway is overrun," he said flatly, "and its garrison ambushed in the night by undead wights who walked the sea ways, followed by the very marines of Kör. The second land army over the White Throat reported by Eirec and his Geyfylla met them in a pincer. A master stroke."

"What say you now, Prince?" asked Renault. "Shall we leave our homes there to orcs and slavers?"

"We underestimated our foe," said Trakhner bitterly. He

paced to and fro, stepping over a puddle where the tent leaked. "We schemed to gain first the high passes, bottling him behind the Vigfils. We thought to engage him far afield, thereby saving our seabound cities." Trakhner's fist met his palm with a meaty thwak.

"You forget, Renault," said Gault quietly, "the lowlands burn already."

"Victory in hinterlands," quothe the knight champion, "to find Sway in ruin behind us?"

"If need be," retorted Trakhner. "Painful as it is."

"Where is our victory?" asked Gault. He pushed his poniard into the camp table, using it as a lever to find his feet, unsteady as an old man. "Yestermoon, I gave king's honors to one Valli, a bowman who stood tall against the Ascapundi, and was burned crown to heel by Kör's ancient sorcerer. He kissed my hand and cried, not with the pain of his charred skin, but because I honored him so."

Gault's voice cracked. "How many survived the night-raid on our hospital?"

Trakhner shook his head, and lines of sorrow weighted his reddened face. "Before he left, Erasmus scryed echoes of a flying demon, lord, and the men had been benumbed. Slain like … like your father."

"Erasmus's heart seemed broken." Gault swayed slightly. "He decried his own failings when he begged my leave. The hospital … so many deaths. He babbled of the red star, saying it was sign of a new millennium, in which the gods shun humankind. Was he insane?"

The others looked to their prince, for his eyes were wild and his words fey.

Renault fingered his square, smooth-shaved jaw. "This *Erasmus*—your Black Merlin, Tallux chief of scouts, Apieron of

Windhover and Xephard Bright Helm, Buthard son of Wulfstane, and now that shuffling bear Sir Eirec who leaves us to join their fools' errand. My lord, what of troth?"

"I think Erasmus had many friends there." Gault's eyes drifted. Exeter favored Trakhner with a meaningful glance at the prince's seemingly random speech. "He oft spoke of plans they hatched, his friends, I mean, for an ecole, a public for many students, held apart from family estates."

"An elysee of arms?" asked Renault.

"Scholars, my friend. Grammar, rhetoric and logic. Arithmetic and geometry, astronomy and music."

Renault was incredulous. "They will breed naught but scribbling troublemakers!"

A thin smile found Gault's face, and his eyes returned to the room. "You cannot read, Renault?"

Renault flicked his hands impatiently from the hilts of his verdigris sword. His gold-fretted mace waited against a stool, as the champion of Ilycrium bore no shield. "Of course I can, but a gentleman has servants to cipher for him. No noble is born to scribe."

Gault sheathed his poniard. "Cipher me this, gentlemen, what news will tomorrow bring?"

Tizil sat upon the upper branch of a forest oak that swayed gently under afternoon's sun. After his foray into the field hospital of the army of Ilycrium, he would rest. *Warding magics, indeed.* He sniffed, no large matter to open a way into the camp. After all, he was small.

He lay back to chew a few dainties whilst he pondered. A mother robin gave up her imprecations once the last of her late hatch disappeared down his throat. Tasty but unsatisfying. Dusk was but a few hours distant, and it would be a dark night after an early moonset. Tonight, the Prince.

Tizil bethought himself of a voluminous eye in a deep place, that of Grazmesnil, eldest of earthbound dragons. *Curse you, bless you, Master!* A paroxysm of rage took the little demon, and the tree's skin was scorched where his flapping wings caressed it. He chewed on something obtained at the hospital; it was good. He tossed the last of the eyeballs up, catching it in sharp teeth like a boy might a grape.

Tizil sighed and reclined against the branch, its rough bark scratching his leathery backside most pleasantly. This time, the job would be more than thorough. *Tonight, Prince, I suck your fucking skull.*

Seamus's paw-like hand touched Gault deferentially on the shoulder. "Something, Sire."

Gault followed the big man to a cordoned paddock reserved by Renault for use of the horse grooms and their charges where the champion was in converse with an unusual warrior. At Gault's approach, Renault retreated a respectful distance to stand near the strange knight's hunched and cowled companion.

"Be most welcome, sir."

A dark-haired elf, splendidly arrayed as a cavalier, bowed and proffered a silk-wrapped bundle. "Galor Galdarion sends his greetings and asks a boon of thee. May my lord be pleased to accept a gift?"

Somewhat taken aback by the haste of the proceedings, Gault looked about uncertainly. Exeter arrived, and coughed in his throat but did not speak.

"An' I am, yet what is the boon?"

"That you wear this always." The tall elf pulled back a cloth to reveal a mirrored longsword of goodly length. It curved gently from its glittering point to the fantastically worked hilts. A woman carved of white opal, platinum entwined, clasped overhead with wings and hands alike the blade's pommel stone, a sea-blue sapphire half as large as Gault's fist.

Gault grasped the brand, shading it from the sun to note the silken luster of elfsteel that glowed with a faintly perceptible inner shimmering. Feather light, it sang to his arm with a harmony of motion. "Never have I heard tell of such a sword." His brown hand bore it aloft to flash in the sun like a sister star. "Wherefore should the lord of Amor bequeath such guerdon to me?"

"My liege commanded me bring this," replied the elf knight, "he does not reveal his mind or counsels to his heralds. Nonetheless, I can tell you somewhat of this brand; its name is Gonfolon and I had not glimpsed it in fifty years. Sadly, I am not a scholar and know not well its powers, although I can tell you one thing of a certainty."

Gault's words were slow as was his wont when perplexed. "What may that be, sirrah?"

The elf's deep voice laughed as he turned to go, tucking the silk into a small bundle. "*This* blade, Prince, will not break."

"Wait, herald!" stammered Gault. "I have yet to ask your name, surely you will take repose with us." The elf was already mounted.

"Nay, Prince. I am overdue!" The elvin knight clucked his stallion to a walk, but his laughing voice carried back to them. "And my name is Galen Trazequintil." He rode off with speed, not pausing for response from the astonished prince.

"My lord, we do not know to what devious end this blade was delivered," said Exeter. "Or if this strange messenger was not a clever spy of Kör."

Renault pressed forward. "Indeed, my liege, it strikes me odd that your father's noble blade and the axe of your grandsire were broken in battle, and forthwith appears this wightish brand."

To their astonishment, Gault shared a laugh only with himself. "Gentlemen, I mean no disrespect. The herald named himself Trazequintil. Dost none of my counselors know a tithe of elfish legend? Galen, son of Galor, prince of Amor. I find that odd disguise for a spy of Kör."

Renault rounded on the elvin chevalier's erstwhile companion. "What of you, silent one?"

The cowled figure's rags brushed the ground. He bowed so low they thought he might not rise. "I too beg a boon."

"Wherefore should my master trust thee? The whispering wind has a face more open."

Candor thrust the sword under his belt, for no sheath accompanied it. "Aye, what of you? Are you also from the fair land of Amor? Alas that the princely knight could not stay, yet would you tell me more of this brand? You seemeth garbed as a pauper mage or p'raps a forest priest."

"Say not of Amor, yet one familiar with it. As for my magecraft, you shall be the judge. In the least, I know much whereof Gonfolon was forged and to what end."

Gault peered under the patchwork hood, and a face he beheld like unto elfkind but with hair aged white. A scar seamed the cheekbone, and the eyes were clear as standing water.

"And your boon?"

"To serve."

Gault's eyes fell upon Seamus and Exeter and Renault, whose

own pierced the robed figure like swords. "I accept. Tonight, join me at table."

SWAY

In a chamber of stone, deep beneath the streets of Sway, a figure crouched. His brown hands cherished a small censure, from which flickered a tiny flame.

All was quiet, for the sounds of suffering and animalistic cruelty from the streets did not penetrate thirty feet of stone. On hands and knees, the figure explored the uneven wall, and with a small knife, he broke free a clay plug and held forth his taper to the gap. Instantly, a blowing flame blossomed.

"Unbroken, fire to fire, we honor your sacred light. Goddess of Mercy."

Erasmus sat back, grimed and exhausted. As he regarded his handiwork, a slow smile found his handsome face, his first in uncounted months. Brockhorst would also be pleased.

Chapter 16

Ilycrium: The Army

An age-pitted dagger appeared in the elf's pale hand with which he sliced a small, perfect portion of his share. The morsels disappeared silently under the drab cowl. Gault's laugh was wry. "Our fare at least, Sir Elf, suits you. This horse was maimed by a wolf yestereve. You see, our camp is cursed."

Exeter took a great bite of meat and followed it with a noisy gulp from his flagon. He fixed his hawk-like gaze on the quiet elf. "Our mysterious guest is certainly a careful eater. Methinks he is careful in all things." The hooded figure gave the slightest pause, then resumed eating without a word, seeming to accept the statement.

"I deem you speak truth, Seneschal," said Gault. "In sooth, 'tis no accident of chance he is present among us. Surely a wizard of lordly standing could repose in distant comfort and worry not a wit about our conflict. No doubt he could scry o'er our travail from his enchanted forest, or wherever he lives, for amusement and not bother to miss dinner."

The contents of Renault's cup jumped. "Rainwater and stewed millet, now we eat our very steeds! 'Tis sad fare for a knight."

"Be glad for what you have," admonished Trakhner. He nodded to Seamus, who industriously scooped the last of his millet paste onto a spoon.

"Might not this mage conjure us some cheer?" continued the cavalier. "This camp has the air of a funerary."

"Funeral, the hospital, so many deaths." Gault held his head on his hands. "I am tired, nigh onto the death."

The elf ceased eating. "Speak not so. I think," he said slowly, "Kör would not be pleased with my presence here, so I beg your indulgence. He who strikes from the shadows may needs strike only once."

Gault lifted his head and shook his auburn locks. "It shall be as you wish."

The elf stood, bowing silently before retreating in the direction of his small tent.

Seamus engulfed his final mouthful, smacking and speaking at the same time. "That one means Kör no goodwill, an' that's a fact."

"Is it?" queried Exeter.

"His kind are long lived," replied Trakhner.

"Wizard elves maybe older yet, and Kör is the oldest creature of aught that walks on two legs that I know," murmured Gault. "Who knows when their enmity began? I guess it was long ago."

He was wrong. In the close space of the elf's unassuming tent, bright eyes burned the darkness, remembering a deeper gloom habited by pitiless laughter amongst pain-wrought shrieks, and the despairing moans of shattered souls. "Gehulgog, well I know thee. Malgrind I name you, for thou made me!"

HELHEIM

The sky fog cleared, and was replaced by burning rain. Henlee turned and spat. "Stuff tastes like pitch." Apieron led them a straight course, at times pausing as if to listen, then resuming his long stride without hesitation.

"As if he is going home," sputtered Jamello, flapping his hands in futile battle against the fiery droplets.

"That is also what I fear," said Tallux.

With the passage of painful miles, the oily rain collected in rivulets and pools, and when fell sky-borne gledes, the foul resin might flash explosively, or merely boil up into sooty billows that none could breathe. In time, there came the sound of a mighty flow, and the party trudged to a crag's edge to look upon a fast river of ink, some thirty feet below. It was wide with the poison that churned its depths.

Henlee pulled his beard. "This creek complicates things. I, for one, do not care to go wading today."

"I see something out over the tar!" cried Jamello.

The thief's thin arm indicated a builded structure nestled against the bank, two hundred yards downstream. The party slid wearily down a slope of crumbling slate to view Jamello's find, hoping for evidence of a dry bridge. The stench of the river was staggering. They saw uspended from an outcrop an iron cage, its ribs pockmarked with corrosion where its lowest portion lay submerged in the dark current. It was empty.

"Whatever lived in that cage was dissolved or eaten," spoke Eirec somberly.

"Or both," added Jamello.

"Whatsoever this was, or is," replied Apieron, "it does not yield us a way across." He eyed the far bank as if by will alone he might draw it to them.

"Aye," growled Eirec. He kicked a rock into the current. "River of the Underworld, what secrets do you hold?"

"A cage, a cage for prisoners," breathed Isolde softly. Her companions looked at her blankly. "Prisoners like Xephard," she whispered, and for a space, they were silent.

Eirec spoke at last. "Lord Mage, do you reckon this is what passes for water in Hel's kitchen?"

Galor shook his head. "Undoubtedly it is poison to natural creatures, as is all else here." Galor lifted an elfin drinking skin. Finely wrought sigils encircled its neck. "Since you speak of water, we must be careful of that we have brought. These jacks I gave you will not spoil, but once gone must be replenished by spell, and the strange magics of this place make any such casting apt to fail."

"Does aught truly live here?" Tallux's fair voice was flat on the insipid air. "I deem this plane and all it contains but an evil dream. Let us destroy it and depart, lest we fade ourselves!"

Cruel and ancient was he that gazed upon the seven walkers. How differently exciting their essences were—and reckless! A serpentine tongue flicked over razor-like teeth, for it had not tasted such in an age. Although Apieron and his friends did not know it, life in profusion teemed here, much of it hidden under ground and under stream, or cowled within fumes above. Only the most bold or desperate traveled extensively upon the exposed surface. Yes, there was much that lived, but none whose scent tasted so sweet to Sadszog. It crept closer.

Whence he had come or why, none could say, for here had he bided since the beginning. No scholar or deified mind could put a name to the sort of being he was. Singular, steeped in ancient cunning with a heart as hard as his horny exterior, Sadszog recked nothing of gods or devils. Content in his power, he bent his will to the span of his own domain amidst the Helfires.

If they were weak, why did they walk openly, seemingly heedless of every danger? If they were powerful, why did they cast about without apparent purpose? All in all, it mattered little. Soon they would become encumbered, then he would feed. With a silent turn of his mighty bulk, Sadszog sank into the Hel floor.

Galor wheeled in alarm, yet found only the dwarf, hands on hips and tapping his foot. "Well, mighty elf?"

"Well yourself, toadstool."

"*Well*," emphasized the dwarf, "twiddle your toes or waggle your ears. Make for us a damn bridge."

"P'raps I might summon you Queen Hashiba's golden dragon to carry you on her royal palanquin, so that your beard does not drag you to drown."

Henlee's retort was truncated by a rising shriek that emanated from a tall form, slender and blurred. Fast as bird's flight, it advanced like a dervish, then proceeded to stalk the elves.

Apieron caressed the twigs and leaves of his living bow, the gift of a barbarian elf who also ventured to the Hel plane, but did not leave. "See thou your twin, turned to evil?"

Jamello cried out in recognition. "The living spear of the druid Sarc the Brave!"

Henlee swore in the rumbling speech of mountain dwarves. "It is an elf-killer!" he echoed in the tongue of men as he ran to the transformed lance of swamp elves. The dwarf two-handed Maul a sweeping blow at the trunk, and was slapped away.

The thing whipped its trailing members horribly in frenzied dance, a grisly semblance of a tree flailed into agony by the merciless gale, and it wailed like a dying forest. Apieron and Eirec rushed to ply their blades to no avail. Jamello tried to topple it with a cleverly thrown wire, and was dragged into unconsciousness for his effort.

Tallux stood aghast, as if struck immotile until he heard Isolde's cries of alarm, "Trolls of fire!"

Three leering apparitions lunged from a crevice before the witch tree to amble like gibbons toward the female cleric. One, too slow to dodge, was grasped and rended in twain by flailing limbs. The second troll was tackled by Henlee and cleaved by Eirec. Its fellow monster began an odd dance with Isolde between long-nailed claws that flickered with flame and her holy spear. Looking down, it gaped stupidly at a hole blown in its chest by Strumfyr. Tallux's second arrow melted its head from its shoulders.

"Galor, quick!" shouted Apieron. Why Apieron acted next as he did, he did not stop to ponder. He sheathed Leitus, and from his wallet, he withdrew the little acorn he had borne from the high camp an age ago.

The elf mage instantly grasped Apieron's intent and the kernel. A drop from his jeweled flask, and the Eldar elf sang an incantation that swelled in vision: brown-cake earth and misty rains became a green bourne that faded onto a white-shored sea. The acorn grew a life span in an instant, until a thick oak towered before them. Its furrowed skin split into a face that roared a leaf-shaking challenge. The elf-killer howled its reply before rushing insanely to tear at its nemesis.

Jamello opened one eye. Before him, an eye in the stone mimicked his, but this one was two feet across. "Apieron. Galor!"

Jamello scrabbled frantically away as a second eye blinked from the slag which swelled and buckled as the colossal shape that was Sadszog emerged. Jamello slid down and away from the avalanche of its passage. Galor flew to engage. "Go back, Apieron," called he, "safeguard the others!"

The oak fell and burned, and the witch tree also lay quiescent, but its tortured and blackened limbs did not smolder. A bell-shaped cloud of dust and raining pebbles blew up from where the elf mage had battled the keeling monster. Now Galor returned to them, and open mouthed, they regarded his soiled garments and sooty hair.

"Well, and well again!" Henlee began to chuckle, as did Eirec and Tallux. Isolde and Jamello were too astounded to say anything.

At a dismissive wave, dust flew from Galor's person, and his robes resumed their flowing motion. "I am weary, and think we all must rest once we cross the dark water."

Henlee happily sunk Maul deep into the fallen elf-killer. "Wood will be no problem; a fine bridge this will make."

"Since it will not burn, we shall cast it into the stream when we have crossed," said Apieron, "a remembrance for he whose lance this was."

"Aye, lad." Henlee's brown eyes softened. "Noble Sarc who vouchsafed for a dwarf in trial for the death of a very kinsman, we will never forget."

FASTNESS OF LLUND

"Axylus. Come!" Xephard whistled. "We go on quest with our friend Apieron."

Xephard stood in the sun of the hippodrome as a spring breeze, pollen heavy, freshened through the training yard. Xephard banged a pail loudly and with little patience as Axylus neighed but did not come. Xephard dropped the grain bucket. Perplexed, he rounded the white wall of the Lampus and laughed.

"Betrayer, false friend!" His mighty gray stood in the temple's forecourt, great head bowed to Isolde. "And I thought he cared for little but oats and mares; you'll ruin that horse."

"He has more sense than you." Isolde stroked the stallion's white forelock. "I think he would rather remain here."

Xephard took Isolde's hand. "Do you doubt he was bred for war, as am I?"

"So? Ride to the battles of men with your troop. Why seek you the beasts of the Pit? Where is the affront you must correct, is your precious honor somehow besmirched?"

Xephard gathered Isolde's other hand. His cloud-blue eyes sought her sky-bright orbs. "That they exist is enough, they are abhorred by the goddess."

Isolde's gaze faltered and fell to her feet. Her voice was small. "How do you know these things, Xephard Bright Helm?"

"Because they are true."

Helpless and spent, Xephard felt like a broken bottle, his mind emptied of all he had ever seen, felt, or known … *the women giggled, playing in the stream as their brown bodies flashed in the late day's sun. The river, glad of their presence, caressed them happily.*

Rudolph Mellor smoothed his fine shirt and stroked his goatee. He tensed and whipped around, panic writ on his features.

"Wash day at temple is wondrous, is it not?" Xephard smiled broadly.

Jamello returned his attention to the spectacle. "Bathing girls, beautiful! Even more so when love lights their eyes. The fault is that I only notice it when they love someone else."

"Reflect on what you possess, not what you lack."

Jamello looked speculative. "When your back is turned, Isolde has such eyes for you."

"Indeed."

"Perhaps we should stay? And let others quest—"

Xephard draped a heavy arm over Jamello's shoulder. "Come friend, the Donna waits."

Focusing as never before, Xephard shaped his thought that it might be a lance to pierce the fog of oblivion. He summoned the face of the Gray-Eyed Goddess as he had ever imagined her, a serene visage, eternally strong. She opened Her mouth to speak.

The face flowed, and seven heads reared, and each mouth roared a churning litany of chaos. Xephard slid, scattered into the flow.

The quick glance of a weasel, muzzle wet with blood.
Two unkempt infants raised by a child, their mother a slattern.
A wracking pain in the gut, a meal best forgotten.
A woman lulls in comfort whilst her husband works,
a lover's arms around her.
The whimpers of a dog that swallows a shard of bone,
punctured from within.
To lose a life's love and gain a poem, who
can say what that is worth?

The paladin wanted to weep, but no tears ever fell in this place. So he bent his head in shame. Adestes watched him, and the man swayed as he knelt in darkness, unaware he did so.

Adestes saw the hand, invisible to others, pass over the man. "Little more than a husk, I will accept his final offering," moaned the undead spirit. Adestes Malgrim, Kör's Malesh, grinned but did not move aside to allow Ufelion full access to their victim.

Xephard's thoughts flickered across what was left of his existence. Tortured tissues laid bare in the Hel shriving, scattered perceptions and points of memories skittered across the floor of his being like bouncing grains from the thresher's flail. "I am no one." The man slipped sideways on the burning.

Adestes' face was impassive, but he observed closely. "He approaches the Void," murmured Ulfelion.

"It is almost done," agreed Malesh.

Xephard's mind unraveled. They were formless, these new dreams, but real. An agonized throbbing of base sensations, bitter taste and acrid smell, a nerve-burning touch, the glimpse of ponderous shapes on the edge of recognition. Yet there was one constant: Illimitable Hel.

Epilogue

A lisping, mesmeritic chant arose in the tent of the Prince, its rhythm nigh inaudible against the flapping of Ilycrium's standard, for the wind blew brisk this night, and chill. Gault stirred but did not wake as a clot of blackness shifted in the shadow from which the spell-weave drifted.

Tizil focused, and felt the sigh of the man's lungs, the thrust of the bellows-like diaphragm. The heart's thrumming reverberated in the demonling's soul. He had fed on both decrepit king and wounded soldier. Each time he gained power, and yet the spirit force of this man was as above those others as the dread dragon himself above the fawning adepts who served in the nighted crypts of the Pleven. How might Grazmesnil reward his servant for this last and mightiest slaying?

Tizil squirmed in anticipation, and the tempo of his conjuration quickened. Gault caught his breath as if to rouse, then sank into nightmare. It was time! A small claw stretched forward to vibrate in synchrony with the pulsing course of the man's great vessels.

There occurred a sizzling like burning leather. Tizil shrieked and his claw recoiled. Before him shimmered a war maiden of blue and white. Gault sprang up. The vision faded as Gonfolon leapt to his hand. Tizil burst into the air, mouthing words of staying and confusion. They availed him not. Like a scythe of diamonds, the sword clove the flapping imp in twain, and black blood spattered fur and weave. Gault held Gonfolon before him as sentries pushed into the tent, led by a swearing Seamus.

"What deviltry—"

Seamus's curse dropped to a stammer as Gault's glowing brand illuminated the scene with a light like summer's sky. The shattered form of the demonling began to stink, although no stain marked the shining blade, and a woman's laughter tinkled from somewhere.

Beneath the king's banner stood a cloaked and hooded figure, his hand clutching a staff of bone. As the watcher turned to depart, no one was present to witness a stray mote of starshine caught in the beggar's cowl that glimmered for an instant like silk-spun diamonds.

Guards wrapped the carcass into the soiled floor covering and retreated. Renault burst into the tent, bearing a flambeau and his verdigris sword. Gault sheathed his own, his eyes glittering in the fluttering light. "No more ill shall be spake of the elf lord."

Book II

The Herald spoke:

I have oft glimpsed the dragon of darkness in
many guises, though I knew it not.
A dark shape, out of focus, beyond every scene of
misery and death I have witnessed. Now the veil is
torn, and I know thee, mine lifelong enemy.

Chapter 17

Helheim

On Hel's winnowing plain, Apieron did not think sleep was possible, yet it took him to an odd place, where darkness swirled and patterns of gray moved against sable. The lighter shades grew swiftly, reducing indistinct shadow into familiar shapes. Apieron flew high as if a spirit that sees and knows every mind. He saw himself—Xephard Bright Helm, peer of the Temple and favorite of the Goddess Who Loves War.

The sun shined brightly on the hippodrome, and a festival gaiety filled the air. There was another knight, a cavalier of great repute. Lances were grasped and clenched as knees urged destriers to a gallop. Isander's shield appeared to inadvertently slip aside, and for an instant, a cleverly concealed crossbow was revealed. A metal quarrel rested its groove, tipped with a lead ball. The horses raced to close.

Isander tilted his shield to aim at Xephard's head. Xephard raised his own to counter and lean back slightly. The bolt glanced off his upraised targe with a loud sprang, and shot up over spectators rising from their bench seats, yet Isander's eager lance-tip caught Xephard first, thudding into his flank and blowing him off Axylus's back. His own weapon caromed harmlessly from Isander's plated chest.

Xephard struck the packed earth heavily and rolled to regain his feet. Faster yet, Isander wheeled his horse perfectly to threaten the paladin's throat with the heavy spear. "Yield to me thy harness and fair, Leitus, and you shall live, Xephard Ass-Fallen!"

Like a blur of steel, Xephard grasped the lance and made to pull Isander forward. The cavalier instinctively reacted, urging his warhorse to backstep, thus propelling Xephard onto his feet and under the spear.

Isander cursed and discarded lance for battle mace, but Xephard closed and plunged his poniard through plate and chain into the meat of the chevalier's thigh. With this painful lever, he threw Isander to lay stunned in the dust.

Xephard sought Isolde amongst the onlookers. She turned away, and he accepted his victory laurel with a wan smile.

Bird-sharp eyes missing nothing, Cynthia departed her shaded seat, instructing servants to bring her paladins to the rooms of healing.

Xephard sighed and lay back. Preparing to apply salve, Cynthia poked stiff fingers deep into bruised flesh. "Ow, mother, do you finish Isander's work?"

"Love hurts, boy. Does it not?"

"What?" stammered Xephard.

"Do not 'what' me," commanded the Donna. "A sybil is not needed to know something is amiss when my perfect knight spends his days holding flowers and mooning about like a dazed calf, only to get himself unhorsed by arrogant Isander. Thou art hardly subtle, Xephard."

The paladin captain gazed from a fretted window, a perforated casement that welcomed a narcissus-sweetened breeze and light cast in pleasing shapes, and the giggles of children, his devotees. "Right you ever will be, Perpetua." Xephard's tones were mournful. "Never have I feared any death, but it seems I am fated to a more tragic doom … that of love unattained."

Xephard continued, unaware of the old lady's amusement,

"The best and most I can do is pledge her my protection and chaste devotion."

"Who is this radiant creature? Princess Kilanda of distant Vafnir, whose brothers are giants and suffer no suitor to enter that place? Is it dark Selene, who lives secreted on the forgotten isle of Prim, and is rumored to be the richest woman in the world? Perhaps it is the Goddess of Love herself who has so smitten you, whose jealous husband you fear to anger?"

"Nay, Holy Mother, if only it were one of those, then I might quest with glad heart. My dilemma is much worse! I love one who must not be loved. The goddess shuns unvirgins, and I who would bear her up, would ... would be her downfall."

Xephard stared. The old woman's cackling laughter rollicked forth. "Silly boy, do you think these old eyes so blind that I have not anticipated this day? My two favorites are attracted to the excellence in the other. By their union, more perfect will they be."

"But Donna, what of the goddess?"

Cynthia gave a final chuckle as she placed her frail hand on Xephard's massive shoulder, holding him steady. "This is the way of the world. Spear Goddess approves. You and Isolde will wed with the advent of spring."

Apieron bent and touched Isolde gently. "It is time to go."

"I was dreaming. I saw the front of a white bull, framed by churning ocean, and its eyes were windows into the waters. Its face was intelligent and strong, and as I passed, it snorted and stomped twice, whether in challenge or affirmation I did not know. He reminded me—," Isolde's voice sank to a whisper, "it was Xephard."

Apieron helped her to her feet. "I think we shall meet him soon."

Isolde's blue eyes searched the terrible expanse awaiting them. "Despite this place, I know it."

Her eyes sought his, but his tenderness had fled. Apieron stared motionless, gazing out over the Hel plane where a vortex in the stone moved laterally before their encampment. Ridge and gully, boulder and stalagmite were erased into powdered rubble. "Hel hath no pit deep enough to covet what we seek."

"What is that?" she whispered, yet he was already gone.

FASTNESS OF LLUND

Xephard lay submerged by weight of spell and wound of sword. Enchanted fire ringed him round, and he was bound by Hel-forged steel. Tormenting litanies marched through his mind. A fell arm and dark will, unstoppable, a whimsical malice that slew with mirth … a malignant purpose bent on a friend he could not name.

The mother wren who swoops from her nest, a moist
and shaking chick on the ground she cannot gather.
The wheeze-rattle of a dying elder, breath too short for words.
The mewling cries of a puppy, abandoned in the cold.
The jaundiced eye of an old woman, who spits ill at you.
The night sobs of a woman who lays with a man who loves her not.

Hopelessness … Xephard's mind received the machine images, and he knew each before it arrived, but was powerless to stop them. Dark healing maintained the merest spark in his tortured frame, although each touch wracked him with blinding agony. In the days of his life, pain, to Xephard—champion of men—was but clay to be manipulated to best serve, strengthening some portion of will even as it ravaged the flesh. Now he knew the endless parade of sounds and sights, driven by hate-filled intent, would in time dissolve his thought irretrievably. His spirit wept.

In the swirling, chanting, hope-destroying miasma, the briefest glimpse of a face would at times appear. He tried to summon it, or at the least prolong the time of its presence, and each time he was cast again into the river of shouting anger.

With the mightiest effort of his life, Xephard summoned a grain of memory, a tiny thing, yet something to cherish more than life itself. He must find a name-place for the woman whose face flashed from the line of gray-shrouded tormentors. He soul-strained to hoard it against the thief of despair who robbed one first of will, then the ability for aught other than to witness its ant-marching order.

She beamed forth again! A sad and knowing smile beneath eyes of unsounded wisdom, a goddess of light and color. *Isolde!* Xephard remembered his love.

The river of despair rose and, swollen with rage, it beat against him in hate-filled cacophony. It did so to no avail. Xephard stood. Legions of howling, grasping forms buffeted his core. Hot irons and vampiric caresses were applied to the shell of his body, so far away. It did not matter, for Xephard, champion of the shining temple and hero of Ilycrium, knew again his betrothed, and the goddess who loved him always, and ever would.

His treasure intact, Xephard sank again under the black sea. As his consciousness was quelled by the devices of his enemies, it was forever melded to the golden key he would never forget. Love.

Ulfelion grasped the man's hair. It had grown long. The touch of the unseen hand caused the comatose man to moan. His throat was bared to the vampire's dagger—a lich blade no other could wield.

"Stay, grave drow!" commanded Malesh. Girt for war, he

flashed in the gloom of Llund where he had hied in great haste, apparently none too soon.

Ulfelion swung his long dagger in line with Adestes' glittering torso. Both wondered whether it would pierce the Helstone cuirass. Xephard's head dropped to the ground. "This one has little left to tell," intoned the undead sorcerer.

Adestes Malgrim laughed. "Soon enough will you feed. But first, the other herald to the *She*, he named Apieron Farsinger, must come."

HELHEIM

The companions leaned forward, ever uphill the journey was. Tallux's hands clasped his ears as each traveler flinched from the evil rhythm, a pulse from the heart of malice. At times it was joined by legion voices taunting from a pillar of black fire that danced to and fro on their vision's edge.

"Can you not dispel it?" croaked Jamello.

"Not yet," said Galor. "It comes partly of us." His glance brushed Apieron.

"Let that thing come closer, and I'll silence it," growled Henlee as the wind, always in their faces, fairly blasted his words away. "And where is that traitorous dog, Turpin? I'd pay my beard's last gem to know."

Apieron turned, his brown hair whipping in the gale, and his teeth grinned without mirth. "He is here." An escarpment loomed, at its apex could be dimly seen the serried teeth of a ruined keep. The fortress of Llund.

Galor sighed. "Despite my shieldings, it found us." His hand waved. "Nay! Not yet, friends." Apieron, Henlee, and Eirec paused a moment in their final preparations. "First, a reconnaissance." A blur of white found the elf mage's cupped hand. It shifted and winged off into the murk. A long minute later, it returned to find a perch on his shoulder. He cooed to the flighting. "Go now, return when you will."

Galor Galdarion turned to the others. "Many demons dwell therein that fly and crawl. There is also a dark spirit, cold with unlife. And a man."

Apieron tightened steel-shod gauntlets and donned the ebon kite shield before addressing them. "Beast or undead god be damned, the man is who we seek, he who walks with darkness. If in the hunting we find the other, so much the better. They have heavy debts to pay."

"Aye," seconded Eirec, whose eyes glinted dangerously in the fitful light. "We have much to avenge."

Isolde's voice seemed strident in the gloom. "Is the life worth of those you seek equal to those who are lost to us? How do we honor them?"

If he heard her, Apieron gave no sign. Galor lifted his arms, and when they descended, each person looked askance at the other, for a conclave of fiends they seemed. Even their weapons were deformed and twisted by the conjuration, save Leitus and Isolde's holy spear. Their bearers hid them as best they might. Jamello fairly laughed when Eirec turned to protest to Galor something about his mien, but the sound that emerged was a harsh croaking in ugly gibberish.

Since no further speech was possible, they advanced to the second battle of Llund.

Chapter 18

Fastness of Llund

"Do you see the standard?"

The companions gazed at Galor. Despite his hanging proboscis and clasping tusks, they understood him clearly, and above the broken rampart floated a banner that, at times, shifted from obscurity into relief. It bore a many-headed beast. Several of these looked backward, the remainder regarded them with unclean eyes.

Jamello gasped, for the unholy magics of the standard, his form and those of the party melted and flowed back to norm. Four humans, two elves, and a dwarf stood in the shadow of the wall. Bowstrings twanged, and javelins began to sigh through the air.

A tall demon drew up. Whether his cap was three horned and conical (or that was his natural physiognomy) was impossible to discern. It hefted a ballista and fired a man-length shaft unerringly toward Isolde. Tallux picked it off in midflight. The famous woodland archer then swung his mighty bow upon the wall missilers, many of whom wielded the steel crossbows of Hel. Apieron also plied his living bow, the final gifting of Sarc, to great effect as Jamello added deadly albeit infrequent shots to the melee.

When the tall demon reappeared, Tallux's arrow, broad and barbed, pinned claw to ballista.

"Bagwart tipped your arrows?" sniffed Henlee.

Tallux smiled grimly and sent another into the thrashing devil. A barked arrow and an iron quarrel joined in flight, blasting the shrieking monster from the rampart. In moments, the wall was swept clean of adversaries, yet as the company searched for a neglected portal, metal balls and flaming urns heavy with naptha were hurled with fiendish calls over the rampart. The taunting laughter of a man lifted from within.

As Galor melted any object that fell near, Apieron unstrung and struck his bow into its back-riding shell. The man's voice sounded again. Apieron ripped free his javelin of white to stride into the open and toward the archway. "Rock-huggers! God's curse on cowards who strike down a man's woman and children whilst he's away … the spears you grasp twist and bite you!"

Apieron began to run to the aperture. "Sharpen your blades or lay them down, it matters not. Soon I'll water the rocks of yon crypt with your foul blood!" The challenge of an iron horn of dwarves echoed him into the keep, and Eirec's war cry joined the battle of sound.

Beyond the courtyard was revealed a dim chamber. Within it stood a knight whose molded cuirass glinted an emperor's wealth of gems. His targe was an argent circuit of many devices—the shield of a hero. The darkly handsome face smiled at Apieron, and the man's raised sword transformed into a whip that flashed and curled about the torso of a captive at his feet, prone and bound. Barely discernible, a moan trembled along the ground.

Sparing no sidelong glance, Apieron careened ahead, neglecting the frantic calls of his friends. Into the cell he dashed. His javelin hummed with eagerness, but he did not cast. The tableau shifted. The captive stood, becoming a woman, dusky and beautiful. "You," he breathed, "what do you here? Why did we lead thee from the pit?"

"Why indeed?"

An awful realization coalesced in the depths of Apieron's brain.

"How goes it, brother?" asked the dark knight. The whip was again a sword, laced with crawling script. It flickered to life.

To the side, a clot of darkness opened. A sepulchral voice arose from an undulant form that grew into substance. "I, lord Apieron, am thy rightful father. Who has reaved thy properties? Taken thy woman?" Cold shadows caressed Apieron, who stood stock still. "I am your god, Apieron Farsinger. Soon only thy naked soul shall be left to look on. P'raps I will grant it speech, that you may worship me." Behind them, in the corner and partially concealed with rubble, was a naked man, pale and unmoving.

"Come my son," commanded Ulfelion. "Come and meet your doom." The female laughed, her fanged mouth parting in obscene glee. Leathern wings floated above snaky hair, and her eyes grew hard and red as garnets. In them Apieron saw:

The nursery of Windhover! Upstairs, protected by thick walls and unflinching men, Apieron beheld Sujita, his little Jilly! and curious Ilacus, who ever tried to climb his crib. He saw Setie the eldest, her intelligent eyes dilated with fear. A succubus danced there, crowned with fire.

When Apieron charged, a trap had unfolded behind him. Jabbering fiends swarmed from the mound like ants stirred by a stick. Eirec, Henlee, and Jamello leapt to meet them. Tallux also drew sword and dashed into the fray, his actions a living blur.

Galor cleared a space about him with his invisible blade. Only the hilts were revealed, gold in his deadly hand as, in one fluid circuit, three demons gasped from rent throats or rolled away from cloven limbs and wings. The Eldar elf sprang atop a block and drew himself up in his full pride. He smote the air, and a shockwave blew into the center of the donjon. Decrepit walls and open towers collapsed as countless tons of hewn basalt settled over the myriad foes within.

"Now it's a fair fight," hooted Henlee. "Twelve to one."

"Blasphemy!" roared an undead susurration in arcane speech. A mesmerization fell from a veiled figure of dark majesty as Ulfelion, vampire lich and Prestidigitator of Hel, joined the fray.

"Liesmith and ill guest! Betrayer!"

Apieron remembered his javelin. He stalked forward, but a slim hand, gauntleted with silvered steel, was placed athwart his chest. "Leave this bitch to me," husked Isolde.

Apieron faced the vampire and Adestes. A fury took him … a crimson wave of hatred. The muscles of his jaw bulged, and his hands worked convulsively, his gaze was terrible to behold. A casting struck the boss of his dark shield, and its ebon surface flickered to life. A speaker's stave was there revealed, clasped in a mailed fist. Its base was planted on a forested mountain, and its top lost in a cloud fretted with lightnings. The lich's efforts fell into nothing. Ulfelion burned Apieron a look that promised death.

From somewhere, a wave of force rippled through the cell, and the decayed roof opened, showering the interior with oily dust and flecks of stone. "Blasphemy!" shrieked the undead sorcerer. He lit through a gap like an ugly crow.

"Excellent!" Malesh lowered his visor. Silver round-shield and lodestone sword led his advance. "Puppet, slave of a boy-king who will soon be dead. Foolish mummer for gods who lose their world." The burning sword flashed against the kite shield of jet. "See how you ran, obedient dog, here to me?"

The two warriors, so similar, crashed together, shields locked. Weapons nicked and parried, but Apieron's rage could not be denied, and Adestes was thrust back as the white javelin was thrown at last. The argent targe was expertly raised so that the lance would deflect harmlessly aside and irretrievably so. The javelin, blessed by gods who also wrought the famous shield, pierced it dead center and the arm of the man who bore it.

"I am my own man," gritted Apieron. A sable-hued javelin now hovered in his hand.

Adestes flung dart and circuit against the wall, and his ensorcelled brand wove a net of trailing flame as he sprang to engage—a sword routine no man or hunted beast or immortal devilkind had ever countered. Apieron picked off each attack cleanly, and his javelin flicked points of steel and blood from the immaculate casing of his foe.

Against a small buttress, Isolde finally closed with the succubus as a man might corner a leopard with a spear. The Hel witch spat and struck with elongate talons, yet dared not risk any caress from the priestess's spear. The demoness paused, a strange look in her feral eyes. Her breasts swelled, and her thighs parted. From her dark nipples and shadowy pudenda, a miasma of buzzing death gathered, then assaulted Isolde.

Isolde backstepped and sideswiped again and again. With each pass, her weapon dissolved a swath of the roiling creatures, but there were many beyond counting, and her arms grew heavy. The succubus screeched with glee and stalked her prey. "White whore! After I feed on thy womb and entrails, a goddess I too shall be."

Isolde frantically batted at the cloud with ever-widening blows. Seeing her opening, the fiendess surged forward and clasped Isolde's front. At a beckoning thought from the demoness, the chittering plume dropped. It began to writhe and fuse.

Spear useless, Isolde punched and struck, elbow and forearm, helm and shoulder with the precision of a warrior monk. But the daughter of the pit was steeped in evil wisdom and the immortal blood of her father nerved her limbs. Canine and talon scored against dwarven mask and plate. Her hair grew vipers that tore at the wodensteel.

"Your lover is mine," she crooned. "Mark my final kiss!"

Arms locked with the succubus, Isolde felt the sting of acid on the other's moist breath. She twisted her head and noted with horror that the swarm had become a tick-like thing, pregnant with blood. Scrabbling to Xephard, its face bobbed with greed.

"Nooo!" Isolde screamed and twisted her enemy. They rolled to the flags, hair flying and limbs entangled.

Apieron saw. His ebon shaft pierced the scuttling creature with a resounding crack, pinning its bloated flesh to the frowning stone. Distracted, the succubus paused a fatal second. Isolde's spear tip, born in the snowy halls of gods, found her breast and quenched her life.

Adestes Malgrim did not advance. Leitus lit the chamber as Apieron tilted the mirror of her blade. "Somehow I knew it to be true, we two are bound by the energies of heaven. Accursed fate."

"Not the same!" answered Adestes. "You walk to slaughter, and I to glory." He stroked the surface of a golden ring. It twisted, and a shadowy serpent launched toward Apieron, red eyes glowing in a smoky head.

With a single stroke, Leitus sheared it in twain. "You do not understand," Apieron's voice was slow and wroth. "For myself, I care nothing." He shook his heavy helm. "Neither is there glory here for you, at the time of your ending."

An icy cast of fear found the belly of the Helknight, his bronzed face grew pallid, and he lifted his visor to breathe. The serpentine ring turned again. Floor stones buckled upward as a braided serpent of aureate plate surged halfway from the cell's floor like the back keel of a mighty fish seen above the sea swell. Adestes Malgrim sprang onto its flowing bulk and shattered through a wall, and was gone.

Apieron and Isolde dashed to cover the captive figure with their bodies while the stonework crumbled into ruin. "He lives," choked Isolde. "Go now. Kill that bastard."

Ulfelion swiveled his cowled head from consideration of Galor. Eirec's great sword, six feet of blued, Nordic artistry, was raised overhead as he charged. Ulfelion blew as if a kiss, and the priceless brand, heirloom of a long-sired house, folded into a useless loop. A bellowing demon taunted as it body-checked Eirec to the ground and lifted an iron-hafted axe. Ulfelion beckoned, and a portion of the sky came to his bidding, and winged devils haunted its interior. The vampire mounted as a man might a stair.

Jamello loosed a metal-shod quarrel with a sailor's curse, then shuddered when the pale face favored him with an evil grin. The bolt was struck into filings.

Tallux sped a half-dozen clothyard shafts with points of imperishable steel. The lich gestured, and three fiends emerged from the shadow, unwittingly interposing themselves, and were summarily punctured.

"Try this!" shouted Henlee.

The dwarf whirled, and Maul ripped the air. Ulfelion might have rued the hammer toss had not a barrel-chested fiend, a captain of the flying squadron, thrust itself forward to retrieve the mighty weapon. Its brow flap lowered in concentration as if expecting to somehow affect Maul's path in flight. The heavy glaive fell to Henlee's feet. A second later, a demon head as large as a basket fell in accompaniment. Henlee kicked it like a ball. As the wraith rose above the companions, Galor unleashed a second wave of disintegration. Ulfelion's tattered mantle streamed before the blast; otherwise the lich seemed unaffected, although around him flying monsters not so fortunate fell in pieces.

Ulfelion's cry pierced mortal hearts like a seeking needle, and he again gathered the darkling cloud to himself. He swelled as shifting unlight fell from his form, and where it touched, a sepulchral chill beleaguered muscle and nerve. Galor spoke an imprecation not heard in a millennium, and drew again his invisible blade. He shot upward to engage.

Jamello ducked after embedding his crypt blade into the chest of a flying fiend who meant to impale him. The devil fell entangled, limbs and wings, hilts of blade and spaded tail into a plume of tumbling blood and dust. Jamello tensed to dash forward and retrieve his thick sword; instead, he crept backward, crouching before the menace that rose before him.

It was a father of devils, clad in enchanted bronze. The beast smiled, showing small pointed teeth in a lipless mouth. "Man, you be foolish to approach with empty hands." The champion of the pit produced a morningstar. Jamello's eyes widened, for its handle and chains were forged of blackened steel, and its spiked globes glowed white hot and swung in unison.

Jamello spared a glance for hidden ambush, then raised onto the balls of his feet for a final rush as might a cat, once satisfied with the vulnerability of its prey as it fixes eyes on target, ears laid back.

The devil laughed and raised the swirling death above its head. The air shimmered behind the incandescent orbs—each straining against its restraint whenever its arc placed it near the approaching man.

Only paces apart, Jamello coiled to spring as the terrible orbs hurtled at his face and torso. Jamello planted his left foot into a crack and stopped, whipping his momentum into his arms. Two streaks of silver left his hands.

The looming monster paused in midstrike and collapsed. The balls twisted weirdly, each seeking vainly to strike at the human as they fell. The devil's face was cast into a mirthless grimace. Two quirt handles protruded from its eyes. "Who said there was nothing in my hands?"

Jamello stepped hard on the corpse to pull free his needlelike darts and gathered the crypt sword. He then ran to help Tallux and Henlee who stood a hillock and fought in tandem. Both, black armored, were silhouetted against the storm-lit sky. Henlee provided an anchor, and any fiend who sought to overrun their position quickly fell foul of the dwarf lord's impervious plate and looping blows. One kiss from Maul was enough to maim or slay.

At intervals, Tallux dashed from the lee of Henlee's broad back into the confusion. A slash, a jab, and he was out as two more Helspawn bled out their lives. Agile as any elf, Jamello found this much to his liking. The three sons of the mortal world pushed ahead and more, soon forcing a general route.

Eirec rose from the dust that swirled gray around his knees. His moustache was half shorn, revealing a crimson patch on his sooty face. His mouth worked, brows lowered over a glare so fierce that his opponent took a backward step. Despite the Hel-wrought axe it bore, the devil cast a look side to side as though seeking aught to bolster its courage.

Issuing a resounding cry that might have echoed from the frozen peaks of the Vigfil Steep, Eirec charged, arms outstretched as if to embrace his foe. Hooves churning in the billowing dust, the fiend heaved back in retreat, as if it sensed the grasp of this wild human would be a permanent doom for one nigh immortal within its native plane.

Ulfelion raised his arms and felt his essence burgeon. Better by far than any rapture known to mortals was the advent of the Gorgon, whose merest glance was death. His dead eyes regarded the struggling fools below and the elvin mage. Toughly knit were their spirit and sinew, yet soon he would cast them into the Sea of Riven Souls ... tides swept eternally against shores of darkness.

The lich raised his fear-crowned head, and then the other, the Herald, burst through a wall atop a serpent of golden braid, pursued by the second child of the star. Ulfelion paused as if listening. His arms fell. The vampire mage gathered himself and was joined by Malesh. Together they streamed like a departing nightmare toward the palace of Tiamat, Queen of the Abyss.

In their wake fluttered a scrap of cloth. It began to smolder. Apieron snatched it up. It was a small thing, a wisp of silk, its rose-steeped dye blanched nearly white. Apieron clasped it to his face, then stood a long moment, remembering the perfume of she whose favorite winding this was.

Isolde tore her gaze from the shattered cell where lay her beloved. As she approached, Apieron gently placed the silk in a pocket against his breast and withdrew a burned and severed weaving, his most treasured possession, carried the long miles from the bridal chamber of the riven keep of Windhover. With a clasp, he attached as badge Melónie's gifting in cream and dun and blue next to the emblem of his father's house.

"Come, Apieron."

"Know you what this means, priestess?" Apieron looked meaningfully in the direction his nemesis had fled.

"But the Donna spoke of her passing ..."

"I have quit service to my king. Now I renounce your temple."

Isolde shuddered at the quiet firmness of his speech, worse than any shout or curse. She tugged at Apieron's arm. "Come," she begged, "the lord Galor watches over he we have found."

Henlee stooped and hoisted Eirec to his feet. The big man stood groggily. He was covered with charcoal, some of which yet bore flame. His armor was muchly scorched and the leather of his arming jack showed through in places where the mighty demon had scored through. "Damned Hel frog was harder to wrestle than a rutting walrus," Eirec spat a mouthful of blood for emphasis, "hopping and twisting and shifting its weight funny."

Henlee slapped Eirec's metal cap back onto his friend's bald head as Eirec straightened painfully. "You're beautiful."

Gazing a final time on his sad and twisted sword, Eirec gathered his foe's iron-hafted axe. He took a practice swing. The man-high shield-splitter was perfectly balanced, its white face slicing the air with a sigh. "I shall take this for Waelwolf." He spurned the thing at his feet. "And cleave more of this one's ilk for my troubles."

"Collect yourself," said Henlee. With his scarred hand, the dwarf swatted out the little kindlings nestled in the Northman's bearskin and bushy beard. "We have won the battle of the pit. The silver knight lays within, like as not it's guard duty for you and I."

"I will bide here a hundred years for him," growled Eirec.

"Me too, lad. Me too."

Chapter 19

Ilycrium: The Army

The army was half the strength it fielded the day it was defeated on Celadon's plain. It tried to move, albeit like one who has been long sick and at last leaves her bed. Despite this, each eve saw more come to join cause with the Candor prince. Merchant and herdsman, lowland lord and highland chieftain alike had witnessed the invader's indiscriminate slaughter of man and beast, and the despoilment of earth and forest. Kör's creatures roamed like plundering ants, and thusly those citizens who survived would fain strike a blow before death caught them up.

"Surely Iz'd Yar knows we are here," spoke Gault to Trakhner. "The attacks grow ever worse."

"And each night, we defend the better," answered the stolid general.

Gault, Trakhner, Renault, and the cloaked stranger observed lines of bare-chested soldiers who dug trenches into which pickets were set at dusk. Armed men stood nearby, hands on spear and bow, for in mounting numbers, the beasts of Kör tested the periphery of the camp by dark. The killing came easy amongst night-blind men who could but strike out inaccurately against dimly seen foes.

"Tonight the moon leaves not her bed, and the woods will howl," mused Renault as he fingered the hilts of his verdigris sword. Just that morn, he had slain a troll that possessed two heads, its mouth dripping crimson with the blood of four armsmen whom it consumed as it fought, its souless eyes fearless even as the champion hewed it asunder.

Trakhner tsked in his teeth and spat. "The last time the moon hid her face, reinforcements from Jolf of Wighelm (a house entire!) were decimated by beasts in the darkness ere they found us."

"Have you stones? Gems of value?" queried the soft voice of the stooped and hooded elf.

Renault was incredulous. "You seek fee?"

Gault pulled five moonstones from a pocket within his belt and placed them in the mage's palm. Renault shrugged, then let fall a fistful of tiger eyes to cover the Prince's offering. They winked in the mage's hand, capturing a portion of the sun's light.

"These will suffice."

"Indeed," snorted Renault. "Lightly you hold a fair ransom, Sir Elf."

"Their value shall you judge when day lights our morrow," replied he. "General, recall and rest the foresters. They shall stand third watch with me."

"It shall be as you say, magician. Though I know not how a dollop of jewelry might defeat the prowling creatures of Kör."

"If they grow bold and seek to pass the palisade, the weremen will pay sore," promised Renault.

The threadbare cowl shook, "They will not pass!"

Guf, son of Dram, crouched beneath a wide-boled chestnut. The dark blur of the forest proper was a scant fifty steps distant and within it, a crashing as if of large bodies sounded more close than before. Behind in the camp, a mule brayed. Guf's longbow fell from his shaking hand. He grasped for it in the dark.

"Steady," urged a soft voice at his side.

Youngest of the king's forest runners, Guf had been accepted into service mere months past on recommendation from his brother. At the river defeat, Erwain had fallen before an Ascapundi's axe.

The woodland sounds grew louder, rumbling grunts were answered by hissing chuckles. To Guf, they smacked of greedy anticipation. "Trollmen, Lord. Gawds! How many?" A wet stench came to them on the wind.

"Near enough to shoot, scout?" The young man nodded, his throat too tight for words.

The cloaked figure stood. A solitary star shined fitfully amongst clouds. The mage beckoned, and the star flared suddenly, eclipsing all else in the sky. Answering orbs of light burst into being at regular intervals along the tree line, the flickering copper of tiger eye and gray-shot blues from moonstones from whence the mage had placed them. Two score pale trolls cowered in the sudden illumination. For a moment, they milled in confusion, then leapt to snarling attack.

It was enough. A hundred bows sang, and shafts of whistling death terminated with meaty thunks into shrieking targets. A second volley stilled any that yet moved. The lights winked out. From the forest, a ragged cheer drifted to the camp. It was answered by thousands, and horns wended the victory call over the nighted woodlands.

Gault beamed and slapped Renault on the back.

Seamus's one eye winked with glee, and the big man downed his ration of winter beer in a single, celebratory gulp.

"Tomorrow," growled Trakhner, "foragers and scouts are to range afield. Tomorrow this army marches again!"

FASTNESS OF LLUND

Isolde breathed deep. Cleansed as well might be, she began her meditation. Entwining her body against Xephard, she winced whenever she brushed against the gruesome wounds on his breast and back. Her chest tightened for the guilt she could not shed, and for the sinful doubt that spawned it. It was a hook through her center.

Was she but the medium for the goddess and Her favorite to be discarded in the end like an empty jug? The youthful priestess gasped, overwhelmed. Then Xephard inhaled, pushing against her chest. Isolde matched his slow rhythm, and let her unfaith slide from her mind like brown water down a gutter.

Isolde touched Xephard's forehead. It was heavy with cooling sweat. She thought of the Temple, of its orderly marble gleaming above vine and orchard, and pastures that climbed olive-green hills whose far sides were kissed by mists arising from the ravine of the Falls of Omens. Isolde summoned a vision of the Donna, invoking the wisdom that walked within that one's venerable name.

Beyond the cell where she lay with Xephard, Isolde had placed Apieron and Henlee. She knew no mortal foe or wight of Hel would disturb her casting. "Apieron Farsinger. Henlee dwarf lord," she said for strength.

"Xephard Bright Helm!" called Isolde into the darkness of the enclosure. Where it was broken, the garish sky squatted in malignant poise. "Childhood companion, the only man ever did I want, always. I pray and thank thee, Goddess, for this one chance," spoke Isolde past her throat's constriction. *How ugly my croaking must be! This single opportunity for redemption.*

"For love." Tears coursed wetly onto Xephard's nape as Isolde inhaled his scent, and was there!

Silver flames danced over water that pooled like mercury. For a moment, there hovered a woman's face, wise and stern, whose gaze fell to a stricken warrior cast upon the lap of a woman mourning. The visage softened into a smile not of the world. An instant, and the fire lake was gone …

Xephard perceived only blackness, his movements slowed as if burdened by a great weight of foul water. The pressure of it was crushing, but he found he could move his arms and legs somewhat, and realized he was breathing the inky substance. "Then I am drowned, or dead, and this be my eternity." His words were muffled.

Suspended in limbo, images clashed in Xephard's brain, more startling than before. His friends came to the ruins of Llund. Above cyclopean blocks, the sky gnashed its fury. He rose as Apieron ran to embrace him. Xephard lunged with a piece of steel, and the ranger of Windhover fell pierced, eyes incredulous yet not angry as they filmed away into death.

"Brother, have I slain thee?" Xephard thrashed against his viscous tomb. A tenuous luminosity paled, and he saw it came from his limbs, clad in the silver raiment of the Temple. He battled the oppressive fluid. Suddenly he stopped, for ever so faint and at a great distance, he heard his name called. Thready and flat it was, but it was a sound not made by him.

It came again, and there were other words spoken as well, too far to discern. Slow and mournful they seemed, but the voice?

That voice was real! One he loved. It came from above, and Xephard thrust out with purpose, flailing the smothering weight, half-swimming, his powerful thews beat in great silver arcs. Up high, he distinguished a glow in the water—a sphere of light that rendered it brownish rather than pure black. The words floated clearly. "Xephard, warrior of Spear Goddess. Come to me, Xephard Bright Helm!"

Isolde! He pushed with great effort. No clotted abscess of Hel would keep him from that voice, for one thought ruled his will: *Whether I be living or dead. Lady, I answer thee!*

With a tremendous heave, Xephard burst the final barrier.

Isolde bent over the paladin, and her face felt drawn as old leather, for the vitality that had left her. She knew ten years had fallen on her features. There were no tears left. She stared unblinking at the warrior's face, and her soul fluttered weakly, a butterfly that lives but a day. Was it enough? Would he wake?

Xephard's broad chest expanded, a breath deeper than any yet. His wounds spread but did not bleed. His eyes snapped open, alert but quiescent, and his thick-fingered hand stroked her face. "In my time of travail, I remembered this." He smiled in his guileless manner.

Isolde gasped as her universe opened like a flower. She discovered she had more tears.

"Never again will I leave your side in this life."

"Not now," she commanded. "Now, the healing of the body. Sleep!" He obeyed.

Apieron stared down at the man on a bed of cinders. Isolde had dressed him in arming doublet and leathers for travel. The flaxen hair had grown long and more pale. Apieron touched his own brown beard. "As has mine."

He gazed at the shield fallen from the stricken hand of his nemesis and ran his thumb along its center boss. The white javelin lay quiet in his back-riding sheath, angled across its jet twin. The shield was unblemished as if newly cast by the hand of the God Who Forges. "P'raps it was." Apieron placed the circuit on the warrior's left, where it appeared perfect, reunited with its rightful owner. Leitus, unsheathed, gleamed when she found the hand of her master.

"No cadaver you! Hope against hope." Apieron kissed the noble brow.

They climbed a narrow fosse. Its banks were clad with heather, and they took their way to a rim graced with stirring trees. A freshet fell fast in its depths, they had drunk of it lower down from bowls of birch bark fashioned by Apieron.

"My brother. I dreamt I had slain thee, and could not—"

"Nay." Apieron's smile was wry. "A different death has invited me here."

"Here?" laughed Xephard. The night was clear, cold, and cloudless. Pearl-frost stars were swathed in purpling blue, garments for an elf queen. The knight of the moon bore his shield, and it blazed argent glory, illuminating all the land beneath him. Xephard laughed again, for a second moon, bright as the first, was revealed on his left arm. "The heavens declare the glory of God."

"Remote and uncaring, my friend. We cannot dance their dance, a fancy for our slumber."

"Then let us walk this bluff a little farther, for this forest brings me joy."

"Very well," said Apieron.

They discovered a foot-worn track where, under a dripping myrtle, a trefoil glimmered atop ghost-lit leaf mould. "See, an omen, and a good one." Xephard inhaled budding, pollen-laden perfume.

A mule brayed loudly from a darkening thicket, where an old woman wept.

"What ails thee, Mother?" Apieron freed the beast where its cannon was captured by clinging thorns.

"My sons are dead, will you walk me to my home?"

"Of course, Mother," said Xephard. "Fear nothing." Tethered in Apieron's hand, the mule allowed himself to be led. The path was littered with storm-swept boulders and fallen logs. They walked far into the dying night until, beyond a screen of leaf-bare oaks, they found her dwelling. It was small but well built, a hut of stone and timber whose steep roof was caked with snow. From a wooden chimney emitted a sweet smoke that hung on the frigid air. "Bless the Goddess, we have arrived!" said Xephard. The last mile had been steep and the mule stubborn.

"Out here, we are our own gods," said she. Xephard colored. Apieron chuckled dryly but added nothing.

"More favors I ask." The old woman clutched Xephard's arm in her shaking grasp. "There are three."

"I so pledge."

"The first you have already fulfilled. Trust is a precious thing." She fumbled with a thong latch and led them to the single room. Sitting on the floor of planed wood, they took from her a porridge served on rough shivs. After they had eaten, she thrust a cloak onto Xephard's lap. Faded from white, it was yellowed and threadbare. "Wear this always."

He nodded.

"And now the last, give me your shield." Apieron stared aghast.

"Though it be the death of me, I own my word." Xephard handed over the mighty circuit. She took it and smiled.

"What needles you, elf?" The black dwarf stood before Galor. Sweat had stained rivulets onto Henlee's intricate plate, furrowing a layer of grime-encrusted blood. He accepted and emptied a skin of dweomered water. "Killing's thirsty work." Henlee nodded his brown beard in gratitude. "But I am content, the lass's dream-walk be a mighty conjuration if it returns the knight of silver to us. Why so stern, Magnus?"

Galor's crystalline eyes returned from unseen distances. He smiled, shaking out his golden hair as if waking. "I have also dreamed, Dwarf King. I thought to smite our foe directly and thereby spare our friend yet more grief. Alas, it is not meant to be."

Henlee repressed a shudder. "Dearer to me than brethren he is, and his losses are mine. This Thing we seek has authored much woe."

Henlee gripped Maul crosswise. "You and I, Elf Lord, do what we can, and I swear by my father's beard, I will not leave without him."

Galor placed a pale hand on the dwarf's shoulder. "Nor I."

Henlee regarded his own chest mail and armored skirts. Burn and stain, rent and corrosion were removed from his harness and person as the eldritch mage removed his hand. Henlee's brown eyes glimmered. "By the way—about the king business. No mention, please!"

Isolde ran her hand over the stubble of Xephard's hair and replaced the stopper onto her elfin flask. Little of her water remained. "You are as handsome as I can make you. It is time to wake." She kissed his forehead.

From within the smoke-blue depths of his eyes, Xephard smiled, and his fingertips brushed her lips. "I am happy. I beheld a distant storm at sun's setting, and from her mists fell purpling streamers onto the window of Westglow." Xephard drew Isolde to himself under the yellowed cloak. "There we loved as if we ever had, since the world's squalling birth. Billows of watered wind kissed away the heat of our bodies, and lo! thus the rains of heaven favored the dying day."

"You speak in poetry," laughed Isolde through bright tears.

Xephard's hand faltered in the stroking of her hair. "I … had much time to compose."

Isolde turned, scowling. "Rudolph Mellor is here to see you."

"That wrap of yours is, er, something. Where is your shield?"

Xephard smiled. "As you well know, my friend, troth comes not cheap."

Jamello stroked his goatee. "I now know why you are a paladin; you would starve as a tradesman, or a thief."

Xephard waved. "What betides out there?"

"Oh, Henlee and I have searched this waste pit till our hands bled. No Helstones! I think I saw the dwarf shed a tear." He grinned conspiratorially. "And no fire ale." The pensive look returned to Jamello's face. "In truth, we found little. Will you bear my shield, the one you gifted me in the Wyrnde?"

"You surprise me, Sir Thief," said Isolde.

"Once in a while, rarely, I assume a mask of honor."

Xephard opened his hand. Jamello took it and hoisted him to his feet. Xephard beamed his smile. "Actually I know of no one who has more and hides it so well." As a brother, Xephard kissed Jamello on the cheek. He proffered an arm to Isolde. The three walked from the cell.

"There you are!" boomed Henlee. "At last we can leave this cursed pit." He smashed a dirty bottle for emphasis. "The gold elf aggravates us all, he bethought himself to control the motions of this little rock."

"In that, I failed." Galor seemed to float to where they stood. "Look."

They stood below the decrepit rampart. The relief, carved in basalt, the heraldry of a many-headed beast with glittering eyes, had been blasted from the stone. Over the block, a milk-soup sky rained fist-sized gledes onto a cluster of battered hills. Each struck with a fantail explosion such that the storm echoed like an angry surf. "With each passing hour, the distance to our final destination grows," said Galor.

Henlee ran his hand appreciatively over the block and whistled. "Even Maul could not raise a chip from the snaky woman."

"That at least I accomplished." Galor lifted an object and placed it upon the stone. "That, and something else." It was an ancient tome, six hands tall and five wide. Its binding appeared of gray leather, warped and cracked. "Of what substance this was fashioned, I am glad I do not know. See, it is too fragile to handle. Should we open the cover, it would break into useless fragments."

"So much the better," growled Henlee.

"The dwarf speaks sooth," agreed Tallux. His emerald gaze looked on with distaste. Eirec spat to ward off a curse.

"Nay, good dwarf," laughed Galor. "This is a discovery more valuable than gems or the droughts of Hel." Over the grimoire, he waved his hand, and thick flowing lines appeared in the air above it. Page by page, strange characters rippled fast as an undulant river. "Ah," breathed the elf lord, "now I know you!" His hand fell, and the device sank to its source.

"Well, what does it say?" blurted Henlee.

Galor regarded them, a strange light made his gaze hard

to bear. "A greater prize we could not have found." With stern eyes, the immortal mage glanced at the book. It withered into blowing dust. "It belonged to Ulfelion. Our next meeting shall be different."

Xephard stared into Leitus's depths. He handled the heavy brand as a lesser man might a carving knife. "I am glad the black book is destroyed, for much that is evil was writ there."

"Why delay?" Apieron's voice rose. "I want that murdering wraith, his doom quickens!"

Henlee glanced to Eirec. "That's settled. Looks like we're in for a bit of a walk."

"Across that?" Jamello flapped his arm in the direction of the storm. As if in answer, a not-so-distant crater erupted into a blowing plume of liquid flame that burned like an unholy candle for a moment, then was gone. The ground, already scorched and twisted a thousand thousand times since its inception, showed no sign that the torch had been.

The dwarf whistled through his teeth, "Of course, if we bide here long enough, the same is bound to happen right under our feet."

"Perhaps we should wait a bit longer," stated Tallux. They followed his gaze to Xephard, who huddled within his tattered cloak as if overcome with a chill.

His head lifted. "Fear not for me. I know what you have suffered on my behalf, thus a second life fills me with the yell and strength of a babe. I reach not for the nipple, but the spear." He stood erect. The yellow garment was flung back, and they saw he wore no armor. "I shun the trappings of war, this earthly skin. I place my trust in the will of God."

Xephard's scarred face furrowed. "Let our enemy shudder with uncertainty, let them moan with fear!" The holy warrior's eyes squinted past the web of pain that lingered in his being. "We shall fill their blasphemous mouths with silence, their unclean eyes with blood."

"Stay, Xephard Bright Helm!" Galor strode to the fore, shaking his head as if returning from meditation. "We shall not tarry here, nor shall we walk."

Galor shouted. Although all their words sounded flat in the dead air, the elf's cry boomed from the rocks and fell from the lowering wrack. Some ten paces before the slender mage, the reverberating words found a focus. A gray-white mist began to swirl and ebb, and Galor's imprecation was answered within the nexus. Hooves stamped, and a rhythmic neighing accompanied flashing movements, ever circling. Woman and man, dwarf, and elf held their breath as the lineations of a mighty stallion coalesced, softly gleaming in the pall. He nickered and surged as if impatient for the race.

"There's a parlor trick!" exclaimed Jamello.

"Seems a bit misty," said Henlee dubiously.

Xephard came forward, his arm reaching for the animal's proud neck. The warhorse swung its massive head to regard him solemnly. Deep through the girth and dappled white, it seemed the echoing twin of the man whose words were barely audible. "I dreamt him slain, Mage Lord."

"His essence lingered. It seems he would not abandon one he loved. What say you, paladin? Will you accompany Axylus Thunderhoof to battle?"

Xephard's storm-blue eyes, flecked with amber, burned like cold fire. "For this I was born." In answer, the huge destrier reared in the gloom and stamped down on stiff forelegs. "But how shall I ride whilst my companions walk?"

"Indeed," laughed Galor and swept back his scintillant cowl to shout again.

As before, a palpable sound cast to and fro, less forceful than before, yet more than one echo answered. Xephard's stallion joined the race of mist around the assembled party, his hooves churning rock and rubble as he blurred once more. Neighs and whinnies carried from the encircling cloud until at last the echoes died. There stood six horses, champing and steaming.

Apieron's aristocratic mare nuzzled his brown beard affectionately. Jamello's palfrey gamboled in the coltish joy of its youth.

Tallux stroked the bristled mane of a thick-framed and stripe-hided mount. "If you will, we shall war together, and may we deal deadly blows for the memory of fallen elves."

A finely knit stud of golden pearl knelt before Galor. "Come, Sir Dwarf. Igwain will bear us easily. You should be pleased, for he is no dream."

Before Eirec stepped a war stallion, a mighty chestnut nigh as large as Axylus. It pranced nervously away from his hand. Isolde gathered its stall. "To me," she said, "you shall bear us both." An odd note found her voice. "Let us meet thy former master."

Leading their mounts, the companions came to the remains of a man. A scorched cloth of vermilion yet swathed its torso.

"Is this what you want?" demanded Henlee. Ungently, he hoisted the corpse atop a block. Its desiccated joints rattled.

"I am weary and loathe this task." Isolde drew up. "Turpin the Fallen—High Cleric of Sky, speak. I command you!"

The shriveled head raised itself to regard Isolde. "Thank seven devils its eyes are shut," breathed Jamello. A shudder coursed through the mummy, and a leathern scrap of a tongue flicked over what had been lips.

"Ah-h," it croaked, "the Little Flower of the Vale. Tell me, does the witch slave of your pitiless goddess yet breathe? Nigh as withered as I she was, and as pure." Xephard started forward, but Apieron placed a restraining arm across his breast.

"Enough." Isolde flourished her holy spear. "By the powers you betrayed, I impel you."

The knobbed head laughed as might a serpent. "You have little power here, and less wisdom. My soul writhes in the embrace of one far greater than thy aloof goddess. Flee now! Or not. It matters little. A heavy foot treads the darkness."

The skull cocked as if it yet bore ears. "Dost thou hear the rustle of dragon wings?"

"What of my wife, you craven bastard?" Apieron grasped the lich by its thin neck.

"On thee," it replied, "a Hate has been cast."

Apieron's hands shook. "Why?"

The reedy shoulders managed the semblance of a shrug, "Ask the stars."

The skull snapped with a crack, its shards falling from Apieron gauntlets. "Then rot in Hel."

Chapter 20

Uxellodoum

Vodrab's tunnel worm at last penetrated the inmost sanctums of Uxellodoum, the conjuration recking not of buttressed stone, steel-clad companies of defenders, or priceless fashionings in crystal and gold. All were crushed into ruin by its frenzied thrashing. Boiling geysers that fell from triggered ceilings scarcely slowed its mile-long length. Chanting clerics and thick-thewed dwarves wielding heavy axes hacked free pieces of the worm that dissolved into poison gas, overwhelming its attackers. Battalions of orcs cased in iron were sent in its wake. Although the writhing hulk of the spell-worm broached the stronghold's many-layered defenses, goblin carcasses were heaped high as dwarves fought to save their ancestral home.

Winter had come to the Axe Grind. Ice glittered on lacquered shields and drooping moustaches as seven thousand Mgesh sat atop grain-munching ponies, disgusted to be left behind whilst comrades fought the famous knights of the Western realm. They, proud lords of the high steppes of Kör, were left to supervise miserable orcs.

Whips of the Cur Quans were scarcely needed as long lines of goblin men fingered crooked weapons, eagerly awaiting their turn to descend and reave the bearded ones. A frigid wind swept snow in slanting streamers from the passes. Hetmen of the Mgesh cursed their illustrious general, Iz'd Yar, and they cursed the races of orcs and dwarves and their own many gods. The horsemen yearned for news of victory, that they might turn the cavalry southward to plunder and glory. Little notion or care had they of the chaos that reined beneath their cold, stamping feet.

Before departure for war in the West, Iz'd Yar had commanded Drudges in their milling hoards to hound the retreating dwarves in their deepest mines. On islands in seas of stone, fierce battles thus ensued in terrible darkness. Lungs were wracked in narrow, dust-filled tunnels while the very rock groaned overhead.

Engineers of both races endured hacking, muscle-wrenching agony as mine and countermine were cut despite traps of sliding stone, yawning pits, or liquid fires of tar that stuck boiling to skin and hair. Inevitably, there would come the moment of collision with the enemy in corridors too close for strategy—or any but the most crude weapons. In life-blood contest, mattock and dagger struck out blindly, and eventually gave way to fisted stones and murderous grappling. Iron-hard dwarves surrendered not an inch to the pale, misshapen humanoids that were the sappers of Kör. Merciless fingers choked off battle cries of the fighting clans of Uxellodoum, and sledge-driven blows silenced the grunts and rumbling yells of the mine slaves of Kör until beneath the suffering earth, there ensued a bitter stalemate.

Taken by surprise and harassed by strange magics, Uxellodoum's mountain clan nonetheless stiffened to a defense no other race could match. Four thousands of their number slept the sleep without dreams, and thrice that many orcs and Drudges had fallen, yet so savagely did the combatants tear the other that the battle's balance grew thin. All knew a sudden advantage to the other would mean annihilation for themselves. Orcs screamed their hate whilst drums of stone boomed to dwarven spell chants. Pallid Drudges obeyed distant masters, heedless of death, and Uxellodoum's living waters dripped tears in their millions whilst hard-eyed combatants slew, and slew again in darkness and blood and filth.

ILYCRIUM: THE ARMY

The wind whispered winter's secret, yet it held remembrance of ripened fruit and smell of fallen leaf. Gault breathed deep. Long had they walked that day.

The army wended along bottom paths, too weak to confront its pursuers, too stubborn to relinquish its quest for the high ground. Above and to the sides of the march, red-orange leaves of ash and oak hung amongst mountain-slope pines like garnets sewn on a dress of emerald. Gault laughed aloud at this whimsical notion. What Tertullion would have said, he could not guess. He was hungry, the men were hungry.

A sergeant's gravelly voice rose over the line. "Get moving, you slugs. We've a job to do, an' the Prince is in a hurry!"

At Wiglaf's side, Cusk willed his feet forward like the others. New holes had been punched in belts and nutrition-starved frames shivered intermittently from chill or fever. Rations were short. Cusk's formerly open mien was lined, his eyes shadowed by the memory of swarming faces filled with hate, and of the dead that had bloodied his legs to the knees, and of Dunstan, who was pierced by a Mgesh horse javelin and hacked into red ruin by shrieking goblins.

Gault sat his charcoal stud, an excellent beast that had belonged to Isander. Deep through the girth and well muscled, the stallion obviously knew more maneuver than the young prince knew to demand. Behind him rode the drab-hooded mage. Before the army had struck its hidden cantonment and field hospital, that one's last request evoked a snort of distaste from Trakhner, but the general waved a finger at a subaltern who had told off soldiers to comply. Thirteen miserable infantry had followed the vagabond wizard as he picked his way over the mound of death. Like a shopper in a market, he selected pieces of ivory and horn, bone and tooth, until each trooper staggered under the weight of his burden.

Gault turned to his silent companion. Without apparent signal, the stranger's steed quickstepped then slowed to match pace with Gault's own. The mage pulled back his cowl. White hair streamed onto his mantle, and aquamarine eyes glinted in the westering sun. "Sir, how did thine hair in color change? As I knew it, 'tis not the way of elfkind, but of mortal men who grow old and feeble."

The stern elf gazed a moment on some distant focus before he replied. "Men say we have not souls, but rather contain a portion of earth's spirit, sea, and sky. I am no sage, but I have seen that which is more eternal then even those. It crouches in darkness and would rend a world not of its making." The elf's gaze grew hard. "It has spawned willing slaves aplenty. Kör is such a one."

Gault was amazed at the frankness of the spellbinder. "You have seen whereof you speak?"

"I have."

"Where then is the balm to ease thy spirit?" The head of the column passed beneath arching trees under whose shadow streamed a cold wind, and Gault pulled close his cloak. The sorcerer's unbound hair whipped free, although he made no sign that he felt the chill.

"I taste not food upon my lips, nor the perfume of flowered boughs. There is no heart in my breast for maidens to hold in gentle keeping. I am but a rod, mighty only in the smiting." He wheeled, and Gault stared at a silvered cloak that flared behind as the long hair shined for a moment before fading into the gathering dusk.

A small force joined the army by night. Fifty armsmen came to offer service, the remainder of the scattered contingent of Windhover, and led by a dark-haired lieutenant named Telnus. Renault tsked at their long hair and beards, although Trakhner gladly accepted them into the ranks of scouts. They were of the frontier, skilled at the stalk and bow, and such had proved their worth so oft in the campaign until even the stolid general came to value them highly.

Late into the night, Gault held converse with Telnus and encouraged the taciturn officer to tell all he knew of the mind of his erstwhile master. When Apieron's lieutenant had taken his erect military stride from Gault's tent, the prince could not sleep. Staring into the darkness, many of Telnus's words and those of the elf replayed themselves time and again.

The next day, the army faced into a wet northern wind as its columns climbed out of the forest into an open country whose weathered hills were tree barren. Yet there were also broad valleys of wild grasses where nestled open glades of yellow beech and dark-leafed yew. A hunting horn sounded. Gault gave the stud his heels and thus came to a high pasturage nigh a sedge-lined lake. There, a score cavalry rode perimeter for an unusual capture.

A great flock of long-haired, upland sheep milled around twelve giant herdsmen. Tall as Ascapundi they were, and thick of hide. Ropelike hair fell from low foreheads. Their gazes were slow and their teeth flat.

"There is also this!" Renault spurred up and with his foot pushed a man who tumbled at the feet of Gault's stallion.

With weasel-quick glances to Renault and Seamus, the man rose to a crouch. He was thin of feature. Dank hair lay over a soiled tunic.

"You have an ill-found look, spy," quoth Renault. "Where were these sheep bound, if not for the bellies of Körlings?"

"I hight Grimm, a better man than you … who will soon be dead by the hands of my masters!"

Renault clucked, and his destrier checked the man to the ground. One of the herdsmen stepped forward, and to the surprise of the Westrons, they understood its sonorous speech. The creature touched a barreled breast. "We slaves to the warlock. He Vodrab, old spellman to Kör king. We Vur always been this."

"Ahh, a name," breathed the hooded mage, who had joined them.

"Then the old tales be true of gentle giants, keepers of the wilds. But you, sir," said Gault to the captive man, "are of our own country. I recognize your dialect; it is that of the peoples hereabouts."

The man cackled then wheezed. "You cannot win! Think you the few legions you fled are the main of his force? A trifling." The man's fingers snapped, and he swayed from where he crouched. "The prince of the Dream Throne summons Snakes from North and East." The man grinned slyly. "And from the *West*." A gaunt arm waved at the sky. "Soon gather the ravens."

"How far to the outcamps of Iz'd Yar?" asked Gault.

Lifting his chin, the man said, "A day, maybe two."

"How far?" quietly asked the elf of the foremost herdsman.

A bony fist raised and lowered seven times. "That many days for walking Vur."

"Silence!" wheezed the other.

"Vur slaves of him Vodrab. Vur not spies, we work!" Gault's questioning glance sought the mage, who affirmed with a nod.

A pair of mighty forearms attached to Seamus hoisted the captive back to his feet. "Liar and traitor," stated Renault. His hand strayed to the grips of his verdigris sword. "Wherefore should you live?"

The man spat. "Noble knight! Had you dwelt in the uplands when came the foragers of Yar, you would be dead. Some of us hide like animals, many have gone brigand." He spat again. "Not a few serve new masters."

Gault dismounted to stand before the man. At a glance, Seamus released his grasp. Gault whipped back his cloak, and the man stared sullenly as the hilts of Gonfolon glowed like a lamp of pearl. Unfastening a clasp, Gault draped his woolen cloak over the man's narrow shoulders. From his purse, he pressed five silver pennies into Grimm's dirt-smudged hand. "A chattel of Kör, be thou no more."

The captive's limbs straightened, yet he shook his head. "Nay, I am pledged to the demon general. And also his he-witch."

Renault sputtered, his face crimson. "You would abandon your natural prince in the face of his generosity?"

The man's weary eyes were pits in the light of the sun. "Then I will gift him in turn. You are brave, Prince, and these others. Soon I will find your graves and do homage." Bowing, he returned to the rear of the herd.

The Vur spoke, "I am Boug. You take dem sheep."

"What of Iz'd Yar's pet spell-weaver?" called Gault.

"We find more, we and dis small one. It probly take, uhmm, ten days' time."

Renault watched their departure as if he might suddenly rowel his steed to a gallop and trample the deserter to the heath.

"Let them go," urged Gault quietly. Fatigue lined his voice. "There are many such as he; I cannot slay them all." He looked to the fading herdsmen, whose slow, long-legged steps carried them off with deceptive speed. "Oddly, I deem the Vur keeps his word."

The rags of the mage's cowled head nodded once in agreement. "Noble."

"Come, Champion," called Gault to Renault, whose steed was yet sidestepping in the direction the herdsmen had departed. "And I shall use Braegelor to better purpose. We have five hundred sheep to see to!"

Bivouac was set as a northerly wind drove ranks of clouds heavy and gray, although it did not rain. From a trailing valley was harvested a stand of yew, evergreen leaves stripped free as was the white sapwood, leaving the inner hardwood to be cut into man-high staves for tensile bows that could be fashioned on the march. Strings were twisted from hemp and linen, and long-tailed horses also contributed, albeit not without bites and bruised feet to remind grooms the worth of their sacrifice.

Cauldrons soon began seeping the cloying smell of simmering malt, while a line of soldiers traversed the pasture in search of heath tops and yarrow, nettle, and yellow dog. The process was supervised by a stern sutler named Kulmbach, whose family inn had lain in the path of the invaders. Thus the day passed in peace as mists laden with wet came and went like slow, billowing waves.

With stomachs full, men took their ease. Many already eyed Kulmbach's stoneware, though the strained elixir had been sealed with honey and yeast only that afternoon. Sedge midges took buzzing nibbles at the host, but halfheartedly as if they knew the still sleep of winter was inevitable.

Crickets trilled their last at the water's edge, and in the east, the moon's lazy crescent hung low over darkling waters, its swag belly almost touching a tree line of nighted hemlock beyond the lake. The moon was orange and cast a glimmering onto the streamers of clouds grown pale against the sable sky. In gaps between high cirrus, star lamps were revealed in pulsing argent, and it seemed to Gault that here they ventured more close than was their wont. He saw the men happy in their ease, and for the first time since that distant spring, he gave over his worries. He would not forget Grimm's prophecy, but for now, this day, it was enough.

Chapter 21

Iz'd Yar

Iz'd Yar fixed his glare on Vodrab. The field marshal's demonic heritage was enhanced by the ruddy light of the moon. "You have located the boy-prince?"

The sorcerer grimaced. Jeweled nails and jeweled teeth flashed in the moonlight. "Nay, Imperitor. Something there is that shields them from my scrying."

Iz'd Yar eyed the staff in Vodrab's hand. Its margins were blurred, and the stave hummed with potency, a weapon of dissolution. At a subtle look, his twins ceased their stealthy advance on the spell-weaver's back.

"Our trap is not prepared, Makis. You have yet some time." The voice took on an ominous tone. "What of the piss-stained Mgesh?"

Gommish advanced on his bandy legs. The scalps at his belt stank, and a leopard skin draped his greasy shoulders. The Mgesh king fell to all fours, striking his forehead thrice on the ground. "Six thousand of my brothers are come from the dwarves' mountain as you commanded, Great Lord. One tribe remains to heel orcs. Twenty hetman have come and sworn to Gommish."

"Who was the last to arrive?" inquired Iz'd Yar casually.

"A Cur Quan," stammered Gommish. "Klegu Beed."

"Chain him over yonder geyser," commanded the field marshal of Kör. "I would have music with my dinner."

In reverse order, the Mgesh chieftain repeated his obeisance, and departed accompanied by the heartless mirth of those nearby, his face burning in the darkness as he made to kick his splay-hooved mount to a gallop. The vicious, hairy-spined animal tried to bite and throw him. He bit-choked the beast until it too hastened to do the bidding of their demon master.

Across the lands, the hosts of Kör likewise gathered. By light of sun as well as moon, Ascapundi jarls mustered their full strength, the very ground cracking before the weighty tread of three thousand battle-clad giants. Peak-helmed warriors of Kör's mysterious East called Meges came with rippling mail, and tall horses behind the red-skinned giants. Twelve thousand silken khalats covered their sun-browned necks, and strong hands bore javelin and bow, while sword and axe were girt to skirted waists. To their rear marched maniples of elite, demon-bred infantry, each a noble well learned in war. As long lived as elves, they were toughened by the ceaseless conflict that surrounded the Living Throne. Praetors called deep-throated orders to these immortals, Hel wise and armed with terrible weaponry. The wrath of Kör had been stirred. All the North trembled its advent.

ILYCRIUM: THE ARMY

Gault and the hooded mage stood a stony shelf where a few straggly gorse sent creepers across the sun-warmed rock. The wizard swept his hand away eastward. The decline before them, filled with shaggy evergreens and skeletal hardwoods, abrupted on its further end against an escarpment of equal height as their lookout, yet of greater depth and becoming a rocky plateau that stretched to the horizon. Gault knew that within the rough landscape were myriad passes and gullies that sheltered Kör's advance.

"Do you remember the march-stores set down in your grandsire's time? With the aid of elvin rangewalkers, such were placed along the route to Kör that armies might move without need of resupply."

Gault gave a low whistle. "I remember the tale, we deemed them Baemond's legends overblown, or at the least, plundered long ago by beasts or two-legged robbers, or fallen into decay."

"The memory of Kör is greater than that of men. He knows they are real, long has he sought them. There are rich stores of weapons and foodstuffs and coin—yellow gold and bright silver. About them are spells of warding and preservation."

To the rear of elf and prince, a soldier cleared his throat. He addressed the mage. "Two turns of the hour clock have passed since foresters reported discovery of yon cache by Kör's advance guard."

The hood nodded slightly. "My thanks, Captain. You may go."

"As you will, Lord." The man saluted, departing in more haste than which he had arrived.

Gault smiled at this, yet no reply was forthcoming. "Come now, good sir. I came alone by your request. Renault doubtless mutters and frets about your fealty, and my good sense! What is our purpose?"

"A gift, from us to Kör. Something I prepared in the night after trail runners of Windhover and I found that for which we searched."

Gault shifted uncomfortably. "One of my grandfather's caches? This is our gift to Kör?"

"Indeed. By now, Iz'd Yar's scouts have reported to their masters, who have hastened forward, eager for spoils. Suspicious of ambush, they will find no agent of Ilycrium within leagues."

Gault shook his head. "Their captains will bring dweomercasters, and your trap shall be discovered."

"There is no deception. The goods exist—some in caves, others in cleverly concealed strong houses. The magnitude of the find will incite the cupidity of the advance officers, who will come in greedy haste with only their personal spellbinders."

"Iz'd Yar will not be aware until it is too late; should any of his captains summon their dread lord, they would lose most of the valuables. The protective glyphing is strong, but not overly so. In the night, I removed those of concealment. Iz'd Yar's edicts will not be heeded, and magelings will quickly eliminate the residual wardings with their masters so near and eager."

Gault squinted against the morning sun. He attempted to pierce the shadows beneath the wizard's hood. "Your analysis seems fitting. I believe Kör's officers will enter the storerooms with their personal guards and spell weavers. What manner of ambush have you hidden so well to avoid the detection magic of the adepts of the Gray Land? Is it worth the loss of the trove? An' we need it sore!"

"You judge." The elf produced a palm-sized, many-faceted amethyst. It was interlaced with tiny branching lines. "Gaze hither, Prince. Tell me what it is you see." Gault took the proffered stone. He appreciated its great weight. Albeit only an amethyst, although its sheer size would make it a valuable rarity. He gazed into its polished surface. The gem was indeed flawed, cracks spidered to the core of the spherical crystal in limitless connections and combinations.

"What you behold are lines of construct that link the jewel to the cache. Every wall, floor, and ceiling, each furnishing and item are present throughout the stone."

Gault stared intently at the gem. He gasped. Within its purpling depths, he beheld tiny figures. He marked plum-helmed

Azgod who plunged hands into bags of coins while mages whisked maps and scroll tubes into robe pockets and belt pouches. Soldiers prodded grain with javelins and fingered weapons taken from racks that lined each chamber as if they had been laid down that morning. "Our friends seem to be enjoying your party, Wizard."

The elf's reply was flat. "They tarry overlong, much more and Iz'd Yar will arrive to claim their treasure. 'Twould be better for them." He shrugged. "I think they will not have that chance."

"What will you do?" asked Gault, enthralled by the wonders of legendary come to life, and by the deific view of his enemies offered by the spell stone.

"May I?"

Gault proffered the gem. The mage took it gently in two hands, then raised the flashing amethyst above his head and with a cry, dashed it to the rocky surface of the lookout. The gem exploded in a flash of violet as it fragmented into a thousand small shards.

Gault blinked. "That was dramatic. What now of the rooms?"

"Gone."

The young man pondered this a moment. "And all that was in them?"

"Gone."

Gault paused. He said slowly, "And the persons within?"

His companion gave an almost imperceptible twitch. "They too are gone, Prince."

The sky was more gray than blue with the lateness of the season. In the distance, birds of some sort wheeled and spun beneath heavy clouds. A brisk wind got up to sweep the hilltop and whipped Gault's auburn hair, he pulled close his fur collar and said quietly, "To where have they been displaced? Surely Yar's he-witch will attempt to recall them."

The cowl shook. "Even he cannot, the rooms were not

removed to another locale, or even another layer of being, they were removed from existence itself. Their entities were tied to the stone, which is destroyed."

Gault glanced at the remains of the amethyst. Its fragments glinted here and there like broken glass. He shivered against a chill and raised his gaze to regard the elf again. Sunlight glanced off tiny diamonds and subtle lines of platinum thread set in the elf's mantle. How had he not noticed them before?

"Who are you?"

The elf gave a long pause as if considering the words. Stepping back, his posture straightened. He removed his cowl as Gault gave back in wonder. He recognized by report the proud features, yet there were changes, for the hair of radiant gold was flowing white. The broad mouth, by many telling always set in private mirth, was now grim and scars seamed the face although, as the histories spoke, the incandescent eyes remained perhaps as difficult to gaze upon as ever.

"The tales of Eirec of Amber Hall were not complete, for I know you, Giliad Galdarion of Amor."

"Amor? No longer." The resplendent mantle rippled. "My tale? 'Tis unworthy. I now beg another boon, Prince. My identity must be secret until we are positioned to strike Kör a wound from which he cannot recover."

"I deem a mighty blow was struck today, Iz'd Yar will not be pleased." Gault's hand raised. "And yet it shall be as you say, none shall name you or inquire. I so pledge."

Giliad bowed. "Best to move your army today. Our adversary will undertake special effort to inquire as to what befell his servants."

Gault placed a friendly hand on the elf's shoulder. He felt the fluid metal links of an armor coat under the silken cowl and the muscles of a swordsman beneath. "It is well to have you among us, Elf Lord. I had not thought to hope for such aid."

"We shall see if it is worth your praise, but now it is time for us to leave!" An escort of soldiers relaxed their grips on halberds, glad to see that no dark curse engulfed their liege or revealed things best left unseen; moreover, the Prince seemed amicably disposed towards the mysterious spell-mumbler. If the Candor trusted him, so would they.

Giliad stood a moment. His cloak fluttered as he stared out over the encampment with its orderly lines, ready to march. After a time, he turned, departing swiftly from the outcrop, his light footsteps belied by the grating of an elfin boot that ground small pieces of purple gem into the rock. Retracing the steps of the Prince, he adjusted again his concealing garment.

IZ'D YAR

Iz'd Yar bent to scoop a handful of blue-violet shards, mixed with pebbles and grit from the scarp's edge. He flicked the fragments with a clawed thumbnail. "Clever."

"A bitter potion was here served us," crooned Vodrab. "Deeply did we drink."

Iz'd Yar turned to a tall half-demon, Shaxpur of Tyrfang. The brevets of an officer stood on the shoulder of his gold-chased hauberk. "You will assume command of the advance guard, I am certain anything of note will be reported immediately and directly to me."

The field marshal's yellow eyes held the other's a long moment. "There are worse fates than annihilation. As for the human rabble, I sense a new presence." He glanced to Vodrab and let the shards fall back to earth.

Shaxpur did not envy the fate of any creature that earned the wrath of these two. So be it. Those fools of captains had disintegrated themselves; the human king's pet wizard was earmarked for death (or worse), and he, Shaxpur of Tyrfang, was promoted. His first act would be to assume the possessions of his late commander. Of course he would slay any of their slaves that seemed too clever. This disaster was shaping up nicely.

"Any further commands, Dread Lord?"

"This old one shall stay with you. He has a revenge to prepare."

The new colonel looked with distaste upon the withered necromancer. The creature's jeweled teeth caught the sun in an obscene grin. Shaxpur yearned to smash that leer into shattered ruin. And yet, even that pleasant reflection was spoilt, the old mummy probably would not even bleed decently.

Shaxpur of Tyrfang bowed more deeply than he had in a century. "It will be as you say, Imperator."

THE GERALES

The day seemed hot to the runner. The upcountry slopes where lay his destination were impassable by horse, save perhaps secret trails known only to the fierce natives of the land. The scout did not have time to spy them out, for his message was urgent.

With the slow jog of a tireless runner, the man traversed windswept heaths dotted with rock-saddle meres—a land of green and gold. At length, Telnus came to the steading. A far-flung tribe of Northern tribals, the Gaxe, had subsisted on the downslopes of the Gerales for untold centuries. A hall of timber stood the high ground of a village, and dozens of outlying buildings huddled behind a low palisade of stone. From the wood-hall's high roof, a smoke drifted white on the gray sky of afternoon.

Cynewulf came to where gate guards stayed the stranger. He was accompanied by a half-dozen carles. On face and arms and chest, scars of blue woad stood forth. A heavy trousse was at Cynewulf's belt, and a wolf skin draped his back. He fingered a torc of heavy gold that depended from his neck. "A long way you have run, Southman, with no horse! P'raps you are lost?"

"I am not lost." Telnus was lathered in dust and sweat, yet his deep voice was steady, his dark countenance observant and thoughtful. "Battle comes. All who would be free, gather to the Tower and the Horse."

Cynewulf frowned at this reference to the standard of the Sea Kings. With the grasp of the Candors grown weak, he and his ilk had assumed the aspect of petty kings themselves. Cynewulf looked to his shaggy-headed kerns, who emitted a rough laughter. "What beggar is this? He asks my hundreds to march 'gainst the Snakes of Kör?"

From his broad belt, Telnus unlooped a string of tokens. He tossed them to the booted feet of the Gaxe chief. They were head pelts, furred but shaped like no natural creature. "If a lone scout might slay five werebeasts of Kör on his way hither, cannot your tens of hundreds easily master three or four thousands of Kör's foot-walking slaves?"

Cynewulf's bearded mouth split into a wide grin. "Foot soldiers?" laughed he, "Aye! with supporting cavalry, and anchored by immortals of the Dream Throne." Cynewulf raised his hands to silence any retort. "And you seem to me more than a mere scout, though your generals cannot count. My range-walkers tell me of six and six Snakes again that gather 'gainst your steel prince. An' yet I like your courage, take your ease at my table."

When their master clasped hands with the tall Southron, boys and women hastened forward, bearing water and cloths to lave away the grime of his journey's toil, that the stranger might sup with their lord.

Cynewulf pushed a wooden trencher away with a belch. Bones were tossed to wolf hounds, flagons of mead and herb-cleansed water were refilled. "Now Southman, Telnus, if that is your real name, why are you truly here?"

The forester stood and inclined his head in respect. "My thanks for your bread, but I have said what I have said." He turned to go.

"Nay," protested Cynewulf. "Tell me more of your mind!"

Telnus of Windhover paused and pondered before speaking. "Eirec of Amber Hall has fought a great battle named Axe Grind. Five hundreds of his fighting men and three hundreds dwarf survivors walk with the Sea King's son."

"What care I for such as he? Tollway robbers, bandits of the ice flats! They seek thy prince's gold."

Telnus laughed grimly. "There is no gold, only hard strokes."

Cynewulf swirled his ale cup, then downed it to the lees. It was refilled. "Better reason for Gaxe to weather the storm as may be. My people need an unrash leader." At this, a mixed babble of approval arose in the hall.

"Uglich has come. He and his beheld the assault of the wraith dragon, and fought bravely at the battle of Celadon. A very hero of Ilycrium he has become."

Cynewulf spewed his ale. "Say not his name here! A greater villain there is not in all the world. I should know; I'm his cousin!" Cheers and banging cups answered this proclamation.

"Then," said Telnus, "I say this last ere I take my leave." The tall forester leaned forward, and the hall grew still. "Apieron, son of Farsinger, sent me."

A fire of green logs trailed hissing sparks to its vent hole. Dogs cracked bones. Otherwise, there was silence.

"Ah, the Farsinger," spoke Cynewulf. "What message from

Xistus's son? I know not why he dwells as do the men of the West, in service to the Sea Kings."

"Only this, war is joined in all places. Snakes nest in one's own stable-yard as well as beyond the fence. Worse, outside the World Gate twists an eldar serpent of Evernight."

As if against his laconic nature, Telnus summoned his words again. "Apieron the Spear Runner sent us forth, some to spy and fight, others with messages. Windhover and Apieron's family are no more. He is grown fey. Farsinger's son seeks again the black lands with some few others, p'raps ill-fated as he."

Quietude again filled the feast hall of Cynewulf, chief of Gaxe. The ranger lieutenant of Windhover gathered his pack. None rose to escort him from the steading.

ILYCRIUM: THE ARMY

"'Twas the animals that first gave us clue."

"Continue," said Trakhner.

"T'easy, birds an' four-footers were afleein' all from one place. 'Twas afore we finded it, you could smell the blood at a hundred paces! We durst not continue further in the dark."

Renault stiffened, but Gault shot him a staying glance. "No one questions your loyalty, man. Speak and leave nothing out."

The lean army scout wiped sweat from his face with a rag before replacing it under his leathern cap. "Thank 'ee, yer Grace … the moon, he rose. Then we saw the corpses, dwarves they were, pale an' naked."

"All a' sudden, one o' them gets up and shambles off like a drunkard, then two, then a hundred or more! We shouted, but they paid no heed."

"Mayhap they were not dead," said Renault.

"Well, sir, you could say as much," replied the ranger. "'Tis true no wolf or raven came nigh that pile."

"You see?" beamed Renault. "A simple—"

"Save the blood," interrupted the man. "You remember the blood, sirs?"

"You are doing fine, soldier," said Trakhner. A scowl found his bluff countenance whenever his gaze chanced on Renault.

The scout faced Gault, although he could not help a few furtive glances at the silent, hooded mage. "There was more blood, yer majesty, than a slaughter yard. Every one o' them dwarves was bled out over that pile o' rock." His voice sank to a tremor. "An' when they left, they left dead."

"Well, Master," said Trakhner. "What have your conjurations told you that my own eyes cannot see?"

The Prince's escort fidgeted while the mage completed his investigations. The great smear of blood upon the tumulus that centered a deep-forest glade startled even Renault, and none had dare accompany the elf.

Seamus flexed the three fingers of his left hand and touched his empty socket with the remembered ache of his wounds.

Trakhner continued, "Dwarves come to aid us, no doubt. Ambushed in revenge for our little trick with the supply cache."

"Just so," replied the mage. "Necromancy is not the way of elves, although I have spoken to the departed spirits of the brave dead. I thanked them for their sacrifice and promised honorable interment of their remains should they be found."

Gault's face was set. "So it shall be." His auburn locks played above the fur of his collar, the cape of a bull elk that had gored a horse.

"In return," continued the cowled wizard, "the spirits revealed a vision of their dying. 'Twas a brave thing, even for a riven soul."

"And so?" queried Renault. "What showest they?"

"Something valuable, the very faces of our enemy."

Trakhner snorted and indicated Seamus and Gault. "Our prince and this one saw them clearly enough at Celadon."

"But I have not!" Giliad seemed to grow in stature; they saw now that he held a staff of eldritch bone, and at his waist was girt a graceful sword. "Our foes are mighty in their evil, yet are not the gods they deem themselves to be."

Gault smiled. Trakhner gave up his scowl and likewise grinned. "A wild ride, Sire. Where will it lead?"

Chapter 22

Iz'd Yar

"I am pleased, Makis," said Iz'd Yar. "And yet how is it that a century of bearded dwarves were running loose in my countryside?"

"Not all rogue tribes of the stunted ones serve men," said Berich, eldest of the twins by minutes. "Some serve your very cousin."

"Impertinent," scowled the field marshal, although he could not suppress a small pleasure with recent events. Messages had come with regularity; wolfling and scryspell, bird and mirror, each told the same tale. A mighty army gathered itself to him.

Fourteen thousand would march from the occupation of Sway. Moreover, thirty hundreds Ascapundi spearheaded a mighty force through the Vigfils in advance of twelve thousand medium horses, as well as five maniples of Tyrfang's immortals. His own army would swell more than double. By report, uncounted orcs formed the rear guard, razing villages and despoiling the land as they went. With the precision of a master Stratego, Iz'd Yar brought more than sixty thousand battle-hardened soldiers onto the foothills of the Gerales. The army of Ilycrium would be hemmed on three sides by a fan of living steel. There would be no escape.

Vodrab's stare had not left the smirking twins. "These were enemies," he stated. He shook his matted locks in disgust and turned to Iz'd Yar. "This country is conquered, Dread Lord. Coast and city, mountain and plain. All that remains is to drain the lees! Their ragtag army and its whelping prince can run no farther; soon you shall drink fire wine from the skull cups of his generals." Vodrab spun about to pitch his words to the entire entourage. "A dukedom for the Cousin Royal?"

"You speak prettily, Vodrab," growled Iz'd Yar. He waved aside the others, save his pale twins. "Tell me now of events beyond the Last Gates."

Vodrab's ropelike hair whipped about in his fervor as the ancient face found an uncanny light. "*She Who Waits* tests her gaol. Its walls crumble, soon an invincible army shall presage Her advent into the world, long have they awaited Her summons! This, Iblis has foreseen, and done much to affect its happening."

The chaos staff fairly shrieked in the air, and the sons of Iz'd Yar hid their bald heads. "Dread Master, soon you shall close with your enemy. I shall offer the blood of our foes to aid Her passage, then shall your house hold sway for a time without end."

"So long," remarked Iz'd Yar dryly. "The Dream Throne for me to share, and might you, Vodrab, stand to gain more power for your mummeries? I deemed as much." Nonetheless, the mighty Azgod laughed long and low. "Bring me forth this Army of Brass so that I might close the trap and crack the Westrons like boiled bones. Then we shall see!"

KÖRGUZ

Sages and historians record that, in many lands when dies a king, brothers oft fly to the seat of government to vie for the scepter; internecine strife commencing under whatever veneer of civilization exists. Much more so in chaotic Kör, where Azgod lords savagely contested with serpent priests and fierce out-peoples. Orc throngs struggled above and below the earth with renegade dwarven clans. Giant Ascapundi in their wintry fortresses were brought to battle each snow thaw by hoards of chanting nomads—Mgesh who acknowledged no sovereign but their savage Cur Quans. And farther east, armies of tall horsemen in silvered mail maneuvered fluid squadrons like hunting eagles across the uncharted lands of the Meges.

Since the Starfall three decades prior, Iblis, by preternatural cunning and sheer brutality, had whelmed his foes, welding the various peoples of Kör into a suzerainty such as the world had not known for a millennium. Those who opposed him, whatever their ilk, had been mercilessly slain, their mouths gaping protest only to the sky and uncaring winds.

In three short decades, his invincible arm and chosen cult forged the spear of empire. "Yet once made, the weapon must needs be wielded, lest it turn on the hand too weak for mastery," spoke Iblis, prince of mighty Kör, high priest of the cult of the fallen dragon. Therefore, his remorseless gaze was turned upon Ilycrium. With her sweeps of verdant pasture and strategic seaports, he might stage a war of conquest to encircle the planet east to west like a serpent of wrath.

"So be it!" The Throne of Dreams twisted beneath his touch, playing over and again the machinations of his thought.

"Your accountings, slave."

In tones devoid of emotion, Alcuin, Savant of Kör, completed his recitation for the final battle. No detail of order and supply, weather or personage was unknown to him. His milky orbs stared as if they pierced the veils of distance and time, seeing everything that moved within the hegemony of Kör and the new land called Ilycrium She claimed for her own.

Pilaster waved an ebon hand. "Satisfactory. You may live a while longer."

Alcuin bowed slightly. The colorless wisps of hair on his chin brushed the robes over his breast.

"What think you, Faquir?" mused Iblis.

"Over seas and on the earth, in the deeps and beyond nighted airs, all moves to your bidding."

"And our general, will he succeed?"

Pilaster ran an uncertain hand over the flat horns of his ram's skull. "He would that he be a mighty duke to the scepter of Kör."

Iblis laughed abruptly, a horrible sound. "This your colorless pet has not seen, eh, Magnus? What of the creature at my cousin's side, this Vodrab?"

"A death finds him," added Alcuin softly, "and Iz'd Yar's sons."

Pilaster's red mouth twisted in rage. Columns of fire erupted floor to ceiling and crawled toward the slender human. "You were not bid speak."

Iblis filled his mighty chest and exhaled, the vapor of which smothered the burnings like blown candles. His metal-grinding laugh came again. "I care not for my cousin's get. Even your precious war-gathering may not be enough to ensure the destruction of the man king, to open the gates of the West."

Iblis' bulk stirred from the throne. Immortal guards crashed gleaming volges and stood to attention. Monk-warriors from the Pleven Deep prostrated themselves. Iblis' black hauberk glistened like polished night as he towered over the demonic arch-mage and slight human. "Am I not high priest of She Who Waits? Three decades past, I summoned an army from beyond the Gates of Sorrow; now it comes! Dragons of earth shall circle this final battle." An imperious arm lifted. "You, Pilaster, send this one to

Archwaze. I would know wherefore our prisoner has escaped. Kill any who betrayed us."

The mage demon flickered gray-white, then subsided to a muddy hue. He crouched his thick bulk and bowed until his horn-bossed front kissed the floor. Iblis appeared pleased. "Go now," intoned he, and the tyrant of Kör's voice boomed from the walls. "Prepare the final summoning."

THE GEHULGOG

Thir looked into Alcuin's scarred and sightless eyes, and heard the savant's halting words.

"May I?" One tentative hand was placed upon the Drudge's cragged brow. "I, who have been blind my life entire, would see what you have seen." Thir grunted but did not recoil from the human boy's touch. One other had touched him thus. Well he remembered.

Thir struggled to his feet as the pale hand was withdrawn. He did not recall falling. There was the sound of water dripping over stone, and by the smell of the air, it was now deepest night out and above—where he had never been, and yet had not ceased to contemplate since the coming of the elf lord. Thir waited. He regarded the expressionless human until at last the adept cleared his throat and stirred as if awakened from the midst of a slipping dream. The strange orbs scanned Thir in every detail head to toe.

"At last … at last I understand."

HELHEIM

"Do not touch them," commanded Galor. "Who knows what bane they will bring you."

"Nonsense," sniffed Rudolph Mellor. Before his feet grew a cluster of living gems, and in their depths, glimmered inner fires.

"A master thief of Bestrand knows a thing or two about jewels, and of this sort, I've more experience than you." His crypt blade slashed down.

"'Tis passing strange that a single, small stone might be worth the life's toil of the average man." Tallux turned the forest steed away in disgust.

"Please, Sir Elf, more valuable than that!" Jamello happily packed his trove and swung upon his palfrey, then clicked it to the lead.

"Slow, my friend," laughed Xephard. "You have already proved your bravery."

"Enough foolery!" snapped Galor. "Delay favors our enemies, for mere minutes here be long hours in the lands of light. Day by day, Kör plunders our world."

"I do not wish to go where we must," added Isolde, "yet I too sense our hour grows late."

Jamello wiped a trickle of blood from his nose, thereby smearing another streak of rust-hued dust over his face. Dimly aware of the soiling, he was beyond concern. How long had it been since he had smelled aught but burning sulfur? He sniffed his new pomander, a parched and droopy thing that remained attached to his blouse. Nothing. He nibbled a petal. It tasted like sulfur. Jamello drew abreast of Apieron and opened his cracked lips to complain, but closed them instead.

Atop his hunter, the tall ranger seemed a ghastly apparition from a child's night-fright. His features were caked with red clay except where flecks of blood had pooled and scabbed from the nicking gale.

Xephard and Eirec and Apieron rode upwind in attempt to

shield the others somewhat from its renewed onslaught. Apieron leaned into the blast as if by so straining he might shorten their passage. The horses needed no sustenance; they walked tirelessly and without complaint. Jamello knew it was he and his companions whose endurance limited the pace, yet he had no doubt that if Apieron should suddenly die, the ranger would remain thus, jaw and unblinking eye thrust into the tempest—unaware that he had expired.

Jamello halted and sniffed. He was wrong; he could smell. Salt-tang wind and sweet rotting kelp. "The sea?" The wind broke his words, and the party ignored him. He pressed his knees, and the pony resumed. Jamello heard the rasp of cordage made fast as vessels berthed. *The sea!* Ships' crews, fat with coin and starved for ale. He clucked his skewbald bay to a trot. Oil lamps and smoke twining in rafters, women, and song! Then to bed, cozened by the mumblings of Father Ocean. His colt cantered ahead.

"Ware the water!" shouted Tallux.

Jamello pulled up, glaring at Isolde, the reins of his colt held in her fist. He jerked them back. How he loathed those smug blue eyes that missed nothing.

"It *is* salt," proclaimed Henlee, wiping his hand on his skirt, "and it burns."

"Our way lies beyond this lake," said Apieron. "Come." He and Xephard stepped their mounts into the brine. Without alarm, the steeds trailed after their leader, even when the solution rose to their gaskins. The sky was brown and the air thick with red haze, a fiery miasma that seared the lungs. Each breath as shallow as possible, and the eight companions sloshed on until the imprecations of dwarf and Northman and even wood elf became nearly continuous. Jamello swayed drunkenly in his saddle.

"Apieron!" called Isolde. The ranger did not turn. "Apieron, it is the Voice of Despair returned! Let us halt, that Galor and I—"

"Not now!" answered the elf mage. "Our enemies have found us."

A line of bull-visaged demons waded athwart their way. Each bore a fauchard, and bellowed challenge as powerful torsos thrust the brine aside in undulant waves. To either side reared obsidian cliffs, sheer as faceted glass.

"These are Arzshenk," warned Galor. "Resistant to conjuration, flesh eaters that consume any weaker than themselves."

Tallux lowered his hand. "I count fifty at least."

Jamello laughed. "Caught betwixt the devil and the deep? Nay, we enjoy the devil in the deep!"

Henlee prodded Galor. "He's going crazy like the first time."

"Stay together!" shouted Apieron. "Myself, Eirec, and Xephard will force the center. Follow close!"

The companions dug in their heels and their horses found a gallop, seemingly as little encumbered by the salt sea as were their foes. Tallux stood, and with uncanny agility, began to wing shaft after whistling shaft into the line of Arzshenk. These wallowed to the point where the grip would come, bull throats filling the narrow place with a roar like an avalanche.

A tall knight, clad in Helstones on sable, crouched before the lapping shore. He poured the contents of a leaden flask into the brine. Immediately, a reaction stiffened the solution into frozen spicules.

"What of the Arzshenk?" questioned the vampire at the man's

side. "They who are slaves of the She." A swell of crystallization raced away and down the length of the lake.

Adestes' darkly handsome face lit into a grin. "Salt beef."

The foremost demon swept its voulge from the water, spraying acid onto Xephard's front. Leitus parried its blow, and Axylus dashed the Helspawn into the lake and stamped with steel-shod hooves. Red blood clouded the water.

Eirec matched strength with a second, his new axe ringing on guisarme. Two javelins flashed by to pierce the beast. Apieron's mare wheeled and stuttered, then resumed her race as the expert horseman retrieved his darts.

To either flank, Tallux prevented envelopment with a frenzied barrage of shafts. Jamello expended the last of his quirts into the bovine snout of a devil that flailed at his screaming palfrey. Eirec and Isolde closed to aid him, and the spear of the goddess sheared off the top of its horned head.

Jamello shouted angrily at Isolde, his words lost in the frenzy. He lay about him, heedless in his seat.

An Arzshenk surged up, claw brandished to disembowel Galor's leaping horse. The elf twisted, and his invisible brand descended. Five severed talons tumbled free. Henlee wobbled dangerously then frantically regained his seat. "Damn it, elf. Dammit!"

Tallux stood again the swamp horse. He cried in alarm, "The lake turns to stone!"

"Ride, ride!" shouted Apieron. An aura spread from Galor as his slender stallion neighed musically. Almost as one, the others answered and lifted themselves, manes streaming, to gallop across the surface of the lake.

"Glorious," cried Tallux.

"Oh gods of the nine worlds," called Eirec, "let one of us live that skalds may have their song."

"Ride!" said Apieron. "I see the shore. By my father's stave, I think I marked a man."

The death moans of Arzshenk carried against the wind to the standing pair. Ulfelion's breath was sapping cold in Adestes' face. "I wonder, Darkstar, what is to be thy fate?" The eight companions, riding valiantly, were less than a mile distant.

Adestes' face darkened. "Was it I whose spell failed on the silver knight? As for the other, I bested him once. Attend thyself, grave-lich, my fate is beyond thy mouldered ken." Adestes leapt back, summoning flame to his blade of lodestone.

Ulfelion's laugh was hollow—sepulchral—an empty place in the air, and like an evil prayer, he streamed into the pall.

"Good riddance!" Malesh squatted to study the foremost man a while longer.

Apieron cast about, but the embankment was empty. As if in mockery, the rocks reflected his rant of frustrated rage. A pillar of shadow flitted, clinging to the ranger. Its whisper became a roar.

"Apieron!" shrieked Isolde.

He wheeled on her, gray eyes aglitter. "Think you I have not carried this thing in my soul since last we came here? P'raps even longer. Dispel it if you will, what matter? Whither do you think we go? We who hie to its source."

"I … cannot." Isolde looked frantically to Galor.

The gold elf regarded the apparition in silence. His sapphire-and-platinum cowl floated about him, undimmed. At last he spoke. "I will risk no hurt to Apieron."

Xephard approached. At this, the column swelled thick with hate, and lightnings fretted its substance. It surged at him. Xephard held Leitus askew, regarding her mirror. He touched the shadowed mass with her tip.

The haunting murmur faded as the pillar fell into nothingness. "I also know you, animus of the void, though I did not wish it." Shieldless, Xephard turned, his tattered cloak hanging limply in the gloom.

Jamello tugged at its yellowed fringe. "I don't suppose you might do something about the sulfur reek? Flaming rain?"

"This place," the massive shoulders shrugged, "is real."

Isolde touched Jamello's lean, haggard face. Of equal height, their gazes met squarely. "Your eyes are sane."

"Thank you."

"Look," pointed Tallux.

The rocky lake shore gave way to an escarpment that appeared a rift of quartz shot with veins of beryl and topaz. Apieron stood its apex, his gaze apparently fixed on an unseen vista. A wind lifted his hair and tugged his beard, and his close-fit mesh was burnished orange as if he faced a dying sun.

"Reckless man, heedless pupil!" Henlee led a huffing ascent to join his friend.

Xephard followed to stand nigh Apieron. Leitus was sheathed as the fringed and yellowed cloak hung limp, and their faces were lit from below by a kaleidoscope light. The others scrambled up to join them.

Galor swept wide his arms. "Behold Cocytus, the final pit."

"Are we home?" breathed Jamello.

Isolde swiveled her look of frenzied worry between the thief and the tableau before them. Tallux sat and hid his face with two hands. Below lay a sea of magma dotted with pinnacles of black stone that rose from its surface, monolithic rods plunged by an angry god. As if twirled in gargantuan glassworks, the pillars were pure as black diamond, their surfaces reflecting orange-red streamers from the magma. Portions of the fiery sea churned in burning spirals, leaving frozen crests of lava in fantastic drifts, some overtaking the black spires like sand against beach pilings.

"The Dark She is there," said Apieron, and the others followed his gaze. Beyond the lake was thrust a shard-like cliff of many thousands feet, a fusion of gleaming crystal and tortured metal that loomed into the seething sky. A mighty shifting and groaning from the cliff came to them as a portion of the mountain, bristling with spears of stone, hurtled free like a Hel-wrought tumbleweed that soared to shatter on its opposing slope, then plunged ruinously into the magma. In its place, new spikes the size of trees erupted from the cliff face.

At the mountains' feet crouched a high-arched battlement and dry moat. Bastioned towers dotted the perimeter, and iron bridges cut these via maw-like barbicans. A demon host thrummed with activity along invisible highways in the air betwixt the moat and the sea of fire. Sooty fiends screamed and struck up at birdlike Helspawn whose skin shimmered like teeming fish. Others marched in ordered companies such as the companions had seen before, for there seemed a general movement. Battalions became regiments, marching away and into the gloom.

"So many." Isolde's expression was bleak. "Our land will blacken at their tread. Who knew Hel could empty itself onto the world?"

"It is only the beginning," said Apieron. "The ungoddess is awake, awaiting something. Can you feel the beating of Her heart?"

"I feel it," growled Henlee. "We all do, the mountain throbs like a drum."

"Tell me, someone," said Jamello. "Are we heroes?"

Tallux grinned cynically. "Martyrs."

"Nay." Eirec shook his shaggy beard. "Blind, stumbling fools."

"Maybe fools, but not blind." In Galor's hand was cupped again the dove-like shimmer of white. It flitted away downslope across the burning and into the shadow of the largest gate tower.

"She crosses the moat and into a peel, unmarked!" cried Tallux.

"Perhaps," replied Galor.

Apieron gathered his reins. "There is something else." He fingered the badge of brown and blue and cream on his breast. "I can feel Melónie, down there."

The strange wind blew Apieron's hair, "She is dead."

Isolde gave a start, an involuntary cry passing her lips.

Galor touched Apieron's shoulder and moved to speak. What he intended was lost, for his messenger returned, although it seemed to shed portions of itself as it landed, a wounded blur. Galor blew it free. "It is as I have feared; there can be no stealth." The gold elf's voice was sad. "I would have shielded us … if I could."

Galor bent and whispered something to his destrier. "Igwain shall lead you over the fire lake. Make for the center barbican—and pray!"

"Can our prayers ascend?" whispered Isolde.

""You are uneasy?" Tallux's green eyes danced with his jest as he swung gracefully atop the forest steed. He held the nose of Eirec's chestnut stallion for him.

"Never!" guffed the Northman. "Although I have some skalding …" He waved his enormous arm in the direction of the fortress. "About that, Thyrmgjol above the Nostrand, the Hel of murderers and thieves. Hey Henlee, how's this?"

Eirec drew himself up, filling his chest with air:

Dark sky
Death sky
Wings of fire
Battle cry.

"Better!" bawled Henlee. "Now pick up that pretty new axe of yours, let us give it a proper baptism."

"I wonder what time it is above?" asked Jamello, "You know, in the light of day."

Xephard turned from where he held close converse with Apieron. "Here too a sun shall rise!" A strange light found Xephard's face. "A noontide of vengeance."

"What the—?" Jamello gave back, his hunter dancing on the quartz scree. Xephard's tattered cloak melded and flowed until it shined purest ivory; its tasseled fringes shook happily as the holy warrior glowed like a hero from legend.

"The war cloak of our Spear Goddess, Sky's daughter," breathed Isolde.

Apieron's grim expression broke into a smile. He touched the shining garment. "At last, brother. The final battle, a fitting end to doubt and fear."

Xephard dismounted and took Isolde's hands, and a long moment they shared before she spoke. "Did you know I have always compared our eyes, mine shadowless, yours muted like the sky before a storm or depthless ocean."

Isolde laughed amidst her tears. "Those eyes should have been mine, Paladin, no tempest bides in your soul."

Xephard closed hers with a kiss. When she opened them, he was astride his impatient destrier. He laughed aloud, and Axylus reared, springing a circle on two legs.

Galor's sapphire gaze fell on Xephard's front. The cloak fluttered aside to show a rivulet of blood, tiny and crimson on the chest beneath. The stallion plunged, and the garment parted again, revealing no stain. A sad smile found Galor's face, then his mien grew stern as the Eldar elf put forth his powers. Igwain neighed shrilly, and the other steeds took up his battle challenge.

Hellish faces, minute in the distance, gazed up the slope in wonderment.

GREENWOLDE

A golden elf sat quiescent on his steed to regard the forest entry. He was a stranger here. Both elvin cavalier and his gleaming stallion stood motionless before the foreboding impasse that once had been gate to the kingdom of the Malave.

Before troubles had set their shadowed hands upon Ilycrium, a well-used highway issued from the forest sanctum of wood elves onto well-traveled paths that led away north to cultivated uplands of men, and beyond to sparsely settled hills and vales that nestled beneath the imposing mountains of Anheg. Winding ways there also were that led away south into sunny meads and open forests before finding the canal gates of Bestrand, city of crying gulls. The principal route, however, lay westward where the subtle trails of elf folk merged with the byways of the man-kingdom of Ilycrium and its capital, Sway, once proud queen of the sea-kissed shore, ruled now by the servants of Iblis.

A setting sun cast slanted rays on the knight atop his warhorse. Their blended shadows fell across the overgrowth of vine and tendril to merge into deeper shade within the barrier. The sinews of the forest itself were wound in a tangled perfusion more unyielding than any steel. A distant wind moaned softly in the forest as it sifted betwixt root and bole, and in time, the breeze found its way past the barrier to stir the elf's dark hair laid over his mantle, spun of blue silk and diamond-beaded gold. Likewise, the stallion's flowing mane lifted in the freshening wind. A dappled gray he was, proud in his strength. His nostrils flared to take in a subtle scent, and the muscles of his neck rolled in excitement.

The elvin paladin seemed to wake, and stood his stirrups to produce neither sword nor spear, but a silver horn. And lo! he was tall and mighty of frame. He sounded a musical note. Guardian trees quivered as bits of dusky branch and hoary leaf fell. His distant master had bade him haste, for his errantry was urgent. Thus the elf blew again, and bright new leaves sprung upon the twisted face of the gate. There came also flowers of blue and gold atop clusters of white berries. Somewhere in the forest, a songbird began to trill.

The golden elf sounded his clarion a third time. With a creaking heave, the boughs before him parted, hastening to open a way. The warrior reseated himself on his narrow saddle and stroked the heaving flanks of the stallion whilst sheathing the horn. He withdrew a white lance and unfurled its long, narrow pennant. The silver tower over sea and mountain of Amor rippled gracefully before the breeze.

At some unseen signal, the charger started forward, and Galen Trazequintil passed the walls of the Malave, Greenwolde of forest elves, to disappear within.

Chapter 23

Tiamat's Palace: Hel's Fortress

Galor stooped to the ground and palmed a handful of powdered iron as he studied the palace's horn work and fronting moat. He blew the material until it was gone. It twisted off downslope to be lost in dark airs.

"That was exciting," said Henlee. He turned to Tallux. "And what are you, a hedgehog?"

Arrows of varied sorts bristled about the wood elf's person, and two spare quivers hung from his back. "I have salvaged what I could, but I fear they will soon be gone."

Eirec pulled at his lips, "Perforce, so shall we."

"Elves," shrugged Henlee.

Jamello heaved up his heavy arbalest. His pony pranced with energy on the shingle. "Shall I lead the charge?"

"Thieves!" said Henlee. Axylus gently nudged Jamello's hunter aside. The paladin shook his head.

"There is something …" said Isolde.

"Wom—" began Henlee. Silenced by her icy stare, he closed his mouth.

Isolde produced a clarion of hammered metal. Xephard took it reverently. It had been his, oft wended by the captain of the temple. Now he sounded a note, clear and beautiful. The brazen blat of an iron oliphant of dwarves followed, enjoined by the bullhorn of Eirec's fathers. Together, four men and a woman, gold elf, dwarf lord, and half-elf scout began their assault on the fastness of Hel.

Their steeds galloped downhill, gliding over crack and burning rift until, streaming from the battlements, the gunnefanes of chaos could easily be seen. A beast guardant was writ there in dark heraldry, and from the banners streamed waves of fear and dissimilation. The nearest bastion loomed. The riders turned to parallel the dry moat and saw its length was strewn with mounds of bone. In places, the walls were honeycombed with burial niches and strangely lit; there was a stirring within.

Veering away, the companions marked the apex of the revetment in the distance. Bows began to twang, and Hel-wrought arrows sighed their deadly paths. Crews of bombards and ballistae strived to take aim on the fleeting targets, while ranger and wood elf returned winged death from their famous bows. An adept of Hel, tall in robes of shadow, hurled a stringer of globular lights that pulsed with eagerness to consume mortal flesh.

Galor raised his fist. It bore a dull stone, heavier than lead, and the eel-glow twisted back on its path, consuming the caster in a muted conflagration of flashing lights and shadow.

Apieron called out, "Slow, Jamello!" The thief bore no crop but made whipping motions, trying to drive his colt to the fore where, in their path, the squadrons of Hel loomed, and a red dust rose at their feet.

"Ware the rear … we are flanked!" shouted Henlee. Quick glances discovered an exodus from the fosse consisting of tall demons of matching harness, and fell warriors from mortal lands who came like ants boiling from a flooded nest.

"Ignore it," cried Galor. "Mind the front!" It was then that his iron-blown tornado struck.

The roar of it whelmed defenders on the wall and tore through the dry moat's ossuary like a geyser of splintered bone. Random shrapnel and razored rocks of its interior shredded flesh and bent steel and thundered against the imperishable wall. The devils and devil-men that habited their honeycombed necropolis like larvae in holes were swept up and destroyed.

Galor spied movement on the rampart, a flash of Helstones and a crimson cloak. The golden mage lanced a thin beam of whitest light across the man. An obsidian merlon, impenetrably thick and spell shielded, was severed across its base to topple ponderously into the moat. Adestes Malgrim staggered back and gazed in amaze at the molded cuirass he bore. One of its ensorceled gems was smoked and cracked. Crouching low, he stared at the stone of the riven crenellation as its bubbling faded orange to black. He touched his armor and shook his head.

"A mighty guerdon you are." Even so, he would bide above the conflict until the fey elf was no more. On legs that yet wobbled, Malesh sought safety in the shadows.

Riding pell-mell through the smokes and random enemy, Xephard led a charge for the open bridge. Isolde clung to Apieron as he bore away left toward the arm of the dry moat, untouched by Galor's twisting storm.

A conclave of arcane priests summoned three funnels to battle Galor's one. Their tops reached aerial highways, sucking portions of the living wrack into their spell-lit interiors, and the flying demons who swirled therein never emerged.

Xephard pulled Axylus to a halt. The warhorse steamed the air with the fog of his breath, and muscles rippled under the dappling sheen of its hide. Looking askance at the environ of Hel, Axylus snorted and stamped his desire to tread it into ruin. Xephard laid a reassuring hand upon the proud neck. "Come friends, do not stand idle! I cannot carry all the battle."

Eirec cursed the paladin but did not remove his eyes from the beetle-like thing that he disassembled with ride-by sweeps of his iron axe. Afoot, Henlee huffed in windy gasps as he strove to catch up the Templar. "Shiny galoot! Dwarves do not need speeches for milksop recruits." He raised Maul and sang the battle cry of his people.

Xephard did not wait, but turned his destrier's head to the next picket, and Axylus fixed the Helkind with baleful eyes. The mighty stallion broke into the throng, biting and stamping as claw and steel and helspun magics were turned by the ivory cloak. Leitus stove in helms to cleave horned skulls, shattered breastbones, and sundered limbs whole. In the midst of swarming foes, Xephard shined like a brave star in the blackest vault of space as his holy garment cast the enemy into a bewilderment of fear, and its tasseled fringes shook joyously.

Apieron heard voices in the wind. Howling spirits of women and men cried out in madness, and he discerned terrible screams and strange brayings such as animals make at their lives' ending, yet worse than all was the strident keening of children as if in mortal fear. To his ears, the entire fosse echoed with the sounds, save where Galor's tornado dissipated against the counter rotations of the opposing funnels.

Leaving his pony, Apieron descended the dry moat. A jumbled

perfusion of bones and desiccated flesh stretched for miles. He fixed his gaze on a not distant pile. He knew what he sought.

Henlee grasped a fiery whip. Its owner, a bony, paunch-bellied fiend of mottled white, yelped its surprise but did not relinquish the flail, thus making its last mistake. The dwarf pulled the devil to its knees, and Maul painted the stones vermillion. A conclave of demons shrieked outrage and pressed hard the black-armored dwarf. Henlee gave back grudgingly whilst Maul reaped grim harvest.

A five-horned giant flapped onto the dwarf's broad back in attempt to drive its spiked forearms and elbows through Henlee's casement. The dwarf lord erupted into a stomping, slashing frenzy and whipped about, slashing free three horns with Maul's razored edge. The Helspawn emitted a horrible piping until Henlee's backstroke exploded its skull. After that, not many cared to face the fierce mask and dripping foehammer of the dwarven beserker, thus Henlee made his steady way, a boar amongst hounds, to where the holy warrior broke the battle.

Tiamat's lieutenant heard the paladin's war song, and rose to the curtain wall to view what portended. Outside, carnage reigned. Eyes squinting in consternation, Aurgelmir beheld fiends converging from all directions, yet unable to encircle the quick-striking attackers on their agile mounts.

"Death cheater," rumbled Aurgelmir's cavernous voice, for atop his mighty charger, the Templar beat a red swath of ruin.

A masked dwarf followed, shouting in an uncouth tongue and laying about him with a wicked glaive whilst two lithe archers bow-dueled his aerial troops and intermittently knived wounded demons. The two bowmen were protected by an enormous, shaggy human who swung a white-faced axe that rended demon hide and limbs, spilling smoking ichor onto the pitiless stone. More destructive yet was a fell elvin mage who was liquefying great swaths of the nearest bartizan with scintillant beams of blue and white. Any minion unfortunate to find himself in their path was sundered in twain.

Aurgelmir bellowed his rage, and imps scurried away in fear, climbing like monkeys. Aurgelmir's troops were not alone in noting his displeasure. A clothyard shaft suddenly appeared in his shoulder, notwithstanding Hel-forged scale and a hide that would shame a grandfather croc. Aurgelmir bellowed twice as loud and drew forth the offending dart. That these mortals had survived and penetrated thus far attested to either incredible prowess or a colossal blunder on the part of certain personages. What the silver knight was doing to his companies was simply appalling; the man deliberately sought out the champions of his reeling formations and crushed them. It was as if some vengeful angel had appeared to exact terrible toll on the denizens of Hel—and where was his daughter?

Aurgelmir, Lieutenant of the Abyss, Lord of the Tower, gathered his powers.

Once he dealt with the paladin, he would have converse with one Adestes Malgrim for letting this one live to escape, and the interview would be thorough indeed. With such pleasant reflections, Aurgelmir descended the inner bailey while dispatching telepathic missives of command. He felt the purpose of the Dark She, to slay these defilers was not enough, their souls would writhe—an eternity's agony for this day's effrontery.

Isolde drew up, Apieron was lost to her, and she cast frantically back to the battle. A power was there.

Ulfelion rose above the strife, black on orange-lit gray. Blades of unlife streamed from the vampire, flickering in and out of phase, and questing for living flesh. They found the party. Horses screamed and pawed the air as pieces of their forms melted into insubstantiality. Tumbling and rolling, the companions leapt free, brains and limbs numbed and cold.

"The Gorgan!" wailed Isolde. "The Gorgan has come!" In awful splendor, Ulfelion continued his ascent, and his pallid features were revealed, implacable, fixed on death.

Jamello crouched, whipping his head side to side with unfettered paranoia, although no enemy approached. Tallux drew Strumfyr but did not fire, his fingers frozen to the bowstring.

"Run!" cried Galor. "Your steeds are free. Run, close with the enemy."

Eirec lifted his head to see Xephard far ahead, cast horseless into a sea of Helspawn. Eirec shook his shaggy cloak and freed himself of the spell. "Charge!" he roared. Tallux and Jamello leapt to his bidding.

Alone of the companions, Galor remained horsed. Gentle words he spoke to Igwain, and swelling in stature, the elvin stallion rose with speed into the air as from the noble head grew a horn of gold and pearl, fixed in aim upon the breast of their foe.

Isolde turned in search of Apieron. Skirting the fighting, she came to the lichmoat. Dovecot holes of ordered remains, some of which began to stir, lined its sides. Ignoring these, she walked the jumbled ossuary that stretched the fosse's length. Removing helm and mask, Isolde stooped over a tangled pile of white bone to withdraw something she cradled gently. Pressing it to her chest with one hand, she drew forth a cloth of silver and wrapped it.

Apieron's face was dark as he turned to regard the battle. Of his steed, his brave racer, there was no sign. New columns of helions issued from niched posterns along the curtain wall, and braying horns sounded from many places. Where the party had been, the airs boiled with battalions of flying demons. In Apieron's hand was the bow of swamp elves, its living quiver, Quq, bristling with leaf growth. When a shaft was freed, another grew in its stead. Glad it was to yield arrows this day.

Isolde saw him as he ripped another bolt through the midsection of a flapping thing that had dared approach. The arrow passed through its target and was lost into the roiling cloud. She knew the famous bow had already slain more than could easily be counted. On Apieron's back were slung the javelins gifted by the matron, their heads clotted with gore.

His words were thick. "And the children?"

With reverent motions, Isolde placed the bundle into her pack. Shaking her blond hair, she gathered helm and mask. "Only Melónie. What will you do?"

The vermillion cast of the battle danced weirdly on the well-surface of Apieron's eyes. "Kill them all."

Igwain's hooves thundered the fractured sky as he ascended, braving the storm of unlife, which like an inexhaustible wave, beat and tore at the pair as the Gorgan exerted its maximum powers of dissolution. Galor's shouting incantation and the challenge of the unicorn were lost in the maelstrom as their forms became obscured to the watchers below. Squadrons faltered in their march, and fell heads were raised to the spectacle. The companions used the lull to consolidate their position, slipping ever closer to the barbican.

Ulfelion exerted his dominion. He breathed a sphere of disintegration into the smoky labyrinth that was the abode of airborne fiends. It expanded hugely in rapid silence to loom over the combatants below. Stricken demons and pieces of demons fell to the ground.

Galor countered. Blinking eyes from below beheld a tiny mote of emerald that appeared at the center of the spell storm. It grew. Soon, a waving forest became visible. The fronds parted to reveal a misted tor, its garment a patchwork of heath and flowering sedge. The mountain bore a silver tower where a single bell tolled clear and beautiful, and trees bowed their shaggy heads as night birds grew silent, and white gulls raced over a burgundy sea to welcome the dawn.

Over the battle, the Hel sky shattered into a concussion of blinding light. Earthbound combatants staggered to their knees whilst columns of rock slid from the cliff face into ruin. It took many minutes for the air to clear, yet gradually the gray-orange of Hel's burning returned to the void.

Of Galor Galdarion and Ulfelion, Prestidigitator of Hel, nothing remained to be seen.

Puffing hard, Henlee pulled up near Xephard, tiny flecks of silvery steel shining on the dwarf's black casement where heavy blows had fallen. Henlee followed the path of Xephard's gaze. "A bat?" he growled.

"Nay. A raven."

"Then bigger than an eagle. Why, he's—"

The dwarf's observations were lost in the flapping advent of the bird. Its eyes glinted an evil crimson, and purplish energies fled from it, branching to lick over the pair. Fed by the metal they wore, it chased its crackling self about their persons as a single echoing caw followed the bird's departure.

Flat on his belly, Henlee hauled to his feet. Wisps of smoke emanated from his braided beard. He discovered a smallish demon also immobilized by the casting. After its lifeless form fell from his throttling fingers, he gathered up Maul and shield. Searching the battle, he found that Xephard now held the level before the bridge arch. Eirec was there, as was thief and wood elf. He did not see Apieron or Isolde. His dark eyes searched the crawling moat.

"Apieron!" Henlee shouted. Slinging his round shield, the dwarf reached to his belt where hung the iron horn of dwarves. He began to run.

"First I will get you to the others."

Taking her hand, Apieron led Isolde a dodging run toward the apex of wall and fosse. Her spear emitted bursts of light that bewildered grasping Helkind whensoever their talons came too close, and Apieron slew any that directly encumbered the way. At length, there came against them a human champion of the moat. In the world above, he would have been deemed a giant, yet here his seven-foot and mightily girthed frame was little more than average of stature. In his massive hand was clutched a scythe of dull metal, its edge alive with white-hot radiance.

With confidence, the risen prince strode to the bloodletting. For had he not been a great captain of his people? Behind him trotted two others, slightly smaller and similarly accoutered. The shadowed eye slits of his helm were fixed on Apieron, and the arc of his raised scythe glittered like diamonds.

Apieron pinned him to the earth, then smashed his lieutenants into red ruin with a lump of jagged stone. Something snapped, and the ranger lord of Windhover, gardener and singer, ran amuck. Bow slung across his back, Apieron surged. Javelins ever-sharp pierced flesh and brains in gory harvest, the soul-shriving moments of Melónie's death playing again in his tortured mind whilst he slew with weapon, hand, and boot like an implacable Fate come for judgment. Crying aloud, Isolde followed, and the agony of his burning spirit clenched in the depths of her breast, catching up her faltering breath.

"Apieron … Apieron," she called many times.

Unheeding, Apieron loomed above the fray, tall and terrible. The red tide of his anger filled his vision while for him all things slowed. A demon screeched, beating down with wing and flail. Its black ichor hissed into the air as Apieron rended it, the edge of his kite shield tearing its form into two pieces. Beating a swath of destruction, Apieron waded knee deep in the limbs of his enemies, their shrieks drowned by the churning in his heart and the song of slaying in his brain. He wept and slew the more as, never ending, the tide of his enemies broke against him like a streaming cliff, black and massive, that looms over the battling surf.

When their foes had fled in yammering dismay, Isolde caught him up and clasped his armored knees to silently beseech the storm in his eyes. There came a sound. Apieron lifted his head as a note, pure in tone, pierced the oppressive air.

"Clarion," murmured Apieron's bearded lips. Joining the silver trumpet, an olifant sounded with the deep shout of a thousand mountain dwarves who ascend from their palace caverns to defend their homeland, eager for war. "Our friends press the gate."

Isolde followed him, her carven mask again in place and spear lofted overhand, a threat to their enemies. As they ran, Eirec blew a full blast that spoke of thunder and ice-clad mountains. It gained force like a mass of snow on a high slope that shifts and stirs, soon to become an irresistible juggernaut of white fury that sweeps the mountain clean.

A wyvern-winged demon swept at Eirec to snatch up the hated horn, and like a hammer, he wielded the instrument to deal a blow on its keeled skull that stunned the flapping fiend. From his hands, the mighty bull's horn, chased with heavy gold and fretted with gems, fell riven. Apieron ran by, piercing the demon twice where it lay.

Isolde severed the last vestiges of its life as she leapt past, garments aflutter on her armor.

"What? Hold!" cried Eirec, but they were gone. Cursing, he gathered his father's shattered horn and followed.

Xephard wore a broad smile as he embraced Isolde. They shared a place in the storm that had been quieted by the power of the paladin's arm. Apieron made to move past where another surge gathered, and saw a dark boulder detach itself from a low wall before which lay a disordered pile of dead and dying Helspawn. The boulder shook free mask and helm. Henlee grinned hugely in his black face.

"Couldn't find you. So we wended our horns and set up in this place." A crawling, eyeless thing sank its fangs into Henlee's boot. "Why the foot?" cried he. Maul flashed and Henlee's other boot kicked the head into a burning hole.

"Plenty to do here," said the dwarf seriously.

Xephard spoke. "Bide, Apieron. The gate is unfought; you and I must force a way for the others to follow."

Apieron paused, uncertain. Lit by the garish light, he stood swathed in the gore of his enemies as a man might don a favorite garment. He regarded the plain of beasts.

"The source," cried Isolde. "The heart of darkness lurks behind those walls!"

"The gold elf is gone," added Xephard quietly. "If not us, who else?"

"Aye. We will go there." With something like regret, Apieron turned his back on the advancing tide as the airs again grew dark with flying monsters, and a wild clamor arose as templar and ranger dashed a straight course for the frowning barbican. The others followed, keeping station to the rear.

A terrible head, bearing a crowned helm of office, rose above the rampart. Isolde gasped, for with true sight she beheld the naked vulnerability of her companions. The voice of despair returned, and it smote her brow like the hammer of malice. The head and cliff-like shoulders ducked beneath the wall arch. He was coming.

Aurgelmir advanced from the ramp step with ponderous tread. A gargantuan arm swept aside all magics and illusions. Eirec's shouted curse carried as their clothes began to burn. Apieron fronted the bridge with Xephard flanking him as fear emanated in waves from the gate warden's milky orbs. What inexorable thought swam behind those eyes, the ranger of Windhover could not guess. The voice spoke, acid on stone.

"Where is thy ring of passage … thy safeguard to the keep of She Who Is? Speak, before I slay thee."

Apieron upthrust his hand. "Only this!" Suspended by her snaky hair was the head of a succubus, conquest of Isolde.

"Daughter!" Rocks cracked.

Jamello and Isolde staggered to their knees, yet with faithful arms, Tallux bore them up. A javelin of white, a javelin of black, appeared in Apieron's hands. "Soon you will sleep again with your slut of the Pit. Come and die."

Iron rods, hissing with fell energies, were clutched in taloned fists. The beast's cry of fury commingled with Apieron's own in terrible symphony, and Leitus shined like the sickle of heaven as Xephard leapt with his sword brother to engage.

The second battle of the wall commenced with utmost ferocity. Ignoring the heat that blistered his skin, Tallux took station before the barbican against the flying squadrons. A shout turned Henlee round, and he smiled grimly to see Eirec beside him, wild-eyed and furious, as a ruck of Helspawn, rank upon rank, braved their threats. Behind him, Henlee heard the first blows of the gate battle struck like the forge hammers of dwarven heroes. A sidelong glance found Isolde and the thief beside Tallux. The three stood fast before the sky's assault. So much the better. He and Eirec of Amber Hall would bear the brunt.

"I think," said Eirec, looping his white-faced axe and shrugging his rounded shoulders as if to loosen them up, "we should attack, lest we be ringed and dragged under—" A masked dwarf passed him by, running headlong into the press.

Shouting his deep voice, the black dwarf smote his enemies like a dark comet. Mortal foes would have taken counsel with their fears and fled, but these were rendered mindless by their master's will. They hissed and threatened the approaching dwarf with long taloned claws and fangs that might easily tear the soft flesh of man or elf, yet like an unstoppable stone that crashes down the course of a wild mountain stream gorged with snowmelt, Henlee rolled unencumbered into their ranks. So great was his strength that Maul slew with every strike, and the passage of his iron-clad body snapped wings and arms outstretched to strike him. Their horny hands and razored teeth rang out on shield and armor but found no seam to pierce or purchase with which to drag him under. Eirec whooped with joy and charged the breach. Buffeted and dazed by Henlee's assault, numbers of Helspawn fell before the Northman's axe.

So great was the carnage wrought by the dwarf lord, Aurgelmir paused a two-maced attack upon Apieron to fix Henlee with eyes of death. Heedless in his berserk fury, Henlee recked not of odds or magics. Well he remembered his words to Melónie one chill morning, but it was she who had fallen. So now, in this place, would he build for her a sacrifice greater than the burial mounds of dwarven kings.

Tallux heard the deafening bellows of the gate warden and the equally fierce cries of ranger and paladin. He smiled grimly when the sound of a blade striking home came to him like a butcher's cleaver into meat, for no other hand could wield such a sword as the white Templar. But Tallux of Greenwolde, Captain of the Foresters of Ilycrium, did not turn to look. He set himself, legs braced wide, his arc of polished yew gleaming red in the gloom as shaft after pitiless shaft found targets that were struck screaming from the pall. Like a hunter fearless before his prey, the bow that no other could wield smote steel-tipped ruin amongst the flying ranks. Never did his emerald eyes flinch or the thick wrists of the half-elf fail their strength.

Jamello marveled at the power wielded by Isolde. At her booming commands, fell radiances erupted from her spear or the ground itself to consume their enemies. An agile devil twisted past her stabbing spear. The thing leapt on kangaroo legs meaning to overwhelm the slender woman by might and momentum. Casting aside his arbalest, Jamello intercepted. Crypt sword and targe picked off strikes of claw and hook as he recalled the lessons of the paladin and took no backward step.

"Ah tahh!" yelled Jamello as he waded in for a slash of his own, but a shadow crossed his eyes. The blur overhead became the creature's spaded tail that struck the heavy shield from him like a discus, and a splash of poison seared his face below the morion's rim. Screeching its triumph like a forest ape, the fiend gnashed its frothing jaws and charged.

Quick as a hornet, Jamello drew his main gauche and peeled one taloned hand out wide as his crypt blade sank its full length into the beast's barreled chest. "There's a trick you don't know."

The demon's baboon maw opened to respond, but black blood welled up, and its curse died unspoken. Sparing a glance to Isolde, Jamello sprang to reclaim his shield. He found another there first.

"Whence came this, Scraling?"

It was a man, tall and clad in ancient harness. He was as dusky in hue as the thief, yet with cruel, aquiline features. Jamello swallowed. Many depictions of that race had he seen in the city lost to the Wyrnde. There came to his memory the prince they slew in his unholy bath.

A corded arm gathered Jamello's shield. "My people made this." A bronze saber nigh as long as Jamello swept the air. "Thy sword also will I take. Well met are we!"

"Meet this!" Jamello backstepped, slinging a tripwire around the man's lower legs.

The twin-edged saber dipped, and Jamello's wire parted harmlessly, the blade then batted aside the two shining balls thrown at the giant's face. They exploded, and he staggered. "I meant to slay thee with honor. Now my slave will you be."

Jamello's voice seemed high and powerless beneath the Hel-torn sky. "Yon shield is mine; drop it and live."

The man laughed as might a lion. His jeer died when a

blue-pommeled dagger appeared in his breast. The plate of his corselet was scorched in futile resistance to the blessed weapon. A second appeared, and a third. Too slow, the sword of bronze and heavy shield weaved their defense.

"Stay dead." Jamello gathered his gear.

The thief yelped in pain and looked to his shirt as it began to yellow and curl.

Isolde beckoned, "To the courtyard, fool. We shall be incinerated out here!"

Henlee and Eirec hove into view. Nothing pressed them close.

Jamello turned and ran. Miraculously Apieron and Xephard had pushed the monstrosity they battled across the bridge, its dark blood staining the walkway. As he traversed the span, Jamello kicked the she-demon's head into the crawling moat.

Aurgelmir, father of devils, shuffled and shouted. Dealing blows with either hand, his ageless knowledge of combat was pitted against the righteous strength of Xephard and Apieron. Jamello took position within striking distance of one scaled leg.

"Is this armor?" Jamello flipped into his right hand the long kindjal he had obtained in the swamp tomb. Elaborate filigree swam below its jade hilts. Many enchantments thereon glowed in this place of power, for the race who forged it had known and betimes battled many creatures of the Pit. With a prayer to any god that might listen, the thief drove it home with every fiber in his sinewy frame.

The kindjal evaporated in a flash. Jamello reeled back and fell to his seat, but a heel kick spun him across the bailey.

Aurgelmir paid no further heed to the gnat that sought to sting him. At his thought, the stone underfoot became an ally to grapple and drown the defilers.

Xephard's cloak fluttered, and the rock grew quiescent. Roaring his rage with the voice of a sudden storm, Aurgelmir struck down at his attackers. They danced aside whilst his adamant rods plowed smoking furrows in the pave. His alabaster orbs wove a spell of mazing. Never had it failed.

The woven cloth on Apieron's breast bore the pattern of his ancestry. Knitted by Melónie's hands of love, it reflected the demon-lord's spell into harmless colors. A javelin of white appeared in the gate warden's throat. An ebon javelin joined its brother. Pitching forward, Aurgelmir struck his final blows, seeking to drive his foes into death's abyss with him. Leitus's flare lit the courtyard when she sheared the waist-thick neck.

"Where are my children?" screamed Apieron. He bore up the crowned head like an onion on a stick.

"No time," screeched Isolde as she dashed past. "To the keep!" Flames danced on her back.

"That's a big lizard," shouted Eirec, leaping the carcass.

From his sooty face, Henlee grinned at Apieron as he followed. Apieron dropped the head and extracted his lances. He fell in behind, exhorting the others to greater speed. Across the rock raced an undulant snake, feet-thick and fat jaws bulging with poison. Its ephemeral corpus was tethered to the ring on Adestes' hand. As if shot from a bow, its length sped unerringly toward Apieron's back. From a high balcony in the shard-like face of the keep, Malesh spat. "Here is my kiss, brother!" The apparition gathered its snaky length for the final strike—a moment's pause that drew its head above Apieron's shoulder.

Leitus flashed once and the summoning tumbled and dissolved into nothingness. Adestes jerked back as a smell of burning flesh arose, and the golden circuit hissed as its twining serpent constricted, fusing onto his finger. Turning from the fray, Adestes Malgrim fled into the gloom-drenched fastness. The keep of Hel's Queen.

Epilogue

"Those were happy days!
When our hands grasped wine full cups,
not the heavy sword,
And Rafters sang to our joyous verse.
Pitiless fire has consumed all.
Like ocean-blown spume, we are borne on Hel's Storm."

"Ha!" shouted Eirec.

Henlee pushed past him. "I'll be damned."

"Droll," tittered Jamello. "What do you see?"

Eirec's laughter lifted back to them. When he turned, his beard sparkled with ice. "It's winter inside."

"If this be a cavern, I see no root," said Henlee.

Apieron strode forward, and the others followed. The ledge on which they stood ended after thirty paces into a rough foot over a nighted drop. Neither elf nor ranger could mark its depth. To either side loomed a hollow edifice of gleaming jet. Like a couloir between sky-touching mountains, it seemed an echoing darkness without end. A frosty rime coated the rocky tongue and the near wall with a glassy sheen. Swirling mists, heavy with biting crystals, lived in the yawning space, and where they eddied against the ledge, hoarfrost gathered in corners.

"I do not think they expected such as we," intoned Henlee.

Apieron sat heavily. "Galor," he said. "He spent his life who otherwise immortal might be." Apieron's fist found his chin, and his gray eyes sought the darkness. "That the wight Ulfelion was destroyed by his passing, I have no doubt."

"His death earned us the gate," husked Eirec.

Henlee stirred. "A great victory."

Jamello's voice was barely audible. "Then he is dead?"

"I … do not know," stammered Isolde. "His wisdom, who can compare?" She shifted uncomfortably and looked down to Apieron. "I will try my best."

Xephard lay a strong hand on her shoulder. "We must have hope. Whithersoever he is, I wish him well."

"Aye," rasped Henlee, "dwarves will not forget his glory. The grand elf."

"In the Malave, our Greenwolde, paens will be sung until saplings grow old," said Tallux.

"And the skalds of the Nortings," growled Eirec. "The telling of his final battle shall rise in the hall until all is forever lost."

For a moment, no further words were spoken. Their breath billowed and took strange shapes on the frozen air. Drifting away in the murk, it swirled, assuming the form of strange, billowing creatures.

Apieron roused as his stern eyes strived to pierce the shadow. "A light, Priestess."

Isolde's spear tip emitted a soft glow. Henlee chuckled grimly. "A thousand more of those, and we might see to the end of his hole."

"You fret like my grandmother," said Eirec.

"Not in this cold; she'd be hibernating," snapped Henlee.

Eirec's red-faced retort failed on his lips. Perhaps drawn by the dwarf's shouting or the fitful light, a swarm of the fluttering, mist-born creatures attacked.

Isolde spoke a word, and her spear flared. The frostings died.

Xephard stepped close and held Leitus into the glow. An airborne path, vaguely serpentine, appeared within her mirror surface. Xephard's cloak rustled its approval. "Heaven's light pierces all falsehood."

"Gird yourselves," said Apieron.

Xephard's clarion gleamed like silver liquid.

Jamello ran to him. "You're not going to blow that thing? Now is the time for stealth … a thief's hour."

"Blow it," said Henlee.

Isolde looked uncertain.

Clarion's tone rose, a feeling into a sound. The mist obeyed its perfect note, solidifying the way as Isolde's spearglow fully revealed a stairway of scintillant crystal. Apieron gathered the oliphant from Henlee's belt. Its blast charged into the hollow place, setting ice devils dancing.

"We are coming, murdering bitch!" Apieron raised kite shield and ebon javelin. Not looking back, he led them into Hel's Castle.

Chapter 24

Ilycrium

As when kindling is laid upon dusky embers, the wise husbandman does not fret the pile and lets it be. First nothing happens, then of a sudden, yellow flames lick up to make a merry blaze. Thus began the rousing of Ilycrium the nation.

Across the country, aged swords were removed from hiding places, and bills were whetted as farmers and yeomen came forth, their work-hardened hands clenching humble weapons. Country barons heard rumor of a brave prince who had faced immortals from Kör lands yet lived. The tales were of a young man, king but for happenstance, whose army endured the hunters of the enemy, thereby saving Sway's complete destruction and that of many castled estates. Cup and plate were thrust aside; armsmen were summoned.

The soldiers of Wulfstane and Buthard also marched, although those of the Boar's Head did not commingle with others and sang no songs. Also from the lands nigh Windhover, large bodies flitted amongst gloaming trees, and hoofbeats thudded on the loam.

"My lord," rumbled Seamus, "a delegation of women awaits you, led by a noblewoman hight Klea. They came in the night."

Brushing sleep from his eyes, Gault followed his ambling companion to a grassy dale sheltered from the sky by a tarpaulin stretched between trees.

Renault and Exeter traded words with a woman, apparently of the city. Tall and well spoken she was, although her blond hair had been shorn short as a pageboy's. Gault felt he had seen her, yet no surname came to his lips. At her side was a peasant woman, strong of arm, thick of frame, and girt as a soldier. Trakhner shrugged helplessly to his prince.

"What of your husbands and children?" demanded Exeter.

"Slain. Or gone off to war."

Exeter's thin face bore a look of one who argues out of patience, yet the conclusion be foregone. "What of your homes? Who shall keep the hearth that awaits your loved ones' return?"

"If the armies of Kör overrun this land, there will be no hearths to keep."

"My Prince!" sputtered Renault. "It is not fitting for a woman to enter battle."

The noblewoman laughed. "How think you we came here, gallant knight? Four hundred women do not cross the wild this land has become without a fight." The tall woman lifted her chin, and her green-eyed gaze was steady. "War finds any who dwell here. Men do not possess every courage."

Exeter tugged his long chin. "Four hundreds? Better than the magical armies of elves that were promised by such as he, and never came." The chin indicated Giliad, who stood in the shadows, his hooded robe again in place and dun as the bark of the pines. A glint of sapphire eyes came from the shadows of the hood; otherwise, the elf did not stir.

"Peace, Seneschal." Gault looked to Renault. "I too deem the quiet courage of waiting and healing to be better than that of arms." The prince stepped forward and proffered his hand to the noblewoman. She knelt and kissed his palms. He raised her. "And yet I gladly accept your aid. It is in our diversity wherein lies our strength; many colors make bright the garden."

As soon as the women departed, Renault protested, "I like this not, Lord. They are vulnerable, and in turn, they will render the soldiery vulnerable."

"Spread them out, Trakhner," replied Gault. "Let the men of each company witness their bravery."

Exeter looked torn. "Be at ease," laughed Trakhner. "It is not wise to cross one of these goodwives. You are better off fighting the men folk!"

The peasant woman faced Wiglaf and Cusk, her face colored from weeping. "First I begged Dunstan not to go, near unmanned him by my tears, did I." Her hair was also blond, although more yellow than white and fell to strong shoulders. She pushed a loop back under her bonnet.

"When he ha' gone, I cursed the very name of him I loved." She nodded sadly. "Lonesome nights I prayed for him, and days turned into weeks. Me an' t'other women put foodstuffs in kit together what as a soldier'd need. We sended them ta' the army with such as would take 'em. Soon there weren't t'any left to go, so we be here, an' help wha' we may."

Wiglaf cleared his gravelly throat more than once, yet no words came.

"We did the best we could for 'im," said Cusk. Tears found the youth's eyes. "He was our family." The woman began to weep in earnest, and Wiglaf gathered her against his chest, shielding her with his arms.

"I know," she sobbed. "I know."

No one had marked his going, but the elvin mage had somehow departed when the company of women filtered into the encampment. Exeter was not done, "My Prince, trust you that shadowed spell-mumbler?"

"Doubt you the elf's tale?" asked Renault.

Exeter's reply was quick. "Men also whisper tales. It is said none escape the Gehulgog save they serve some evil purpose, even unwittingly."

"I had my doubts," admitted Trakhner, his weathered face crinkling into a wry grin, "but this old war dog has learned something of the elf's mystic. Kör must be mighty indeed to casually break such a one and return him alive."

"Who knowest what plan the demon-lord conceives? What sorcery he plots against us?"

Gault spread wide his hands in appeasement. "Sirs, I know something of our guest. His name is Giliad Galdarion, and I think he would allow his identity known if only by our few leaders, and we will not speak it again after now. Be assured, his only muse is revenge, and for that, Kör had best plan long and well."

Done with his argument, Exeter continued to stroke his short beard. "That, Highness, was never in doubt."

TIAMAT'S PALACE

"Listen!" said Tallux. The seven companions stood before a split in the passage. Long had they traveled the invisible stair until it debouched onto a concourse wide and tall.

"A city," whispered Jamello. Humming activity—the voices of thousands drifted from the rightward passage.

Apieron joined the sharp-eyed elf and master thief. "Our way is left."

Henlee and Eirec shared a look, relief writ large on their craggy features. "Caution. It is down, and steeply so."

Xephard's cloak, having taken no stain in the gate battle, shifted like a white shadow. "Thus the burden of Her sin hast weighed Her to the lowest Hel."

A brief rest was called within hearing distance of the turnoff. When the march resumed, the way grew narrow and frigid. Knees and thighs burned with the strain of the descent, yet no rope was called for. Each companion felt the pressing urgency, a menace more potent than the milling foes left behind. In time, the tunnel opened into a nighted valley. Jamello and Isolde gasped.

Rifts of frozen ice, glacier like, descended from cloud-obscured cliffs to the right. Slick surfaced, the ice was faintly lit and oily blue. At its center was a larger flow where a river poised in stasis overhead, its feet splayed into a mile-wide forest of ice-boled columns. "An apt home for the frozen devils of Hel," rumbled Eirec. "What will befall, Priestess, when we slay their Mistress?"

Isolde spoke in hushed tones, even so, her voice carried in the icy silence, "Galor once said this place was birthed by Her advent, a creation of Her thought." The warrior-cleric of the Lampus shrugged against the weight of her doubt. "If She is slain, it might cease to be."

Jamello dropped a spiculed shard. "That's encouraging."

"What matter?" answered Apieron. They walked toward the gap betwixt river and cliff.

Isolde caught him up, and her eyes flashed. "Do not forget the world we've left, we too deserve our place therein."

Ice crunching beneath Apieron's boots was her answer.

"Or," added Tallux, "we have wandered into Her dream, where She cannot be defeated."

"I deemed it to be something like that," mused Eirec. "My father—"

"What do you think, Apieron?" interrupted Henlee. "These holes look much the same to me." The dwarf gestured to where shadowed recesses in the near wall opened in the ice-bound stone.

The ranger of Windhover stood a moment before the seventh. Nodding to Henlee, he strode in. Climbing a twisted course, in time, it became a carved passage, and script lifted from the stone, taking shape as they ascended, and seeming to shift within its own illumination, then it began to crawl across the frozen rock.

"We have seen this before," breathed Jamello. "But not so … so powerful."

Apieron tried to pierce the meaning of the glyphing. Mesmerizing and elusive, it fled from him. His legs were weary. How many miles had passed underfoot since that wintry day at the Oracle? Isolde was wrong; he had walked in Hel from the moment Windhover burned. The places his feet bore him were irrelevant. He looked down:

His form was much the same, but swathed in a cloth-like mesh of gray metal. He bore a dark sword, and at his command, flame rippled its length.

An apparition rose before him, its backdrop a roiling sky. Speaking, its voice hung like smoke, animate with power. "What welcome this? Am I not thy true father?"

"Think not to lay a chill hand on me. I will smite thee, and my brand drink the unlife that moves thee!"

Ulfelion laughed. Those thralls that served Llund's pit fell to their faces at the horrid sound. "Thy blade hast no power to drain that which is empty. The force which binds my essence is greater than the warming blood that moves you. It is everlasting."

The vampire drew itself to a mighty height, a tower of seething blackness. "I cannot be undone by mortal weapons. Its passage through me will reform, stronger for the vengeance I will take. You mayest be a god amongst unworthy men, Malesh, yet to me, you are but a lesser priest. Command me, you cannot."

Apieron shook free the vision, but a dark wisp teased the corners of his mind, refusing to depart. He ground his teeth. "Thou art not my father, shriveled ghost! Met you my friend, Galor Galdarion?"

Henlee came close. "I heard you mumbling … what is that!" At his tone of alarm, the others rushed forward. They halted abruptly.

Barbed like a lamprey's mouth, the corridor before them rotated and surged with liquid peristalsis. "Hel's asylum," answered Apieron. Before any could stop him, he strode into the fanged tube. Like quicksilver, the illusion fled, leaving him fronting a door of gold-chased iron. The point of his shield broke the lock, and Apieron kicked open the valve to step within. A girl looked up, her black eyes asmolder. She stood behind an astrolabe heavy with diamonds and blue enamel. Over it she leapt to attack.

Apieron's grip shook her wrist, and a dagger fell from her fingers. Around the companions stretched an apartment, dark and sumptuous as befitted a lieutenant of Hel. Platinum frieze work bordered its many angles, and there was a translucent vase of sensuous carnelian in which black symbols flickered, marking the passage of time.

Twisting free of Apieron, the woman dashed headlong into Henlee. The dwarf's black mask and adamant armor loomed menacingly. "Tell us of him we seek," growled he. Defiance without fear was stamped on her face.

"Never!"

Xephard locked her black orbs with his own. "Know you we can deliver you from this place?"

Her answer was spittle. Apieron took her, and grasping the woman by her hair, he shook her mightily. "Where is thy master, slut?"

Isolde came forward. She touched the girl's face then jerked back her hand from a savage bite defeated by her gauntlet. "There is no evil in her, and yet her life has ever been caught in its web. If indeed she knows aught, nothing she will reveal of his intent or purpose." Isolde's voice was heavy with weariness. With a gesture of disgust, Apieron spurned the woman from him. Jamello produced a length of rope.

"Bide here, wench," commanded Henlee as a dog might growl a warning. "Do not let us find you elsewhere." Apieron stormed out, and Rudolph Mellor followed last yet not without many a sigh and backward glance at the unlooted apartment.

Apieron frowned. "This is not the way."

Jamello walked to the edge. "You are wrong." His face and shirt were suffused with the warm glow of amber.

Henlee moved to stand with him. "Boy's right." As he gestured the others forward, they could see a dreamy smile plastered the dwarf's begrimed face.

"Such treasure!" muttered Eirec.

"A world's worth," breathed Jamello.

Tallux smiled darkly. "I deem here is the wealth of more than one world."

"Wait!" Henlee braced Jamello with an outstretched arm. His hands were aquiver. "Contain yourself! For there lives an order in such a pile, runways and balconies, diamonds and soft sapphires, gem-crusted weapons and precious drinking horns …"

"You are becoming excited," said Tallux.

"Observe, elf." Henlee brandished a wisp of white hair pinched between two thick fingers. "Sprig of my uncle's beard, Ohm Runemaker."

"We should leave," murmured Isolde.

Henlee thundered words of old dwarvish. Cast into the receding cavern, they reverberated, losing themselves in golden shadow. Nothing stirred, yet in that vast space lived a quiet expectation. Muchly pleased, Henlee turned to them. "If you only know a little magic, it should be grand as this."

"Grand as what?" asked Isolde.

Far below, the great mound began to shift. An aureate arch reared itself, and bastions of ingot and coin of every valuable metal were revealed in orderly array, passages and rooms receded into the pile. Jamello stooped for a heavy broach that was fashioned as a leaping jaguar at his feet. Ruddy carnelian and yellow jasper winked at him. Jamello pushed against Henlee in preparation for his descent as he fiddled with the broach, affixing it to his blouse. "What was the good of your casting, Master Dwarf? Now we must explore an entire mansion. Better to sift a mound!"

Henlee sniffed. "The shapespell overlooks such trifles as your kitty. Each chamber here is enclosure for a singular and mighty item. Beyond yon arch, there are many rooms!" The dwarf rubbed his hands in excitement.

"Shall we enter?"

"Nay," said Apieron.

"We should leave," said Isolde.

Jamello fairly wheeled on her. "You said that before."

"How much can bear you hence, Rudolph Mellor?" The wood elf's emerald eyes seemed to war with the harsh glowing of the gold.

"More than you think," blustered thief and dwarf simultaneously.

"Stay!" commanded Apieron.

He eyed the image reflected on Leitus's mirror. Xephard angled it, gently rocking the blade to and fro so that all might see. The cavern, a full furlong wide and many deep, began to fold in upon itself, its immensity silently and inexorably compressing by half and again until at last resembling a golden egg. It drifted into the abyss like a beetle floating a dark stream, and after a final wink, was gone.

"I think I might cry." Jamello rubbed his eyes repeatedly. Henlee added nothing, but the dwarf gazed up as if beseeching the heavens. The ceiling collapsed.

Save Jamello and Henlee, the others had stepped away, already making for the main corridor. Agile as the hunting cat he bore, Jamello leapt aside, although a jagged piece of steel rent his cloak. Xephard, Eirec, and Apieron ran to where Henlee had stood. A heap of rubble overtopped a twenty-foot plate of iron, inches thick. From underneath came the muffled curses of a dwarf.

"Three … two … one!" called Xephard. Dust blew and lungs heaved as they hoisted the lid, slowly overtopping it into empty space.

Henlee crawled free. "What took you so long?" His ankle was twisted back on itself. "Missed a ceiling trap? Fine thief you are!" Beard abristle, the dwarf continued to remonstrate Jamello as Tallux realigned the joint with a pulling snap and wrapped it snugly with a winding.

"I think the impervious steel of the dwarves saved your life," Isolde looked up from the limb. "Both bones were broken. I've healed what I may, and yet my powers grow weak. You will need a crutch."

"Nonsense, Maul is stick enough."

"Shall I fetch you another blanket, Grandfather?" inquired Eirec sweetly.

"When I stand, I'll fetch my fist into that blowhole you call a mouth."

"Can you stand?"

"Oh?" sputtered Henlee, rising awkwardly to his feet. "And where were you when the hoarfrost froze the beards of I and one other, and the Sons of Scotti whetted their knives?"

Apieron lowered Henlee gently to the pave. "Rest, Uncle. So must we all, I deem it might be our last." Apieron turned to address them. His haggard face was seamed, his gray eyes those of a man a score years his senior. "Whatever our hardships have been, the greater trial awaits."

Xephard pointed. "Then it is good we stay for now. Look to the Rudolph Mellor—" Jamello lay wrapped in his blouse's remnants, sweating and shivering. His eyelids were shut, but they fluttered with his mumbling.

"And so Her malevolent presence afflicts us all." Xephard knelt to lay a cool hand upon Jamello's slick brow.

Jamello's dark eyes snapped open. "I dreamed … a woman, so beautiful, clad in scarlet."

Isolde scowled. "A false vision," scolded Xephard gently, "follow it not." He leaned to whisper soothing words to his young companion.

Henlee followed his lips and nodded appreciatively. "You cannot possibly hear what is said," said Isolde.

The dwarf's brown eyes gleamed in the small light of her spear. "He speaks of honor."

Isolde sat down heavily. Mask and heavy helm were laid aside as she tugged at a tangle in her hair. "How I hated that word when it took him from me." She looked to her gentle warrior, pure in the gloom. "But it is water to him I love."

Henlee pulled her fretting hand to rest in his calloused paw. "Aye, honor is the bread a true warrior needs." He smiled. "If I die today, 'twould be amongst men and women more rich in this than any I know."

When the last scraps of food and precious water were consumed, the remaining gear was tightened and shields hoisted. "Are you ready?" intoned Apieron. Six faces regarded him.

"For what?" whispered Jamello.

"To kill a god."

Chapter 25

Iz'd Yar

Shaxpur of Kör scowled. "Scout, what betides?"

Odikine, a steppesman hunter, hoped the demonoid could not smell the fear that crawled from his bowel up to his sweating face. He unloaded the body his steed had borne. "Only a Westron spy. I feathered him when he made to sneak our pickets."

"What of his kit?" demanded the officer.

The Kör lord loomed half again the height of the Mgesh, and twice as broad. Odikine wished he had something, even water, to wet a mouth gone suddenly dry. Odikine looked to his pony, and the agile little horse returned his glance. In three seconds, he could be on it and spurring away. Three seconds would be too slow.

He proffered a bundle wrapped in the blouse of the man he had slain. "Only weapons, and these." He opened the punctured garment to reveal a pouch of wheat grain, spoon and flint, a wooden box containing cloth and unguent, and a sketch painted onto fiber paper and folded in half.

Shaxpur dashed them to the ground and slapped the Mgesh,

who stood stoically. "Fool, these are nothing. Bring me a living captive before tomorrow's sun sets!"

"Greetings," said Iz'd Yar smoothly. He stooped to pick up the scattered items. One at a time, he eyed short bow and dagger and the other things. He finished with the likeness.

"Waste not your time on the scrap, my General," said Shaxpur. "Merely the dwelling and female chattel of the dead wretch."

Iz'd Yar placed a hand lightly upon his subordinate's shoulder while his lambent gaze fixed the scout. "Trooper, you are dismissed." The man bettered the three seconds of his fantasy. The clawed hand dug painfully into steel links. "Colonel, these tokens speak more of our foe than maps or weapons. This carrion had concerns for his miserable hovel and breeder with her puling brats."

More than fear, Shaxpur's face revealed deep puzzlement. "Any wise soldier cares for his possessions."

Iz'd Yar released his grip. "You have courage, Colonel. Now learn wisdom. Regard his chit, do you see the trees?"

Shaxpur focused on the strange lines of the human artist. He was able to discern a house, the female and pups, as well as a grassy expanse with blue lines depicting water. "My lord, I fail to see the trees of which you speak."

"Because there are none! Most of this cursed land has them, save the swamp meadows nigh Bestrand. See you this?" The depiction waved before Shaxpur's face. "It is papyrus, a water weed beat into pulp and dried into paper. Know you why?"

"Because there are no trees?" ventured Shaxpur.

"Thrice a fool," stated Iz'd Yar.

He spurned the body at their feet. "Here is no horse-knight, this man obviously traveled on foot half the breadth of this heathen kingdom, leaving the breeder for which he has affection to hie here and spy on me!"

Vodrab's evil laughter hissed behind them, the escort of the general had come.

Iz'd Yar stepped back to include all in his glance. "Young Candor has roused this land more swiftly than you idiots reckoned. This rotting meat was a man of duty, such make dangerous opponents."

Vodrab raised withered hands, making as if to push down the anger of his master. "We mobilize a force he could not equal in a hundred years."

Iz'd Yar drew a benighted dagger and pointed it at Vodrab's thin breast. "You, Makis, signal my marines at port in Sway. They are to harry the Ess." He kicked again the corpse. It folded with a wet crack. "Yon crowmeat was not starving. Our enemies are resupplied somehow. Burn, loot, and rape the Western coast. Many peoples live thereon, and I want these sons of slaves to fear for their homes more than they honor their boy-prince."

The half-demon's eyes blazed again upon Shaxpur and Vodrab. "Why are you still here?"

SWAYMEET

Shadows and light played in the council chamber of Swaymeet, royal palace of Ilycrium. The smoke-blackened faces of its stone-and-bronze kings glowered on the beings who shouted and gesticulated within the room. Ascapundi war leaders bellowed and drove bucket-sized fists onto the mahogany slab that served as table, sending cracks into its buckling length. Orc chiefs screeched and waved scimitars.

Sisteros, commandant of royal marines, had what he needed. The last drommond of the fleet would depart as soon as he boarded. "And none too soon," he murmured softly, surveying the gathering with distaste.

Well he remembered the long hours of darkness preceding his

final attack. Ghouls summoned by the black druid had stalked riverbed and harbor floor. Circumventing strongpoints, they had infiltrated the city like a plague, thereby breaking the spirit of Sway's defenders. Under X'fel's sky-smear of crimson, neither armsman or child or the feeble aged were spared undead thirst or the clutching claws of grave wights that stank of decay and sea slime. Yet, with the coming of day, they had been called away and not seen since. That was good, deemed Sisteros.

After the devastating losses inflicted by the harbor Sisters, Sisteros's crew had fired the dockside and subsequently much of the city. Then had come the waiting. How many weeks? His men were soldiers, not despoilers. Sisteros had no taste for the unsavory appetites of giants and goblins. Let Goz keep Sway! The city's back was broken; marines of the Dream Throne would off to seek more worthy opponents. Sisteros stood to depart.

"Where are you going, hairless ape?" shouted an orcish hetman, spittle on its lips.

"Apparently, nowhere," came Sisteros's even voice. His indigo-plumed helm nodded to the bivalve doors of ironclad oak. A statue of a fierce sea king, spear out-thrust, stood before the entrance where none had been before.

The goblin turned and shrieked louder than the others. The babble dwindled as a shaman advanced on the towering figure. He bore many totems, some of bone and some that squirmed as if alive. Mouthing an incantation, he touched the spear that threatened the room. It took him in the chest.

Giant Ascapundi swore and stared. Orcs gave back and scrabbled frantically for weapons. One statue stepped from its pedestal. Metal and stone flowed as a robed arm shot out to grasp an Ascapundi by the shoulder. Frozen by the irresistible strength of that grip, the giant had time for a single yell before an iron scepter cracked its brainpan. Flickering bronze censors were ripped down, plunging the room into near darkness lit only by a gray aperture high against the outer wall. Frantic shouts of outrage and bestial roars were intermixed with the sound of fearsome blows. Soon all was still.

Outside, in a silent corridor, Erasmus withdrew his brown hand from the chamber doors. Pulling low a coarse woolen hood such as a laborer might wear, he joined a second figure. Together, Brockhorst and he took their quiet way from the palace.

TIAMAT'S PALACE

Henlee pulled his beard. "I guess if a mountain were melted and dripped down a hole, it might look like this."

Eirec rapped the structure with his axe butt. "Not stone, wood."

"Nonsense. Not even the ironwood of the Malave is so hard." Henlee pointed. "And that one's master, King Dryas, sells it dear."

Tallux jerked his chin, emerald eyes alive in the gloom. "Look again."

The corridor the companions walked had buckled in ages past against a whorled buttress of the substance in question; the enormous diameter of which could be guessed by its slight curvature across their path. Where the floor of the tunnel was riven, the structure fell into yawning darkness, its bulk intricately twined and divided into countless offshoots that quested their own path or rejoined the main above and below.

"Are you saying it's a giant carrot?"

"I would rather not guess," whispered Tallux.

Jamello ran his hand along the slick surface. "What plant could live here?"

Eirec's eyes held a strange cast. "There is one."

Apieron's voice lifted up from below, urging them to follow.

The ranger already descended below the level of the floor. Xephard and Isolde already climbed after.

"No ropes," mumbled Henlee, "an' lame foot."

Tallux chuckled. "Jamello and I will search the easiest path."

Eirec's voice was like syrup, "Shall I bear Maul for you?"

"Bald-pated lout," muttered the dwarf as he limped to the hole and gingerly lowered himself down.

"Do not fall!" Apieron grasped Henlee's coif, hauling the dwarf to a stop.

Henlee rubbed his ankle beneath his high boot. "Just sliding a bit to ease my broken dog."

"How far does this go?" asked Jamello softly. "We've hugged this thing a half day by my guess, and no change," his words fell to a murmur, "not that we have any choice." He waved his bloused arm to the surrounding night. Far distant and gone with the blink of straining eyes, flickered tiny lights.

Eirec's response was solemn. "Yggdrasil goes to the end, to Nastrond, Shore of Fallen Corpses."

"Hsst!" All heads tracked Tallux's lambent gaze. Below them, approaching rapidly, was a colossus.

"Thing climbs like a spider," grunted Henlee, yet awe tinged his voice. Four arms aided barrel-thick legs in the ascent, four arms more bore titanic swords. Its skin was vermillion and crawled with yellow flame.

Tallux's command was soft and urgent. "Quick!" The wood elf severed seven sprigs from the root, more tendril than leaf. He placed one in each mouth.

"You too," urged Isolde. In a panic, she confronted Xephard who was reluctant to accept his portion. He fingered Leitus and eyed the flaming monster that loomed at their feet. Isolde grasped Xephard's jaw and forced the leaflet into his mouth. He disappeared.

The apparition approached, and its burning flickered into the frigid air with the stench of burning rock. Its great weight shook even the mighty structure the companions clung to. The ponderous head swiveled side to side, and the eyeless sockets were wells of night, yet resuming its rapid ascent, the monster faded above like a slow red flare.

"Climb," said Apieron, and they continued down. Hel's vibration returned, at first as a nigh imperceptible tremor in the twisting surface on which they walked and slid and clung, it grew and throbbed.

"Just what I need," gritted Henlee. His veins bulged and teeth ground with the efforts of his toil.

The cadence deepened, and Jamello imagined himself to be a crystal cup filled with water, the surface bouncing and fretting to the infernal tattoo. He licked cracked lips with a tongue that felt like a shriveled lizard, long dead in the sun. "Stop those blasted drums!"

"Silence, fool," shushed Isolde.

Shadows detached themselves from nighted crevices, unwinding from the middle airs. If one stared overlong, faces materialized into hulking forms, animate with malice.

"Do not meet their eyes." Against the light of Isolde's spear, no shade approached, yet their numbers grew until they swarmed like schooling fish, swimming and angling in cadence with the rhythm that quivered in the waste. Caught between its silent command and the antipathy of the spear, the creatures accelerated their movements.

"Damn things are making me dizzy." Henlee began to falter.

Grasping the dwarf's braided hair, Tallux followed with a steadying hand and quick, sure feet on the twisting descent.

Xephard nodded to Isolde and slid ahead with Apieron. Leitus caught the argent light of his cloak and reflected Isolde's spear globe. The light of the paladin's brand cut swaths in the swarming flock, dissolving shadows into nothingness.

Isolde kept the rear whilst Eirec warded her, glaring and swatting with his white-faced axe any shadow that lurched too near.

Fluttering scores of shades now assailed the party, as semi-materialized fingers plucked at beards and garments. When light of cloak and spear faltered behind twists in the way, talons clinked on armor or hooked in flesh. Apieron's ivory lance pierced the batwing that tugged Jamello from the bole, the javelin's crackling energy scorching the shade to a dry husk. Still the party descended, and the ranger of Windhover led the fighting climb.

At length, a gray light beckoned. With no apparent source, a luminescence bleached of color lit the zone they pierced, and as the companions found this new level, shadows fled for the cold blackness above. The companions stepped from the falling way, for it had grown thinner with many branchings, some of which pierced the very stone at their feet. Jamello leapt eagerly from the root, followed carefully by Henlee, who was aided by Tallux. Despite his burns, Rudolph Mellor sighed with relief from the long cold and attempted his old rakish smile.

Something tapered and eel-like thrust itself toward Apieron. He kicked it away.

Xephard spoke at his side, "We are close."

The warming air became thick and wet. Amorphous shapes, tattered and incarnadine, drifted as Her rhythm deepened.

Henlee batted the air before him. "Damn stuff's like honey."

Save for Xephard and the environ of Isolde's spear, the others grew encumbered. Each of Jamello's footfalls slowed before touching ground, as if the lithe thief trod on liquid. He adopted a gliding, half-swimming gait.

Tallux held up his hand. "A sound, like water rushing!"

"Not water," said Apieron. "Blood."

Jamello stopped and stood quivering. "What is this place?"

Isolde's response caught in her throat, finally she croaked, "A womb."

The flags at their feet erupted. A crested head was joined by two others as the bulk of a tri-part beast shook free. The charnel reek of death flowed from it as three skulls searched the wastes and roared, its breath blowing foul skuthers of bloody ice. A six-eyed gaze lit on them, whilst its fury seared their minds.

"Foul get!" Xephard fronted the beast as its trailing bulk heaved onto the slag. "Hie back to thy bitch, dam, lest we slay thee."

"If that's a whelp," gasped Eirec, "where be its father?"

When the monstrosity spoke, its voice issued simultaneously from three mouths and was terrible to hear. "Why dost thou not speak, Star Child?"

As the creature moved, pieces of it shifted into nothingness and rippled back into view, like ink thrown onto glass.

Apieron drew up. "You have not yet been born."

It gurgled, "We await consummation. Thou and thy dark other grow close, Herald. Thus we are formed." The beast lurched forward. "Why slew you my sire? Thou, and this fated one?"

The heads snapped down, and a triple blast of reeking sputum struck the paladin. His white cloak flared, and a harmless frost fell onto the ground.

"Futile sin!" spoke Xephard. "Your end was writ ere your conception." Wisdom's perfect warrior strode to the attack.

Henlee, Eirec, and Jamello sprang, then stumbled. Even Tallux's movements were hampered in the pulsing, gelid air.

Isolde jerked her gaze to Apieron, and blanched when she beheld the foreboding on his face—a flicker of pity in his gray eyes—as he tracked Xephard. Then he surged, quicker than the others to the aid of their friend. The jaws again gaped wide and a jetting arch of intolerable cold crystallized the miasma as it struck elf, dwarf, and man into a tumbled pile of frozen limbs over ice-slick stone.

Encumbered and lame, Henlee heaved Maul two-handed at the head that overtopped Apieron. Eirec's hurlbat followed. The dragon's sail ducked, only to meet the cleaving momentum of a white javelin alive with fell purpose. The head split asunder, and its contents fluttered like wounded bats.

Xephard battled two foes. One swipe of Leitus sheared a pointed horn, his back sweep splintering a canine as long as his forearm. An arrow from Farstriker cut a sluggish path to rebound harmlessly from a crested brow. Panic nerved Apieron's limbs, and he hurled his ebon javelin with all his strength and skill. Flying true, it cracked into the dragon's tri-part pectoral at its nexus. Black lightnings vied in the scaled breast, yet the beast was not slowed. Apieron cursed, for his dart had not penetrated.

Xephard drove Leitus through the jowls of one plunging maw. Shearing through hide and teeth, the sword caught up crossways, either end out of the mouth. A malicious grin found its visage as the skull-like head was destroyed. Too late, the deception was revealed. Darting in whilst Leitus's stroke was yet in play, the last head gathered up the paladin and shook him like a hound with a rabbit.

A woman's wailing floated eerily as Xephard fell broken to the pave. His hand felt blindly for a weapon as the beast locked its crucible eyes on his own. "No other can aid thee!" It lunged, gurgling in triumph, "Consuming thee, I am *now*!"

Xephard grasped the sheared horn of the dragon. As the implacable jaws closed, he drove it into a smoldering eye. Apieron fell to the ground beside Xephard, and together they beheld the dragon. It fell upward, pulling apart as it rotated and dissolved into the ruddy gloom of the cavern's top. "My heart is glad. Ever thus will our enemies be vanquished." Xephard's breaths labored; a pink froth flecked his lips.

"Do not speak of a time without you, brother. Directly the cleric you love comes, an' her leechcraft make you whole." Xephard softly patted Apieron's iron-gauntleted wrist as he would a fragile bird, then Isolde was there. Apieron drew aside and sought the others.

"You seek to bear my pain for me, lady?"

"I do," she whispered, hair and tears falling down.

"Nay, that can never be." Xephard's face paled, yet he smiled. "When I die, Priestess, and go to the arms of the goddess … will you in some future time search me out?" When his weak cough ceased, Xephard continued, "Can it be so that two shades clasp one the other as have we in this world?" Isolde gripped him fiercely, and pressed her lips to his. Like a sound suddenly still, he died.

Henlee drew Jamello to his feet and strode haltingly to place his heavy hand on Apieron's shoulder. "What happened?"

"Darkness falls." With no further words, Apieron stooped and gathered Isolde from Xephard's body. She moved woodenly, her face a mask of anguish.

With solemn steps, Eirec and Henlee, Tallux and Jamello cleansed Xephard as best they could. The shining clarion was placed upon his breast under folded arms, his cloak shrouded around him.

Isolde knelt before Leitus. The famous brand bore the

luminescence of the paladin's body. She turned to Apieron. "You must bear this."

Apieron's gray eyes caught fire, dancing with the rhythm of the chamber as he took the blade. "Aye, a final time will I wield thee, White Lady, then nevermore."

"It is too wet to make a pyre," muttered Tallux, "and we have no fuel."

"If he stays, we stay," growled Henlee.

"Then we must bear him," answered Tallux, "and gladly."

Eirec's voice was touched with awe, "I too am honored to be the bearer of a hero. The slayer of Nidhogg, Corpse Tearer."

Isolde wheeled, panic writ on her features. "Where is he?" Cloak and body had faded.

"Back to his goddess, lass." Henlee steeled his face. "She claims her own. Now hurry if you please! This be no place to tarry."

Long they walked, but how far no one could say. Isolde clung stumbling to the fur of Eirec's cape, carried blindly to where she cared not whither. The bitter cold had returned with the advent of the unborn dragon, and it burned as fierce as the fires above. They halted, rooted in morbid awe.

"How … came they here?" stammered Jamello.

Tallux likewise stood aghast as Eirec fretted and cursed without pause. Rows of mortal souls, waxened and imprisoned, lined a mausoleum like the pupae of bees. King and priest, cavalier and spaedam, all good men and women worked grimaced mouths and bulging eyes in silent screams for ingots of iron had been riven into each gorge.

"The elf mage is no more, Priestess," choked Henlee. "Do something."

Isolde regarded the dwarf's impassioned face. Her eyes lanced blue in the dark, revealing the true forms of the horrors about them. "I know not if I can …" The soul minds in their multitudes beat upon her. Torment. Futility. The fettered spirits, dependent from a spiked and twining lattice, bobbed obscenely in cadence with the pervading rhythm.

The throbbing struck Apieron's chest with soft heavy blows as if forcing the rampart of his breast to that which lay within. Jamello crouched like an animal and darted looks between dimly seen walls and buttresses of slag stone, as if afraid they might yield to the vibration and collapse.

Gathering shadow, a fiend slunk toward Isolde's back—a gibbering thing. Apieron slew it. At his glance, the companions took station in a ring around their cleric. "Rouse thyself, sister."

Isolde drew herself up. "This was Xephard's."

Apieron poured from the flask she proffered, and with the last dash of water they possessed, Isolde cleansed her face and trembling hands, its runoff freezing on her leggings. She grasped tight her spear and summoned an image: the white grotto of vestal maidens. Generations of world-wise women, pure in their devotion to the goddess, filled Isolde's bosom with their shout and song. Isolde's eyes flashed, and she pronounced a word.

The captives screamed, iron falling from their throats. Jamello fell stricken to his knees. Tallux covered his ears and wailed as Eirec and Henlee whipped their heads wildly. Apieron stood, regarding Isolde with eyes like a gray and restless sea. She wept, but from her spear hand, a pale cleansing fire leapt body to body, consuming all in funerary rite. There was no stench and no remains. Silence welled up.

Isolde collapsed onto Apieron, whose strange eyes sought the shadows beyond the Hall of Riven Souls.

Chapter 26

Dungeon of the Hel Queen

There was a narrow introitus, cast in shadow where the stone had frozen in its flowing. A liquid of some sort pooled there, set hard as granite by the frigid wind that soughed from the opening, and the cadence slapped against the companions' brows and breasts.

From the lead, Henlee lurched. "Whew … what a stench! Thank the bearded fathers that my nose is frostbit."

The channel wrapped close as on stiff legs barbarian and dwarf, half-elf and thief, woman and ranger strained forward until the walls fell away to an unknown distance. Isolde's spear pushed a sphere of radiance into the shadow—small and blue, a bitter diamond on a sable cloth.

Then came Her greater light. It hulked amidst clouds of chromatic spray—an Ungod, knowing no glory, no power save Its own.

Its hate shimmered in visible halos while the remorseless heart thundered, demanding obeisance. Behind Her, a well-forge churned like a machine, the elements of a world blended in its depths, as in the upper spaces far above the gaping companions, strange shapes glided to the unholy dance.

«Are you gods to stand thus before me?»

Apieron remembered Sarc, whose tawny hair had blown on the Hel wind as they stood on storm-swept Pankaspe, and recollected the words of the valiant swamp elf. "*There is no beauty here.*" Apieron saw the apparition, and knew Sarc had been wrong, for Her darkling beauty was beyond anything he had ever imagined, sinuously strong, ancient and ever-young. Her seven heads, crowned with many horns, bore galaxy eyes that kenned wisdom beyond his mortal world.

"The eyes! Look at Her eyes," gasped Tallux. "She ... *It* is glad we have come."

"Nay," corrected Isolde, her voiced cowed to a whisper, "that *he*, Her second herald, has finally come." A solitary wind whipped Apieron's hair and began to tug the little badge of homespun from the clasp on his chest.

Jamello beheld a raven-tressed beauty clothed in red. Crimson were her lips. Her dragon eyes smiled and beckoned with living grace—a very goddess. He went to Her.

"Stay!" thundered Apieron, but it was too late. Jamello ran to the embrace, and she cupped heavy breasts in welcome. Her scaled arms beckoned wide, whilst with rolling words, She pronounced his doom.

An ebon javelin struck the woman's chest. Half its length protruded quivering. She did not fall. A horned head drew back, the dart deep in its neck. Jamello fell as the crowned head snapped down. A dwarven shield of black adamant, bearing a single scratch, settled with a clang over the thief, who pulled it close as the Beast's scything fangs failed to find purchase. The head reared and, joined by six others, writhed chaotically while roaring litanies of destruction.

The companions froze, hearts straining fitfully. Isolde tried to scream and could not, and Jamello groveled. Yet brazen and pervading, an olifant of dwarves blared its challenge. Jamello rose and clawed for his arbalest. Tallux sprang to Apieron's side, although when he beheld Apieron's expression, the wood elf's hand paused on the helve of Strumfyr. The others, following his glance, gave back before the ranger of Windhover. His face had grown so terrible that Isolde held up her hands in placation and warding. Unheedful of his friends' distress, Apieron advanced on the Demoness.

The Beast, Mother of Dragons, affixed Apieron with Her baleful glare. Tallux's great bow began to sing. Eirec gave vent to the war cry of his people and charged, but with the weight of a toppling tree, Her lashing tail struck him down and his axe clattered aside. Henlee leapt in support, bringing Maul from an overhand sweep that ended in a crunch, twisting and cracking the spine of one mighty pinion.

Pieces of the vault were riven as Tiamat screamed in affronted rage. She pinned the dwarf with a scaled claw and bore down to crush him like a shelled insect in his armor. That was when the spear of ivory, hurled by Apieron the Javeliner, found Her eye.

She howled with all the fury of eternal Hel, and whipped Her long neck round to extract the bitter dart as its magic played about Her skull, and ichor from the riven orb bubbled.

Three heads gathered and breathed. Held high to port, Apieron's heater-shield flared its warding against the violence of Her blasts—frozen fire, burning cold, and the vacuum of the abyss. The speakers stave, planted in green and sky and secreted within the steel, endured. A sweep of the opposing wing cast Apieron through the air to strike a buttress, and the offending shield spun away. The blow snapped his arm at the shoulder where weakness remained, a gift from Malesh.

Laughing Her triumph, the horned heads rushed in like

sharp-muzzled wolves, each straining to grasp their share of a trapped fawn.

Isolde had been paralyzed by the impact of the Dark She, albeit now, at the very last, she beheld the Being who slew her love and reaved her land, and in her heart knew that Cynthia, Perpetua of the Temple and mother of her rearing, was also dead. Spear raised, Isolde glowed with an argent nimbus that magnified her stature. Her casting smote like a storm come to bide in the deepest recess of the earth.

In all Its bulk, the Beast rocked back and settled. It revealed Its saber teeth and chortled, «Spent is thy spell, little witch. Here is mine.»

Raising Its claw from the dwarf, She lurched forward to vomit a void that overtook Isolde and drove her to her knees in position of supplication. Tiamat's deriding laughter raked down her spine. «Now you behold your true god!»

Lamplit eyes blazed forth. Isolde saw therein the insanity and disease of the world entire. She screamed, and her heart thudded to a stop. "Mother, why have you abandoned me?"

The Beast wheeled again to Henlee who brought Maul down on Its foot, smashing flat one taloned toe. Jaws champed after the dwarf, seeking to rend him where he crouched, too lame to flee. With his good arm Apieron jabbed It away with Isolde's spear, but two mouths snatched and flung it away. Seven heads joined their gaze on Apieron, and the eyes of nightmare drew him forward.

Something in him twisted. Apieron lunged aside and drove Leitus under one winged scapula. The protruding sword blazed with the light of an avenging sun. It exploded.

The She recoiled and scampered aside, then paused as if

perplexed, but the dark animus returned to Her eyes, and She stalked again. Weaponless, Apieron stood without hope. Bitterly he recalled the hurts done him, as in Her malevolent shadow, he relived the destruction of friends and home, the diminished voice of his twin gods, and Melónie. First and last, his wife touched a place in him that as a man he could never define yet was inspiration for every worthy act he had ever lived. Grimed by the blood and gore of friend and enemy, battered and harried over countless miles by fell design and self-loathing, Apieron woke.

Touching the little badge of cloth on his breast, Apieron began to sing. It was a sound never before uttered there. He sang the true honor of friendship, the unabashed love children give, and the untainted spirit of Melónie, her invisible devotion stronger than the thrones of gods.

The Demoness opened wide her central maw to engulf him, and six brows, crowned with tall horns, lowered to witness the consummation. Apieron saw something deep in the Beast uncoil. It felt like that within him, twisting to escape. The jaws gaped. Apieron fell back as his body immolated with pain, and a diaphanous essence fled him into the looming gorge. The She thrashed back, Her jaws yawning impossibly wide. They erupted from within.

A spherical being of radiant energy hovered above dark goddess and faltering man, then surged upward through the roof, leaving a tunnel of burning stone in its wake. The Beast fled and plunged into the well grist. Excepting the companions, the cavern lay empty.

Rudolph Mellor hopped into view tearing madly at the jaguar broach on his blouse. The thing had grown animate and sunk its small but steely claws into his skin. Cursing as only a wharf thief of Bestrand could, he threw it down and stamped it into shining pieces.

Apieron raised Isolde with his broken arm, and worked it loosely.

"I heard it snap," she said and bowed her head when he returned her spear.

"Healed by the star surge, by my guess." Apieron looked to a puddle of orange-hot stone that dripped from a wide aperture in the ceiling. "I wish him well."

"And he reveals the way," said Tallux.

Henlee looked up from where he tended his ankle. "Good, but listen, it grows dark again, and I do not wish to grope and stumble from this hole."

A tremor rocked their feet, then settled. "Quick Jamello! Up the wall and drop a rope." Apieron caught up the dwarf and prepared him for the hoist.

"It is quite cool," called Jamello as the last of the light failed. "You beautiful little star!" The thief's elated voice floated down to them. "The way is not too steep."

A violent shudder shook the cavern, and the swirling well moaned as bits of multicolored slag popped from its surface, and from its depths gathered a stone-tearing shriek that grew in intensity. The seeds of riven worlds plumed from the well, but the companions spared no glance. Minutes of frantic hoisting on a spliced and frayed rope gathered them into the borehole. Using hands to pull, they staggered up its angled length.

Jamello led as Apieron shepherded them from behind. His last backward glance found the well fountaining its strange elements into the vault, destroying the space it had reigned for millennia.

"Haste!"

On and up, straight as a mason's rule, they ascended the

tunnel. Three times, it traversed sections of the great root, cut clean and smooth as the stone had been. In the center of the second, a fluid dripped sluggishly top to bottom. Henlee pursed his mouth against the feathered ends of the wood, then turned and smacked his lips. "A little burnt, like dwarven molasses." So overwrought by thirst were they that each consumed what they could of the thick sap.

Isolde pulled back and wiped her mouth, for even she drank heavily to assuage the torture of her parched throat and mouth. A vibratory groan echoed down the length of the structure. "At least that's not the Black She's blasphemous heartbeat."

Tallux's emerald eyes searched all aspects of the bole in which they stood. He nodded to Eirec, who spoke. "Mayhap this is worse. Outside and above, a storm rages, even Yggdrasil trembles."

Henlee's voice was flat as it seemed finally his hope fled. "And we walk to meet it."

"Out! Up!" Apieron pushed them on as fast as their battered limbs could bear them.

Hand flat in gesture of warning, Tallux spoke, "Do not touch the water. It is foul." The temperature had warmed somewhat. A brown trickling flow from somewhere ahead found the middle of the tunnel. They straddled it as best they could.

"Hel's sewer pipe!" sputtered the dwarf. His lame foot dragged in the muck as he caught up the others who stood below a lip where their way coursed through a greater passage and the source of the effluent. It stank.

Eirec swung his axe blade flat against the bare tunnel. It drummed loud enough to rattle teeth. "A gnat." He frowned at the others' startled expressions. "Big as a sparrow." With apprehension, he angled the axe blade as if expecting some insect horror to burst forth. It was smeared with blood. "See?"

Henlee shook his head. "Churl, kill a bug with an axe."

Jamello pulled himself into the upper corridor and called down, "It's a big one, and to find the star's cutting again, another climb and rope trick. A light, Priestess!"

Like a pack of starving lions, they rushed, leaping above the slime, save no cat of the world was ever so unkempt. Matted fur and scabrous skin gleamed in the light of Isolde's spear. White madness lit their eyes, and their coughs were choked with disease.

Tallux whipped two arrows into the darkness. Eirec and Henlee splashed forward, axe and glaive dashing two of the seven pony-sized bodies into the muck, braincases shattered. Others leapt agilely over their stricken mates. Tallux shouted, the last of his arrows was expended as two more forms hurtled to splashing ruin.

"I'm out!" cried the wood elf. Apieron tossed him Sarc's living quiver and dashed ahead, unslinging his javelins.

Fronting the ranger's charge, three of the cats back-crouched but did not spring, their tails lashing fiercely as they screamed challenge. A shadow detached itself from the wall and became a man. Unearthly gems gleamed on his molded cuirass.

Three skeletal humans crept before him; they bore the accouterments of sorcerers on rotting garments, and staves were clutched in blackened claws. Around their shriveled necks floated a serpentine mist, an ethereal chain of gold to a ring on the man's finger.

"Leaving so soon?" asked Malesh.

The Hel knight was obscured as the fetid water under the

companion's feet was sucked into a towering wave that fell and kept falling upon them. Apieron's brazen yell echoed in the tube, and with a sprinter's speed, he dashed to the side, catching only the fringe of the cascade as he bore down on Adestes Malgrim. Tallux followed. In a tumbling rush, the remaining cats bowled into them.

Behind the churning water, Isolde heard the moan of the lich mages and Adestes' mocking laughter. Her mouth and eyes were filled with slime with each attempt at casting. She screamed and began to tear at the barrier with her spear. Like Northman and dwarf, her blows were futile as the parted water instantly reformed itself.

Jamello found a shallow niche where uneven stone deflected a portion of the cascade where wall met water, and he wiggled through. A shriveled face locked eyeless sockets upon him, pinpoints of crimson mocking him from their depths. Then he was pinned aloft, limbs splayed helplessly against the ceiling.

"Help me through the water!"

"What?" sputtered Eirec.

"You heard me. Punch me through that cesspool!"

Grunting with the effort, Eirec gathered Henlee, for the dwarf weighed nearly as much as he, and heaved Henlee into the barrier, pushing the soles of dwarven boots at the very end.

Henlee dashed reeking liquid from his eyes and was buffeted back off his feet by a whirling battle in which Tallux parried with his sword three biting, slashing cats, each as large as a bear and quick as the elf.

Face up from a pool, Henlee followed the upward gaze of a lich, its face a mask of grinning death. There he discovered Jamello, who emitted strangled cries as he was progressively crushed into the corridor's roof. Finding his target, Henlee hefted Maul and began his charge.

The spirit leash tightened and Malesh bellowed his commands, "Come, Asuaps—and you, Salthok. Slay me this man!" A nest of rubbery limbs burst from the floor at Apieron's feet. Like frantic cilia, they beat against him and seared his skin as they entwined his leg armor.

From the depths of the bore whence the party had come, the deep rumble of settling rock preceded a pressure wave and swirling grit that burst into the corridor. The exit hole collapsed in a downward spray of stone. Rippling unsteadily, the water wall fell into a low wave against Isolde and Eirec to drain as they waded forward.

The undead necromancer who had been folding Jamello into the jagged ceiling glanced to them and the charging dwarf. Triumph lit the mask of its face, there was time yet for another death.

A small item fell from the thief's mouth and fell slowly as if in liquid. A dozen feet from the ground, it burst. In its place, a yellow butterfly fluttered a dizzy circle. For an instant, the wight stared, then Maul burst its head into splintered bone and ash. Jamello fell face-first into the feculent chyle.

"Ahh, the dragon's hair." Adestes addressed the twain drow before him. "I had not thought you so potent, my pretties."

Apieron's javelin licked forth, but the illusive, rubbery appendages deflected his blows and ripped the darts from his grasp.

"Now, finish him!"

Held immobile, Apieron beheld a crimson storm birthed in the recesses of the liches' sockets, but the humble scrap of clothwork on Apieron's breast, Melónie's gifting, took on its colors of cream and blue and earthy brown as if under an untainted sun. He pushed free of the tentacles. Empty-handed, he approached Adestes while the three gravedrow shrank from the light of Melónie's weave.

The scarlet cloak flared as Adestes' scrollsword was drawn. "As it should be," said he, summoning fire to the dark metal of his brand.

"Not this, at the last!" cried Isolde.

There came a second burst of collapsing rock, and a great portion of the tunnel's roof and side fell into nothing. A wave of light and heat struck them. "I don't believe it," gasped Henlee.

A spade-headed beast thrust its long neck amongst them. From its frill, stone masonry cascaded as if water off a turtle. Its rider was a golden elf, and his aura filled the corridor. The beak snapped and dashed a sewer lion into ruin. Eirec's iron-hafted axe severed the spine of a second, while a lightning thrust of an elvin sword found the heart of its mate. Two liches cowered from the golden radiance that proclaimed Galor Galdarion. Isolde's spear flared with joy as it bivalved the stricken wights.

"Stay, Tallux!" commanded Galor. "None of you can catch him."

"About time you returned," sputtered Jamello. Henlee hoisted him from a puddle. The thief swayed, "I've used my last trick."

Eirec touched the beast's cobbled hide, then jerked back his hand, wary of its beak. It ignored him. "Yes, the same wyrm as by the dark stream," snapped Galor. "Mount up; this place collapses anon!"

"What of Apieron?" Isolde reluctantly extended her arm to Galor, whose surprisingly strong grip swung her behind him.

He smiled like dawnglow. "This beast swims in stone."

Adestes ran lightly down the corridor. Killers descended from the lands of light!

More terrifying, in that they seemed to lack any concern for self-preservation, their vengeance halting at nothing to slay him, and by the sounds of it, would bring this plane into ruin about them to boot. He, for one, would not be present for that eventuality.

"Tiamat be damned!" Adestes chuckled at the irony as he sped down a jet-glass tunnel. Random apertures in walls, ceiling, and floors admitted the glow of the Hel burn, and brighter flashes of demon fire where the fighting had been.

Adestes ran with easy grace, navigating the dangerous windows, some mere inches, and some dozens of feet across. He sailed over the larger ones, scarlet cloak streaming, and heeding not the scalding winds that emanated from without. Fast as he moved, his mind wandered quicker yet, and bethought himself of the invaders and the clean radiance they seemed to carry. Perhaps he had lurked too long in this gloom, mayhap it were best he return to the realms above, but first, he had errands.

The Ghaddur blocked the corridor where it narrowed. Its hulking form cast an enormous shadow to the fore. At its back was a fiery chasm. Its bulging belly and muscled chest filled a third of the passage. Adestes doubted not that its razor-clawed pinions and the black edged all-bard it bore could reach easily across the remainder.

The heavily jowled and fanged mouth opened. Although its speech was so low and thick as to seem a mere rumble, Malesh had little trouble discerning the words within. "Overlong have I awaited this moment, spawn of slaves."

Adestes' lips put name to the creature. "Malvoisen!" Malesh's long blade was drawn in a blurred flash, and in his left, he produced the golden dagger as he slowed to a crouch some ten paces from the mighty devil. Despite his hurry, it would not do to underestimate the brother of Bolechim. The Ghaddur had chosen its ambush well, for the yawning pit eliminated a flanking dodge, and the play of light in his eyes made it difficult to discern the beast's exact movements. To retreat was impossible, for there followed Apieron Farsinger.

"Hairless ape," frothed the giant, lightly testing its fifteen-foot glaive as if it were a mere hand wand. "Fall now to your knees, and pray that I be merciful to thy shriven soul."

"Are you wroth with me, Lord of Pigs, that I butchered thy sibling? P'raps he was more to you than I thought?" Adestes' face assumed a lascivious leer.

With a roar of outrage, the behemoth charged. Adestes crouched lower, hoping for a leg- or groin-strike under his opponent's overtopping rush, yet Malvoisen was a savvy fighter, and its rush was clever, as a thick left pinion swept round to bounce Adestes sideways into the path of the descending pole arm. He rolled with the blow, not pausing to counter with his longsword as the demon no doubt intended. He sprang up from the tumble inside the chomping arm and kicked the fat, snapping maw. The Ghaddur moved to gather him in, yet when it tried to drop the all-bard, its meaty hand was pinioned to the haft by the golden dagger, and the bite was deep.

Adestes continued his roll over the outside of Malvoisen's limb and onto his feet, then bounded back, parrying wildly as the Ghaddur bull rushed to stomp with its feet and batted its deadly wing tips.

Bellowing in frustration, Malvoisen yanked the poniard free of its hand and buried it with a screech into the stone of the corridor, until only the hilts showed. No doubt it meant to snap the dagger, thus denying its enemy a weapon. Adestes was pleased, apparently the roundrel Blodig was not made to yield to even the giant strength of a lord of Ghaddur.

Malesh's taunting laugh was curtailed by an underarm toss of the all-bard, expertly thrown at four-feet height, wicked edges whirling around its long axis. The glaive crashed into his torso and rended his armor as the man was hurled back into the shadows with a broken cry. His dark sword went cartwheeling out of sight. Malvoisen screamed in ecstasy and leapt to strip the last vestiges of life from this impudent worm.

Malvoisen caught up to his pole arm, which lay benignly on the rock. Of the man, there was no sign. Malvoisen spun suddenly, receiving a sweeping cut from the dark sword across the throat. His hands flew up as a back blow opened the distended belly. The Ghaddur sank to its knees with a bellow of disbelief as its black, snakelike intestines boiled onto the steaming pave. Undamaged, Malesh stood over the strickened devil of the Pit. Hoisting the voulge, he drove it into the coiled pile of writhing viscera.

"Why, Malvoisen, you *are* much like your brother."

The Ghaddur's mangled throat produced only animal sounds, yet the hate-filled eyes never left Malesh as the man turned to go. He tested the priceless dagger and sighed. It was buried uselessly in the tunnel rock.

"Pig demon!" spat Malesh as he floated over the fiery cleft. He would indeed be glad to quit this place. First though, his remaining errand: the woman he had secreted and would salvage. Touching down, Adestes Malgrim resumed his run and disappeared into the tunnel.

Apieron burst the door of iron. He bore both javelins in his right hand, shield high on his left. Running into the dark apartment, he found a length of severed rope atop a silken couch. His rising scream filled the room. "He was here!"

And to Apieron's maddened ears, the space echoed its mockery.

Outside, a storm raged. Cliffs toppled beneath the wyrm's feet, yet by the power of the Eldar elf, the companions would glide to the next buttress or passageway as, around them, Galor spun an expanding sphere of calm that warred against the roiling chaos like the meeting of two mighty rivers, a battle of flying foam and churning waves as each tries to win dominion over the other, brown versus green. With its beak, the wyrm crushed a dome of basalt and halted. There Apieron stood amidst the wreckage he had made in a once-sumptuous dwelling, and as if he did not see them, he turned to leave.

"Apieron!" screamed Isolde. "We must go … this plane collapses!"

"Malesh has fled," addressed Galor to Apieron, "although I believe you will meet again."

The wyrm surged through walls of rock and burst into the Hel sky. The companions saw battalions of flying demons scattered pell-mell, smitten by crackling lightnings and waves of dissolution. Isolde pointed, where across a collapsing atmosphere, a silver streak hung in the air. "The path of the comet!" With a cry to their steed, Galor propelled them on its line, while below, entire mountains and lawless seas swirled into ruin.

"The ash plain, and Duskbridge!" called Jamello.

Indeed, echelons of marching figures stretched for many miles, and Hel's spinning light glinted off armor and weapons and proud banners. Even chariots there were, pulled by flaming steeds. The terminus of their march was beyond vision in the environ of the Gate.

"The Army of Brass," gasped Tallux. "Woe to mortal lands."

The storm encroached upon the host of Hel's rearward ranks, catching them up and pulverizing ground and air, but the vision was lost to the companions who beheld that their silver way ended in an eye of blackness. Lights wheeled as they raced into its void.

THE WYRNDE

Sunrise found the Wyrnde. Rising in humid airs, its pallor lifted the slate of retreating night. Mists uncoiled from moss and fern as coverlet for toes of forest denizens. Cypress and willow, birch and sycamore, albeit none as great as a furrow-barked redwood, four hundred feet of mast-pole majesty, its lowest limbs rising above its tallest neighbors, and its bristled top was stirred by winds unknown to the marsh below. From the highest boughs, lifted a mighty head. Feathery feelers, broad and sensitive, twitched to messages wrapped in currents of air. Sights and sounds it perceived, never dreamt by aught that walked on two legs or four.

Wings lifted and pinions strained. One, two beats, a third, and it was aloft! Its brethren sang to it and rose to follow on the long-streaming breeze. Finding sun-warmed thermals, they turned north, from whence came the taste of war.

Chapter 27

Bishop's Gate

Dawn came pink and fair, and a lay of frost glistened on trees and grasses. The horizon sharpened, and low mountains appeared in the north as the sun crested the east rim. Night's watch paled to blue, and clouds smoked in the rays of sun's rising. Night birds fell silent and retired as others stirred and began to sing. In the growing light, the landscape gained depth, distant hilltops leapt backward, and Apieron could see a streamer of ground fog folded into a depression beyond miles of rolling grass and sparse trees.

Galor spoke, "Yonder lays the river Sval, whose cool waters we must cross before afternoon wanes."

Apieron turned in astonishment. "You carried us far, Magnus. Sval winds far north of the Gorganj."

Galor gave a slight bow. "Soon I'll leave you." His luminous glance surveyed two men and a woman, woods elf and dwarf as they rose from a fireless camp. In the night, they had cast themselves down, overwhelmed by burn, wound, and hunger, and the terrible grinding fatigue of body and spirit.

"Beyond Sval is a traveler's haven known to men as Bishop's Gate. Goodly monks have dwelt there long, even by the counting of my people. Their lord is said to be the King's vicar, a high priest of Ilycrium east and south."

"I have heard of Bishop's Gate," said Apieron.

"Was not Turpin the Accursed such a man?" growled Henlee. "What would we there?"

Jamello made a gesture of warding. "Do not speak his name! 'Tis ill luck."

"Never in life did I meet the man." Eirec tugged the remnants of his moustache. "But I have seen his shade."

"Healing, rest, provisions," said Isolde. "The good abbot of Bishop's Gate will not deny a sister prelate."

Henlee was stubborn. "Apieron can gather for us, and the woods elf hunt what we need. Even my foot is in fettle, must 'ave been that root sap."

"I think we should go there," added Jamello. Nobody heeded him.

Isolde sighed. "There is the beer." She eyed Henlee and Eirec. "I said it, the monk's guard a recipe six centuries old." And so they walked.

Henlee snuffed the air. "Feels like late winter."

"It is," said Galor.

"A week in the Pit," mused Eirec, "a season of the world."

Henlee chewed a thistle heart, unmindful of its sharp spines. Lavender petals adorned his front as he limped. Earlier that morn, they had chanced upon a hot spring where things yet grew and bloomed. "A warm kitchen in winter," Isolde called it. Henlee had gathered thistles.

For a time, Apieron had stared into vapors that billowed from the water. Where the mist caressed border stones, rimes of red and yellow molds glimmered softly, but no voice sang to him, and when he left, Apieron did not name the waters friend.

"Time enough in that black hole, Eirec Alkeim," said Henlee. "So I wonder of the boy-prince, and dwarves, and also of Darla Brownhair." The dwarf glanced slyly to Galor. "I also wonder, if the hill-humper and the popinjay stumbled upon a good idea." Eirec scowled, but the dwarf ignored him. "Perhaps we might winkle a bit forward. I am fine, of course, for walking, but these others—"

Jamello looked hopeful. "Cut him a stick, Apieron," replied Galor testily. "Hobble faster, Sir Dwarf, that you might sooner know the answer to your many meanderings."

Apieron led them. He heard the honking call of high-flying geese borne aloft on frigid currents, their living wedge piercing the sky, vibrant with innate purpose, and from a far distance, an elk brayed its full-throated challenge.

Tallux was nigh and shared a look with him. The elf's moss-bright eyes gleamed something. *What was it?* Apieron walked, beyond travail and fire, he was alive. Why? He touched the patternwork scrap on his breast. Why should he doubt? Was it Xephard? Melónie? *I remember thee, lady of Windhover. Mother of quick-witted Setie, and handsome Ilacus, and the infant child Sujita—my Jilly. And thou Xephard Bright Helm, Son of Morning, thee too I did love.*

Behind him, Apieron knew was Galor, whose feet seemed ever to tread on air. Stalwart Henlee kept pace as best he could while Eirec fingered the edge of his mighty axe and chuckled darkly, lost in memories. Isolde leaned on Jamello's arm, whose face was grave and noble. One by one, Apieron met their eyes and nodded. There was much to ponder.

They came to Bishop's Gate.

There was a stone bridge and a waterwheel, and a small skiff was tethered at the quay. Leafless, white-skinned poplars overtopped stream and priory, a rambling multi-storied affair dotted with lead-latticed windows. Gamboled roofs bore many chimneys, and its sides were timber, stone, and plaster. A pasture could be glimpsed behind, where boys tended white whorl-haired cattle at grass.

Henlee studied the sluice wheel, parallel to the stream and connected by clever gears to a gristmill and wood saws. The abbey's master greeted them himself at the door with a courteous bow. He bore a light and honeyed water in hand. Even Eirec grunted his approval.

"Thrice welcome! Nobler guests Bishop's Gate has never seen, though she is seven parts of a thousand years. I am Nogaret." The man was thin and eloquent. Sparse hair swept back from an intelligent brow, and the face tended towards the severe, yet his mannerisms seemed genuine. His black cassock bore buttons of gold, and his cap was silk. Two cowled monks stood in waiting.

Nogaret clapped long, pale hands. Baths were poured, barbers summoned, and clothes taken for mending. At sup, Apieron felt an overwhelming sense of exhaustion summoned by the mere comfort of a chair and the smell of food. After the briefest of inquiries, the master and notables were politic enough to cease all questions and spoke instead of events in the wide world.

"Blessedly," said Nogaret, "Bishop's Gate stands overlooked and unmolested by the ravishments of the enemy, who despoil all the land, burning what they cannot use. Iz'd Yar occupies what once was Ilycrium east and west, save the most remote marches under the Anheg, and the uninhabitable bogs of the South. Yet we of faith have a duty to hope and hold in stewardship many traditions lest they be forever lost." The hands clasped, a graceful gesture. "And to pray when hope wanes for the boy-king, who is leaguered by foes." Sensing the fatigue of his guests, the master shared a final toast and bade them rest. Feet sore with each step, the companions trod to their beds, a dorm for men and a single chamber for Isolde.

In the darkest portion of the night, Galor rose from where he lay. He ghosted through walls, moving deep into the monastery. He passed a dozen armsmen clothed in leather jerkins. They bore daggers in hand. Felt-wrapped boots stalked the silent halls of Bishop's Gate.

Galor materialized within the private suites of the master. "*You!*" Nogaret branded a cleric's mace, its diamond-shaped head gleamed wickedly. "You have no right, no authority here!" An Azgod, tall and blanched white, stepped from the shadows of the wall.

Galor paused, and raising no offensive hand, he replied to Nogaret, "That is true." He nodded to the chamber's door. A booted foot kicked it, wrenching it from the frame. A spear-wielding figure entered. "But *she* does."

Shouts of alarm and clash of arms echoed from the hall. Battle cries of dwarf and Northman rose above the fray. Apieron dashed into the chamber, bypassing Galor and Isolde to close with the pale half-demon, a terrible fury in his eyes.

Nogaret waved his hand, and the chamber's floor sprouted the orange flames of Hel. Isolde lowered her mask and advanced. The master called, and a howling being of fire gathered itself around her. The holy spear wagged dismissively, and the creature wailed its dissipation. Heavy mace raised in fury, Nogaret charged.

The Azgod's yellow eyes danced with glee as simultaneously Berich, son of Iz'd Yar, leapt high and struck hard with gleaming blades in either hand. They ground and sparked against Apieron's kite shield. A staff and fretting lightnings glimmered on its surface as the Azgod's castings failed, and Apieron laughed grimly. Defeating a blinding attack worthy of a fencing master of Tyrfang, he drove his ivory dart into the scaled midriff of his foe. The slit eyes bulged. An ebon lance pierced the larynx, silencing a death curse. Apieron looked up as the Hel-lit flames faded, leaving only the reek of scorched stone. Galor had departed.

Isolde rose from the still form of Nogaret. "We will bury him as a true priest; mayhap his soul will find redemption."

Apieron spurned the corpse at his feet. Its black mouth gaped wide in the pale face as if in jest. Small teeth glittered like those of a fish. "This one I claim as my own. He burns."

Isolde turned her head rapidly at a small noise and, dropping down a flight of steps, she entered a chamber lit by niched candles. Shadowed by Apieron, her hard eyes fell on three tiring women who sat at bench with floating hair and expressionless faces. A mighty loom was before them, and on its shutter lay an ebon standard that was near complete. It depicted a many-headed dragon, the central mouth clasping a red star. A dimly heard clash of metal on metal and falling bodies came to them from without, and the outraged shouts of dwarf and Northman surmounted the clamor.

Isolde's voice boomed in the close space. "Why do you spin the heraldry of demons?"

The eldest, bedraggled and thin, lifted one foot. An iron ankle circlet rattled against its chain. Although slender, it was bolted to a pin driven deep into the floor. Her response was flat, without hope of mercy. "We are slaves."

Apieron ripped the dark weaving from its shutter. Isolde readied her spear, but she allowed a small smile. "Will you labor this night for your freedom?"

The women shared a long, wordless look. "Tonight, Priestess, we will twine the stars if you so command."

The imperishable steel flashed. Chains were sundered. "So I do."

Eirec grunted with satisfaction and wiped the keen blade of his Hel-forged axe. "It seems Fleshgrinder likes the throat yokes of thralls as well as the necks of orcish men."

"How many did you free?" asked Isolde.

"Two hundreds we found working the winter crops for the slavers of Kör," replied Henlee. "As for the whip masters?" The black dwarf shrugged his incredibly broad shoulders. "Fertilizer."

"I also found slaves," said Isolde. She wore the dark circles of another sleepless night, although she appeared pleased in the thin light of wintry sun. "They labored well for their freedom. Giftings they crafted you."

"Magnificent," boomed Eirec. He accepted and lifted aloft a scabbard with harness that was supple, yet tough, for his broad-bladed axe. Runes of keeping adorned its surface, and it snugged over shoulder and back in tailored fit.

Jamello caught something soft. He bowed laughing, and placed atop his head the silken slouch-hat preferred of thieves. Henlee pulled on high boots that were fashioned after the manner of dwarves. He gingerly tested his ankle, then stamped down. "I feel quick-footed as I've ever been, like a dancer."

Tallux grinned widely and accepted jerkin and breeches of black leather, barely visible on which was a front tracery of dark green in threaded design of his forest home. When he rustled the garments, they emitted no sound.

Isolde's gaze fell on Apieron. "And you, ranger of Windhover?"

"I need no emblem."

"What of thy badge?"

Apieron's hand flew to his breast. The patchwork cloth was gone! He bowed deep to Isolde and gathered from her a knight's tabard whose pattern fused in radiant array around the little weave borne from the ruin of Windhover. Under his fingertips, its magic thrummed and called to him. Apieron pulled the garment on and spoke softly to its center. "Thus my bride, we go to war …"

Jamello pointed again. "And you, Priestess, where is your gifting?"

Isolde pushed aside her cloak. Revealed was the shining robe of a high priestess, a garment of power. "There is something else." She lifted a mace whose long, cylindrical shaft was of leather-bound iron, perfectly balanced against a diamond-shaped head of blued metal. "This was Norgaret's." She slung it from a belt loop.

Henlee's dark, scarred hand touched it. "The steel is glad at last for a worthy hand to wield it."

Jamello wrapped close his cloak. It was brown wool of a type worn by the monks of Bishop's Gate, most of whom were ignorant of the conspiracy and had gladly supplied the companions with small packs and equipage for light travel. A cold wind gusted, and they saw cattle hunkered down in rows, facing into the wind. Jamello shivered, "Too hot, too cold! I miss Bestrand—and what became of Galor?"

"And his pet?" added Henlee.

Apieron took up a stave of green birch as tall as his shoulder, its white wood smoothed free of bark. "We will not see him again on this journey."

"And his wyrm?" asked Eirec.

Isolde laughed, "You have not the true sight of the Gray-Eyed Goddess. It was released into the barrens of the Duskbridge as we flew."

"Remind me never to walk there again," said Jamello, "as if the place needed another monster!"

"Too bad about the wyrm," mused Henlee. "He was a good one."

The entire day, over their plodding course, the sun was veiled behind undulant clouds as if removed behind liquid, and as evening gathered, the remote orb gave up its futile efforts. Even so, a shaft of light pierced the wrack, filling a high-tree canopy from below, much like the glow of a taper beneath a lampshade, and the previously dreary landscape softened to gold. A murmuring creek called to them, and the companions laved free the dust of their march from arms, breast, and brow.

"Might be chilly tonight," said Henlee, busying himself with a fire. "The Gerales hinder much of the snowfall hereaways south. This would be nice country, if it wasn't for the war."

Jamello and Eirec stretched out on packs, too tired to assist the dwarf. Jamello vented a drawn-out sigh. "Apieron says battle crows gather above those hills. The foam-stepping Horse of Ilycrium is brought to bay."

"A great battle comes," agreed Henlee. "I can smell it."

"Don't fret, Grandfather," mumbled Eirec, half-asleep. "We'll be ready."

Henlee wheeled, but the big man was already snoring. Tallux favored Isolde with a small smile as he moved toward their back trail to assume first watch. Isolde followed him with her eyes, for even the wood elf's gait was stilted. "It is too soon," she whispered to herself. "We bear many wounds."

Isolde found Apieron beside the slow rill. Past the horizon, the sun's final illumination caught on a scar of limestone above the bank and reflected its yellow cast to Apieron's feet. He crouched and cupped in his hand was a wild rose, a single flower amongst winding thorns.

Setie stood blinking in the light.

Melónie's garden rose was in full bloom, and five dozen crimson heads wagged their slow wisdom. Apieron stood the child in front of the bush whilst his wife captured the image, paintbrush in hand.

"Just a little longer," he promised.

Setie squinted into the sun's brightness and tried to smile. At three, she was merely a fraction heavier than her brother, two years the younger. "A bit more," urged Apieron.

The garden was alive with a growing things and summer's birdsong. Melónie's little stream laughed its merry course, while Setie clasped her hands and tried to strike a pretty pose, her pale olive skin taking up a translucence in the sun, the health of a growing child. She would be as beautiful as the mother.

Apieron sighed and pulled his beard. It had grown long, perhaps he should cut it. What became of that sketch? Gone, like the rest.

Isolde touched his arm. "Where are you?"

Apieron pulled his gaze from the wildflower he held. "Home, for a moment."

Isolde's voice grew choked. "It is still too soon for me. Memories come, I push them away—"

"Mayhap I sinned against her." Apieron touched his temple. "Here, in my defense, 'twas unintentional."

Isolde's eyes glistened with moisture. "You have returned, that is what is important."

"Aye. Thanks to you, and Xephard, ever he gave with both hands."

Isolde's tears fell onto winter's dead grass. Apieron gathered her to him. When she could speak, "To die in such a horrid place, you don't think—?"

"Nay, his spirit flew the fetters of Hel, as did the living star."

Isolde's clear blue orbs searched the gray ocean of Apieron's own. "It is so hard to know. How much easier 'twould be to drift, to lose oneself."

Apieron searched a distant place on the northern horizon that lay under the nightfall. "I have wandered that lonely darkening." He regarded her and smiled softly. "Such paths are not for you, Priestess, nor would I wish them on any other." He took her hand. "Come, I've something to show you."

There were votives that had fallen into the stream. Legs buried by silt, two wooden pilgrims shaped as man and woman lay face down in the water. Apieron breathed low over the rickle, "Release them, gentle spirit, that we may set them aright."

Isolde swept clean a small space atop a moss-grown ledge, and Apieron placed the offerings there amongst fern bracken, turned yellow and russet by the season.

"They again have their place," said Isolde, "a giving remade."

Apieron's eyes had again grown wan, but he touched her shoulder with gentleness, and together they climbed the bank.

SWAY

"What are you doing?" demanded the man.

"Preparing to exit this rubbish heap. Iz'd Yar commands our presence, it seems the boy-king of this dung-hill country has been brought to bay. But enough banter, manling, step aside!"

The man did not move. Darkly handsome, he wore his superb plate like a second skin. Its molded front bore a rainbow wealth of gems. "And the city, what is to be her fate?"

Goz, Iz'd Yars commandant in the West, and this other stood in the windowed throne chamber of Swaymeet. The giant gazed out at the city. Terra-cotta roofs of many colors there were, and cobbled streets framed by masonry gutters. Here and there, a burned-out frame or a building pulled to rubbish opened a view to winter's gray harbor. He faintly sensed rather than heard waves roar against the two rocky islands in the bay. That there was not more destruction vaguely bothered him. Precious stones glittered on his own hauberk as well, the occupation of Sway having been profitable.

Goz shrugged. "Dexius will hold it in surety for us." The minister stood nigh, his normally pallid skin seeming even more so, and his hand shook where it clutched a short stave, an ivory rod of office.

"I think not," opined the dark warrior. "The priests of the *She* require blood, dragons stir in the East. Fire the city!"

Goz's eyes fairly bulged, and his voice grew to a roar, "I care not what moth-ridden deity you serve!" His choleric face turned to the diminutive minister. "What's that you say, slave?"

"Kill him now," whispered Dexius.

The dark blade licked into Goz's form and out again. "Too late," quipped Malesh.

The half-giant's hands had reflexively moved to strike; now

they sought vainly to gather something back into the wound. Goz sank to the floor.

Beyond the windowed portico, the western Ess surged its eternal rhythm against the Sisters. Two Ascapundi, bearing mighty guisarmes, gawked in surprise, unsure what they had witnessed.

"Follow your orders, knaves," snapped Adestes. "Gather your kind and leave the city. Join the war gathering." The Ascapundi grunted and left the hall with a bang. Adestes regarded the corpse at his feet. "Rather like letting the air out of a bag, don't you think?" The other man seemed to shrink further still. "Shall we discuss your treacheries?"

Adestes Malgrim pushed the poniard slowly, and Dexius' hands futilely grasped the gauntleted fist that held the weapon while the minister's eyes widened as never before. Malesh twisted the narrow blade, placed deep enough to incapacitate, yet not so much as to cause an inadvertently quick death. Dexius's hands fell from Adestes' wrist as wordless sounds issued from his gaping mouth.

Malesh leaned forward, his ear to the other's white lips. The knife ceased its twisting. "What is that you say?" The minister's eyes rolled, scanning the room for anyone, anything.

"Do not worry, there are none about to aid you. People are such distractions, are they not? Always meddling, always wanting." Malesh placed his other hand on Dexius's shoulder. "You never allowed anyone nigh your beloved person, yet I am close now, am I not?"

The man's eyes bulged. He nodded vigorously, clamping down his screams so as to not provoke Malesh. Blood started from his lip where he bit through.

"Come. I tire of bearing up your end of the universe." The

dagger tilted slightly. Dexius rose to his toes. "You have ten seconds to justify your continued existence."

"Apier—" Dexius choked.

The blade withdrew a fraction. Dexius swallowed bittersweet blood. His words came in a rush. "—scry spells. Apieron of Windhover … survived the Hel shriving … goes to mountains … Gerales."

"Congratulations, you've saved a city," whispered Malesh. "I go." The diffused sun of the throne room burnished Adestes' sable hair copper and gold, although his eyes remained utterly black.

Dexius wanted to fall, to cover his wound, but the well of those eyes filled his vision. A shape began to grow, tiny and rising with speed. It uncoiled, gaping wide its many mouths. The blade surged through the diaphragm into the great vessels and finally the chine. When he died, Dexius's expression did not change. The corpse lay supine, a look of horrified fascination fixed on its pallid features.

Adestes Malgrim, Kör's Malesh, strolled down the wide avenue that fled from the palace. There was now no time for proper arrangements, but happily, he smelled smoke, as behind him the first hungry flames framed the once mighty home of the Candor kings.

Chapter 28

Ilycrium: The Army

The night air was cool on Gault's chest where sweaty rivulets had trickled through the grime of the day. Renault had tsked when Gault doffed jack and coif to labor beside the men. Once the army set its back to the Gerales, revetments of earth and stone had needed to be raised behind ditches and faced with sharpened timbers, for scouts told of an unending river of reinforcements that swelled a valley gathering of Kör. Should the enemy suddenly assault the heights, the men of the West intended to defend from a strong place.

Gault dreamed: He surveyed his camp by moonlight, and was pleased. Ilycrium's men would fight the final battle under the royal banner, a marsh stallion that reared against a field azure with peaks and waves of white. The moon rose to confront Kör's red star. Dry lightning flickered, and from somewhere, a dog howled. Gault saw a keep perched behind towered walls atop a sea-battered tor. He knew that place.

A man walked the storm airs to stand nigh, his face as cragged as were the cliffs of Varkold. The Duke, Gor du Roc, took Gault's hand and beckoned to the tide rush where a second figure emerged from ocean's darkness. Bel Candor came to them, the thin crown of Ilycrium about his shock of white hair and furrowed brow. Together, Gault's fathers searched his face from shadowed orbits. Gault's hazel eyes gave back the gaze; he would be judged as he may.

The lords of Ilycrium bowed and beckoned, and their gesture revealed the kingdom entire. To it, darkness gathered, and as Gor du Roc and Belagund sank into stone and surf, they implored him in silence, ghostly arms shimmering.

Trakhner slapped his neck and regarded his hand with disgust.

"Blood fly," chuckled Exeter, "here for the battle."

The general wiped his palm on his breeches. "Thing's big enough to fuck a turkey."

"What betides in the long vale?" asked Gault.

Trakhner hitched back his broadsword and fighting knife and swelled his barrel chest to speak. "Iz'd Yar's twenty thousands have doubled and nearly so again. Also, a Snake of the Mgesh has wound its way hither from Uxellodoum, whether this bodes good or ill for the bearded folk, I do not know. Counted amongst the enemy are twelve or more thousands horse-knights with peaked helms and swift mounts. It is said they hie from Kör's hinterland as vanguard for three legions of Ascapundi plus orcs." Trakhner rumbled deep in his throat. "And who can count the many thousands were-creatures to which our scouts can put no name? Some are tall and terrible; these last march under many banners and bear the stamp of the abyss. Lords of Kör I deem them. Tertullion put the name *Azgod* on them—mayhap the foul get of demons who bred mortal women."

Gault groped for a stool and sat heavily. "So many." At length, he sought the faces around him, and not even irrepressible Renault had aught to bolster the dampened spirit of the council. Only Seamus seemed unperturbed, his one eye bright upon the Prince like a watchful dog.

Giliad spoke, "There's more." His cowl was gray in the shadow of the tarpaulin, and his voice grim. "A very great army prepares its advent from the Matog, called by men Duskbridge. Twice the strength fielded by Kör, it will flood up from the south like a dam bursting. There will be no escape."

Renault rounded fiercely on the mage. "What then do we do?"

"What we already intend: defeat Kör soundly. We have allies you do not see. Even now, there are those who strive beyond the Last Gates."

Gault looked up sharply, a small hope flickered on his face. "Apieron Farsinger?"

Giliad nodded. "And others."

"We have heard this tale afore time," Exeter harrumphed. "Runagate knight at best, and if he indeed passed your foul Matog, he was lost to the world."

"Good news?" asked Gault in a small voice. "Anyone?"

"Aye," said Trakhner. "A borderer's tale of a mixed bag of Ascapundi and fell goblins who have filtered hence from westwards."

Exeter colored. "Poor jest, General. How is that good?"

Trakhner's bluff face grew redder still as he looked up at the beak-nosed baron. "Sway is west! I deem she survives."

"To starve?" asked Renault.

Trakhner looked to the entry flap and smiled. "Here is a man, my lords. Judge this yourselves."

Gault brushed back his auburn hair—and the worry from his features. Trakhner beckoned, and Seamus admitted a young soldier who bore the thick brow and jaw of the highlands, yet the tawny hair was cropped short, and his stature was one of the blend races that had sprouted in the colonies founded by the Old Marshal.

"What is your name, scout?"

"By your leave, Duskene, my lord."

"What news of Sway?"

The man shook his head. "I hail from Teraza on the strand, far north of the fair city. Gray-and-black drommonds reave our coast, three maybe four hundreds Kör marines to a ship. They kill some and loot, and burn what they can't steal."

"Invasion?" queried Exeter.

"Nay, sir, though they could at that. Fisherman brave enough to sail in winter tell of gatherings on the water. Forty or fifty black sharks of Kör at a time."

"What tell, man," asked Renault, a mounting exacerbation in his voice, "of our coastal garrisons?"

"Companies to resist brigades, that choose when and where to strike? None can match them, save perhaps Malchar of Denfirth, but he has fought a long war, and his numbers grow few. I was such a one until he dispatched me with missives up coast, and my home." The man shrugged. "Now I am here."

"What of the people?" asked Gault. "Your kin amongst the coastals?"

"They are brave in defense of their homes, Lord, but when overmatched, they fade." The man smiled raffishly as might a hill-man who has won at gambling. "And live to fight again, yet we do not forget the gifts of your grandsire, Highness. Kör would return us to the dark days and worse. Aye, Sire. For *you*, they will fight!"

Gault stood. "When you go, scout, remove your corporal's chevrons." The man bowed his head.

"Think you, General, we might find those of a sergeant for this man?" The soldier's rough face beamed.

"We might indeed, Sire. Dismissed!" Shoulders squared, the

man executed a crisp salute and about-face. Seamus escorted him out.

"Kör does not have a great navy," said Trakhner evenly.

"And we, none at all," quoth Renault.

"Cursed Farsepians," growled Exeter.

"Nonetheless, forty or fifty troop ships to harry up and down the coast, and the siege force here. It means but one thing." The general's meaty fist smacked his palm. "Our prince has reasoned well. Iz'd Yar summons his Snakes to chase us whilst his sailors seek to prevent reinforcements. For the nonce at least, Sway is spared."

"Then she will live or die with us," mused Renault.

"Aye, we are hemmed." Exeter stroked his creamy doublet. "'Twill be the death grip."

Gault chuckled grimly. "Just as well, there is little enough left to eat. I'd rather fight than starve."

"You heard that half-wilding scout," said Trakhner. "Sire, take the Crown!"

Seamus proffered a bag of purple silk. Trakhner withdrew a delicate fillet of gold, nearly white in its purity, it had been worked to fit over a battle helm of the type worn by Gault. Renault's red glove touched it reverently. "'Twould be a mighty symbol for the men."

"I made a vow," said Gault,"it seems long ago."

Trakhner's hands pushed out in protest. "A land without a king is no country at all. Your grandfather knew this. Think you he warred thirty years in foreign lands for personal gain? Bah! He was rich and settled already."

Gault placed a strong hand on Trakhner's shoulder. "Peace, old warhorse. I have said what I have said." To the others, it seemed the prince had grown much from the coltish youth who sat council in Swaymeet before the advent of Kör, and as one they bowed and exited, and Gault followed them, coming close to Giliad.

"Walk with me if you please, Magnus."

Seamus followed the pair under pine boughs and a clear sky, where stars winked blue and flashing yellow, like diamonds suspended in night's weave. Gault touched Giliad's robe. "What do we now? Men and brave women gather to our cause each day. In days or short weeks, we will boast our greatest strength." Gault swallowed. "They honor me, an' yet Trakhner's tallies and your dire warnings make me afraid. Exeter is right, his falcon's eyes miss little. Kör has found us, we are trapped."

Giliad ceased his slow stride. The waxing moon forced its frosty light through needle-waving pines. The elf lord's hood was gone, and on his breast, fluid scales rippled like the flash of a swimming trout. His eyes glimmered ultramarine as he studied the prince.

"What to do? You know better than I, who are lord of this land."

"Am I? Or the last of a proud line?" Gault swept his arms wide to indicate a thousand fires, most well shielded, that dotted the near slopes of the Gerales. "These are Ilycrium's only shield by land or sea, our best and bravest. Am I he who lost a kingdom? Who betrayed his people to their doom?"

There was a pause broken only by wind moaning in the pines; no insects stirred on the wintry hillside. The mage spoke at last. "Do you wish to know more of thy brand? Of Gonfolon?"

"What? Very, though I have been afraid to be deemed unworthy."

"It has never known defeat, and will not serve the hand of dishonor." Giliad flicked back his mantle, his wide shoulders sparkled with dark sapphires and soft pearl with diamonds strung on nets of platinum. "It chose you, I merely guided it hither."

The noble elf's eyes flashed under moon and star. "Powers gather, gods are watching! and you are an instrument of their will. You and I (and Seamus) stand on a piney slope of eastern Ilycrium, we also walk within a nexus from which will flow the momentum for an age." Gault stood stock still, listening to Giliad's final words. "Fear not! I pronounce no rede," said the grim elf. "I, too, will here live or die; for in the end, I have business with the minders of Kör!"

THE GERALES

Dawnbreak limned the Gerales purple, although the ancient mountains were still far to the north, and the intervening low country rolled and beckoned. Jamello poked at the ground with a stick. "Those don't seem much closer."

Apieron hitched tight his belt. "We have two days."

It was midmorning when they came upon the farm croft. Scavengers had destroyed what they could not carry. Centuries-old grapevines were slashed to the root, and the field was weed-grown and pockmarked with debris. At its center was the burned-out shell of a steading, and its timbers, end-on to the sky, looked like the ribs of some stricken beast. A man was there. Stripped to the waist and back turned to the six companions, he labored to repair a garden wall. Between its two faces of fitted stone, he packed red clay and gravel.

"Emplecton," said Henlee, "trick o' the army."

They saw helm and shield; the former was buried to the nasal, a planter for garlic flowers. The other a basin for dew, and birds watered therein. A lance, cracked and molded, was struck point-down into the earth, and to it was tied a sapling pecan. A stained and faded pennant lifted fitfully in the chill. Its ensign was a lamplit door under which a dog stood guard.

"I feel I should know this heraldry," said Apieron, "from my days at Court."

"I too," added Tallux, "although this was not the home of any noble."

Henlee rumbled, "Deserter? Surely he hears us." The man continued to work.

"Leave him be," said Apieron. "This day ages, and we have miles to go." With little pause for rest and snatches of food, the party strode across woodcuts and tall grass fields as the plain rose into stair-step hills. Twice they caught sight of people who scampered into cover until they had passed. Eirec caught up one white-haired dam, hurrying from them on wobbling legs, and they could feel the eyes of many others from a stand of laurel.

"Why flee you, Mother? Are you in danger?"

She jerked free her arm and signed against evil. "Perdition-scorched devils!" Her bleary eyes searched their lot before she fled. When she gained the shelter of the trees, she cackled in triumph. "Gremlins … knaves!"

"You scared her," accused Jamello. Eirec shook his bushy beard.

The companions struck a game trail that climbed gently as grasslands surrendered to rock and wood, and they chanced upon a rare find, an abandoned apple orchard overgrown with red sumac. A ground-hugging mist lent the place a forlorn look, and tree trunks glistened wetly. The travelers spread out to harvest a quantity of the wind-burned fruit. Yet more fortuitous, Tallux felled a fat doe as she leapt from a brushy thicket of sorrel. The deer had fed well on apples, and Eirec grunted with pleasure as he hoisted it atop his shoulders.

That night, air from the swale they had quitted rose to warm their camp, and its tugging breeze fanned the flames of a cooking fire. Jamello removed his boots, and his toes nearly touched the blaze. A split log fell from the conical fire. "I am too lazy to gather you up."

Tallux chuckled. "The fire does not mind."

"Perfect night, thief," quoth Henlee. He raised a small skin of wheat beer, last of the monks' winter brew. Eirec nodded sagely.

"Almost perfect," corrected Isolde quietly. They followed her gaze to Apieron, who sat opposite the fire, unheedful of their conversation, and his eyes glinted unblinking in the smoky light.

The final day's ascent was the most difficult. Spurs of granite thwarted their path and forced the party into bramble-choked ravines or another steep cleft, necessitating a hard-pulling climb. Jamello groaned when they surmounted a fold to behold the largest of these, for it opened into a gaping fissure as far as they could see east to west. Stunted, splay-rooted pines lined the rock cut, and a reddish stream trickled in its depths.

"Not without rope," said Henlee. "Lots of rope."

"There is a bridge!" cried Jamello.

"Out here? You dream!" rumbled Eirec.

Tallux shaded his eyes. "He is right, although its presence seems impossible."

An hour's scrambling effort took them down a loose-rocked bank to the approach of a stone span, muchly weathered but intact. "Look there!" urged the elf scout, "on the foot of the bridge."

Yellowed bones were there piled. Of varying shapes they were, yet all were humanoid. A blanch-skinned ogre hulked from the nearest buttress. "I am Black Hogstyrgger. No mortal may cross."

"He's as white as snow," exclaimed Henlee. "*I* am black."

Tallux drew Farstriker into its deadly arc. "Kör's slave."

The creature's fanged mouth chortled. "You lie, spriteling. Hogstyrgger is masterless. Many of your kind have I slain, so your head will I mount on thy twig, a feast for crows."

Apieron waved back the wood elf. He jumped lightly to the approach, no weapon in hand.

"Take my spear!" cried Isolde.

Apieron paused slightly and shook his head, a grim twist to his mouth. "I retain *something* of the Starfire."

Cresting a saddle, the companions descended swiftly into the dusk of the southern Gerales. They stooped to avoid silhouettes, and checked any wayward step that might loose a stone to alert the spies of Kör. Guided by night-eyed elf and sure-footed ranger, they ventured close to the horseshoe vale until moonrise set it aglow.

Apieron signaled a halt. "Too dangerous to go far in this light."

"Thank you, Lady Moon!" whispered Jamello.

"Rest well," said Apieron. "But no fire! Two awake, two asleep. Tallux and I shall walk and watch apart."

Jamello looked out and gasped, "Gawds."

"Aye," breathed Isolde. "So many."

One by one, growing numbers of distant fires glittered into view, in a trickling, random cascade. "If each elf, maiden, and child alike of Greenwolde were to hold a taper," spoke Tallux, "there would not be half this counting."

"Eight or ten thousand camps," growled Eirec. "Maybe more."

The terrain below was laid out in a cul-de-sac, with arms of the Gerales upflung on either side. "Stepsons of the Vigfils these mountains be," said Eirec. "Slow going for any army in retreat."

"There will be no retreat," said Apieron.

On a west shoulder and hidden from the vale, they could see some hundreds of fires were scattered among copse and ridge, yet no individual figures could be discerned. In contrast, the valley's center and its open, northern approaches were lit like a candled mass. "No need to ask which be friends," grunted Henlee, "or which be foes."

"By the norm," asked Isolde softly, "how many soldiers to a fire?"

Henlee shrugged. "Twenty or so."

"Great Goddess!" whispered Isolde.

From their right, the fat moon gained height. Of brightest argent, it became painful to gaze on for long. A high wind drove rank after rank of scudding clouds across the moon disk, taking up its glow in pallid luminescence until fleecy grays and blacks were fringed with silver or shot through with dancing lights. The sky beyond was of deepest indigo, yet against the brilliant moon and cloud-rush, no stars were visible. Save one.

"Evil comet," grumbled Eirec. "How I hate thee!"

A flap of wings gathered above them, and a low-honking call sounded once. "Goose," said Henlee. The dwarf looked meaningfully to Farstriker.

"Swan," said Tallux, "black against Father Moon."

Isolde touched Apieron's sleeve. "A good sign for you, they are favorites of the Far Darter, he of the bow and of the harp, the Shining God."

Apieron watched the bird until it was lost over the sentry-lit vale. "Fate rules the gods as well as men. Sleep now."

"Tomorrow, I slay Adestes Malgrim."

Staring upward, Isolde attempted her final prayer before sleep. The Lady of the Moon was fickle, and thus Isolde would not call upon Her. X'fel gained in its ascent, the bloody light piercing low pines to light their camp with its cast. Isolde felt her spirit war with the star's malignant purpose. Closing her eyes, she breathed deep and pushed into her meditation, then they opened, her link to the Divine restored.

"How many must die, Apieron, before you rest again?
Will a sea of blood drown the fires of thy guilt?
Apieron Forest Walker, singer of gentle
songs, wherest fled thy soul?
Love knowing Melónie, and Xephard—favorite of
the goddess, guide thy friend, whose feet tread sunny
paths, though his heart bides in darkness."

Chapter 29

Ilycrium the Nation

"Rouse! Children of the West. Cast aside shackle and fear!" Doughty heralds dared the land. From wintry crags to fens brown and silent with the lateness of the season, they bore a message. Over lonely wolds to hidden garths they came, and many listened.

Intrepid frontiersmen, fathers and brothers of children slain, ventured deep into the land of their enemy. They sang their song before halls of Eastern dwarves who paid tributes of gold and levies of arms to the Dream Throne. They conversed with slow-speaking Vur who shook shaggy heads and revealed not the workings of their hearts; even so, they harkened to the full story of the heralds.

There was one, apart from all others, who held a gold-chased skull, and touched the spirit of a dead king of dwarves. Alcuin cast words, whispered in iron-barred darkness to silent Drudges whose black eyes glittered in the gloom-drenched Archwaze, the Gehulgog of Kör.

"Sometimes we saw the oddest things." Cusk stirred up the cooking fire with a richly worked poniard that a year before he would have feared to touch lest he be accused thief.

Byrinae tasted their broth, bubbling in a sand-scoured helmet. She scowled at Wiglaf who was reaching with a spoon. Grunting his acquiescence, the sergeant leaned back against a crate, folding his enormous arms across his chest. A handful of mint and winter leek found the mixture. Byrinae smiled at Cusk, bidding him continue.

"One night we stood th' lookout on a ridge. Like waves t' battle 'ad washed the dead t' the foot of our hill." Cusk gestured over the fires of Ilycrium's encampment. "A thousand men, ours an' Kör's, die on such a day. 'Skirmish' the lords call it, or 'probing attack.'" Cusk's mouth formed the strange words clumsily. "Anyways, th' moon was up like this one whilst we watched. Who knows what stirs a night air? Th' corpses was ghastly pale in that light, but we tried t' ignore 'em. Instead, we stared at the far trees, ears strainin' like rabbits for clinking armor or mutterings such as troll-men and ghouls 'ill make."

"All o' a sudden, one of the bodies shambles to 'is feet! Slowlike, he stiff-legged it to the tree shadow. If'n 'twas a soldier that had laid stunned ha' the night through, or a witchspell, we never know'd. T'either way 'e was cursed or blessed by a god, an' not a dog amongst us darest hale or hinder 'im. After a time, he disappeared, gone to where he'd been, I'm guessin."

Byrinae's thick face was pleasant in the low light. She smiled. "Eat, boys. Noble Klea says we 'aven't many peaceful nights left. Tell me more, and 'o my Dunstan."

UXELLODOUM

As one, pale unlovely Drudges turned on goblin engineers to strike down the weaker creatures in silence. Wending their way from assault tunnels, misshapen hands fell upon orcin rankers arrayed at the passage mouth, and no other stayed them. Placing knotted backs to Uxellodoum, Kör's slaves faded into upland shadows to begin the long trek back to Körguz. Once these departed, dwarves sprang a trap long in the making. Sappers chopped through the final feet of narrow tunnels in descent to those crowded with goblin pioneers. Above them, sluice gates were raised.

Mugul, war chief of orc runners, swore by the dog teats of his goddess when he beheld a diminutive goblin backing *out* of a tunnel mouth. The very same hole into which Mugul had driven so many hundreds of the creatures to kill dwarves. The orcling reeled, its head lolling dazedly. Mugul drove it to the ground with a mailed fist. Spitting bloody teeth, the miner's eyes cleared. It spoke a single word, "Water!" Mugul lowered his arm, and felt first the vibration in his knees, followed by a geyser of brown water, blasting him back against the stone. He heard his spine crack.

Mugul watched as the water rose up his body. Shattered wood and mud and broken goblins filled the ravine where he sat. His guards were either stricken as he or fled. As mud swirled and bubbled up his neck, Mugul cursed the cleverness of dwarves, that he was to meet his end by the absurd notion of drowning on the side of a mountain.

Dwarven officers were quick to follow up their victory in the tunnels. Iz'd Yar had invested the mountain with twenty thousand. Of these, a full legion had been lost in the siege, and a second Snake of steppesmen had been summoned southward. The remainder was not enough, and for the first time in many months, dwarves breathed the clean air that climbed Uxellodoum's frowning steeps.

Axe and mattock swung freely as nakirs of bronze and stone echoed down the mountain. Mgesh and goblins, spurred by whip masters and the notion of Iz'd Yar's wrath, howled their affronted rage and charged upslope.

"So much the better," mused Stumfurer Broadbelt aloud. "No need to chase the foul creatures through snow." He turned to Draliks, his granite-faced captain. "Today, a red reckoning."

"And then?"

"Ravens gather southward."

ILYCRIUM: THE ARMY

Tall barbarians, survivors of the Axe Grind, shared wary looks with wode-tattooed hillmen. Tannhauser, captain of the Northrons, grinned in his beard and tapped a yellow cendal sewn onto his surcoat. Each ally had a matching circuit of the cloth somewhere on breast or shoulder, that the disparate clans not mistake the other for the wildings of Kör.

Uglich placed a restraining hand upon a bare-chested carle.

"Another time, shithead," called Tannhauser pleasantly in his native tongue.

Uglich's woad-beaded face broke into a wide smile. Bobbing his head agreeably, he echoed the Northman's sentiment in the language of the Seod.

Cynewulf, chieftain of Gaxe, the Gerales highlanders, and sworn enemy of Uglich, eagerly watched the departure of the contingent from Amber Hall. He shared a wolfish look with a dozen muddy-locked retainers and eased a bone-handled scramasax from its hairy sheath. Stepping from a copse, they began a stealthy advance on the unsuspecting Seod.

Renault came striding forward. A moment's hesitation soon turned to innocent stargazing when Seamus hove into view. Weapons were hastily sheathed, and rude, gutteral voices attempted amicable greetings. Cynewulf slapped an underling's head for the idea and led his party back to where Gaxe kinsmen waited on the far end of camp.

Renault followed the flashing gold of Cynewulf's torque with a sour look.

Seamus smiled, making his face wounds all the more ghastly. "Kör or no, we'll be havin' a fine fight sooner or later."

IZ'D YAR

"Two thousand lost in the occupation," reported Shaxpur. "Three more on the march from Sway."

Iz'd Yar's displeasure rumbled deep in his chest. "From Uxellodoum, I sent three Snakes to invest to Sway. Eighteen thousands!" The yellow eyes narrowed to dangerous vertical slits. "Now you tell little more than twelve return? By their looks, a third wounded or too exhausted to fight! And where is fat Goz?"

"A long march," explained Shaxpur. "Pecked at by man-creatures the entire way, and yet, Dread Lord, we control the coast entire. Their cities are starved out or burned. No force of size can come thence."

Iz'd Yar's talons clutched Shaxpur's shoulder. The Azgod officer winced inwardly at the memory of a similar grip. It rotated him to face a curtain of stone and living timber that lay adrift the high vale, and up the frowning aspect of the Gerales, where lurked the Western enemy. "Does this look like a fucking beach?"

Vodrab twitched forward, clutching his blur-margined stave. "Sixty thousands and six have you, Dread Lord, a mighty anvil to break the man king. And the hammer hies from Hel itself, the Army of Brass comes anon!"

"Your devotion is inspiring," responded Iz'd Yar dryly. He wheeled on his son. "Where is thy brother?"

The pallid Azgod blanched whiter still. Overlapped plates of ebon lacquer rustled over Astorath's muscular torso as he licked black lips. "Tardy, from Bishop's Gate. Gone for foodstuffs and slaves, and … an item of power."

"He'd best return soon—or not at all." Any further threats from the field marshal of Kör were interrupted by deep shouts and the call of brazen trumpets. Five hundred immortals of Kör had arrived in the night. These marched in ordered ranks to join the numbers of Shaxpur's battalion, while behind them a greater host poured into the valley. Horrible creatures these were—an abominable mating of orcs or orcish humans with bestial demons, the dregs and outcasts of Tyrfang. These had come in their unnumbered thousands to bolster the ranks of goblin men. Although degraded, the strength and fury of the abyss nerved their sinews.

A raucous squabbling erupted as the newcomers displaced purebred orcs from the best cover against the unwelcome light of the sun. Iz'd Yar turned to face Shaxpur. "Our royal cousin favors us, see thou your gift from the Dream Throne. Congratulations, Quastar."

"Provisions are thus, my lord." Gault nodded. His supply master continued, "Every beeve has been slaughtered, the last grain ground, and any root edible (or not) dug from the Gerales."

"It does not matter," replied Gault softly. "Iz'd Yar has flung wide his net across the hills. We can expect no laggard aid. Gentlemen, are you ready?"

One by one, Gault's officers rumbled, "Aye."

Renault laughed grimly. "Tonight they eat their last bean, yeoman and knight, and tomorrow, they'll fight!"

THE GERALES

The white lamp of the moon rode high in night's vault, and no stars shined, save X'fel, its illumination bathing hillbacks that dwindled to the open north into flats where encamped the army of Kör. Watch fires burned low, yet a brooding presence dwelt there.

To the west and south, the moon's pearl radiance held sway on the heights of the Gerales. There were no clouds, yet winter's breath stirred frost onto leaves and grasses that crackled underfoot.

Apieron led his companions down an undulant slope toward the benighted vale. They had miles to go in the darkness, wending their careful way amongst rock-rib shelves and watchful trees. Apieron could see small lights wink in rhythmic fashion on the heights where the men of Ilycrium waited. And below, the camp of Kör crouched in its immensity like a hidden beast, pregnant with malice. Bold signals flared across its length. To the unspoken question, Apieron answered, "Generals do not sleep this night."

Nothing more was asked, and the party moved with the unthinking precision of long familiarity, each action unconsciously coordinated with those of every other. Thus they walked, thus they would fight on the morrow.

ILYCRIUM: THE ARMY

The dark of predawn was close, oppressive. Despite the chill, Gault felt he rebreathed the very same air he had just exhaled. "This night lasts forever. Will blessed Helios light yon vale today, Magnus?"

The cowl moved. "Think you Kör's evil star swallows the sun?"

"Speak no ill redes," protested Renault to both. "All is set. Dawn or no, today we must strive with the black prince."

Gault Candor did not know how he felt, and wished he was as steadfast as Trakhner, or better, Seamus. He could not help but ponder that so much ill afflicting a basically good people seemed more and worse than the mere vagaries of fate. That Ilycrium was abandoned by her ungrateful gods, or afflicted from realms beyond, as was Tertullion's fearful guess, scarred the face of universal justice. The hurts he and so many others had suffered rose in Gault such that he thought he might suffocate or burst.

Braegelor seemed to sense Gault's mood, and the stallion jerked his powerful neck. Vapor from the restive destrier rose in the still airs as uncertainty and fear, spawned in the long night, rose palpably from the army. Men were up and spoke in hushed tones as they shifted feet or slapped the cold from loosening muscles. Frugal meals, the last of the provisions and prepared the prior eve, were hastily eaten on foot as gear was stowed and rigging tightened. The draw and balance of weapons were tested, and nervously tested again. From above, came a swift flap of wings as three geese wended swiftly from the north, their honking calls drifting forlornly over the encampment.

"A sign," said Renault, "and a good one."

"I hope so," muttered Gault.

Trakhner harrumphed, "At least they be not the war crows of Kör. I'm off, although I don't think I'll need to boot any laggards awake this morn!"

"Go with God," said Gault quietly. The man bowed and was gone.

"Where I come from," mused Seamus, "when someone is dying, a prayer is spake for them. Will you, my prince, say such a prayer for me?"

Gault turned, astonished. "Are you afraid, Seamus?"

The armsman's scarred face looked perplexed. "No."

"Then, why?" stammered Gault.

"It seems the gods must hear the prayers of a king. And you are the only one I know."

"When I asked you not to leave me, Seamus, I meant it."

"Never," rumbled the giant, but his face scrunched into a muchly pleased grimace.

Gault looked back. Behind a band of knights picked by Renault for their exceptional valor was strung the heavy cavalry. Gray ranks of Trakhner's infantry of many sorts flowed in an ill-defined mass from the western slopes into the valley's cup. The polyglot army of Ilycrium, beaten and harried, would not await the Snakes of Kör. It would advance perforce to settle the fate of the West.

Gault knew also that royal scouts, muchly augmented by foresters led by Telnus of Windhover, lay scattered in a screen of crafty hunters and skilled bowmen who do not sleep. They marked a path such that the army's attack be swift and sure come morning. Such was their proven skill that he had not feared a surprise raid by the enemy's prowling monsters in the long dark.

Gault startled. "Where is the mage?"

"Gone, Lord," tsked Renault. "Never a by-your-leave in his comings and goings."

"Peace, Champion. I deem he has his own preparations to make."

Gault's charger shifted impatiently, and Renault's stallion also reared. The knight wheeled him into a croupade to calm him. Gault leaned forward. "Did I tell you, sir, how my grandfather's father came to our land?" Renault and some others pressed close.

"From the Northron coast, the Wgend rode ocean's highway down the Ess, for they sought lands hospitable for farming. At length they discovered a bay sheltered by two prominences, whereon was a fishing thorpe. The rising rays of morning's sun slanted through fog on the sea marsh. There, 'midst the tall grass, Baemond and his father heard nickers and splashes, and for the first time, the Candor kings glimpsed white horses of the seashore. Heartened by this omen, he made a city there, Sway, and took for his house oriflamme of the Silver Horse. The Old Marshal was but five then."

A soldier hastened forward. "Trakhner sends his respects, Sire. The foot stands ready; he says also that Telnus, the forester of Windhover, has reported. There be no change in the lair of the Körlings, but their lights have dwindled, and the calls of foul beasts mingle with the voices of Iz'd Yar's man-slaves."

Gault nodded, and noticed something, and walked Braegelor forward. While most eyes were cast anxiously to the north, he searched the eastern horizon. It paled, and though yet unseen, the sun spread golden wings into night's yielding. Where they met became a zone of ephemeral blue. There hung a white star, herald of the day. It challenged the red smudge of X'fel.

Gault gazed left, and like a window that opens to a shadow-filled room, dawn's level found first the uppermost heights of the Gerales in slow descent. Gault took his newly made standard from a squire named Baudalino. Gault stood his stirrups and hoisted it high. It appeared a black flag against the waning gray above. A western breeze lifted over them, and Gault shook out the banner. The rising sun struck it, and lo! threads of gold and silver and sparkling gems caught and reflected the sunrise. It depicted a lordly stallion set over mountain and sea. Braegelor reared such that man and banner appeared as one.

Each knight raised and shook his lance, and the tips burnished fire in the dawn-rise as they gave vent to a mighty shout. Bordering the valley below, hunters grinned in their camouflage and hidden places, knowing their labors had not been in vain.

Gault returned the banner to Baudalino and prayed aloud. A

great surging wave filled his breast, and he raised up with outflung arms to the shining gods of the morn:

Keen glancing dawn,
Promised light,
Shatter darkness,
Render right!
Aid us, Helios, friend of man.

"Poetry milord?" called Renault.

"King's Prayer," whispered Seamus in awe.

Gault responded with a laugh clean of foreboding or weariness. "Summon the horse, friends. It is time to reclaim our land."

Redoubled cheers of the waiting cavalry rippled through the ranks of footmen such that the southern end of the valley resounded. Splendid colors, painstakingly tailored on the long march, fluttered over the armor worn by Renault and the other knights. Proud gunnefanes fluttered also over a thousand Northmen who would again fight in wedge with dwarves of Uxellodoum. Twenty-two hundreds of these fingered beards and weapons, and looked to the dawn with dark eyes. Tannhauser laughed and called greetings to his thanes in their native tongue. "The eyes of many are upon you, and a clear path to our foes for thirst of axe and sword. A fine day!" Dwarves did not cheer or jest, yet brandished whetted steel in grim salute to their tall comrades.

The host of Ilycrium surged forward. Once the cavalry found the ridge-lined floor of the vale, where darkness lingered, officers summoned infantry brigades to intersperse with the mounted companies. Night shut her doors, and day came to the valley's sky like silvered glass. Sun's fiery chariot leapt into the vault as hunters' horns called one to the other amongst slopes and fells, and war trumpets answered from Gault's vanguard. Incandescent rays of the risen sun found the red star, banishing it from the heavens over Ilycrium.

So began the third battle between Kör's hegemony, and the men of the West.

Chapter 30

Orrustudale: The Battle Valley

The men of the West learned a bitter lesson when Ascapundi had smashed Ilycrium's played-out charge before the Celedon, thus allowing swift orcs and galloping Mgesh behind them. Many companies had thereby been trapped and annihilated betwixt rampaging flankers and Kör's fresh troops from the river. Trakhner and Gault therefore arranged the infantry into separate squares sixteen men wide and twelve deep. Side by side, these would advance up the valley—near enough to support the other, yet with gaps such that cavalry reserves might dash forward to stymie enemy penetrators or to exploit any break into the foe's rear.

Many a cavalier grumbled for the imagined slight. "I hope they grouse all the worse and evermore," smiled Gault grimly. "That will mean they are alive."

The griffin on Renault's red jupon gleamed its cloth-of-gold in the morning sun. The knight champion beamed to behold Gault in the fierce gear of a horse-knight. "When they behold their prince beside them on brave Braegelor, men will stay!"

Gault slipped a hand under Braegelor's crinet to stroke the

charcoal stallion's proud neck. "We shall ride together, brave one, and hope not to shame the memory of thy noble master."

Renault dismounted. He placed his gloved and gauntleted hand on Candor's knee. "You, who are our finest cavalier, honor *us*, Highness. Win or lose, live or die."

The verdigris sword was proffered. Gault touched it. "May the blessings of Our Lady be upon you, Renault. Rise, my friend, and when it is time, lead us to victory."

The army debauched onto the rounded butt of the vale and advanced, and from shadow and mist came a stirring, then a rumble as the great beast that was Kör's army was roused to wrath. Against the walking squares of Ilycrium again came the Mgesh. Their exalted shaman Rhocuus, who wore many totems of power, waved his sun-blackened arm, and ten thousand Mgesh who had never known defeat kneed their agile mounts to a gallop.

"Ware all," cried Trakhner, "behind the steppe-riders are many Meges."

Rhocuus ceased his chanting. His arm fell, and a sporadic lift of arrows shrilled overhead, noisemakers marking their trajectory. The range found, a sky-darkening barrage ensued. With the killing shafts were ballistae spears and weighted chains that struck with great force to bounce bone-snapping paths amongst Trakhner's squares. Into the teeth of the arrow storm these marched—sturdy pike and shieldmen to the fore, archers to the rear.

The yew bows of Ilycrium responded. Clothyard shafts flashed up in well-timed volleys. Tapered bodkins of Bagwart's design whistled from high to puncture the leather and laminate armor of Mgesh. Special attention was paid to Kör's artillery; the Western longbows easily overreaching advancing horsemen to pierce man and orc who manned Kör's war machines.

Mgesh again filled the sky with their deadly rain, then galloped under its cover to the valley's edges only to find the

Gerales's upslopes occupied by horse-riding clans of Seod and Gaxe. Uglich and Cynewulf scowled at where they guessed each other to be across the divide, whilst their carles poured frantic counterfire down upon any Mgesh squadron that ventured near.

Spurned by the fierce return volleys, the Mgesh center roweled their steeds to a gallop. Charging and wheeling with precision none could rival, Gommish's squadrons closed again, this time directly into Ilycrium's squares. Powerful laminate bows drove killing shafts from murderously short range while yet out of reach of the ponderous weapons born by Ilycrium's footmen. Many front rankers fell pierced as the steppe-riders yelped with glee and rode pell-mell between the squares. In the gullied terrain where night's mists still crawled, it appeared the lines of Ilycrium were already fractured.

Without betraying horn or shout, Renault's cavalry poured into the gaps from holding positions deep to the ranks of infantry. Thick-limbed knights on armored cold-bloods spurred north in flying columns. Their thunderous charge struck the closely channeled Mgesh like an avalanche of steel. Once lances were splintered or entangled, the knights plied axe and sword. The gold flanges of Renault's blackened mace shattered the top knot of an Eastern Hetman whilst his cavaliers trampled their lesser foes.

Wildly retreating Mgesh left two thousand of their brethren on the valley floor, and the wounded living were quickly dispatched and trampled over by Ilycrium's vengeful footmen. Compressed by Iz'd Yar's next wave, and goaded by the black fury of their Cur Quans, Mgesh streamed loosely to the fringes to grapple in desperation with the free tribesmen of Ilycrium.

Short bows from either side loosed shaft after shaft from mere paces into the breasts and throats of their enemy, yet the Seod and Gaxe were fresh and held higher ground, whilst the Mgesh grew desperate in their failure. Soon the lines mingled, and where they flowed down against Ilycrium's outlying squares, yeomen infantry plied heavy polearms and mattocks against the curved blades of the beleaguered Mgesh. Strong bands of Ilycrium's tribals shouted with glee as they broke free to ride through the milling chaos, counting every steppesman they butchered.

Flutes and timbrels sounded from the north. Although the day had come clear and crisp, dust from the battle already obscured the middle distances. The flash of silvered armor revealed the cavalry of the Meges nations, their proud riders galloping noble steeds with easy grace to succor the harried steppesmen down the valley's center. As with their Western foes, a Meges horseman's tutelage was an arduous lycée. Adept at maneuver and every knightly skill, each was expert with javelin and scimitar, and in their midst were war chariots on scythed wheels that bore archers and spearmen.

Despite their loss of momentum, Renault's horse-knights charged, and Meges signal horns blew. Pennants dipped and raised as clever officers who loved their soldiery called for a reverse before the irresistible Westrons. Nonetheless, Ilycrium's heavy destriers punched deep into Meges' lines to meet well-armed men with steel bucklers and burnished mail. Feathered plumes surmounted helm-fixed khalats of watered silk, and electrum and gems sparkled from harness of man and horse, years wise in the dance of battle. Two hundred Meges fell at the first crunching shock—never to return to their Eastern cities. It was not enough, and the belly of the Meges line stiffened before Renault's outflung chevaliers. Knight slew knight. Many beasts were stricken, and their thrashing whinnies added to the din.

Trakhner's footmen were hard put to support their mounted brothers in the wake of the cavalry charge. Saber and spear wielded by unfought Meges brought them to a staggered defense furlongs short of their mounted kindred. Flying squadrons of Mgesh, maddened by shame, crashed repeatedly into the eroding squares, and were now supported by bellowing half-trolls armed in riveted brigandine. Soon the Chaos Standard shrilled to packs of orcs and slavering creatures who ran in like hyenas, yelping to the taste of blood on the wind. Unlike the disaster of the river plain, however, the were-creatures of Kör could not flank their prey by creeping on the edge of battle. Gibbon-armed trolls and fiend-spawned wolflings were forced to climb rocky buttresses where Gault's huntsmen had concealed themselves in the predawn. Unbeknownst to the combatant's below, fierce conflicts soon erupted amidst tree and stone fall.

From Gault's position, a single clarion sounded.

"They listened!" shouted Trakhner when Renault's cavaliers reigned in to fall back as best they might to the royal banner.

The old general laughed through the tears of a proud father, and slapped Gault's back when his infantry closed ranks such that chevaliers rode safe from pursuit. Runners removed the dead and wounded from the many-legged squares that paused, then resumed Ilycrium's advance.

TYRFANG OVER KÖRGUZ

The palace of Tyrfang brooded over Körguz. Like mountains in winter, countless spires glinted with black majesty over a cold, slated sea. Within the dread walls, a perfect mirror reflected turmoil in the heavens. X'fel loomed at zenith—paling all other bodies by its ascendance. Votaries in their hundreds chanted in cabal, evoking the emergence of the chaotic deity they revered—ancient and ageless, Eldar yet consummate with a new power harnessed by an implacable will that suffered no doubt in the design of Its malice.

Her advent was near.

Strange-eyed priests, nigh immortal and steeped in evil

wisdom, slit the throats of a thousand Westron hostages whose tortured screams lent power to the unholy symphony, and an incense of burning flesh clouded the innumerable corridors of Tyrfang. The city's very foundations trembled, whilst an unquiet sky parted. Orange and lurid, X'fel loomed like a falling planet.

Iblis' heart beat wildly. What exactly portended, he could not discern. Even scaly-skinned priests would not answer when his impatient talons had bulged eyes and collapsed skulls. Nay, they did not fully ken what they did, enacting their role just the same. Iblis wondered at the location of Pilaster and the pale human abacus that groped at his heels. The prince of Kör chortled deep in his chest. Pilaster had never been one for religion, the squid-skinned mummer probably had his white rat bolting the doors to his chambers whilst he made to hide in a closet.

Iblis laughed, and the magic of summons throbbed. It ebbed and shrieked, nearly lifting his feet from the floor. Wonderful! Soon he would know.

THE ORRUSTUDALE

The squares were moving, their fronts engaging milling orcs and ragtag units of Mgesh. A few score trollmen and Ascapundi blundered into the ordered ranks where even their stature and great strength availed them not. Dragged down by the press, these were slaughtered like tossing bulls. A leftward battalion of Meges charged forward as timbrels and pipes heralded the Eastern knights in their silver-chased armor, and their horses' feathered headstalls danced to the music. Little impeded by Ilycrium's archers, they peeled to either side in graceful feint to disgorge a pounding wall of red-fleshed Ascapundi.

"Steady!" shouted Trakhner.

"Pikes!" called officers as entire squares buckled. Men died.

Hulking bipeds with ropelike hair and slow, thoughtful faces pushed forward. A cry went up as Vur were touched in awe by many farming men turned soldier, whose legends held that the gentle herdsmen were good luck, and harbingers of mild weather and numerous flocks. Yet ungentle were the booming shouts and fierce blows as Vur drove headlong into the Ascapundi salient.

Giant tore giant as great feet stamped plumes of dust that arose to cover the squares. The Ascapundi, surprised and beyond vantage of their mighty king, were driven back, although at great cost to the Vur. Two-thirds of these lay dead on the field as the remainder folded into the slow progress of Trakhner's formations. Meges again filled the opposing distance, but their horses shied from the crumpled bodies of Vur and Ascapundi.

Trakhner cursed. "See how these knights of the East, these Meges, are too wise to dare our squares? They remain mostly unfought whilst our men toil in the sun!"

Gault looked to Renault, whose red glove tugged his strong chin. Gault grinned, and the knight champion nodded his affirmation. "They will come, General."

"How?"

"Two minutes after they do, order the foot to quickstep forward."

The ensign of the Silver Horse, three cubits broad and nine in length, was set into motion. Braegelor snorted his satisfaction, long had he waited. His broad hooves spurned the rocks of the valley as Gault's mesh glove lowered his bevor. Through its slitted apertures, he nodded to Baudalino, who grinned like a madman as he struggled to pace his prince with the great streaming banner atop a tall spear set vertically in its leather cup. Gault beheld the infantry, who shouted and raised weapons in a rippling salute as he pressed from canter into a smooth gallop. His iron-shod lance waved once its pennon, then was lowered.

Gommish frothed in rage. Dashing heedlessly before a Meges chariot, he jerked up his bow and loosed an arrow into the looming boy-king. A second, then a third followed. Gault angled his heater shield so that the first shaft deflected away, the second shattered on Braegelor's peytral, and the last caromed off his sallet. There was no time for a fourth. Gault's lance took the Mgesh king square through his barrel chest, splitting breastbone and chine before ripping free. Renault dashed Gommish's son from his saddle, thus ending their line of kingship forever.

Gault's van rolled over scattered flights of remaining Mgesh steppesmen before colliding with the surging Meges. Braegelor staggered when Gault drove his lance through the base of a splendidly gilt war chariot, spilling its thick-legged driver and javeliner under the hooves of its horses. Gonfolon shrilled through casque and shield like living flame. When she encountered the upraised sword of a Meges emir who bore a blade of eel-like patterns folded fifty and fifty times on a master's forge, there ensued a flash that rocked Gault back despite his plated armor.

Blinking sparks filled his vision within the sweaty confines of his close helm, and he thought he discerned a woman's tinkling laughter. The Meges noble lay supine, his breastplate scorched, and the pattern-worked heirloom riven into scattered shards. Even so, the forces were closely matched and neither gave thought to retreat. Nonetheless and contrary to their headstrong nature, Renault's cavalry held up their ingress once the charge was spent. Gault heard Trakhner's frantic whistles. He had no time. A snarling troll bared yellow fangs in its blue face and clawed at Braegelor's head, foiled by the metal chanfron as the destrier reared and plunged. Gonfolon flashed, and the creature's strange skull was riven.

Gault shouted to knights, "Hold!"

He heard salvation in the running tread of heavy feet, and from the swirling dust and brushy cuts on the valley's uneven floor emerged the infantry, sturdy yeomen armed with poleax and halberd who ran in amongst the horsemen. Pressed close, Meges found little room to maneuver, and there was no stopping eight-pound axes that clove with the pendulous force of man-high hafts, and on the reverse swing, the Eastern riders were billhooked to tumble irresistibly from their saddles to be speared or trampled. Maimed horses screamed horribly, and the hardscrabble was churned into red mud that painted the legs of the swirling warriors with bloody paste.

Rudolph Mellor cursed his fate. "It never ends ..." he gasped, "errands for priestesses."

Best as he might, the nimble thief avoided the stomping, shouting skirl of battle, and instead cut a devious, westward path across the ravine and ridge-cut vale, yet even so, outlying conflicts occupied every niche. For the most part, these encounters were unevenly matched, violent and brief, as men locked in perverse embrace with the servants of Kör clawed, bit, and hacked with primal savagery. Jamello saw a half-wolf run a circular path around a beleaguered pikesman. The man's feet crossed as he strove to keep his ponderous weapon between he and the snapping jaws of his adversary. From the lee of a boulder, a second wolfling leapt onto the man's exposed flank.

Jamello pulled his crypt blade from the spasmodically champing jaws of the were-creature. The sword heaved free with a crack, as it must have been wedged in the throat cartilage, and bloody froth and fat and bile speckled Jamello's jupon. Wiping his sword on the creature's greasy pelt, he looked to the second where his leaping downslash had opened its gullet. Whilst a man, it must have consumed a meal of garlicked sausage. The food-like odor was overpowering, and the meal lay upon the steaming coils of bowel amidst clot and waste.

Jamello swallowed. "Sausage on sausage, I'll never eat wurst again." He covered the pikesman's face with the soldier's homespun cloak. "Sorry, my friend."

Uglich jerked his straggly beard, indicating the flat of the vale where mounted companies of knights on brightly caparisoned coldbloods swirled against the heavy cavalry of Meges, and steel flashed in the midday sun. Uglich spat and turned to address the person at his side.

"Man for man, my gallachs can match any nobleman, but I'm not such a fool as to lead them into that!"

"For you, I have a plan," winked Rudolph Mellor, the thief's handsome face lighting into his most winning smile.

"Brighthelm!" shouted Jamello each time he slashed with the blade of the crypt, and a creature of Kör spun away trailing red. The muscles of his arm felt as if they were torn from their roots, and the membranes of his throat were chaffed dry, for breathing the rock-grit dust was like inhaling needles.

"Brighthelm," he croaked. There came a roaring to his ears.

His sword rebounded from the sallet of a trollman, who loomed from the smokes that wound up the scree and bracken of the eastern upslope. The half-troll grinned as it closed front to front, for Jamello's heavy blade was trapped against the scales of its bosom.

The creature leered hideously through its broken teeth, and gripped him up against its swag belly. With his shield, Jamello tried to batter the sallet aside. The troll leaned and bit him. The shield dropped. Jamello twisted frantically, seeking some dodge or purchase or weapon. He felt his spine yielding. Bits of meat, raw and rotten, heated the thing's gusting breath.

Blood pounding his temples, Jamello faded. "Brighthelm," he whispered as his thumbs fumbled under the low-slung helm for the beast's carotids. He could not inhale or feel his legs.

Jamello Edshu, who was Rudolph Mellor, thief and jongleur, gave over trying to straighten his spine or even to preserve consciousness. "Xephard Brighthelm!" he exhaled his last. Like machines, his hands tightened; nothing else mattered.

Jamello retched, then stood. The purple-faced thing below him was unmoving. He slung free a wad of bloody phlegm that was choking him. When it hit the ground, he could see one of his teeth in it. Not pausing to stare or curse, he ran. His first errand accomplished, he would obey the will of the young priestess.

Cynewulf released the hairy scabbard of his scramasax when he discerned the identity of the figure who came pelting up to where he held council with two others on the valley's eastern uplift. Apparently the newcomer had traversed the entirety of the battle floor.

Jamello collected his breath. "I have spoken with Uglich.

Seven hundreds of his wild kerns remain to him, all mounted. They will slip on the fringes, opposite the west wing of Ascapundi. When those big bastards come onto the flats, his Seod will feather as many as they may, hit and run."

Cynewulf scowled, then grinned mightily, and his carles relaxed their suspicious posture behind him. "What that brown-skinned, tattooed Western toad can do, we will do better! The Eastern Ascapundi are ours."

"Praise the goddess," breathed Isolde, "thus you save many lives." Tallux nodded and gripped Strumfyr, a gleam in his emerald eye.

Cynewulf fingered his golden torque. "Will you accompany us, Priestess? I like the look of your silent archer, and your swiftling spy."

Isolde shook her honeyed hair, gathering up mask and helm. "We go to find a makis of Kör, he named Vodrab. I will pray for you."

"Better you than me," cheered Cynewulf. He turned the head of his mountain pony. "And I think you need my prayers the more." At his shout, the Gaxe were gone, wending north up the rightward edge of the valley. In moments, they were lost to sight amongst bracken and fell.

"I know you wish to follow," said Isolde to Tallux. "They will hold the Ascapundi a space, and hopefully lead some a merry chase."

"You misread me, Priestess. I admire their courage, and such a bow duel suits me well, but we've a greater task, and more dangerous."

"Of course," added Jamello in plain tones, no sarcasm detectable in his voice. "So why delay?"

Isolde gathered her long-shadowed spear, and looked to the sky. Although blue and bright, it was heavy with expectation.

"Mighty omens are writ thereon. We will join the others on the far side of doom."

"Excellent," said Jamello. "Let us haste!"

Adestes Malgrim liked well the chaos of the field, much blood had been spilled this day, more would follow. The essence within him pulsed with power, it was nearly enough. His red charger flexed with anticipation and reared, forelegs flailing. He jerked its bit savagely. "Not yet!" He hauled the massive beast to a halt, although its muscles gathered for another attempt to break loose upon the field. Adestes laughed, for had he not infused the creature with a portion of the star burn?

Iblis had been well pleased at the return of his favorite slayer. Adestes inhaled, relishing the rich airs of the surface world and tasted the sweet-sour smell of the battle. He laughed again.

Behind, the wings of his company were silent. Adepts they were, masters of the spear-like yari and many other weapons unknown to the Westrons. To the Dragon Rift he had gone to make summons, and these had come to kill under the implacable gaze of their master. Grazmesnil had shattered his earthbound prison: a triumphant scream and a burning wind were loosed in the deepest hour of sable night. Twain brothers had likewise raised horned heads to the dog star and roared their answer to his call. Today, *dragons* flew!

"Remain until my signal. We will choose our moment."

War masters of the Pleven Deep bowed low. Ensconced in a cut behind the left wing of Iz'd Yar's position, Adestes felt the vibratory tread that marked the initial advance of Kör's center. Already he could see the streaming darkness of Vodrab's casting.

Sensing his distraction, the red charger wheeled and tried to bite him. Adestes nearly broke its jaw. It would not be long.

"Scribe, set down this order: That the family hostages of Meges guested in Körguz by our royal cousin, be slain."

"And the Mgesh here?" asked Astorath. He poked the slave scribe as a man might a roast. A bloodthirsty leer split his face.

Iz'd Yar surveyed the war plain. "They are dead already."

Arrayed on Iz'd Yar's fore was a flat of Kör's immortals. Elite units among them flanked their general in a three-sided box, and to either side were placed battalions of Ascapundi, backed by goblins in their thousands. Yet the first troops to action would be a thick line of half-breeds. Tall and strong they were, more so than any man or goblin. Those most akin to their demon ancestors bore Hel-wrought bows and were clad in sophisticated gear of war; those resembling rather their orcin heritage stood as shock troops, crudely armed and thirsty for the blood of Western men. Iz'd Yar could see that the squares of Ilycrium had advanced to within two furlongs.

He turned to Shaxpur, "Give the order, Quastor. We go to meet them."

The black dwarf stood atop a rocky pile one mile north and west of Iz'd Yar's position. Here the forested slopes dwindled to low hills that in turn fell onto the northern flats above the mountainous horseshoe that was the Gerales. Although the black-skinned dwarf was ringed by three thousand foes, he removed helm and mask.

Burn and scar marred his dark features, and sweat rivuleted his face from a toiling run in armor.

"Some have said," began a yellow-haired dwarf whose bodily stature was nearly as imposing as Henlee's, "that in dying, Bardhest Redhand named another king under Uxellodoum."

"I have heard this as well."

"Know this," growled the yellow-haired war leader, "that no Eastern dwarf took part bodily, or by design, in that siege."

"I believe you," said Henlee.

Balverk, war chief of mountain clans that dwelt in Saurdraven, the jagged crown of Kör, scowled under his magnificently braided moustaches. He looked to the singed brown hair of the other and sucked his teeth.

"A vow we swore."

"Oh," said Henlee, "my wishes for your fortune." The black dwarf made to depart.

"Wait!" said Balverk. He held up his hand, brows furrowed in thought. Henlee paused.

The yellow-haired dwarf smiled, dropping his hand. "The oath we made to the Kör prince cannot be broken: *Dwarves will come to the Waelstow; not one will depart whilst any foe stands.*" Balverk's thick hand found Henlee's.

"This oath we will keep."

Henlee grasped the hand. "So be it."

Many orcs and bestial humans had been sent to guard Kör's baggage train. Among them there were also fell creatures that went on two or four legs. An arrow barrage smote them like a storm.

Man-high bows wielded by hard-eyed woodsmen reaped a full

harvest of orcish men, as more than half a thousand frontiersmen converged on the supply depot. At a word from Telnus, sutlers and wagoneers were slain whilst slaves and animals were set free. All supplies and loot, save wholesome foods, were fired and soon an oily smoke arose behind the swarming formations of Kör. There, atop the provisions of war, was raised a simple standard, its heraldic design was that of a horse head in chief, over a field vert per bend sinister.

Thus converged the woodsmen of Ilycrium to honor the emblem of the king's scouts. So silent and swift had been their attack against thrice their number that few had fallen. Telnus sent some to patrol the wooded heights above the battle; others raised their bows in victory and shouted to cheer their countrymen who marched and fought in the long vale.

Shaxpur bowed low before Iz'd Yar, then rose and pointed a vambraced arm behind the conclave where stood Vodrab and other notables. A dark smudge lowered over the valley's mouth northwards. Iz'd Yar's vertical pupils squinted as might a raptor's, piercing the distance. "Did not spies report to us that the human general has little use for rangers and such?"

"They did, sir."

"Then why is there a horse head on a rag over my supply dump?" shrieked Iz'd Yar.

The field marshal of Kör fixed his gaze upon Vodrab, whose own bodyguard glowered back under low-slung brows. The makis could be vaguely seen behind their wide bodies, beckoning and chanting to the northern sky. "Useless old lich."

Iz'd Yar's clawed hand found Astorath, creaking the forge-blackened armor. "You go! my son. Find Iblis' pet assassin, something tells me he will warm to this task." Iz'd Yar's eyes were impossible to meet directly. He focused them on his subordinate. "Now, Quastor, crush those fucking squares."

The bowmen of Ilycrium called to one another with sonorous chants that carried over the resurgent swell of the battle. They had fought well this day. The horse-archers of the Mgesh with their powerful laminate bows, proud Meges, and even Kör's skirmishers had ceased to be unified forces, yet only now was the principal foe revealed. As soon as Ilycrium's archers found maximum range, yard-long arrows began to fall amidst the outstretched wings of Kör. Although fewer in number than the Mgesh, Trakhner's archers had been preserved in their rearward positions, and with smooth ease, each man drew and released, up to twenty times a minute, his killing shafts.

The missile storm of Shaxpur's immortals responded. Impossibly strong arms bent bows of some unknown alloy to the nock. Four-foot shafts of a similar metal, heavy and bitterly sharp, were released with a resonant thrumming. Lifting over any arrow drawn by mortal hands, they ripped the air with awful passage. Shaxpur bellowed a command, and scaled arms fired at will, expending innumerable forge hours in minutes. Ilycrium's squares could not hold, for no targe or byrnie could stay the murderous barrage.

"Close with them!" screamed Trakhner. Whistles blew and marshals shouted, panic rising in their voices. The infantry blocks lurched forward, leaving shield mates pinned to the pitiless earth.

Apieron smelled smoke. It was not the bitter stench that wafted in oily plumes from the wanes of Kör, where he hied. Apieron looked left. The western downslopes of the Gerales were draped in a pale haze, heavy with the smell of woodburn. Far distant, an occasional tongue of flame danced in the creeping pall. Apparently, foragers of Kör had likewise fired Ilycrium's base camp and the fortification so painstakingly reared over the preceding weeks. Any thin hope for retreat withered in the burning forest.

Apieron did not pause, his errand was more urgent. Apieron the Runner flew across bramble-choked watercourses and leapt stonefalls along the valley's rim.

Morning brightened to blue noon over the vale's center, so Apieron sought shadows under copse and ledge as he wended swiftly northward. Word had come to him in the darkness that Telnus of Windhover had resurrected the king's rangers; only they could have penetrated Kör's screen of crawling beasts. Apieron's mouth twisted in wry grin of irony, for his goal was obvious. Smoke and flame.

Apieron passed Iz'd Yar's shining legion as it mustered. He sensed the island of conflict ahead, whence he sped. He opened his mind. A chill breeze stirred the haze from the north, where greater darkness gathered. Something slapped at his brain, and he stumbled, then righted. A shadow flashed across his vision.

"A *door*," he gasped. Wolf cries shuddered eerily on the wind. Something came. Apieron dug in his feet, willing lungs and legs to greater speed.

Ilycrium's mounted knights began to surge between the squares, but the immortal general, Iz'd Yar, Strategos of Kör, would not allow the full weight of their charge to fall upon his Azgod. "Unfetter the half-breeds."

Iz'd Yar surveyed the mob of fiercely loyal demon-orcs that surged end to end across Kör's front, and nodded to Shaxpur. Oliphants blew, and the crooked-faced mob pelted forward.

"Gods save us," whispered Cusk.

"Stay, lads!" shouted Wiglaf. "Keep the pace and hold yer lines even, an' we'll skewer Kör's swine when they come."

"'Tis not them, Sarge." Cusk fought for breath. "Look what's next!"

Beyond the frothing charge of the half-breeds loomed the perfectly ordered echelons of Kör's elite legion. Their ranks, bristling with steel, advanced parade-crisp, and the ponderous echoes of their tread were as the footsteps of doom.

"The boy-king's farmers scythe mongrel men and Iblis' wretched goblins like this land's yellow wheat," mused Shaxpur.

"Where are my Ascapundi?" bellowed Iz'd Yar.

Skegga attempted a lunging swat at a mounted tribesman. The man fled, but in doing so, turned on his saddle and shot the Ascapundi in the thigh.

Skegga yanked the dart free but three others dangled from his hide at angles too awkward to reach. The skulking human galloped to a new vantage where he repeated the maneuver on a new victim. Ascapundi milled about on the wings of Kör's legion, where Seod and Gaxe synchronized their attacks on either side of the valley. Thick tongues in giant faces swore their frustration, unable to close with the darting humans who stung like buzzing wasps.

Shaxpur signaled, and the metal bows bit again. This time, the iron rain sought the edges of battle. In less than a minute's time, Seod and Gaxe were scattered, and their remnants pounded frantically upslope while pursued by vengeful Ascapundi. A full third of the hill riders lay unmoving on the field amidst not a few Ascapundi, stricken by the indiscriminate Azgod deluge.

Skegga paid no heed. He wheeled and bellowed his charge anew, this time back to the vale's floor. He was followed by wrathful giants in their tens, then hundreds. Trakhner's squares dissolved. Forced by the Azgod arrow barrage to scramble forward heedless of formation, they could present no pike hedge to the red-skinned behemoths who smote their line from either side.

"Well done," grinned Iz'd Yar.

Chapter 31

The Orrustudale

On either side, Ascapundi waded into the fray. Skegga stood as a boy might athwart a puddle, threshing minnows with a stick. Some of the giants swung bats of hardwood studded with iron, called godendiac. They laughed and chortled in red-wattled throats, and strangely muscled legs were spattered with human blood as they breasted the battle surge.

Gault shouted, signaling the charge. Muddy turves were tossed aloft as horse hooves dug for purchase. Gault knew that only minutes remained to the infantry before they were broken into chaos or perished. Amidst the pounding onrush of his cavalry, there sounded a curious piping, hollow and deep, and Gault laughed aloud, for shaggy-haired Vur were with the horse. Surprisingly, their presence did not startle the chargers. Candor called to Boug, and the Vur leader waved a knotted arm in reply. He bore a wagon tongue for a club.

Skegga beheld the Vur and emitted a wrathful bellow. Picking their foes, his battle thanes closed.

Braegelor snorted and strained forward as the cavalry rushed the final yards to the enemy. Lances lowered, it was a rolling wave of bitter points. The lines struck like lightning on cliffs. With a buckling groan, the first rank of demon-orcs were dashed under, then the second, but the wildly ferocious half-breeds could not be turned by fear or even self-preservation, and they flung themselves upon plunging horse and armored knight alike.

Boug dealt crushing death amongst the wildings with each flailing stroke of his stave, yet the wild creatures swarmed like ants that whelm the greater foe, until at last he fell under a pile of stabbing spears and notched blades.

Iz'd Yar's immortals arrived, and Hel-forged weapons flashed in the sun.

Ilycrium's foot soldiers ran into the lee cleared by knights to hew at demon-orcs and Ascapundi. Others gathered themselves, looking to reset their ranks and provide lanes for the chevaliers when the recall would sound, although not a few simply sat to weep or stared at nothing whilst forgotten weapons dangled in twitching fingers.

Horns sounded, and pennants dipped. The cavalry whirled, then charged again as the battle achieved a strange balance. With headlong horse sorties, the Westerners barely countered the weight of orc-demons and Ascapundi and the press of immortals behind. Trakhner and his marshals went amongst the infantry, which again found its feet, although it could not yet advance. Gault swallowed, hesitant to give his next command. He searched Seamus's face to gain strength from the armsman's steadfast mien, then nodded to Renault.

The red glove rocked a slow signal, and an unrevealed contingent pushed through the ranks. Squires watered horses whilst riven shields were tossed aside in favor of others that littered the field. A murmur arose. Knight peers stayed minor repairs, and even the staunching of wounds, to gaze upon the grim newcomers.

Serfs and freemen of middle or late years they were, girt with sickle and threshing fork. Many were lame or otherwise infirm, yet each was bereaved of son, daughter, or wife, and united only by a fanatical hatred of those who had shattered their lives. Rapine and slaughter and the burnings of homes and lands painstakingly cultivated for generations was a debt that could be paid only in blood. Too empty of spirit to function in company, these broken men had gathered to the army by a final desire to rend a Körling ere death. Renault's war horn wafted a dolorous note, and a primal scream ripped from soul-anguished throats as the unlovely charge of the lost began. These emerged from the center of Ilycrium's formation and crossed the flats in seconds to smite Iz'd Yar's close-ordered legion with a sickening crunch and rising clamor. Sword and axe, heavy and long, rose and fell as the warlords of Kör plied their trade.

A crazed villager leapt upon an iron spear, taking it through his midriff, as with a gurgling scream, he heaved forward to puncture the neck of an astonished Azgod who bore up the human's body with both hands. More oft, however, the untrained civilians were butchered without hurt to the looming Azgod, resplendent in their armor and perfect in their craft. Passion and valor bled out futilely on the war field beneath the mighty blows and booming shouts of the nobles of Kör. Renault's knights could no longer bide the slaughter and spurred recklessly to strike the line where they could. Trakhner's squares also witnessed the sacrifice and lurched forward. It was not enough.

Each Azgod was centuries wise and in the prime of strength. Many were adepts of the arcane, ever seeking clever ways to discomfit a foe. Their lord was the mightiest of their kind on earth, and wealthy beyond reckon, thus their war raiment was unsurpassed by any nation or force under the sun. Rearward arrow barrages kept the Westrons in the slaughter zone as the three-sided square of Iz'd Yar's immortals flattened to a line, each half-demon eager to slay the berserk humans whose front rank was struck down again and again.

Renault's knights flung themselves on the enemy in desperation; the shrieking faces of demon-orcs and Ascapundi flashed before their sweat-stung eyes. Random Meges, horsed or afoot, rejoined the fray whilst the shining legion of Azgod walked forward like a bloody machine. Gault's heart was riven, and he turned an anguished glanced on Renault whose face also burned with the suffering of the lost company. They were now nearly all killed. The red glove signaled a final charge of the royal van.

"So be it!" cried Gault.

Gonfolon and Renault's verdigris sword were drawn as one.

A scarred, blanch-haired elf stood a low rise several hundred paces behind Ilycrium's advance. His clear eyes missed nothing, and the small detail of soldiers assigned to him shifted uneasily and mumbled amongst themselves. Few of the swirling enemy opposed the cowled elf and his encumbered armsmen, who bore heavy burdens. A score of goblins had tried and been crushed by Boneslayer, the elf's strange sword dealing quick death to the dazed survivors.

He beckoned, and soldiers dragged thirteen bulging sacks to him to spill the contents on the ground. Bone and tooth, tusk and claw of myriad animals and men were there heaped in jumbled perfusion. Tooth ivory and gray bone gleamed wetly. Gathered from the Hill of Death, each had been slain by the reavers of Kör.

The elf stooped and lifted the mandible of a boar. His soldiers licked their lips nervously. "Wise men say the farmlands of Ilycrium were once a teeming ocean. Therein the bones of strange and fierce sea creatures, as large as dragons, are occasionally unearthed. I have added some of their remains to our gifting."

He gazed at the jawbone in his hand. A two-inch tusk protruded, yellow and sharp. "Wilt thou be as fierce as they?"

The elf's cast-off garments streamed weirdly on the breeze as he spoke without looking at his armsmen. "Gentlemen, return to your companies." Making clumsy bows, they departed in haste. The elf surveyed again the battle and raised his eldritch staff. As ancient ivory it appeared, cracked and stained. At his feet, bones began to shift.

The elf lifted his head and straightened, and would stoop no more. The beggar's garb flew away on the wind and his mantle came alive, sparkling with threads of gold and bluish platinum. Diamonds winked therein, as if glad to forget the dun and threadbare past. Giliad Galdarion, formerly of Amor, spoke gently to the remnant of the animal he held. "If you so wish."

It shot from his hand downhill and on unerring course toward the immortals of Kör, as one and another from the piled bone followed to become a flashing stream. To Giliad's magesight, each piece was girded by a hazing nimbus—the vengeful spirit of a creature straining with eagerness. Down the course, random warhorses reared and bolted as man and goblin alike fell flat or cast themselves into ditches to avoid the skeletal river in air. It struck the shining legion as a wave of biting, clawing, thrashing frenzy. Azgod flailed uselessly as their front was mauled. The rear fell back in consternation as howls of pain and the fighting growls of myriad animals lifted over the battle.

Iz'd Yar yanked Vodrab by a rope of the sorcerer's matted hair. Vodrab's gaze was vacuous, and Iz'd Yar shook him until recognition flared into the black eyes, followed by swift hate. "Do something useful, Wizard! Else I'll let out your wind with this!"

The demon-lord's benighted blade swam before Vodrab's vision. The sorcerer shook himself free and stalked into the mist he had coiled around their hillock of vantage. Iz'd Yar waved him away in disgust. He regarded an imposing immortal, a subaltern who waited patiently, utterly confident in his master's wisdom and his own strength. "You! Summon to this fracas the dregs of the miserable goblins, and as many of my cousin's creatures as you can find." The taloned claw pointed to the center where Ilycrium's elite knights drove deep after the onslaught of the lost and the tearing fury of the bone-wight casting, which faltered at the last due no doubt to some mummery of Vodrab's.

"Deep indeed," rumbled Iz'd Yar. He marked the boy-king but a furlong distant. The whelp was brave and skilled, and the Field Marshal's eyes burned when he beheld the laughing essence of his enemy's brand. He hoisted his vampiric blade and gestured to his guards, the most elite of his Azgod. Trumpets brayed and whips snaked forth as Shaxpur threw in the last of his reinforcements, and five thousand orcs ran pell-mell into the fray, raising the noise and chaos to greater pitch. Skegga, mightiest of Ascapundi, had regrouped his own and tramped behind.

Both lines were shattered, the death grip had come.

The battle seethed like a foam-throwing wave that breaks against rocks. Gault kept his van together as best he might, although he despaired for the infantry, for only by sheer discipline could the army hope to survive against the press of numbers Iz'd Yar deployed. Albeit and with no small irony, Gault perceived that the reinforcements cast at him by the Strategos of Kör had separated Ilycrium's army from the shining legion for the nonce, and against mere goblins, they might survive a little longer!

Iz'd Yar stayed his followers as Vodrab reappeared below the overlook. "You appear a peasant woman, Makis! Come to pick over the fallen."

The unclean sorcerer raised up, his voice cackling like a lost wind over winter's dead grass. "I have sent the Chaos Standard before your precious immortals. They rest while orcs and Ascapundi do the dying."

"So?"

"Observe, Master."

The thrumming staff and withered arm beckoned. Half a thousand figures shambled from the mist. Körlings and Western men alike gathered to the necromancer on clumsy legs, their garish wounds fresh with clotted blood. Vodrab's jeweled nails flicked, and his ghouls lurched away.

"Cheap labor," mused Iz'd Yar.

Vodrab keened eerily, his face lit with pride in his lich craft. Soon new monsters of a type unknown to even the field marshal of Kör slunk from the crawling vapors. Their faces were gray, and black veins throbbed their dark essence over corpse-like features. Three hundred of these caught up the undead and filtered into the battle. Vodrab rejoined Iz'd Yar, and together they watched, shielded by the sorcerer's cloaking from unfriendly eyes.

"A corruption fills their mouths," crooned Vodrab. "Should prey survive the rending, soon he will fall stricken with fever."

"Congratulations, Evoker," pronounced Iz'd Yar. "Eight hundreds new pets have you. I go now to join my legion, we will seek the man-king."

Vodrab stepped back, bowing once. "I must off, for a magic far greater than this have I made. Darkness comes."

A horse-scout crouched on his haunches before his prince and chewed a stem as if all was not turmoil. Gault had found Trakhner when the Azgod had unexpectedly pulled back, and even mighty Braegelor needed a respite. The black horse steamed and champed. Seamus and Klea were there, as was Giliad. The brave calling of Renault's war horn and the roaring of Ascapundi drifted over the tumult, which seemed to have lessened somewhat.

Trakhner scuffed the dirt. "Kör's foul standards cover the plain before and behind."

"We are flanked?" asked Gault as he wiped sweat and dirt from his neck with a rag, his great helm beside him on a tuft of grass that had somehow survived the mud-churning battle.

"Not yet, Sire," responded the pathfinder. "Your foresters and wild tribes still patrol a thin screen around the warring. For now, it holds."

"Good news."

The man stood, apparently already rested. "Nay, Prince, there is the other." He spat out the stem. "The Ensign of Madness. Where comes the black standard, we are routed."

"And your brethren?"

The scout waved at black smoke that wafted from the north. "Telnus made true his promise. Iz'd Yar's supplies were fired, but at cost. Scouts stayed to complete the burning. They were trapped, and a pitched battle has arisen there."

Gault turned to Giliad. "Tell me, Magnus, of thy foretelling. What of the army of Hel? Do they also come against us?"

"What use—" began Trakhner, but he fell silent under the elf's crystalline gaze.

Giliad nodded. "They indeed walk our earth, although a mighty blow has been dealt them. Half their number was harrowed beyond Duskbridge, the remainder come hither at great speed."

Gault's face was haggard; his front was smeared with blood

and dust. His hands fell limp. "Is all then lost?" Seamus steadied him with one great paw.

"I do not know what will happen," replied Giliad softly. "Many dooms are writ here today. A year ago, I could not have imagined them. You, who are young and strong, must have hope."

Trakhner smiled in his weathered face. "At last, a decent rede! Maybe the squares can be mended. Come, sir!" the bluff general addressed the scout. "P'raps we can win through to your rangers."

Klea lifted her prince's chin, favoring him with a smile. She then followed Trakhner. Seamus helped Gault remount, and the prince looked to Giliad. "We broke through once, before Iz'd Yar's foul brood came between us. Will you help us do so again? Unless Trakhner can do what he aims and flank Tyrfang's immortals, we'll die here today."

Giliad bowed. "I will serve you here to the end. Go to your cavaliers! I deem your army needs to see the face of a king." Gault returned a salute with Gonfolon as Braegelor reared and moved off. Seamus ambled after him.

Chapter 32

The Orrustudale

Giliad picked his way forward. When he encountered leaderless squadrons of men, he sent them to Trakhner, urging them to reform their ranks. When he met those of the enemy, Boneslayer feasted. In this way, the lone elf came to a cairn of stone placed by unknown men in bygone days.

Weary of slaying, he rested. There was a woman, one Vigfus—a spaedam who had followed Klea's four hundreds. Giliad's hand found hers to stay her casting. "Look not with true sight on the empty cendal of Kör. All who do so fall into madness." The old woman's lined face searched that of the golden elf. He continued, "The fear that ripples from yon standard is only a trifling of its magics."

"And you, lord, why are *you* not stricken?"

The elf paused, his crystalline gaze hard on the van of Iz'd Yar. There the golden serpent clasped a red star in its teeth. "Of that bitter cup I hath drunk deep." His hand gripped hers again. "Harken! Anon comes one who will challenge the banner of insanity. Aid her as you may."

The chaos staff thrummed a living blur as Vodrab performed a small, formulaic step. Air hissed past his jeweled teeth. He wheeled, alarm tugging his wizened features. "Ah, I tasted wizardry on the wind. Were you not Pilaster's pet elfin? Purchased from death?"

Giliad's gaze sought the northern horizon where dusk's shadows already crept from the lee of the Gerales. White hair played in the wind, and the glance that found Vodrab's face made the necromancer give back.

"Thy plaited locks stink, old witch."

Vodrab flashed a grin and stroked a flattened pleat. "Greased with the fat of infants from pathetic Sway. With it, I can fly."

"Fly then, or stay." Giliad shook his head. "Fear not of me, thy doom was spun ere came I. Your Mistress awaits thy shriveled soul."

Vodrab's eyes boiled with hate. He mouthed a word of slaying, and jerked forward, staff leading. With an arresting cry, Giliad brandished Boneslayer. A crevasse found Vodrab's feet. Arms akimbo, the necromancer staggered back from the edge.

Giliad looked left, where a woman and two others toiled nigh the cairn. A quirk of a smile lifted the pale scar on his face. He vanished.

"Look at them," laughed Telnus. "Like bees that return to find a bear has reaved their hive!"

Horse-scouts and frontiersman stood a small knoll at the open northern apex of the vale, where the proud horse head and slash green of the king's scouts floated over the plunder they salvaged from the burning. Mgesh and orcs detailed to safeguard Kör's supply dump returned in wrath. They stamped and swore but kept distance from the leather-clad Westrons atop the hillock, for three-foot shafts had already skewered those that dared approach.

"What next?" asked a pathrunner named Rubens.

Telnus surveyed the tableau. Southward the battle raged. "Toss into the fire what we cannot easily carry. We leave as we came, in the cuts. Mayhap we can then steal unmarked onto Kör's rear."

"What is that?" The frontiersman's brown hand indicated a scrub-fringed ravine. Fog billowed in its mouth. "Odd," added he. "Sun's chariot remains high."

Telnus's face was perplexed for a moment before he sprang to action. "Quick … make barricade!"

Men rushed to do his bidding. Casks and burned-out wagons were overturned hastily as from the dry wash emerged a heroic figure, an emperor's wealth of stones flashing on a silky steel cuirass, and in his upraised hands was a fiery mace. His uncanny red charger reared and plunged, then came straight for the knoll. A scarlet cloak trailed behind.

"Arrows!" shouted Telnus.

A half-dozen shafts splintered on the cavalier's harness and the charger's peytral as some hundreds rangers formed a defensive line at the mound's foot. Behind the fell knight emerged a running wedge of agile monks come to fight from the Pleven Deep, Rift of Dragons.

The mighty knight blew through the outliers as if they were straw. His adepts followed. Many a frontiersman had hand or foot stabbed by a yari thrust, his enemy now past him whilst a second monk slashed his life's ending. The spearheads were oak-leaved and quillonless atop shafts of tensile wood—the whole less than three pounds and appallingly quick. Inner positions of the flying wedge were occupied by slashing swordsmen who exploited rents made by the spearwielders. Once upslope, however, accurate fire from the scouts kept a tenuous perimeter.

A quarter-strength of Telnus's foresters were slain in mere minutes. A Cur Quan of Mgesh set five hundred steppe-riders to ride the periphery of the hastily assembled redoubt, shooting from horseback into the barricaded position. The hetman waved, and two hundred more horseless Mgesh drove an equal number of orcs at sword point up and over. Half fell pierced, yet the remainder scaled the piled debris to leap amongst the Westrons.

Adestes screamed a taunt but held up, wheeling his mighty charger at the base of the knoll, for a block of Ilycrium's infantry approached, bolstered by horseless knights. Trakhner had kept his word. Adestes could see more Westerners as they filtered up from the south to join the newcomers. Apparently, the order of battle had dissolved. Fate lines were converging. He looked to the north, where the high steppes were tinted with a purpling dusk.

"I can feel him, moving in darkness."

The warrior-priest at Adestes's side made a sign and fell facing the distant night. When the man rose, his face was stern. Under his hood, lines of knowledge cut the man's features. His sword and khalat were secured over belted robe by a knotted cord of twisted silk. Beneath the garment would be other weapons, Adestes well knew. More skilled than any assassin of sunny Bestrand or worldly Farseps was this one. Ismay, Prelate of the Pleven Deep, looked to Adestes for orders.

"Lead us a path to ambush yon square."

"And the leather men? Will they not come down on us from the rear?"

"I will ensure it," laughed Adestes. "When they do, destroy them."

Clambering up the short steep without pause, Apieron burst in amongst the orcs. An infant's head dangled from a shaman's waist. Apieron slew him and five others in seconds. Telnus's woodsmen saw, and rallied to drive shrieking goblins from the redoubt.

Smiling greatly, Telnus gathered his liege to him. "Buthard and Wulfstane proclaimed you dead."

Apieron grasped Telnus warmly, yet his voice was solemn. "I think they spoke truth, I have lived the life of the damned."

"But no more," laughed Telnus.

"If we survive." Apieron released him. "For now, gather the Scouts."

Below them, the peril to Trakhner's square became manifest as its infantry made for the hillock, keeping loose formation over boulder rift and tree scrub. Oblique to their path, however, was a broad ravine wherein flowed a river of robed men.

In manner like to the reinforcements that joined the trotting square, Mgesh and orcs attached themselves to the votaries of the Pleven Deep. Even Azgod and random trollmen, carried far over the field by their wrath, joined their fellows. They closed the final yards and surged up onto the flat and into their foes.

Henlee spied his friend moving with purpose amongst the frontiersmen of his estate. They made to scramble down a stone fall where two thousand Körlings, led by yari-wielding monks, clove into a loose square of equal numbers.

"Apieron!" Henlee began to run. There was no mistake. Despite the distant whirl of battle, a crimson cloak and flashing armor marked a mighty knight atop an incarnadine stallion. Gasping for breath, Henlee blessed Isolde for his boots. He ran faster.

Leaning from his destrier, Adestes smashed a knight to the ground with his ruby-faceted mace, its spiked head crushing the man's breast armor like soft tin. Such as this one, if rendered horseless, had attached themselves as champions to Trakhner's squares and greatly bolstered the much-suffering infantry. Incredibly, the warrior braced himself on one arm and made to rise. Dismounting, Adestes ripped a rondrel from his vambrace and drove it through the slitted eyelet of the great helm. Blood started from the aperture, and the knight sank back with a groan.

Adestes leapt back onto his red stallion. From this vantage, he noted with satisfaction the deadly skills of his silent killers. The leaders of the Westerners, invariably heavily armored, pushed to the fore to face their attackers. Even thus, each monk of the Pleven possessed fighting reflexes unequaled in speed, and metal-cased knights soon found themselves isolated in a sea of stabbing spears and slashing tachi in which expert thrusts found the vulnerable flesh beneath Western armor.

Adestes was pleased, for soon the infantry square would be sundered, and more of Iblis' minions joined him by the minute. Mayhap in time he would give over four or five thousands fresh troops, newly victorious, to Iz'd Yar's degenerate son. The pale mutant was ahead, deep in the fray. Spiked hammer and whetted axe slid from the demon son's black-fluted armor whilst his own twin swords keened melodies of death amongst the despairing Westrons.

Adestes rowelled the stallion, and it executed a perfect capriole, blasting away a leather-clad woodsman who was creeping behind. Adestes laughed to see the man pinwheel away. Then he saw Apieron. The object of his regard had filed his troop through a sidecut to strike at the triangle formation of Adestes' adepts.

"Too soon," Malesh rumbled.

He bethought himself a moment. Fiercely driven blows and the grunts of surprise of the dragon votaries marked the impact of the flanking rangers. Already, satellite groups of Ilycrium's infantry attached themselves to this new column as the monk wedge buckled from the side. Heartened by the appearance of their brethren, resistance to the fore within the square stiffened, and a new clamor arose.

Across the space of battle, Apieron saw white teeth in the darkly handsome face. The full lips puckered. A kiss was blown and waved forward by a hand gauntleted with steel …

Apieron knew the room. Well he should, it was his own. A rushing wind gust struck Windhover's upper floor, opening a heavy casement. The dog star's sickly light illuminated a diminutive figure on her great bed, ensconced in a pile of fleece and silk. She sat up, brushing back sable tresses to see. A dark paen, low and silkily feminine, slithered through the house. Melónie gasped as finger-thick bars of her window frame bowed inward, then ruptured.

Melónie hastily sobbed an incantation, and a pinkish fanglow leapt from her hand. She screamed, for revealed by her spell light was a pallid face with feral eyes. A wizard-prince he was, dead before her father's line was begat in the sun-kissed East.

Melónie found again her voice. "Ulfelion. I name and bind thee, servant to my spell!"

The figure paused, and there appeared a second, tall and broad of shoulder. His rich laugh filled the room and fire found his blade. Melónie's scream was echoed by a laughing succubus, its macabre song rising to a shriek.

A gurgling scream erupted from Apieron's gullet. When the vision cleared, his eyes were not human. A dozen yari were lowered in his direction.

"Apieron!" croaked Henlee, his throat too dry to carry.

With a final burst of speed, he caught up and buffeted Apieron aside. The massive dwarf struck the bunched monks like a battle wagon, sending a ripple amongst their rank.

Henlee shrugged off their frantic blows whilst nearly each one of his ended in a crippling crunch or fountain of blood. The shock of Henlee's charge allowed Apieron to slip into the belly of the wedge, where he simply ran amuck. The crimson wave of fury rose again within Apieron's breast and filmed his eyes. Reinforcing squads of orc and Mgesh barked into position by Adestes were swept away before they could react.

Harnessing his javelins, Apieron gathered a heavy scimitar from a kneeling monk who gasped his last breath through a blowing chest wound. With one hand, Apieron swung the five-foot blade into the neck of another. He slashed forward like a barracuda amongst schooling fish. Each bone-crushing thud of the steel reverberated into his arm with muscle-paining joy while in his mind played the actions of his enemies in his absence. How many decades had these ground-dwelling maggots plied their trade of murder, and the sacrifice of innocents to the maintenance of their sun-shunned god? Apieron severed limbs and gutted his opponents with vicious twists and lunges too shallow to grace a quick death. He glutted himself in their agony and destruction.

A sergeant of the Royal Scouts and several gambesoned woodsmen bearing axes followed the rent Apieron made, but he could not be caught, even by Henlee. Adestes' taunt pounded

Apieron's ears, and he found himself on the flats and in the open, sword arm and front caked with clotted gore.

He sheathed the scimitar into a Mgesh bowyer's body and pulled forth again his stabbing spears. The dust-and-filth-smeared man had been dazed and lost, his eyes finally opened with clarity to behold the great weapon through his middle. He sank with a groan that was ignored by Apieron, who listened to hear that the dwarf yet lived by the ruckus behind him. The rain of blows upon Henlee's adamantine casque was like the frantic hammering of a score of smiths on sheet metal, and Apieron knew that once the dwarf's thick legs were set, nothing short of a god could move him. The ebon javelin's vapid blade flickered like lightning from a fast-scudding cloud while Apieron's running feet gave his opponents no clear target and removed hope of flight. Three monks swarmed him, two stooped to tackle in a valiant act of sacrifice, whilst a third leapt high, downslashing with his yari. Three died.

The throng around Henlee sensed their supporting ranks melt. They glanced fearfully over their shoulders while attempting to keep sight of the unconquerable dwarf. This only gave Maul's bitter edge room to swing. The dwarf fought in silence save for the death cries of his enemies—and the blows he dealt and received. The time for slaughter was come. Each Körling that fell before him meant one less that could wheel and entrap his maddened friend. Of Apieron, there was little sign save random groupings of crawling wounded or mangled and deathstill corpses. A sideways sweep of a yari struck Henlee's heavy mask, stopping his musing and painfully wrenching his neck. Maul responded with a satisfying chop into the priest's breastbone, severing the heart and dropping the assassin-monk like a flopping fish.

Apieron delighted grimly in the play of his weapon. Nothing was better suited to laying low a fleeing enemy than the quick-darting javelin. Its eighteen-inch, flawless edge and tapered point sheared with delight the laminate armor and flesh of his foes. If the Spear-Wielding Goddess herself had guided his arm, She could have done no better! Time and again, he caught them up with blows to vulnerable backs or hamstrings, leaving them to await his woodsmen. The votaries of the Dragon Rift were agile athletes, experts at all manner of edged weapons, garrote or by hand, and shrived since childhood of all hesitation or mercy. Against the ranger lord of Windhover, it was not enough.

Apieron drove his lance through the dorsal spine of a half-demon, dropping it face-down onto red clay. The creature crawled painfully forward on its elbows, paralyzed below the waist. Apieron leaned onto the spear butt, driving it through the Azgod's form and pinning it to the earth like a gruesome butterfly. It bellowed in rage and pain. Apieron laughed like a Fury.

Each gut-wrenching death eased, for a fraction, Melónie's hope-ending wail that had been revealed by Malesh. Leaving the dart in place, he drew his truss and stooped down. Bloody moments later, Apieron lifted a steaming mask to place over his head and shoulders in gory mantle. Squadrons of the enemy gave back before this apparition. The fact that only one stood against them fueled their fear more than two score opponents could. Surely some vengeful god of fate assailed them!

Apieron leapt amongst the minions of Kör. With his heater shield, he crushed feet and up into chins—or whirled it sideways to snap arms and mangle throats. The javelin licked out like a many-headed hydra as the War Dancer's eyes lit his foes with a baleful light.

Henlee led scouts and woodsmen to the gulley's mouth, occupying the space recently held by the enemy. The press of battle was yet ahead, where Trakhner's much-suffering square strove to right itself. Despite the space cleared by the companion's wild rampage, the great numbers of roaming Körlings had swelled Adestes' force to twice their own.

Apieron's feet slipped in a pool of gore. He gathered himself like a sprinter, searching ahead for Adestes, but a figure in black-fluted armor stood athwart his path. Its white face spoke, "You have traveled far, horse-ranger. Son of an infidel beggar, scree blown before the Helstorm!" The words continued, strangely formed and reptilian to Apieron's ear. "You've stretched your fateline a touch thin, don't you think?"

Wiglaf and Cusk beat down a pair of orcmen who had turned, astonished to find two of their enemy so deep in their formation. Wiglaf stayed Cusk's arm. "Come, boy. This fight's a free-for-all." The youth had continued to flail his prostrate opponent long after the body ceased to move. Cusk wielded a plain-hilted, sturdy hand-and-a-half, the weapon of a professional fighting man.

"Where to?" Cusk gasped. He wiped sweat and dust from his face. It did not help. From somewhere, a horn was blowing. Deep-toned yells and the shrill neighing of horses drew their gaze. The Silver Horse of Ilycrium galloped its oriflamme above the dust-swirl and ruck of battle but a short stade distant, and the bellowing roar of Ascapundi echoed from the melee. Cusk looked to the grizzled sergeant.

"There!" said Wiglaf.

Cusk nodded and smiled. "To our king." Together they hastened forward.

There was a man, a young Meges, who kneeled in the dust. His torso and hands were splashed with blood-streaked mud, although he appeared otherwise unhurt. Bodies of many sorts were strewn about, and his horse lay behind him, its neck severed by a voulge that was lodged in the spine, angling upward. Cusk heard himself chuckle to see the weapon handle sticking up like that. It seemed darkly ridiculous. *Why didna' someone take it?*

The Meges ignored Cusk and Wiglaf, his handsome, olive face drawn in sorrow as he wailed in prayer, arms outflung to some god. Wiglaf and Cusk hastened by, leaving him to his bereavement. They approached the nexus of the melee, where huge bodies dimly seen ambled in the dust. A Mgesh forager galloped past—quite dead—his body pinned to his maddened pony by an arrow of the Azgod.

"Oh shitballs," stammered Cusk.

An Ascapundi materialized out of the miasma before him. Cusk glanced to Wiglaf who was encumbered by a pair of scaled half-breeds, more troll than human.

Cusk sidestepped the Ascapundi's blow, although its enormous glaive scythed his side. The fine mail and padded jupon he wore deflected the convex cutting edge, yet his ribs and flank were painfully bruised. The Ascapundi's polearm continued sideways to split a low thorn tree and bury itself in the ground. Cusk dashed within its reach. Yelling furiously, the youth thrust his bastard sword into the torso of his opponent. The point snagged! Cusk growled and thrust again. It was useless, for he saw that under a loose garment, the Ascapundi wore a baldric of bull's hide, boiled and layered over the giant's choleric skin.

Releasing its trapped weapon, the Ascapundi bit Cusk's head, lifting the youth to dangle a yard in the air. Growling itself, the Ascapundi tried to drive its short tusks through tippet and arming cap atop Cusk's skull. Failing this, the nine-foot behemoth began to savagely shake Cusk's head back and forth in attempt to snap his spine.

Cusk felt more than heard the thunk, as if a hoe driven into clay.

The Ascapundi emitted a curious squeak, too small for its frame. It released Cusk, who collapsed in a faint. The Ascapundi looked down and toppled sideways. Its own glaive had severed its foot. Wiglaf's enormous arms hefted again the eleven-foot weapon and swung it overhead to split the struggling, barreled breast of the giant.

Roaring like a mastodon, Shabla, underchief of Ascapundi, bull rushed the thick human who had dared strike down his thane. Two others followed close, clad as he in bronze plates, and bellowing only slightly less.

Wiglaf set himself, then quickstepped forward as he has once seen a champion at hammer-throw do. With all his strength and momentum, he whipped the spiked glaive from his hand. It caught Shabla in the gorge above his cuirass, nearly severing the waist-thick neck. The remaining Ascapundi stepped carefully over their dead leader, wary yet lustful for the blood of this manling who had already slain two of their number.

Wiglaf gave back until he stumbled over Cusk's prostrate form. He halted, then braced wide his legs and gathered Cusk's fine sword. He would retreat no further.

Cusk woke painfully. He struggled from beneath a tumble of bodies, and his head swam atop a neck that screamed with each slight turning. He vomited, and his head cleared enough to gaze about him. There were four Ascapundi and one man. Wiglaf's eyes were open and the grizzled lips moved feebly.

Cusk fairly pounced, "Oh Sarge, ye've kilt 'em all. What can I do?" Cusk's voice broke. "Help me help you."

"They're beautiful."

Cusk wept. He gently shook the man's shoulder. "I know tha' sky's pretty!"

Almost imperceptibly, Wiglaf shook his head. "Most beautiful thing I have e'er saw." He died.

Cusk covered Wiglaf's eyes with his hand and cried aloud his anguish. He heard the flap of wings. Lifting his head, he saw them.

A winged elf was there—bare chested and bronze skinned. Cusk could see that the wings were neither feather or skin, but of the same ephemeral, hairlike substance as spun gracefully down its back. The strange elf bore a hooked blade and a twined lasso. Raising a muscled arm, the elf signaled, and a squadron of his fellows swooped to join. Together they assaulted the Ascapundi that stamped and shouted nigh the white horse. Crooked lance and leafy arrow, bolo and slingstone, pelted into the bellowing wall of red flesh.

Confronting Apieron was a pallid warrior as tall as he, although more muscled, and his eyes and mouth were black as was his fluted mail. Twin swords danced lightly in either hand to caress the air before Apieron's breast. Both blades bore an oily sheen.

"I killed your brother at Bishop's Gate."

The weapons dipped, and a bow was given, yet the creature's eyes never left Apieron's front. "You see well, human. His name was Berich."

Apieron studied the poisoned blades. "Is that alchemy for me?"

"Just so. I know you, son of Farsinger. Vodrab sang of your blood."

Apieron lifted a javelin. "And your name?"

"Astorath."

"I will remember yours, and Berich, in a future time."

Seamus raised himself on one arm. The other hung useless, broken above the wrist. An Azgod had laid open his face from brow to chin. He shook blood from his remaining eye. Heaving with effort, he made to jerk free his leg. Looking down, he grunted to behold the taloned hand of a wolfling driven to the elbow through the fat of his calf. Its full weight was on him, and each time he tugged, the creature twitched weirdly. His belt hammer was yet embedded in its skull. Apparently Gault's sortie had swept beyond this spot, and the fate of the Prince was veiled.

A gauntleted hand pushed him gently back. "Bide." A sword flashed, and the wolfling's arm fell free. A figure bent to tie a strip around the red-mouthed wound, and a second around his face. His rescuer's thick blond hair fell free.

"You are a woman?"

"Here is an intelligent male! Perhaps you be worth savin'."

Seamus kicked the wolf thing's carcass away. "I hate those dastards! Fly, lass. A better fate for you than the dogs of Kör."

The woman laughed at this. "I 'aven't been a lass for twenty years, but I thank 'ee." She hoisted him to his feet.

Seamus grunted again, impressed by her strength. He fumbled for his pouch. The woman helped him, her hands lingering on the healed scars and missing fingers of his hand. "A sorry state, woman. Ah," he touched a folded rectangle of leather, "just the thing."

She helped him wet it, and wound his injured wrist. For the first time, he regarded her closely. "Gault's woman's maid o' arms!"

"Glad to meet you." Byrinae's smile was rose-hued in her dirty, round face. "You mention fate. Our men and children are either dead, or lost in that ..." Her chin jerked toward the battle. "We mean to get them back. Comin'?"

The thirteen feet and half-ton of stamping fury that was Skegga, overload of Ascapundi, crushed mounted knights and their destriers with a godendiac large as a tree bole. A maddened Vur swung a length of ship's chain against his flank. The twenty stone of chain thudded, snapping plate-size scales from his bronze casement. Skegga staggered slightly, then the mighty chieftain returned two blows in quick succession. The Vur's great arms dangled limply—both its clavicles broken. Skegga heaved the lesser giant over his back to fall amongst his house thanes, who howled and chortled as they rended the Vur into pieces.

Gault felt as if he were hollow, nothing but painful emptiness within him. After the charge of his royal van, a wave of Azgod had counterattacked and swept over his position. His squire Baudalino lay at the foot of the great banner, stricken by many wounds, though somehow the Argent Horse still rode on sea and cloud. The prince of Ilycrium's eyes were caked dry and could not weep.

Of the twenty knights who rode his sortie, only he and Renault were unscathed. Three men had been sent back with Braegelor and Renault's charger. He and the redoubtable chevalier would stand to defend their egress. The battle was like a chessboard dashed into chaos by a child.

Seeming to float in the dust behind and to either side southward, the majority of Trakhner's stalwart infantry fought in clumps against Azgod who made to regroup whilst driving lesser allies to encumber the Westrons. Behind them away northward was a scarp fringed by a screen of immortals where he knew

Iz'd Yar lurked. Gault smiled grimly to see the oily smear yet more distant and hoped Trakhner was alive. His own sortie was a success, albeit costly, having fractured the envelopment by Ascapundi. "We hurt them, eh, Champion?"

"Truth, Lord. Look what approaches!"

In loose formation, thirty or more of the greatest Ascapundi rambled through the hanging dust toward them. Gault looked about. There was no one else. This time, there would be no charge of shining Templars to succor him. Xephard was dead. Isander was dead.

"What say you, friend? Have the others been given enough time?"

"I fear not, my lord."

"Then we stay." By way of reply, Renault grinned like a maniac in his strong face and lowered his visor as the red glove and verdigris sword saluted. He stepped forward, the griffin of his house fierce on his breast. Gault joined him.

Eirec marked the young prince as he ran. He shouted others to greater haste but did not loose his gaze from the stranded men. A pair of Ascapundi outstripped their mighty king and closed the distance. From the scree of bodies, a troll man leapt upon Renault, tearing his mace aside with clutching talons. The verdigris sword cleft its skull, but at the same instant, an Ascapundi punched with a phalanx spear, the long, tapered point driving through Renault's plate and into the soft flesh beneath. The champion's limbs sagged. A roundhouse blow from a twin-bladed axe, driven by all the monstrous strength of the second Ascapundi, crashed through Renault's aventail to shatter the spine bone beneath.

Gault leapt forth with a cry, and with four sweeping blows

of Gonfolon, removed the offending arms of both spear and axe wielder. Bellowing like gelded bulls, they caromed off. Surrounded by his battle thanes, Skegga stalked forward, his twisted mouth agape and drooling with lust.

For a flickering moment, a notion played in Eirec's mind: a prosperous land, bereft of king and nobles, a land where a strong man might earn a throne, should he be wise enough to embrace a new order, even as it was also ancient and wise. His task was easy, simply rest and witness the birth of his kingdom! That the thought did not originate of his own ken came to him, and he swiveled his head, searching as he ran. He saw only the swirling battle, but the vision pushed into his brain like a relentless surf.

Eirec gritted his teeth, and touched his axe sheath given him by Isolde—cleverly woven of beaded silks and leathers by loom women who served Wisdom. The vision swirled, and the tempting notion to abandon his oath to the young prince was replaced by the visage of a man whose unnatural life of fermenting evil wizened the features beyond human, and a sharp-toothed grin and witch-wild locks flashed with gem glow and the power of his casting, but Eirec heard again Isolde's benediction when she bestowed gifts in Bishop's Gate, and Apieron had met Eirec's gaze when the ranger received again Melónie's weave, his friend's gray eyes smoldering with purpose in their shadowed depths.

Eirec scrambled down and up a creek bank, stamping through mud and water in his haste. Farther ahead, he beheld a scarred, enormous man who hefted a mighty bone of some long-dead creature. That one limped to the Prince, accompanied by a stolid woman with fine, wide hips and blond hair.

Seamus and Gault climbed to ease Renault against the base of a jack oak. Like the tortured knoll against which it fed, the tree held no beauty, bent and dirty. Byrinae lowered Renault's bevor and studied the face. The quizzical mouth was closed, and the brow unfurrowed. "He's gone to t' Halls of Honor."

Seamus limped a step forward and snarled, clearing room for his curious weapon. "The big one's mine."

Gonfolon traced the air easily beside him. "Get you back, woman. At least *you* shall live."

"No, Sire!" Byrinae grimaced apologetically, taking Gault's other side. "What would my Dunstan 'ave said to hear me speak so?" Her words were drowned as Skegga and his angry-skinned giants came on like a red wave.

A shadow passed overhead. Gault glanced up. Another strange shadow ran across the ground, and the devastation began. Two parts of the peoples of the Wyrnde had come to war. Finding a height beyond orcish archers, swamp elves loosed scything fusillades with matchless accuracy. Skegga stumbled, pierced by a dozen living shafts, and twice that again found his prostrate form. He never rose. In mere minutes, it was over; thirty Ascapundi lay twisted and still.

"Strange angels these be," husked Gault.

Eirec trotted up between the bodies of giants. "Friends, come from the Wyrnde. Apieron told of them."

Gault grasped the large man, kissing the sides of his beard. "You survived?"

Seamus and Byrinae smiled to hear Eirec's booming laughter. "I should say the same to you!"

"How?" stammered Gault. "I thought a valiant end surely befell you on the dark shores Apieron sought."

"But for him, Lord, a second host had assaulted you by now. One spawned in the very depths of Hel!" Eirec's deep voice growled, "A World Storm accompanied our flight, that hurt the Helspawn sore, I deem."

"*Apieron* is here?"

"Aye, and others."

A party of horse-knights reined in. One led Braegelor and Renault's charger. Candor knelt before Renault. "Thus the brave die," said Eirec. "I wish him well."

Gently they lifted Renault onto his horse. A squire would lead him rearward. Squadrons of swamp elves moved over the battle's center. The black missiles of Azgod plucked elves from the sky as a ferocious arrow duel erupted. A strong unit of dwarves and Northmen came forward. Eirec placed Seamus and Byrinae and Gault into their ranks.

"Go now, Sire. We will meet where stands the Strategos of Kör."

Chapter 33

The Orrustudale

Iz'd Yar screamed his fury. His baggage and spoils were burned, and only one in five of his Mgesh and Meges survived. Shaxpur now swept orcs and orc-demons into the Westrons so that Azgod might reform their ranks. Never before had their front been breached, and now, elves? *Elves in the sky?*

"Elves in the sky!" shrieked the field marshal of Kör. He wheeled on Vodrab. "Why are you grinning like an idiot?"

Jeweled teeth flashed. "Many have died; there is much blood in the air."

The withered arm pointed northward. There, black in the distance, hung the soul shriving. Every man, woman and creature of Ilycrium slain during the invasion months, every tree felled, was summoned by Vodrab's dire casting. A twisted, gibbering portion of each essence flowed from the northern sky. Shadows fell, and the day grew chill. Minions of Kör howled with glee as the flapping pall put fear into the minds of men, but more terrible yet were the hate-spawned beings it heralded.

Dragons came. No dream mists these; but three sons of Tiamat who cleaved Vodrab's spirit cloud with living tissue, iron hard and nerved by revenge plotted down the unnumbered centuries.

Grazmesnil glowered at a brother who made to pass him by. Eldest, he would be first. Wings tucked, he dived. His great tail down-lashed, and a Vur twitched feebly on the stone, its body broken like that of a clay doll. A crooked javelin rebounded from Grazmesnil's horned snout. His jaws snapped up the swamp elf, and sweet juices flowed down his gullet. It was good.

Grazmesnil bellowed his hate, and a squadron of the creatures fell from the sky, hair and wings melted. With a thought, the Eldar dragon sent his brother to the eastern lay to scatter mounted tribesmen who harried Ascapundi away from the army of Ilycrium's flank. "And thou, Cygunddfel, find the dark star child, who does the will of Our Mother. Aid him."

The ancient dragon turned north to obey, its gray back trailing streamers of howling souls.

His attention thereby undivided, Grazmesnil smote the center of the Westrons with the fury of a slighted god. He was heedless of their pricks to his material form, which felt glorious and strong in its freedom. Heedless as well was he of the Körlings interlocked with his enemies and who also died in number, victims of his roiling breath.

Iz'd Yar's picked followers advanced at leisure behind the folded wings of his reformed legion. Once the immortals of the Dream Throne began their advance, no foe could stay them. He would meet Iblis' pet wyrm in the middle. Iz'd Yar drew his soul-rending sword. It was destined, for somewhere within the melee, he would greet the boy-prince to make a final ending.

Adestes looked to Ismay, prelate of the Pleven Deep. Blood crusted the mouth of the man's silken scabbards for tachi and tanto. "Pull back your adepts. Let Mgesh and unclean orcs front these forest-men and mud-sluggers. A Son of Chaos comes anon!"

Reborn in wrath, Cygunddfel shattered Trakhner's northward square with gouts of dissolution. The bravest orcs and Mgesh were likewise caught and consumed. A few pathetic cavaliers broke lances on the impenetrable hide before Cygunddfel crushed the metal-clad warriors with wing and tail, mangling them with claw and fang. He then swept skyward, low over broken terrain to alight again and upon a salient of men clad as hunters.

Cygunddfel laughed his derision. He fixed a man, tall with corded muscles that gripped a bow, with his lambent glare. Mazed and unmoving, the man did not quiver as the wyrm feasted.

"Back!" screamed Apieron.

He yanked men behind him whilst Henlee broke a path to the fore by punching and kicking woodsmen aside. Telnus was there, and from a shieldburg of bodies and rubble, he confronted the dragon with an eighteen-foot phalanx spear. His sergeants were with him, plying shaft after shaft into the dragon who had lighted to consume the dead. Apieron called out in horror. Too late. Cygunddfel concentrated his breath, annihilating the men and blackening the very stones.

Tears for Telnus and those others stung Apieron's face as he leapt upon the blistered stone.

Cygunddfel focused the full power of his gaze upon the man.

Apieron tossed aside his shield which yet blazed its defense from the dragon's casting, and drew both javelins.

"I'm keepin' mine!" called Henlee, who stalked around the edge. Maul's gleaming edge led mask and his ebon round-shield.

The advent of the dragons changed everything. Byrinae sat on the ground, weeping under the terrible spell cloud, and Gault's grip was fierce on Eirec's arm. "Take your tall Gefylla east to Fuggo and Tannhauser. If they break, we are enveloped."

Eirec chewed his lip. Above them, winged elves milled ineffectually about the greatest of the three wyrms. Another dipped and swooped across the eastern field where red-skinned giants led Kör's assault as the Prince had said. The remaining winged lich had soared northward. Apieron and Henlee were there. Eirec ceased his fretting and grinned, his unruly black beard nodding.

"A sooth plan, Highness. Save I will stay with thee and these others."

Seamus touched Byrinae's sobbing shoulder with the remaining fingers of his hand. She gripped them and pulled to her feet. Red faced, she brushed aside sweat-slicked hair to don her metal cap. She favored him with a tremulous smile.

"And now?" she demanded of the Prince.

Gault mounted Braegelor. A loose company of horse-knights gathered around him and three score infantry. Eirec turned to a dwarven chieftain, red-bearded and fiercely mustached, newly come to the battle. The dwarf grounded his mattock, as tall as he, and bowed.

"We will slay many of Kör's giants that you call Ascapundi ere we die," said Draliks. Departing at a run, he led his column east. As if they had not journeyed the many leagues from Uxellodoum with little rest, two thousand dwarves and four hundred Northmen rejoined their kindred who had withstood the hurtling bodies of Azgod and thundering Ascapundi. With the smooth precision of long-lived dwarves, they formed new echelons and pushed forward. Axe and mattock, hammer and sword threshed the red harvest.

The great wyrm hovered there like a prey bird whose hunger is never sated. It released a mangled pony and dangling tribesman to break and hang in a pine. Circling once to gain speed, it plummeted in full spate upon the dwarven brigade. Twenty perished in the first onslaught, and the immortal dragon raised its hoary head to trumpet its glee.

It stooped again, exhaling the breath of dissimilation, and a dozen Northmen fell smitten. Still the dwarves advanced. Clad in imperishable steel, the secret of whose making was perfected ere the first man walked the fertile valleys of Ilycrium, they recked not of skyborne missiles or scything sword. They tore the heart from the Ascapundi assault.

Singing a slow paen, mountain dwarves and Northrons closed ranks over their dead. The tall survivors of the Axegrind and veterans come from the battle of Uxellodoum would not flinch before any foe, whether earthbound or spawned of the abyss. Stepping over war-strewn bodies, they kept their wedge and moved north, reversing Kör's flanking salient.

Cynewulf's tribesmen saw this and were heartened. Only one-third remained, yet amongst hillside trees, they gathered themselves, binding wounds and resting their wiry steeds for a final charge.

Buthard pushed up his visor. His low-slung brows jutted forward like those of a bull, thick with slow-witted belligerence. "Ho, Exeter! I will have your properties soon enough. You might as well die now."

Exeter's narrow beard jerked in disdain. "Where skulks thy father, whelp? Why not wear his treason for all to see?"

"*I* am here," replied Buthard's gruff voice, "and these others."

The cry and clangor of close-quarter strife came to where the ensign of the Boar surged against that of the Hawk. Exeter's house troop fought with outraged surprise at a neighbor suddenly turned enemy. Buthard's knew the grim purpose of a battle long prepared, and the confidence of new allies, numerous and strong.

Exeter's glance strayed to where the Argent Horse surged again against Kör's massive center, even as the dragon pall darkened the field. When he spoke, his voice was heavy with wrath. "Because of you and your father, more men will die today than should be."

The wide-rolling shoulders shrugged. "Join them if you will, Seneschal."

Exeter was a crafty and proven swordsman, but the hard years had frosted his beard and his once-steel-spring muscles had slowed incrementally under his elaborate harness. He abruptly yelled and step-lunged, the larger man grunting at the aggressive maneuver and flinging up his bearded war hammer, thin and wicked, for the parry.

Exeter's attack was a feint. His hand-and-a-half whirled over the lesser weapon in a vicious swipe at Buthard's extended limb. There was a crunch, and blood spurted onto Exeter's bright sword.

Buthard grunted again and bulled forward. Exeter's eyes widened—his blade caught in the interlocked plates of Buthard's vambrace. The hammer spike split the creamy surcoat and mail beneath to transfix Exeter's heart.

"I name you traitor and accursed," gasped Exeter. He sank to his knee.

"I call myself rich, Seneschal." Buthard wrenched free his weapon. "And *you* dead." Exeter did not hear him. The ivory tabard was splattered crimson, and his hawkish features regarded the troubled sky. With a guttural curse, Buthard jerked free the offending blade and tossed it aside. From the strife of man against man, where the yellow blazons victored over Exeter's men at arms, a fighting squire approached his master. Buthard cuffed him roughly on the head.

"Fetch me a chirurgeon, knave, and bind up this wound. I think the old witling hast cracked the bone."

TYRFANG OVER KÖRGUZ

Alcuin raised his head to the inky gloom that was his cell. What need a taper for the blind? An unwholesome wind stirred his wispy beard. It was a casting!

A half mile through glyphing corridors and yet within the palace, Alcuin's thin body shuddered from the power of Pilaster's incantation, as the Faquir of Kör hurled his full might into the making. Vodrab's dragon pall was not enough. Unexpected foes had succored the Westrons, and more came. Heavy hooves thudded in his mind.

Pilaster's skin rippled a dozen colors, and his flat-horned skull swayed as syllables were dredged from his frame. His mouth pronounced them like chewing glass. Iblis would have his victory. Impelled by the final coming, sounds never heard on this world grated from Pilaster's mangled lips, boiling air and splitting stone.

Half a thousand leagues distant, strange lights stirred the dragon cloud. Like ball lightning come to plague the middle airs, the incandescence streamed at blinding speed toward the foes of Kör. Grazmesnil roared with glee, and nightfall streamed from his wings.

Alcuin stroked the gleaming skull. It was heavy on his lap. "Wake up!" A filmy vision flickered for an instant in the murk. "I call and name thee, King Bardhest Redhand." The apparition returned. It solidified. Alcuin regarded it solemnly with his opaque orbs.

The Redhand frowned. He was perplexed, for before him was a puling manling, pale and weak. Pathetically the chin displayed the merest fringe of colorless beard, although the creature did hold something that seemed of great interest.

"Why name you me?" Redhand's voice shook the close cell. "Know you not my wrath?" Bardhest was pleased, and flexed as the sensation of weight fell into his limbs.

"It is thy wrath I would summon. Pilaster prepares a mighty magic, and the Western prince will fall."

"That it aught to me?" Bardhest was not fooled by those scarred white orbs. He made his best frown, the one he deemed implacable as stone. It felt good.

"Dwarves in number have come swiftly from Uxellodoum where Iz'd Yar's leager was broken. A new king thou named, he and they will die in this storm."

Bardhest stamped his foot. "That is different!" Stone chips and dust fell on Alcuin. "Where be this demon wizard?"

"He holds close, doubly warded against mortal foe and sendings of the arcane."

Bardhest pulled his magnificent gray beard. "I am neither, am I?"

The pale locks shook. "Nay," whispered Alcuin.

Bardhest Redhand's visage split into a fierce grimace. "And Sage, should you survive … bury that skull with honor."

"Though I have little to give, it will be so. My word at least is true."

"Fair enough." King Bardhest Redhand favored the man-child with a departing wink. Too bad he was not a dwarf!

THE GEHULGOG

In the night preceding the Western battle, glooms hung frigid and sullen in the prison mines of Kör. There evolved something, an expectation that lived in small silences between the toil and the grind of machines. It grew, and with strange harmony, Drudges turned from their labors. They died singly, in twos and threes and by dozens. By the hundreds, the demon masters of Kör slew them, but it was not enough, and like a boiling geyser that cannot be stayed, they erupted from the Archwaze.

Blinking against light of star and moon, they joined a chaotic, slashing battle without line or formation. At the first, Azgod called joyful shouts and taunts as they slew while Drudges died in silence. Then a deep, unreasoning fear seized the masters, for the slaves of the Gehulgog were not easily numbered. Alarms sounded by steel horns went unheeded as Kör was muchly depleted of its swaggering soldiery, and no Drudge revolt had ever occurred. Ferrymen were slain without knowing why, and broad, misshapen backs pulled oars, propelling ungainly craft low in the black, frigid waters to Körguz.

Thir averted his gaze from the painful glow of star-filled heavens and looked instead to the oar-straining efforts of those beside him. He knew as did they: all were soon to die. Thir looked again, not one shirked or hesitated from his grim purpose. For the second time in his life, he felt something he had never imagined. It was love.

Thir remembered the golden elf whose name he never knew. That Drudges were created to die in thankless toil or gloryless strife was given. But he, Thir, would ensure it would be whilst breathing the same air that flowed under star and mountain and had caressed the tree he had once seen, the gifting of the golden one.

Barges thumped on quays and were cast off to swiftly return. Drudges assembled quietly ashore to await their full strength and gazed up at the many spires of the Palace Tyrfang that glittered frostily on the dark isle.

Deep in the gloaming of enchanted Amor, a gold elf, fairest of her people, began to sing. Twenty of her sister priestesses, daughters of ever-young gods of clean light and nature's bosom, and starshine that grants the arbor its silvery crown—queen and maidens lifted faces wise and beautiful.

Their lilting voices grew, evoking the living power of Amor, subtle yet giant. A song spell, slowly gathering, lifted from the tractless forest and wended its way south by east. To battle.

Chapter 34

The Orrustudale

Vigfus stood amidst the strife like a bather stands a foamy surf. If she desired, she might stretch an arm to touch the back of a Meges who dealt wide blows with a flashing scimitar against the wooden targe of an axe-wielding highlander. The Seod parried as best he might, but the graceful blade found its range, severing tendons behind the knee. The kilted tribesman fell with a yell as the other's scimitar slipped past a desperate parry to still the axe hand forever. Not pausing to exalt or pillage, the Eastern knight moved off to seek the remnants of his kind.

Vigfus saw all. Her witchy hair blew in the dragon wind. There! The elf's woman came into view. Tall she was, and the robes of a high priestess fluttered over her mail. To Vigfus's sight, they shined bright as day amongst the smokes and reek. At the woman's side was a stocky elf warrior, dark clad and stern of mien. This one sped bitter shafts into the swarming mass of foes, and a swift-footed swordsman danced around the pair, hindering any that would thwart them.

Above, in the battle's center, Vigfus saw revealed the godlike essence that was Grazmesnil, its eyes flaming the fires of Hel as the greater dragon stooped to assail a struggling formation of Trakhner's infantry. An airborne echelon of winged elves moved to interpose, confronting him with a gossamer net slung between two of their strange steeds. Grazmesnil dissolved them instead. Swamp elves cried aloud as the spirits were riven from their graceful bodies.

Spheres of glowing energy raced from Vodrab's spell wrack. Where they touched swamp elf and armored knight, there was a crackling implosion of living flesh and collapse into darkness. Men began to falter. Before and above them, and now from the air itself, death reached out to claim their lives. Vigfus hastened her steps as the fey elf had commanded her. She would aid the girl-priestess.

An odd stalemate occurred on Ilycrium's eastward wing where dwarves and Northern weaponsmen had cleared Trakhner's right of grounded foes, yet caused little scathe to the second brother of Grazmesnil. Under cover of the dragon's diving assaults, Shaxpur ordered, on pain of death, the last cohort of mounted Meges to complete the envelopment begun by Ascupundi and twice repelled.

Confined in their boar's wedge, dwarves could do little against the skilled cavalry that came against them. These were not lightly clad skirmishers, but the cream of their nation, well armored and on noble steeds. Thrice Cynewulf's tribesmen had pelted down and been thrown back from the valley's floor, and any dwarf or Northman caught in the open was summarily leaguered by the fleet horse-knights and struck down to join the unlovely heaps of dead.

Low and murmurous, the arrival of the main of the Liflyne people began like the speech of trees on wind. It grew like deep forest rills, spring fed and pure that conjoin under shaded boles to form flowing concourses that sparkle with rock-chasing life and sunlight. Scattered by the great dragons, aerial scouts were now joined by the bulk of the winged nation, and thrumming signals filled the middle airs over the battle.

Iz'd Yar slid his benighted sword into the breastplate of a mighty human. The man was the last of a handful of brave chevaliers who had sought to hue the Golden Amphiptere. He withdrew his brand, and the man slumped, drained of every essence. That they had penetrated so far was testament to their skill and courage. What next?

Iz'd Yar, Field Marshal of Kör, gazed up to behold entire squadrons of winged elves. The dragon to his left was caught in a filamentous web woven from strings of fluid silk, thick as cables and stronger than steel. Clouds of woody javelins and arrows harried the beast. Three giant steeds of the Wyrnde and a dozen elves were melted by the dragon's thrashing fury, yet many more kept station. Straining wings and singing Liflynes bound their quarry and hurled it to its doom.

Iz'd Yar's yellow eyes closed; he found Vodrab in his mind's crypt. "Get you and your dweamor-banner to Shaxpur!" Vodrab's mummified face leered. The vision fled.

More of the awkwardly graceful, mothlike creatures approached. From each floated lines hundreds of feet long.

Barbarous elves hung thereon to launch directly into battle, agile and deadly swift. Leafed shafts began to fall amongst his immortals. Iz'd Yar's hulking bodyguard stared stupidly.

Kör's field general wheeled on a bashar, a commander of archers in splendid harness. He pointed. "Ignore the others—shoot elves!"

The dust and grit hurled skyward by the dragon's tumble had not settled when Gaxe riders crashed down wooded slopes at full gallop to find and strike again their Meges foe. Haphazardly armored, the tribesmen suffered fearfully in close quarters with the Eastern horsemen.

Hope then lifted the faces of Cynewulf's clansmen, for the boar wedge of Uxellodoum arrived. It became a slaughter. True to their bonds of vassalage, Meges kept the field until there were no more.

Fuggo punched Tannhauser's mighty chest with glee. "Is that thing still hungry, Ice Walker?"

Eirec's lieutenant hefted his morning star, a two-handed affair thrice as heavy as any great sword. "Always, friend."

"Then assemble your slackers," cried Fuggo. "Our black king and your half-bearded jarl are lost somewhere in that!"

The cacophony to their left grew into one continuous climactic roar. "Lead on!" bawled Tannhauser, but the mountain dwarf had already moved off, yelling and slapping his battle thanes into formation.

Iz'd Yar stood on the back of a swamp elf. An Azgod shaft had skewered the creature from groin to shoulder. That it was alive was evidenced by a rhythmic flecking of blood on stone.

The Dream Throne was awake.

Ibis' demon warlock had conjured mightily! and the spell lightning under Vodrab's soul-rack drove Westrons to cover whilst the Eldar wyrm swept winged elves from the sky with his lashing tail and mangled their mounts with the scything of his breath. It mattered not that one of the dragons was lost, for behind Kör's general to the north, another dragon roared its fury, no doubt consuming the last of his rearward enemies. A fitting end to slinking spies and thieves.

Led by Vodrab's banner, Shaxpur's immortals advanced the field again in good order. Iz'd Yar removed his iron-shod boot from the back of the barbarian elf and strode off, leaving his hulking bodyguard to trample the life from the creature.

The dragon came gliding forward, sinuous and slithering, uncoiling himself, proud in his strength and beauty. Cygunddfel tasted the essence of Quas in this place. Heady indeed!

The ancient wyrm gathered itself, poised as if to strike. Instead, it breathed.

The seething cauldrons of its eyes widened as a small nimbus played around the cloth weave on Apieron's tabard, and the son of Farsinger ran toward it, accompanied by a mighty dwarf. The vaporous remnants of its discharge streamed from this one's adamantine casque. Cygunddfel recoiled in amaze. A mistake. Two javelins, both imbued with the powers of heaven, flashed from Apieron's hand to disappear into the deeps of its bosom.

Cygunddfel recoiled end over end. His wings flared against

the ground, pushing the great bulk into the air. More swift was Maul, as the dwarf's weapon tumbled to crack against the dragon's pinion where it sprouted from the great muscles of the back. Cygunddfel breathed again as he died, his last flickering notion to destroy as he crumbled into ruin. A full third of Adestes' monks, come from the Pleven Deep, were destroyed in the wyrm's fall and conflagration. Yet on Trakhner's infantry square, the dragon's vengeance had been most thorough. Many woodsmen were also slain, although the remaining scouts and foresters of Windhover surged past their champions to engage the milling enemy.

Swinging the red stallion's nose, Adestes spurred his force of Körlings and monks to counter, and his flaming sword cleaving any that were laggard, his ruby mace invincible. Rangers and scouts soon found themselves pressed by a crescent of Kör's minions. They traded blow for blow, but the calculus of war was against them.

Henlee brushed smoky wisps from his armor and round shield, and after examining them closely, he scowled at Apieron's humble tabard. "You look better than you should."

"I need your help." Apieron indicated a long and vicious spike atop Cygunddfel's many-horned skull. Maul cracked once, twice, and the spear fell free. Apieron snatched it up, and leveling the horn over his triangular shield, he leapt into the fray.

At full gallop, a line of clever Mgesh crashed their horses into the lightly armored foresters as trailing orcs and a dozen Azgod flew into the gap. The convex arc of the Westerners was cut.

Adestes shrilled a command, and the press rolled up either end.

Apieron and Henlee hacked their way to the breech in attempt to stay the hemorrhage. Apieron's new spear impaled a roaring half-troll, piercing its swag belly as Maul swept a Mgesh chieftain from his steed, then backslashed his maddened pony for a kicking barricade. Apieron's shield deflected a thin lance from his throat, and his spear licked in and out of a steppe-rider's shoulder. Apieron spun, shield leading to decapitate the Mgesh. The little horse bolted, and the rider swept by as a headless corpse.

Burning with intensity, Adestes forced more of Iz'd Yar's creatures into the rent. None hesitated. Malesh liked well these half-trolls, twice man-sized and utterly fearless. Soon the encirclement became complete, and such archers as remained to Adestes Malgrim began to play havoc among the dwindling pathfinders.

Odikine looked to his companion. The man's flat, leathern features held the same question he felt. Cavalry. No steppesmen could mistake the crescendo vibration under hands and feet.

"At least two hundred," said Mangut. "Heavy Northerns!" Odikine gazed in disbelief at the eastern defile. No cavalier would risk his destrier, each the worth of a sizeable burg, on such a dash amongst rock and tree.

Cur Quans had posted the two scouts in the bay, for it accessed the northern plateau and slope where the Hel knight and his sky wyrm leaguered the Westron spies who had fired Kör's baggage and spoils. Should any renegade dwarf or woodsman sneak hither, the twain would ply their powerful short bows in the killing zone. The men stood, for the pounding could now be heard by unaided ears. Gravel began to shake from the embankment.

"They do not swerve!" shouted Mangut.

Odikine stood rooted, awestruck.

To the men of the West, centaurs were only a legend of the deep woods, a beast they ascribed to the fancies of children and old wives. To Mgesh from the open steppes of Kör, they were unimaginable. Odikine and Mangut shed their bows, and fleeing back toward the flats and the chancy safety of battle, they were overtaken and crushed.

Vergessen wielded a twin-bladed and spiked halberd as a man might a woodcutting axe. In his left, he bore a shield of ironwood. Painted green for the forest, it displayed a stave held in gauntleted fist for his friend Apieron. The charge of the centaurs took Adestes' forces utterly by surprise. At first, they guessed them enormous primitives on the great-shaggy horses of northern Ilycrium. It was much worse.

Apieron pulled Henlee back a step, his teeth flashing in the near dark. "*Friends.*"

With thunderous onslaught, centaurs tore first into Mgesh ranks. Men and horses alike were spilled to the ground to be stamped, while knotted arms swung axes and clubs or thrust crude spears at those struggling to control their frenzied mounts. Bagwart had fashioned for them riveted plates into clever chanfrons and peytrals. Some wore peaked helms with elaborate head stalls. Unhindered, centaurs in their hundreds struck the enemy crescent with the momentum of a snowmelt river, swollen with mud and timbers. Even the walking beasts of Kör could not abide this galloping wave of flesh and steel, and the crescent was fractured into clumps of dazed and harried fighters who forgot their encirclement to frantically track this agile new foe.

Henlee waved and shouted to Bagwart, who bounced atop a centaur's broad back without reply, wildly swinging a smithy hammer and cursing because his arms were too short. "Thought you were with the army?" bellowed Henlee, yet the matchless iron shaper floundered past, trailed by a graceful killer, a gray shadow on four legs. Sut had also come.

It was an unhappy day for the wolflings of Kör when the mighty war dog found the field. Iblis' cursed creatures either snarled, slouching to the attack, or loped off yelping. Either way, the result was the same, and the way was opened. Apieron sprinted ahead, his dragon spear, black and clotted, bobbing frightfully before him. None dared face him.

Adestes Malgrim, Kör's Malesh, stood his steed and perceived the stirrings within Tyrfang while his eyes tracked the living apparition that was Apieron. He pondered the doings of the great battle. Obedient to his will, the red destrier turned its hindquarters to the field. Apieron shrieked aloud his frustrated rage, but the crimson cloak dwindled north and away.

Alkdog grunted and grasped Iz'd Yar's arm, painful even to he. Iz'd Yar wheeled at the affront but lowered his lifestealer when he beheld the cause in his bodyguard's eyes. A mass of dwarves had crashed into the rear of his very van. Their broad-shouldered leader wore a yellow beard, and incredibly, the standard that braved above them was of a dwarven fiefdom sworn to serve the Dream Throne.

To the fore, Vodrab's withered lips emitted a shuddering cry of summons that pierced the soul-wrack, and was echoed thousandfold. Grazmesnil burst through the leager of swamp elves, and like a pitiless bird of prey, he shot straight for the dwarven press.

"They are dead," said Iz'd Yar to Alkdog. "Advance."

Grazmesnil did not waste his breath on the armor of the stunted ones. In a controlled crash, he struck amongst them, thumping his tail like a falling tree and thrashing his body like a crocodile. Dragon's blood welled from a score of wounds as his hide was pricked by enchanted steel. In return, his claws tore and crushed, and his mouth was filled with the broken remains of his enemies.

The final survivor, a yellow-bearded dwarf, spoke as the relentless jaws champed down. "The black dwarf will know … we were true."

Grazmesnil consumed entirely this one, for he discerned a power in the dwarf. The dragon reared its head and bellowed his glory amidst his conquest. The scratches they had dealt him were nothing. Later, he would return to feed. He sped aloft, seeking the heart of battle before Vodrab's lightning scattered all the prey.

Chapter 35

The Orrustudale

Grazmesnil burst over the conflict. Counting his evil years, never had he witnessed such naked, glutting strife. He exalted. No man-loosed bolt or device of winged elves could stay him, and wheresoever he glanced, Vodrab's ball lightning brought brilliant destruction. Grazmesnil rolled over in midair, graceful as a falcon, to catch and mangle the bronze-skinned king of the Wyrnde. Consuming the sweet essence, he perceived the flashpoint memories of the centuries-old elf.

Bragen, this one was called. No longer!

Grazmesnil scowled at tiny, ground-bound figures. How they scrambled this way and that under his shadow! He was a darksome deity, born again into the world to feast on mortal men. The spirit pall moaned and flapped its concord.

Grazmesnil found the banner of the Argent Stallion. Well he recalled it!

Gathering his power, Grazmesnil dived to loose his full spate of breath. It broke, rolling aside before a golden mist. Suffusing the battlefield, the haze rose to diminish the wailing of souls. Vodrab's murk faded, dwindling to natural sky.

The maiden song of Amor had arrived.

TYRFANG OVER KÖRGUZ

Far to the north, Pilaster fled down a writhing corridor. A strange apparition resembling a lord of dwarves had assailed him, shattering his conjuration and nearly battering him to death, and only by the narrowest margin had he escaped the gray-bearded specter.

Pilaster pulled up. A Drudge and a palace guard rolled into the corridor. Blades useless, they throttled one another with bone-breaking strength. From somewhere, a wailing alarm sounded. He waved a crooked finger, and the clawing pair turned to stone. He would sort things out later, but first things first. Alcuin must die. *No essence, indeed!*

A mouth yawned into the tunnel wall. Pilaster stepped almost daintily into his private wormhole, it would bear him wither he willed. He summoned an image of pathetic Alcuin who had taken to dwelling in the mines, a journey of some distance even for the spell tube. Fine, he, Grand Faquir of Kör, would immolate the treacherous human in minutes rather than seconds.

THE ORRUSTUDALE

When the lightnings dissipated, Grazmesnil held up. The greatest son of Tiamat thought within himself. His allies were weak, the better so! He would fall and rend the boy-prince as he had countless others in many ages. Wings tucked, he began to fall.

The embryo star Agelos found the battlefield. Not long could he linger, for Quas called to him. Men who later recollected his flight said many things. Most remembered a sky blazing that emerged from a golden mist, and scarcely marked when Agelos traversed the valley faster than eyeflight, and was gone.

The mighty skywinger, Grazmesnil the Wicked, looked down. A blazing hole transfixed his form breast to back. Powerless, he died.

A fragile lilt of singing voices lived in the mist, benisons from the elf maidens of Amor. Ordinary men and women wiped the sweat of effort from their eyes as the life surge of water running and wind in trees came to them. Fading and lingering, it seemed that angels sang. The aureate glow faded, and lo! day's natural ending was over the land as Helios took his westering way behind the Gerales. His passing painted flags of carnelian and purpure on the vault, as if some god took up his knife to open the veins of the sky, and thereby a russet light bathed the hills in blood.

Brutish figures hulked from rock and shadow. Scraps of leather and bronze adorned their sun-blackened skin. They howled curses through knobbed teeth, as knotted muscles drove sharpened iron into the ranks of Ilycrium's armsmen with animalistic ferocity. Vodrab flung wide his arms, unnaturally long and crooked—the joints of no man that walked the earth, and the day howled its ending. From somewhere, fires sprung up and blazed before him across the field. They lifted their banners of crimson and soot to the blood-drenched sky.

Trakhner released his breath, not knowing he had held it. His troopers recalled something of their training, grueling hours snatched from repast of sleep or meal, most often after a toiling march. Stations were reformed. Woman and knight, Northman and dwarf, and even winged elves too weary to fly took a place, each ready to defend his neighbor, selfless unto death.

Trakhner found Gault at the fore. He was afoot; no horse would be sacrificed in the final grip. Behind the Prince loomed

Seamus, his halting steps aided by Byrinae. Eirec was there, as were those knights who would be first. In his left, Gault bore Renault's gold-chased mace. To Trakhner's questioning look, Gault gave a slight shake. He who bore the scarlet and the griffin was no more.

Gonfolon flashed keen in the leveling sun. At a distance of no more than fifty paces, Kör's immortals loomed like demigods of steel. The pitiless eye sockets of helm and mask were black. Cusk was also there and breathed thanks he could not see the faces beneath.

Iz'd Yar's forces were set in three rectangles; the two on either side angled inward to face Ilycrium's lesser numbers. Like a spume-tossed beach, the interval between the armies was littered with crumpled bodies of the slain, the detritus of war. The demon-lords of Kör did not advance, for they had learned that even mortal men might break their rank. Theirs was the stronger position, and night was falling, soon their foe would be helpless.

The line of Ilycrium shifted into final position. Allies and countrymen looked to their prince who had endured every hardship, who had grown from boy to man under their tutelage, leading and led as brother and son. No shouts or horn-blown challenges came. Breath was now saved for the fighting.

The army moved when Gault's skirted leg took the first step toward the death that awaited. There they would follow, and beyond.

Field doctors had bound the wound on Buthard's arm. The long bone was intact, and so a mighty shield was slung over it. He had barely stood when a lieutenant's outraged shout brought him round to behold a tall, blood-smeared man with an upraised lance who dashed two of his yellow-clad armsmen to the earth with torn throats. Before he could bellow an order, the man sprinted off to the main of the bloodletting. Buthard's thick brows beetled in outraged consternation. The man's carriage was unsettlingly familiar.

A deep-throated yell brought him cursing around again. An enormous, ebon-harnessed dwarf cut the legs from his lieutenant. With a running start, Buthard launched a mighty hammer strike at the casque and face of the smaller foe.

The black dwarf deflected the blow aside with a harmless clang. "Is that all you got?" Henlee's hip pivoted as Maul licked out at the out-thrust shield.

Buthard screamed when his arm snapped. Half of his heavy shield fell to the ground, the other dangled painfully from the strap on his wrist. Maul swung again, and the man's steel hauberk screeched the song of rending metal. Buthard folded.

"Dog! That is for Melónie. The children will I avenge on thy father." Buthard's thick lips gurgled a red-frothed protest that no one heeded.

THE GEHULGOG

Pilaster bethought himself. The way was deep indeed, but he was almost there. The white grub had apparently crawled to the deepest hole in Archwaze, as well he should! The tunnel worm opened, and Pilaster strode into the hollows. The extreme depth made them warm. At his thought, orange flame burst from rough walls, evaporating oily with a noisome hiss.

"Savaunt," spoke the Faquir of Kör, "a weasand will I fashion of thy soul."

Alcuin stood, pallid in the glare. Pilaster unfolded his leathery wings, and flapping once, he scooted to within twenty paces of the slender youth. Whirlwind fires stalked the boy, corralling the puling manling to the arch-wizard. Alcuin's robe caught fire, and he fell choking to his knees. Pilaster screamed his fury and rained blow after blow, exposed talons scoring the naked flesh.

A tearing of the very stone brought the tableau to a standstill, and a gaping, light-filled fissure split ceiling and floor. The hollows moaned, and Giliad entered. Pilaster howled like the fiend he was, his ram's head tossed, casting the magics of petrification followed by incineration. Boneslayer brushed them aside. Giliad's white hair and scarred face were fey, and his cerulean orbs were glacial deeps. Alcuin crawled to a cragged buttress where he collapsed. "Another victim, Nightwing? Do the mighty thusly prove themselves on the weak?"

A crooked blade found Pilaster's hand, and its chill sent spindrift dancing aloft. "I know thee, elf. I have studied thy essence and mind, thy broken spirit." Pilaster's red eyes and scarlet mouth appeared as if they brimmed with blood. Smiling hideously, he vanished.

Giliad drew sword, his lambent gaze frantically searching the hellish murk. It was futile. His glance fell on blind Alcuin, who had risen to his knees. One white arm pointed a trembling finger behind the elf mage.

Giliad ducked. A hooked blade froze the air in its passage above his head. He spun and backed away, resheathing his vorporal blade.

Pilaster appeared, then fell into upper and lower halves that rippled insanely before becoming the hue of stone. Alcuin gripped the buttress, wrenching himself to his feet. The frail youth had sustained a terrible beating, his pale skin bore bloody furrows and one elbow was fetched the wrong direction.

At length, the golden elf spoke. "There is no one else, come with me."

There was only the sound of water dripping on stone, and

the slow exhalation of the mines. Alcuin listened. For the first time in over a millennium, the Gehulgog was silent. He held up a glittering skull.

"I must stay, a task undone. He would be buried with honor."

Giliad's scar lifted into a smile. "I know a place."

Alcuin felt the smile in the voice. He did so as well, something he was not certain he had ever done. Tucking away King Bardhest Redhand's gold-chased skull, he clasped Giliad's proffered hand. They disappeared.

THE ORRUSTUDALE

Tallux's muscular arms sped deadly rain into the rear of the Azgod ranks. His own arrows long since depleted, he had salvaged several wood-and-hide quivers from stricken Mgesh. These arrows were shorter than his own, but nonetheless cleverly fashioned and devastating in the hands of the half-elvin archer. The barrage began to tell, and a handful of Azgod bowmen gathered to return fire with their fearsome weapons, yet their metal-girt shafts were slapped from the air by Isolde's passionate incantations. Jamello dashed here and there, slashing the wounded.

Distracted from the clashing press before him where the human line bent like a green stick, Shaxpur snarled an order, and a squad of immortals peeled off to deal with the trio.

"Trouble," gasped Jamello. Twenty looming Azgod trotted toward them with deadly intent. Three fell to Tallux's archery. He drew sword.

"Ahoy!" shouted Bagwart.

His own centaur slain, he now swayed and bounced atop Vergessen at the fore of one hundred and fifty pounding centaurs. The enormous creatures collided with the echelons of Kör like a rolling cannonade. The rear of each cohort became an ear-splitting bedlam of fierce shouting and vicious blows given and received, but unlike the centaurs' previous foes, the immortals of Kör would not yield or break. Even when royal scouts and foresters yet able to fight, and Cynewulf's remaining hillriders joined the fray, Shaxpur's legionnaires held the advantage of numbers and discipline. They advanced like threshers in wheat.

"Where is Apieron?" screamed Isolde to Bagwart. The smith leapt free, bringing his hammer hard against the inner cuisse of an Azgod, staggering him. Vergessen shattered clavicle and neck with a stone.

Bagwart turned. "Who can know? Probably in that!" His knotty forearm indicated the central press where pandemonium reined, only five hundred steps, yet impossibly distant.

Isolde felt a keening on the spell wind. She focused, piercing the obfuscation of war to see the Standard of Chaos. Withersoever it went, Kör was unconquerable. "Punch me a hole!"

The forge-scarred dwarf grinned and pulled Vergessen down to confer a moment. The mighty centaur fluted his hands to emit an undulant cry. Six centaur chiefs reared and charged. Iron spears impaled them, a score of wicked blades and heavy axes cleaved them, but a fleeting rent had been made.

"Come!" shouted Isolde. Tallux and Jamello dashed behind to fend chance blows from her body. Tearing free, they found a clearing in the press where not even the immortals of Kör dare tread. Vodrab wheeled on the companions, his wizened face split into an anticipatory grimace. The blur-margined stave gestured, and his bodyguard lurched forward. Living golems these were, tortured men and Drudges force-fed powdered iron and clay, ensorcelled to grow until muscle and bone grew strong beyond reckoning. More dead than alive, twelve of these constructs closed on Jamello and Tallux.

Jamello's crypt blade sunk deep into the side of a blue-skinned golem. His yell of triumph turned to dismay when the machinelike creature ignored the blow. In turn, it punched Jamello's shield, driving the slight thief to his knees.

Isolde's spear pierced the snarling face and burst its skull.

Tallux frantically slashed and parried three of the beasts as his straight sword bit wedges from their bodies, yet they pressed relentlessly on. Jamello rolled clear to leap behind and hamstring two before backpedaling from the clutching arms, their skin scabrous and hard.

A centaur burst into the fray. His name was Charops. A trio of Vodrab's ghouls fixed upon him. One was smashed by hoof and club; not the chemicals that it imbued nor the dark magics woven into its flesh could forestall the strong doom it found there. The other two latched wickedly upon the forest beast's back and flank. The centaur glimpsed up and beheld the standard of the abyss, and his craggy, bearded face broke into madness. With a sickening moan, the noble centaur fled, the two golems dangling from his crashing body.

Vodrab's staff struck the mailed back of an armsman who bravely parried an Azgod two heads taller than he. Metal links parted, and the stave slid through the man's form until its length protruded from his chest. The half-demon laughed and turned to strike down a dark-faced fisherman, come to fight from sunny Bestrand.

Rudolph Mellor grew wroth. His heavy shield, recovered from the tomb of fallen kings, slammed Vodrab aside. A nearby Azgod roared and rose up from a yeoman's shattered corpse to launch an overhand blow with a flail. Jamello's shield rang but held firm as the crypt blade screeched its delight, severing poleyn and the mighty knee beneath. The Azgod staggered, and Jamello took its head.

Vodrab lunged back in, his matted hair whirling. Jamello twisted frantically away, the stave just brushing the shoulder of his sword arm. Jamello dropped his blade from a nerveless hand, falling face up as Vodrab's jeweled leer loomed in his vision. Tallux and Isolde screamed their frustration, hammering frantically at Vodrab's creatures. Behind the eldritch sorcerer, the midnight heraldry was revealed in its terrible true essence to the prostrate thief.

"How like you my oriflamme, mortal man?"

Muscles twitching convulsively, Jamello was unable to rise, yet his mind was clear. "Screw you, Grandma. I knew Xephard Bright Helm, Son of Morning." Vodrab stepped back, and his staff quivered for the finishing blow.

Tallux burst into a superhuman flurry of wild, slashing attacks at the faces of Vodrab's remaining stalkers. Isolde remembered her gymnastae. Running forward, she planted her spear to vault over the heads of the blockers. Tallux removed a pair of clutching hands and tossed her the spear.

Jamello's eyes widened. In slow motion, Vodrab's stave burned the air on its downward arc. The spear of the goddess was there. Silvery, unblemished steel met the rod of dissonance, and a concussion staggered priestess and necromancer alike. When her vision cleared, Isolde's blessed spear hovered before Vodrab's breast. He began to twirl and fade into nothingness, but a woman stepped forward.

"I *see* you!" said Vigfus. Her withered arms shot forward and grasped Vodrab's hair. His claw made to vibrate into her breast. It broached the skin a second before Isolde's spear transfixed him. With a resounding cry, Isolde then slashed the midnight banner. Tallux slew the thing that bore it. The air cleared as Isolde turned from Vigfus, and her hand touched Jamello's breast. He remained cold, unmoving. The youthful priestess leaned forward, and her breath flowed into him.

"I guess that's as close to a kiss as I'm likely to get."

"Get up," she said. "Kiss girls later."

Chapter 36

The Orrustudale

Iz'd Yar frowned and expressed his displeasure by removing the head of a human female. Notably, she had led some hundreds in a desperate assault upon the very pick of his house. How his van had scythed a red harvest amongst this softer foe! Men-at-arms and occasional knights, maddened by the slaughter of the women, hurled themselves futilely against his immortals. The castellans of Iz'd Yar's house wore realistic steel masks with golden brows, and in their splendid harness, they appeared very gods of war.

Iz'd Yar studied the woman. She had been tall for one of her kind. Beside his foot, the pale hair was cropped short, and her green eyes stared at nothing. The broodmare's apparel was that of a noble. *Klea*. The name came to his lips, perhaps mentioned by one of his spies. Iz'd Yar clucked a note of self-reproach; overwise had he become in the ways of this lesser race.

That Vodrab was dead he had no doubt. *Too soon have you died, old dweomerlich. A fight for the eons this was!* The Azgod left wing had collapsed, pinched between centaurs to the rear and a new brigade of bearded ones on the southern edge, bolstered by berserk Northrons. Iz'd Yar roared an order. Kör's right swung hard against the enemy's center, compressing them for the kill.

Shaxpur detailed cohorts to prevent centaurs and dwarfs from adjoining the dwindling ranks of the man-prince. Iz'd Yar looked to his bodyguard. Alkdog grasped a corded lariat, yanking a winged elf from the sky. Enormous for even one of his kind, Alkdog snapped the creature's spine over a scaly knee. Dusk gathered. It would soon be over.

Henlee came pounding up. Three demon-orc heads dangled from his left hand, Maul dripped gore on his right. "What's all the caterwauling?"

Jamello cleaned his sword on a scrap. "Isolde killed Iz'd Yar's he-witch."

Henlee stared at the tattered chaos standard, its magics fled, and Vodrab's brittle form. "Good! I don't like witches." He spied Vigfus. "Er, excuse me."

Isolde glared at the heads. "Trophies …" began the dwarf defensively. "Never mind." The heads thunked down. "What's next?"

"Where is Apieron?" Isolde demanded.

"Running around like a maniac! Who can catch him?"

Vigfus's strange face regarded them. "Beyond us he has gone."

Companies of running Azgod fell into place, sealing off rearward gaps in their echelons. A hedge of bristling steel lent emphasis to Vigfus's words. "Prevail or not," said she, "the star child cannot prevent the slaughter that will ensue in darkness. Allies are our only hope, we must aid them."

"Fair enough, spaedam." Henlee dressed his adamant shield. "We'll stand here."

Tallux's bow began to sing and Jamello took position as bodyguard for the two women. Centaurs and woodsmen found them, and to them Tallux detailed scouts where he might as the iron legion of Kör closed in. Isolde called spell-fire from the heavens, her spear's point shining star-bright to become a beacon for winged elves, and also for Azgod rankers who peeled away to crush this salient in their midst. Yet by virtue of Isolde's castings, the breach was thereby widened, sparing the lives of many Western men.

"Lawks, sir!" spake Brunhelm, a square-jawed captain of infantry when he beheld the pitiless masks of the enemy. "They cannot be flesh and blood."

Trakhner's bluff face broke into a smiling grimace. A pike butt had splintered his front teeth and mangled the lip. "Come, let us go inquire. If I am right, I shall claim what is owed a captain. If not, a general's wage you'll earn in Hell."

The captain stared, then guffawed, and for an odd moment, both men were rendered helpless by tears of laughter. Their troop had returned southward, and the golden serpent was nigh. Together, they led the strongest corps of Ilycrium's infantry direct onto Iz'd Yar's invincible center.

Alkdog, Kör's champion, stood on wide-braced legs. His pendulous blows shattered byrnie, shield, and helm. Ilycrium's patchwork mob pushed flat against Iz'd Yar's immortals, and as the last smoldering embers of the day winked out, Gault beheld his general's fate. Iz'd Yar found Trakhner in the press, and his benighted sword howled its triumph as it sheared Trakhner's hauberk and delved deep into his flank, yet even as he fell, the unyielding soldier gave back a solid blow that struck Iz'd Yar's upper arm, only to slide without harm from the rippling mail. Alkdog clutched Brunhelm in mortal embrace, his fang's deep in the man's thick neck.

Outstripping his companions, Gault screamed and plunged forward. He was the first of them to strike the whirling chaos that was the line. The scene was lit eerily by silvery spell-fires emanating from Isolde's position, and the calls of dwarves with centaurs and their Azgod foes rose to a pitch as both sides sensed the final grip. Winged elves found fire, and many shot flaming shafts or dropped torches to aid night-blind men.

Gault hacked at snarling faces and surging bodies like a wild dervish. Tears of grief for Trakhner and Renault creased his face. Gonfolon glimmered as she slew, and so brightly that the monsters of Kör near to Gault were illumined within his sphere, the ensorcelled brand carving through steel-clad thews as if they were wicker and parchment.

Gault met the slit gaze of the field marshal of Kör. A dozen chosen Azgod of his house loomed nigh. The duke of Kör raised his midnight blade in salute. "Speak, cub. That scribes might well record my triumph."

"Only this." Gault drew himself up. He produced the circuit of gold fashioned to fit his helm and placed it confidently. "No longer boy and prince. Today you face a man—and a king." Gault stood amongst the twisted bodies of noble Azgod he had slain, and strangely, he laughed beneath his nodding helm. His left bore Renault's gold-chased mace, whilst Gonfolon weaved lazily in his right like the bitter hand of doom. Iz'd Yar paused at the majestic and terrible sight, though the man was but half his weight—and he only one against many. The man-king strode confidently forward.

Two Azgod, nephews to their great lord, pushed forward with intent to seize as captive the king of Ilycrium. Gonfolon clove two grasping arms at the elbow. The sharp flanges of Renault's mace smashed free the mask from one of the creatures, the back blow crushing its skull. The other's luminous gaze met Gault's for an instant, then fled to be lost in the battle scud.

A score knights and stout armsmen surged around their king. There were few left. An Azgod spear pierced one in the midriff, levering the helpless man overhead. "Brave spear!" shouted Iz'd Yar, as before him Alkdog smote a yeoman in twain, shoulder to hip, with an axe he had found.

Gault was there. His flashing mace pinned the axe for Gonfolon to sever the helve. Alkdog was stooped, and Gault's steel-clad thigh found his face. Alkdog stumbled, but Gonfolon's heart thrust was deflected by an ebon blade, a shadow in darkness. Iz'd Yar's blows thundered like hammer strokes and, where the brands met, vivid shards of night sprang free. A weight buckled Gault's knees as Alkdog clubbed him with the axe haft. Gonfolon parried a sword stroke an inch from Gault's face, and he sensed Alkdog stand to loom behind him, the splintered iron of the axe handle poised to thrust.

Eirec and Seamus surged from the side, each gripping one of Alkdog's mighty arms. They bore the massive Azgod to the ground. Cusk screeched his hatred and drove the bitter point of some noble's sword into Alkdog's throat above the cuirass, pinning his neck to the earth. The youth surged free and leapt upon the back of another whose iron-shod boot had kicked Byrinae in the stomach. Cusk yanked back the mask and opened the Azgod's larynx with a basilard.

For Gault, the blade strokes came too fast. Iz'd Yar had

been sword master of the Dream Throne before Beamund Candor was whelped in frigid Varkold. Iz'd Yar's eldritch brand sundered a pauldron to bite deep into Gault's shoulder, and next, his breastplate was riven as Renault's mace cartwheeled away. Gonfolon glowed like balefire, yet she was remorselessly driven crossways athwart Gault's face and neck.

Iz'd Yar's scream of triumph fell to a gurgle. A black and jagged horn of a dragon burst through his breast to quiver a yard before his yellow eyes. Gault sprang to his feet, and Gonfolon's shining arc took the demon's head from his neck. She swept down again, snapping the nighted blade against the metal of Iz'd Yar's body. A woman's tinkling laugh lilted and ebbed.

For a timeless moment, the men regarded one another. The one young and hale, whose trim, reddish beard was visible in the fading glow of his sword. The other, empty-handed, his tall form spattered black with battle stain. The conflict forced them apart.

Leopards snarled and swiped, chained to the great wagon of the Mgesh king whereon was piled the spoils of Alkeim and Uxellodoum, and of Ilycrium. The high shaman of Mgesh wheeled in startlement.

"Stone walker!" shrilled Rhocuus in fury.

He flapped his trailing cloak as might a bird, and indeed, countless beaks and talons and the eyes of prey birds glinted from the strange garment. He stalked forward, and a summoning blew from under Rhocuus's wings as he fell upon Ohm.

The dwarf's living mantle stiffened. Pure and hard, gem flecks and minerals sparkled therein. Ohm's black eyes gleamed obsidian in the flash of canceling magics, and his hands became mallets. He struck once, twice. It was over.

Few remembered with clarity the final moments of the great battle. Anchored by her victorious prince and the champions' return from Helheim, Ilycrium's army lived beyond the darkness. Dwarves and Northrons, Liflyne and hillmen, and a handful of centaurs and vur survived to meet in wonderment when no foe walked the field. The clash and fury faded, and even the lamentations of the wounded were stilled below an exhausted sky and over the sodden earth.

Chapter 37

The Orrustudale

Gigantic in the half-light, the figure approached. As he drew near, others could see in his slow advance that he nearly faltered. Crusted blood matted his features, and his fine chain mail hung in tatters as he limped; nonetheless, a grim determination was stamped on his features. A vital power within him was evident with each breath and step. Word traveled, for men knew he was one of the rare survivors of the last crush around prince and banner.

"Nay, the *King's* banner!" Hardened veterans stood aside for the ordinary man who had fought and lived where devils and generals had not, one who witnessed the rebirth of a kingdom. Half-lights of the hellish strife yet flickered in Cusk's eyes. He walked alone.

"My hand," Gault raised his clenched hand—it trembled—and he smiled whimsically, "may never release its sword grip. I wonder, what befell the Army of the Abyss?"

Henlee sat upon a rock and lovingly honed Maul with a whetstone. "More than two parts in four we saw crushed, these others and I."

Gault searched their faces. "The Lord Giliad said friends we have … do they battle for us? Comes anon an army of Helmen? Win or lose, I would know those who fought." Gault rubbed his palms, blistered by mace helve and sword grip. "So many have fallen, I have learned how precious is friendship in honor."

Henlee grunted. "I know a few—"

"I'm too tired to stand and bow to you, Master Dwarf." Gault's exhausted chuckle ended in a cough. "Although my pillow does stink." Gault made no effort to rise from the broad back of an Ascapundi over which a canvas had been tossed.

Vigfus gazed hard on the young man; the brave face bore new lines of sorrow. Her hair was witchy white in the darkness. "Hold forth thy ancient brand, the sword of a *king*."

"Its glow has faded, Mother." He stretched it forth, and Gonfolon burst again into blue radiance.

Vigfus cackled dryly to their exclamations. She daubed her hands into the churned-up clay at their feet. "Dragon's blood and the willing valor of good people slain. Doubt you the magic of this night?" Her age-knobbed hands moved quickly.

Jamello gasped, and Henlee mumbled his recognition, for the spaedam molded a skillful replica of the Duskbridge, and their gazes were drawn through Gonfolon's aura into Vigfus's construct.

Isolde's blue eyes were very bright. "See this, and learn wisdom," said she to any who approached from the darkness. Brandishing her spear like a shepherd's crook, she gathered sundry men, dwarves, and elves to witness the tiny battle that grew until it stretched from the arid shelves of the Haunted Vale to the storm-battered plain of the Starfall, the very gate of Hel.

DUSKBRIDGE

Goffnu the Scout observed the proceedings with interest, for had not the Bashar, Torgut of the living whip, blithely informed him that his continued existence depended on the veracity of his report? The Khôsh's great desert city of Mogush had disgorged her finest soldiery a week past, six thousands expert horsemen, all fanatical servants of the Duskbridge.

Each of the desert monks had felt in his bones the storm beyond the Starfall Gate, and now a piled cloud of brown, fretted with lightnings, hovered across the dweamor-door that had disgorged the marching legions of Hel. A scaled, flame-eyed demon who rode as knight atop *something*, led ordered columns through the Matog's furrowed gullies and onto the last plain. A mighty host, ten times that of the Khôsh, thusly came hence. Even so, hoary priests murmured dire forebodings and shook wintry scalp locks. "Some disaster has befallen," said they, for the expected army was lessened by three parts in five, perhaps as the She had escaped Her fiery prison.

Goffnu lightly touched the dull badge on his breast in which was set the Serpentine Goddess. The metal was hot and had grown so since the Helstorm. He gazed up at the escarpment, where a strange new enemy, these dwarves, thronged the heights and already reshaped its face to their liking. The bulk of them had arrived soon after dark, and by starlight and firelight had fallen to work immediately. Above, like an angry lamp, X'fel hung low and huge in the north.

The low thrum of dwarven nakirs grew louder. Goffnu's Bashar had remarked on them, saying they seemed not like instruments, but the muttering voice of the earth, or mayhap a somber heart of stone pulsing through the bleak hills.

Until yesterday, Goffnu had never seen a dwarf. Now there were thousands of the creatures. Occasionally, hidden in the whistling texture of the wind, he perceived the sound of deep voices in chant. Fleeting it always was, and left Goffnu to wonder if rather he heard the piping of some mournful night bird. Whatever the source, it kept the rhythm of the drumming.

Torgut had responded only, "Tuton Nakaa," to Goffnu's question. The Bashar then remounted and sped to place other scouts.

Drums of stone? Goffnu snorted. What magic could there be in a scrap of cowhide? Let the ugly, stunted folk prattle and dance! Yet he could not deny the beats gave hint of a force that at times bounced his chest from the prone, as they did now. Instead of breaking cover to crouch to another vantage, he rather hugged the grit of the slope even harder.

With tireless limbs, the forces of the abyss had covered the leagues from Duskbridge to the rim overnight. A quarter of their number angled north in darkness to seek the Gorganj and the soft underbelly of Ilycrium, whilst the remainder debauched onto the barren scarp below the Haunted Vale. Thus, the Army of Brass had come. Princely, gray-faced men in ancient harness gripped spell-woven brands and heavy spears and gazed up at their enemies like hunters that spy game fowl at roost.

The lord of the Abyss raised his scaly arm. Firetrolls and winged demons, hulking and crawling forms, ceased their clamor to wait his bidding. Dawn's weak offering reached the foot of the ledge. Something stirred above, and Goffnu cursed himself for dreaming. He shook his head and stared again.

A forest? Materializing over the bleached stone, mighty trees stood, as if they had always done so, in shadows of mysterious blue. Goffnu glimpsed a subtle motion. By peering under his hands against the level sun, he perceived a vast shifting, and it seemed that the ground itself flowed beneath the canopy. Here and there, he caught a flash of color or the glint of metal. He waited. A song burst forth! An host wended through the trees, fair voices raised to greet the dawn.

Upon the rim, Goffnu beheld what seemed an endless river of mounted knights astride great destriers that pranced with eagerness. Behind these were orderly columns of bowmen and foot soldiers. Goffnu remembered the old tales that bespake of times wherein elvin lords who marched but infrequently to war, yet possessing the longest memories of its art, did so to dire effect. By reckoning of their life spans, the most ordinary elvin ranker could be sire to any aged and retired human battle sergeant. Presently they merged into seamless formations beside the bearded ones. At their head rode a proud castellan, his mail and surcoat blazing the dawn-glow. His horse was a purest white, its plaited mane and tail twinkling weaves of gem light. An unquenchable energy was apparent in the animal's high-stepping walk. Goffnu mumbled his rapid counting and gaped at the shear size of the elvin host.

Twenty thousands or he was blind! And it had come as sudden as a desert flood.

A second force glided to the fore. By the summons of Galen Trazequintil, the leager of Ilycrium's wood elves was opened, and from their Malave came three thousands bearing heavy bows. Five hundred light cavalry accompanied them, armed with spear and saber. While less resplendent than their Northern cousins, they moved in compact echelons, and fell intent was writ on each fair face. Their ensign was a stag that leaped rampant on field of green.

A bellowing echoed up the cliff face, and the bestial din rose to a hate-filled cacophony, for rather than easy passage into this frail green world, there now stood an army to dispute the hosts of Helheim. On the rightward heights were serried rows of the immortal cavalry of Amor. Proud golden elves who had learned all the skills of knighthood when the very stars were young. They sat matchless steeds and were still, save for their scarlet-and-gold banners that stirred to the dry wind. Before them was a captain whose aura brightened the wan day like a lamp in a darkened room, and wheresoever his glance fell, his enemies drew back in apprehension. Drust, Champion of Amor, was come. His surcoat bore tower and ocean, and stream beneath tree.

To the left, Hel's legions beheld a regiment of mountain dwarves. They bore axes, mattocks, and spiked hammers whose edges had been honed a thousand thousand times. Goffnu rose and spurred his horse back to his brothers. Hierophants of the Khôsh had asked a boon and would receive it; to them would fall the honor of the first assault.

Dismounting, each man ordered his many weapons and touched the iron badge on his robes. A twisted serpent dwelt there, and a portion of Her ancient strength flowed into the sun-browned thews of many races of men. The proud slaves of the Matog would take the cliff or die in the attempt. Not one needed to search the pitiless face of Hel's general to know that no retreat would be granted, temporary or not.

Goffnu dashed forward, and his brothers moved with equal swiftness, maximizing the scant cover provided by the hardscrabble while running as fast as any creature that went on two legs. In moments they seized the base of the cliff and began their ascent.

Dislodged reefs of stone and clever rock chutes fashioned by the bearded folk blew Khôsh from its face. A volley of coordinated javelin throws ensued as wood elves hurled once, twice, and thrice with the practice of decades. Heavier than arrows, these decimated the flowing front of Khôsh.

To Goffnu's side, a man fell, a small spear lodged in his skull. Goffnu resumed his monkey-like ascent as a cloud of arrows raked into them. He survived. No more shafts came, for the Khôsh were amongst the dwarves.

Assembled from far-flung settlements west of Uxellodoum, dwarven tribes heeded the summons of an ancient who wore on craggy shoulders a mantle of living stone. He had departed to an errand with the army of Ilycrium of which he did not speak, but his two thousands from Saemid were joined by an equal number en route. Few in comparison to the teeming minions of Hel, nonetheless they came with great haste to defend their land far from its borders. From these, hundreds of volunteers, mostly aged warriors or those to whom the accumulation of days brought joy no longer, had detached themselves in ambuscade ahead and along the march of the abyss. Gripping axe and spatha in hard hands, these had struck the first hopeless blows in the night. Each hoped to smite and slay at least one fiend, for a single such being could wreck unguessed destruction amongst innocents inland. Unencumbered, the cohorts of Hel had rolled over them. Now Khôsh encountered the main body of dwarves.

The slave-warriors of Mogush, servants of the Skyfall Gate, fought uphill in the face of prepared positions. Lithe and incredibly skilled, they would have been well matched against mountain dwarves, those who claimed the mightiest giants of Kör as their most hated foes, but after the attrition suffered on the climbing assault, it was no contest.

Goffnu tumbled a one-eyed dwarf from its roost like a flightless hatchling, the armored body breaking on the scarp far below. Leaping into the creature's nest, he garroted a second whose attentions were elsewhere. A heavy hand grasped Goffnu's scalp lock and spun him about. Goffnu's kindjal pierced the dwarf's brigandine low in the abdomen. That same instant, a stone in the dwarf's fist crushed Goffnu's jaw. He staggered to a crouch and saw to his horror the leap of two elfish war hounds. They bore him back, extinguishing the taper of his life.

Iskhtmanur, master of the march, shouted like a blast. Khôsh had served their purpose. The way was cleared, and demons easily scaled the rampart. Wood elves began to die.

Iskhtmanur, General of the Deep, surveyed the scene with the eyes of one who had beheld countless battles and kenned every calculus of war. He measured the force behind him—a fraction of its splendor had the Dark Queen not been driven forth. It was mighty still! Beside the Army of Brass came walking and winged demons, and many fell denizens of the abyss for which there was no name.

Iskhtmanur could feel Her presence. She was here, somewhere on this frigid world, and Her dark will filled his mind and breast. This skirmish could be no drawn-out match of strategies and attrition. The enemy had seen to that. If they broke in any part, they would be enveloped and slain against the high ledge—a quick embrace into death. So be it!

Iskhtmanur nudged his mount forward. The lizard-like thing scrambled to the rock face, crumbling old stone with its talons as it began to climb. Eastward and beyond the Duskbridge, the world storm churned the firmament and vault into oblivion. The Guardian of Hel there stood motionless. As it slowly sank into the boiling, its westward gaze, alert as it had ever been, never faltered. His adamant crown disappeared at the last.

The final dissolution of the Helplane saw two figures stride from the shattered Gate, unlike the others and unlike each other. They had no need of speech. One was bare chested and well muscled, with long, tawny hair and graceful wings. In his hands, he bore a twisted lance of living wood, his angular face beautiful and wild. At his side walked a man, massive of chest and breadth of shoulders, whose dazzling, tasseled cloak gleamed like surf foam, and seemed as alive. The warrior's scarred hand bore a mighty, mirrored blade as lightly as a common man might a willow wand.

Who could know what strange magics ruled the Matog at that time? Certainly not the laggard Helspawn who were driven over the bitter plain by two that no weapon or claw could harm, and whose fearsome blows reaped utter destruction on their rear. Howling their dismay, fiends fled before the avenging angels (or so they deemed them), and the great press of Iskhtmanur's ranks, flapping in chaos, were thusly pinned against the cliffs. Governed by unreasoning fear, they redoubled their assault on the scarp, for there was no facing the silver paladin and winged elf. As the conflict reached its midportion, the high butte witnessed such devastation as had not been since the Starfall had vaporized fecund wetlands and scoured the valley down to bedrock.

If the battle was less in scale than its counterpart northward, perhaps it was more terrible for the frenzied death strokes of immortals on either side, who spent their long lives like water running. Charge and countercharge, peerless knights of forested Amor grappled and smote gray princes, newly risen to breathe the moist airs of the world and walk paths prepared in eons of darkness. Monsters of the abyss and gruesome demons pulled down destriers and cavaliers to bathe their muzzles in hot, sweet blood while fearless war dogs leapt to the defense of beloved masters.

A mighty clarion shod with silver filigree sounded against the edge. Its bright note rose up the cliff, like an open door into a dark room. The great paladin and his Liflyne companion surged into the swarming helions. It was then that Drust, Warder of Amor, drove deep his gilt lance into the black heart of the beast from Hel.

Iskhtmanur flapped from its ruin to assail his shining foe. Drust dismounted and stepped to meet him, and more bright than the pallid sun shined his shield and brand. Both hosts paused, attuned to the issue. Fate's balance was poised to fall either way.

Rising into the air, a joyous cry rose to greet the victor. Many horns sounded and echoed amongst waving trees. The hunt was on.

The feeble day ended and, with it passed the rippling arbor. As tree paths faded, Drust bowed deep to two figures who walked an aureate mist to the setting sun.

THE GERALES

Gonfolon's lamp light faded. The last image of Vigfus's construct was that of burnings southward that marked a ruinous passage cut by the last escapees of Hel, murderous even in defeat. Gault sighed, letting fall his sword. "I had wished to go home." The air was chill. It began to snow. "Thank you, Vigfus, for your art's gift." To their surprise, Gault then stood and bowed deep to Isolde and Eirec, and to Henlee and Jamello.

"Never had I imagined a king might bow to me," stammered Jamello.

"Where is Apieron?" Gault asked softly. "Will he see me? It is to him I owe the most."

Eirec slowly shook his head. "I do not know."

Having resumed his labors, Henlee ceased them again, cradling Maul gently in rough hands. "One of Apieron's woodsmen told Apieron that Melónie defended his choice to any and all that would listen. None would gainsay the Lady." Henlee's gruff voice thickened with emotion. "I think that helped him. Apieron'll be all right."

"Behold," stated Gault, "I name Apieron of Windhover hereditary baron as long as this land shall last. March Warden of Ilycrium's lands south and east."

Jamello beamed and clapped Eirec hard on the shoulder.

The Northman scowled, then grinned toothily. Henlee looked to Isolde who stared thoughtfully away, and the dwarf doubted not she looked across beleaguered night and distance, to their friend.

SWAY

Vilmar was accustomed to the creak and sway of his ship anchored at sea, save when something was amiss. It was.

"What sayest the missive, sir?"

Vilmar's face was pale in the darkness off northern Ilycrium. A single ship had found her sisters after midnight. Despite rough seas, she had gracefully joined his own. It was Kör's flagship, although Sisteros, Commandant of Marines, was not on board. Vilmar knew Sisteros would not come, for whispered words had reached him of a strange reckoning in the occupied halls of Swaymeet, and of a bloody vengeance.

Vilmar was now senior officer. "Home port," was his first command.

"The war—" began the ensign.

Vilmar waved him to silence. "You and I, and every jack one of us, are to be palace guards. Seems a storm has come to Körguz. The Dream Throne beckons." One by one the gray ships hoisted sail. Slipping into file away from Ilycrium's coast and setting sail for Kör's inland sea, they glided into shadow, as if they had never been.

THE GRAY ESS

Fuquit the Fat stood on the prow of his ship *Avenger*, the most proud galleon to ever slip quay from Farseps, Bride of the Sea. Headed north, the *Avenger* rode the long combers of Ilycrium's southern coast. Soon she would raise harbor at Sway, she and twenty of her sisters, heavy with goods and sun-browned stalwarts. The oaths of men would be honored.

Far ahead and small in the distance, Fuquit beheld tall Iphus and sturdy Scyld as they rose from ocean's mist. Fuquit stood bold on the prow, and shoreward he fancied he heard the faint neighing of horses. He glimpsed a flash of silver amongst tidewater reeds.

"What do you see, Captain?" asked Greco, a curly-headed youth of fifteen and first boy. He was Fuquit's favorite, for he was his son.

"What's that, lad?"

"On the shore, you marked something."

Fuquit placed an arm around his boy's shoulder. Together they gazed to shore where marsh horses, white amongst green rushes, splashed after their lead mare. An arch-necked stallion guarded the rear. Seeing *Avenger*, he neighed and pranced the water.

Fuquit smiled. "Hope, son. Hope."

Chapter 38

Tyrfang over Körguz

As if reluctant, the Herald shook his glorious head. He spoke anyway:

Something moves in darkness, even sinful men grow fearful.
Something stirs the Deep.
Rains lash, thunder peals, the wise man seeks shelter.
Woe is come, Leviathan rises.

The heart of Tyrfang pulsed frantically as the final barrier was breached. The thrashing deaths of so many great ones at last rended the veil, and Tiamat clambered into the material plane.

Statues fell, and columns buckled. Tapestries of eldritch lore, woven over centuries and darkly beautiful, were ripped into rags, and priceless casements of glass annealed from ruby and diamond were likewise riven and fell into clashing shards. That Her sons perished, in part empowered Her ascent, and fanned the hate-furnace of Her will. In the final surge, a full third of the chanting priests who yammered before Her were consumed. The Beast raised Its bloody maw to the dark heavens and roared.

Iblis raised himself from a bow of deference. His first.

Resplendent in his satin mail, he regarded Her with fearless eyes. She was pleased. Her thought flickered southward, twitching in the mind of the tall man who rode hither, his crimson cloak alive in the wind. A survivor, that one. Excellent.

"So tell me, Kör King," crooned She, tasting earth's air for the first time since gods dwelt thereon. "How shalt we order this world?"

THE GERALES

"I remember one eve in early spring," said Apieron, "when the labor of the day was done, so that the folk gathered to my hall, armsmen and red-armed farmers, wives and bains. The smell of a roasting feast mingled with fragrances cast in beeswax candles.

Maids bustled happy under Melónie's loving governance, under which no child ever cried hungry, and the dogs crunched fatty bones before the fire, cackling bright in our hearth.

"Setie shushed Jilly when she cried to follow Ilacus, who tottered amongst the wolf hounds, his pudgy hands grasping their shaggy pelts like they were ponies. No child was ever so safe!

"Then came the skald. Music we'd had and sweet, though dwindling to a soft background when his voice rose resonant in the hall. Gods and virgins floated there, and goddesses whimsical or stern, but soon the song rose to the valor of men who, noble in cause, yield like maidens their bodies to the fickle scythe that is war. Babes were gathered, and arms clasped loved ones, as my people heard of elders and women wise in counsel, and of mothers who give all of themselves to children, and men likewise to kith and king.

"King, country." Apieron paused, then gathered himself. "When he ceased, there was no yell or acclaim, too tight were their throats for speech, and nobly he sat, observing his true reward in the shining eyes of my people. And noble, I gifted unto him silver, for I am, or was, merely a minor fief holder within a rich kingdom. Yea, I filled his lap with one-tenth of Windhover, and named him *Bard*.

"The timbers are blackened and the hall broken, yet his song happened, and must be alive somewhere in the hearts of those that heard him. Those not slain in the reaving."

"Who was this minstrel, who sang so worthily?" asked the other, even as he remained frustratingly removed from recognition, although the voice was soft and near.

"It must not have been important at the time, yet I heard tell the singer was generous in his passing, to where I do not know."

"He seems passing familiar," said the other, a slight undertone of humor in the voice as he faded, and Apieron woke to the waelstow grown still in the night, and under stars very bright.

Dawn crept from her night cave with timid steps, as if afraid to unveil the horror of the battlefield, and yet over iron-cast hills, she eventually rose in the east with feathery pinks and grays to presage the glory of the sun.

Apieron looked up, and sun's chariot pleased him. He sat on a rock-rib outcrop. He had lost the dragon spear somewhere, and the crooked bow was unslung and clothbound beside the javelins of black and white, his heater shield packstrapped, and the blazoned surcoat folded away. He sat, fist in hand, while his gray eyes sought the vast northward opening where had fled survivors of Kör.

"Apieron," said Eirec. "World Candle rises, will you not greet the day?"

"The murderer is there, where I cannot follow … for now,"

mumbled Apieron, who now stood and regarded them. A chill wind lifted his brown hair and beard, touched with gray.

"My friends," Apieron smiled, "there has been news in the night, from centaurs." He grasped both of Eirec's arms, a world of feeling in his eyes. "My children live!"

The dwarf fairly yelled as Jamello, Tallux, and Isolde rushed forward, shouting and pounding. Maul's silvered edge caught the risen sun as the mighty glaive was hurled aloft.

Gault touched Renault's face. Soldiers had raised a cairn for him to be buried with Trakhner and others. The trophies of many enemies were placed below their feet, and silken oriflammes were their winding sheets. "A greater love shared no man than this." Gault stood. "Write that above him, please."

"It will be so," said a man called Teucer. Once a colonel of Trakhner's infantry, he was now general of the army.

Seamus pawed at a tear with his crippled hand. "More poetry, Sire?" His basso voice filled the enclosure.

"Wither came those words?" Gault touched his tattered surcoat. "I know not; perhaps I saw it once elsewhere." Gault handed his general a scroll bound with a string.

The man Teucer took his leave. He picked his way across the battlefield. It was eerily silent, and fibrous mists crawled across the wreckage and stricken dead. He found the companions. Bump looked warily at him, although Sut did not growl, and Teucer halted a respectful distance. "The King sends his regards."

Apieron met the man's steadfast gaze. He liked him. "For that, we are grateful. We take our leave."

The man nodded. "Then there is this." To their surprise, he proffered the scroll to Jamello.

"Well?" barked Henlee after an interminable interval. The man had gone.

It was a waxed parchment that bore the creases of many foldings, and smelled of cheese, yet the royal signet was pressed in scarlet wax: top, bottom, and sides. A ribbon of stained white depended from the uppermost and largest stamp.

Isolde touched it. "A portion of the king's standard."

Jamello perused it with total concentration. His hand fell, face blank with astonishment.

Henlee snatched it up. "I'll read," he said meaningfully to Eirec.

"You do that," rumbled the big man.

"—and by decree, we name Sir Rudolph Mellor of Bestrand, Knight of the Body, and Servant to the Royal House. This Writ supersedes all claims and warrants, and expunges any crimes recorded, or yet unnamed to this day."

Jamello stuttered, "I'm not even a citizen of Ilycrium."

"You are now," said Isolde.

"Taxes," winked Henlee.

Jamello secreted the document away. "Let us go!"

Swift was their passage night and day through winter's weakening grip. There were frowning keeps of rain-wet stone perched on eminences, and cold border towns avoided when possible. If necessary, a coin and a nod procured hearth and sup, although simple folk were wary of the blackened scars and haggard visages borne by the wayfarers to evidence the haunting of the abyss.

Henlee spoke with a dwarf who led a passing column from the battle of the Duskbridge.

"So, how was it, Stonelord?"

"How was what?" demanded Henlee.

"Your journey … beyond."

The black dwarf growled, "I don't like Southern vacations. I burn easily."

Bump had met a Mgesh mare, and she followed him from the battlefield. The new dwarf looked askance at them as they frolicked beside the road. "Oh yeah," said Henlee, "she's small, got bristles like goblin wire on her coffin head. O' course she's ill-tempered." Henlee plucked his teeth in reflection. "That black-faced, she-horse is knobbed-kneed, stubborn, and just flat-out mean."

"So what will you do with her?" queried Rudolph Mellor.

"Keep her, naturally."

Eirec soon departed the company to join Tannhauser and his battle thanes. "I too have received word," he explained, "from White Throat."

Cani was there. Apparently, she had swept into Eirec's rebuilt skalli with the gusting of an ice giant's daughter, her frigid looks and biting tongue sending bondmaids scurrying and setting hulking thralls ashudder. *Eirecstead*, she had scoffed. *Canistead it shall be when I am done!*

Eirec laughed nervously, mopping a hairy hand over his bald pate. "Fate," he shrugged, "a man must meet it bravely."

"I will remember you," said Henlee. Eirec's black brows scowled, then he was off.

One day they came upon a plowman, and Apieron stared. The winter's crop was churned under by the passage of someone's army, but the farmer tilled in hopes of a late planting. His mule was lame, and it seemed the man pushed his plowblade as much as the gimping beast pulled. Jamello tugged repeatedly at Apieron's arm until they left, although not before Bagwart, who had followed them, whetted the crude iron of the plow into a gleaming edge.

For two days, they skirted a lake where reeds rustled from the tug of invisible breezes. Far distant, a dogging crow called mournfully under the cool sun. Otherwise, no life stirred placid waters that patiently waited the advent of spring. The path the companions followed gained the makings of a road, and a traveler, a young and handsome gentleman, joined them, his greetings as well dressed as he. His banter was infectious to all, save the ranger, whose gaze was ever ahead until the newcomer asked a strange question. "Tell me, Lord Apieron. Have you found your god?"

Isolde fell back. She trembled.

Apieron's flinty eyes found the deep brown pools of the stranger. "That is an odd question, and yet you obviously are a man of fortune. I will answer." Apieron's face was set in concentration, yet his steps never slowed. "She whose voice is heard in the brazen shout of trumpets, whose breath unfurls banners … and He whose far darts heal or slay, they have made the way before my feet."

The traveler was not deterred. "Then you serve these gods? They have preordained thy life?"

"A man, p'raps more so than a god, can choose his path, be it ill or sooth. I have chosen mine, and drunk deep the cup fate hast stirred me."

"Fate?" asked the other. "You, who wield the terrible spear of choice, that is greater than the might of the Spear Shaker (or her brother), would cast the cloak of blame before the feet of *Fate?*"

Apieron conceded the point with his best-attempted smile, and as they walked, his words were soft, such that only the newcomer heard them, and also Jamello who was near. "Mayhap a man may sleep in God's service, although ignorant of his sin. Once awake, he might realize how poor a servant he has been."

The stranger spoke no more of these things, and by nightfall, the road gained relatives to join it. The young man took one of these. The last rays of the sun glinted briefly from a slender harp they had not noticed he bore. Refreshed, the companions felt as if they had not toiled the long day through. Isolde spoke to no one of their erstwhile companion, although her hands at times shook for weeks thereafter.

Before dawn, Apieron stood lone watch. The air was thick and still, pregnant with the promise of rain. Henlee found him.

"I never said it."

"Said what?"

"I love you."

"You rebuilt the castle to her liking, provided every—"

"But I never really said it." Pallor lifted night from the land, and they saw that the sky was awash with gray clouds. Apieron shook his hair over his face.

"What—nonsense!" sputtered the dwarf. "You sang of love. You planted and planned and made children for love."

"She was the woman I had, but would not hold … She is the woman I lost, and cannot find again. Ah, Melónie. I will ever owe you this debt, wife." When Apieron raised his face, his gray eyes were strange, one angle of each was kindled by a reflected spark, the last ember of their campfire.

Henlee grasped Apieron's forearms and bore the man up. The dwarf's incredible strength would have crippled a lesser man for days. To Apieron, it brought a painful start.

"She is dead, man! You are not. Honor her with dwarven dirges that ring and echo unending in stone, but live!" He grasped Apieron fiercely. "Live man, free."

Apieron lay quiet, but his eyes were open. He had traveled far. Night was clearing, and an upper wind pushed aside a clouding veil that lent the sky of the Lampus a milky hue. A single star crossed the door of night to twinkle with growing strength. Then came its sisters and brothers, near and far, in shining myriads until the celestial family entire was gathered for their timeless dance. Apieron studied the positions of those known to him—there was the Anvil and also the Winged Hero—yet residing in the house of spring when they should be in autumn's by the day count of the journey.

"What have we lost?"

Points of silvered starfire glistened, unchanging. To Apieron, they remained remote and unheedful of the waking world of men, minutiae beneath their cold glance.

Apieron stood and made ready to take up again his tasks, for the others were gone.

Isolde first to lay her matron to rest, followed by Jamello and Tallux with Sut to the greenways of the Malave, then perhaps to Sway. When the northbound way to Saemid appeared, Henlee had instead turned south to Windhover. His near-black eyes held Apieron's for an instant. With a nod to Bagwart and Bump and the little mare, they left together. Apieron smiled, he would see him soon.

A frost-tipped wind lifted Apieron's beard and cloak, its breath full on his face, clean as any born on icy peaks under stars such as these. From somewhere came a small hope to nestle in his breast, there to fill in part the void he bore always. Apieron chuckled.

A strange sound. Unheard in how many months? Years?

He remembered he had once often done so. Thoughtfully, his fingers touched his breast, and the little hope trembled. He shrugged on his pack and strode along a hillcrest toward the Falls that waited. Stars lit his path, and his feet measured their long pace without falter.

Auroch's foam-chasing water bounced from moon-bright rocks as it ever had, and yet different as the sound of water rushing seems more frigid in winter's lingering grip. Apieron gasped, for it was beautiful, simple, and unstained. He had expected anything else, especially ruin and condemnation.

Auroch's rhythm took him as the women of Apieron's life walked through his mind. His mother Astir, magical and remote. Cynthia of the vale, helpful and wise; and the Sybil, herald and prophetess. Both slain. Melónie, his garment against the cold, reaved from him. Apieron thought of his dark other, but it must bide for now. Lastly, Buthard's face came to him, thick with the slow malice of a betrayer.

The man is dead. I shall think of you no more.

With a barely audible resonance that matched the voice of the Falls, Apieron began to sing—a paen as had his ancestors when the world was young and their singing wove spells of wonderment. Apieron chanted forlornly of man's primordial humility in the face of great unknowns. He cried the losses one must bear, mortal and alone under enduring heavens, and finally, he sang the godhead's flicker, fanned by courage to become the conquering flame of destiny, of poets and warriors, craftsmen and wise women, of mothers and kings.

A woman's voice answered his. Isolde came and took his hand. For a space, they watched the cascade of white and dark. Apieron's song rose a final time:

"Her high-lilting voice nestled in water's flow and sang in trees. E'er I sought it. Never came I to her, or in the end, my Melónie to me."

Apieron looked at Isolde's face. A fillet bound her hair. "Beyond my guilt and anger, there is this. I simply miss her."

"I know."

Apieron studied her. "You travel swiftly."

"And you, slow," laughed she. "You should know that a high priestess of Wisdom does not reck of distance and time as do others." Isolde led him over the Fall's rim to a place he had never been, and Auroch's voice faded. The sky grew light where they stood a high place. Wind waves rushed up the forested belly of the hill, and rippling treetops brought a mighty soughing that surged off the granite. Up and over them it passed, up and away to the tor's darkling shoulder, draped by mists. The air grew still, for here there were no birds, and squirrels were abashed. Hand in hand, they saw a white-flowered dogwood, the first promise of spring, its twisted bole dark and perfect.

Apieron kissed her lightly. "I will love you always, to care and protect. As a sister you shall be to me."

Isolde searched his face, and a slight smile found her lips. "Perhaps."

THE GEHULGOG

On the mountain, it was cold, yet neither of the two persons who stood there seemed to mind the wind that tugged their garments, for it was a free wind. From the distance grew a speck that became a winged horse, gold and swift.

"*Ingold*?"

"Yes," Giliad laughed. He stopped abruptly, startled to hear such a sound. "Thir told you?"

"Yes."

"Come." The long white hand was proffered. Alcuin took it in space.

Ingold neighed as her filmy mane shook free. Elf and man mounted, and the horse sprang forth. Over ice-draped mountains, her flashing coat merged with the rays of a new sun, and although his companion was blind to see, a faint coloring of gold found again the hair of Giliad Galdarion.

WINDHOVER

Windhover lay under the next gentle ridge. Apieron kept a late vigil and pondered the night entire how he would go there on the morrow. That morrow now hovered in the east, but his legs remained leaden. He chided himself, afraid of something. "Xephard," he whispered, "lend me your courage."

"His star has gone into the darkness, my friend. It will rise no more."

Apieron turned. Well he knew that voice, for Galor was there. Side by side they stood in the chill predawn. Already the sky paled eastward, now deep blue rather than sable, a faint yellow tinging a horizon of deep forest hills. Overhead, the morning stars gleamed bright, and lo! One light soared the vault, a lonely meteor that disappeared close into the growing light.

"Ever are you eloquent, Galor Galdarion." Apieron smiled sadly.

"That may be, but yonder was no device of mine." The tall elf touched Apieron's wounded shoulder. There was no pain. "You have grown. Through darkness you have passed, and darkness remains before you. Yet I think your journey done for now." Apieron did not reply as the elf released him, turned to the west, and faded.

Apieron gazed for a time at the coming dawn. Night's deep colors yielded to a rising splendor of gold and scarlet. He wandered aimlessly, chiding himself for this last apprehension of a homecoming, after a year's toil to that very end. *The Year of the Dragon.*

Some distance ahead, Apieron spied a game trail that wove amongst boulders to the low hills beyond. His feet carried him until the path bent to follow the direction where the star descended and where the little trail mounted a hillock. The knoll's head was bare excepting a jumble of stone blocks that stood like a rough altar, natural or otherwise. Perhaps some Eldar people had worshipped here. There were many such fains in these ancient hills of Foslegen. The place bore no taint of evil and seemed a splendid place to greet Holy Sun.

Apieron whirled, cursing his inattentiveness as he whipped forth the crooked bow. An imposing figure stood before the altar. It was a man, tall and strong, with a naked blade in one hand and a wooden rod in the other. A weave of laurel-bound, thick brown locks and a simple tunic hung from one muscular shoulder.

Astonished, Apieron let fall his bow. The man stepped forward on golden sandals to face him eye to eye. He began to sing.

Hail Apieron, son of Renown. Mighty is your arm.
Truth before your eyes! Of thy valor, I have sung
before the Godhead, shining and ever young.

"Nay, father," Apieron said softly, nearly breathless with sudden wonder and confusion. Bowing his head, he pretended to look for his discarded weapon.

"My son," said Xistus smiling, stowing the sword and rod somewhere within his garment. He reached and took Apieron's hand between his own, raising him. "Bow not, gentle warrior. Today, I honor thee. You will not be forgotten."

To Apieron's surprise, Xistus lowered to one knee before him and proclaimed, "Hail Apieron, beloved of heaven." This he said three times before rising and stepping back to admire the confused warrior as a proud father does his son.

Dark eyes watched the twain as a sighing wind swept the hillcrest where Apieron and Xistus stood exchanging intimate words.

Henlee felt nervous whenever Apieron wandered alone. Xistus he knew of old; nonetheless, he shuddered at the sight of a man who did not die but passed into the twilight realm where no dwarf had been. Henlee saw Xistus raise his hands in final salute and embrace Apieron, then stride into a bright glow around the altar.

Apieron stood blinking into the morning breeze. Henlee shifted uncomfortably and turned to meet him further along the trail, telling himself that Apieron was safe enough even with disappearing elves and haphazard Olympians popping out like kettle corn.

Henlee sped up. He did not wish Apieron to see him waiting and worrying so. "'T isn't moot," grumbled the dwarf, "damned wind stings the eyes."

Apieron stooped and gathered something. He inhaled the clay of Windhover, musky, fruitful, decayed, and rich. He cast it from him. Air expelled with a sigh, he turned to Setie. "We are home."

Her face beamed like that of a nymph newly created by the gods. She gathered her siblings in spindly girl's arms. Setie, Ilacus, and Jillia rushed him, rubbing and poking without cease. Apieron was glad he had shaved.

"We love you, Daddy."

Beyond their heads pressed into his neck, Apieron smiled at the sun. His god raced a golden chariot across sky's azure bosom. A tear hung on an eyelash, turning the world to a warm comfortable haze.

The End

Index of Names

Ascupundi, choleric giants of Kör
Adestes Malgrim, Kör's Malesh
Aerald, winged steeds of the Liflyne elves
Aetterne, daughter and consort of Aurgelmir
Agelos, the embryo star
Alcuin, Savant of Kör
Alkdog, Iz'd Yar's bodyguard
Amber Hall, renamed the Axe Grind
Amor, kingdom of gold elves
Anheg, border mountains of northern Ilycrium
Apieron Farsinger
Arzshenk, bull-visaged monsters of the Abyss
Astir the Evoker, Apieron's mother
Aurgelmir, Lord of Tiamat's bastion
Auroch, Falls of Voices
Axebreaker, Henlee's ebon shield
Axylus Thunderhoof
Azgod, half-demon rulers of Kör
Baemond Candor, Gault's grandsire, the Old Marshal
Bagwart, Henlee's forgemaster
Bardhest Redhand, King of Uxellodoum
Balverk, war chief of dwarves of Kör
Baudalino, Gault's squire

Belagund Candor, Gault's adopted father
Betelgeuse Candor, Gault's great-grandfather
Berich and Astorath, Iz'd Yar's younger sons
Bestrand, coastal city-state, Ilycrium's closest ally
Bishop's Gate
Black Hogstyrgger, the white ogre
Boneslayer, Gilead's eldritch stave
Boug, Vur leader
Braegelor, Isander's charcoal destrier, later ridden by the King of Ilycrium
Bragen, leader of Liflyne folk
Briesis, Sybil of Western Lands
Brockhorst, police lieutenant of Sway's city guard
Buthard, son of Wulstane of Wicklow
Bump, Henlee's mighty burro
Byrinae, Dunstan's wife
Cani, Eirec's leman
Celadon the Mighty, site of river battle
Cocytus, the final pit
Cur Quan, title for hetman of Mgesh
Cusk, young peasant foot soldier
Cynewulf, tribal leader of Gaxe
Cygunddfel, dragon-son of Tiamat
Cynthia, Donna of the Vale
Dexius, Minister of Sway
Dorclai Translucia, the Grey Lady, Dorclai Trazequintil
Dream Throne, Living Throne of Tyrfang
Drudges, underdwellers of Kör
Drust, Lord of Waters, Champion of Amor
Duner, Apieron's castellan at Windhover
Dunstan, slow-speaking farmer soldier
Duskbridge, the Matog, the Skyfall Gate

Eafora and Scipflot, names put on Aetterne
Eirec of Alkeim
Erasmus, known as Black Merlin
Exeter the Hawk, Seneschal of Ilycrium
Farceps, Capital of Prebanks, the Saad Isles
Fafnir, Ring of the Dragon
Farstriker, Tallux's famous bow
Fogleaf, Liflyne home
Foslegen, forest nigh Windhover
Fuggo, dwarven captain
Fuquit the Fat, merchant captain of Farceps
Galen Trazequintil, son of Galor
Galor Galdarion, the Golden Elf
Gargantuel, the Eternal Watcher at Sky Gate
Gault Candor, Prince of Ilycrium
Gaxe, Ilycrium's Eastern tribesmen, Gerales highlanders
Gehulgog, prison mines of Kör, named Archwaze by Azgod
Gerales, mountains of Final Battle
Geyfylla, Nordic Barbarians of Amber Hall
Ghaddur, fiend of the Pit
Ghar, the khan who rode not to war
Gilead Galdarion, formerly of Amor
Gommish, king of Mgesh
Gonfolon, the sword
Gor du Roc, Duke of Ilycrium, Gault's birth father
Gorganj, high country above the Haunted Vale
Gorgon of Hel, manifestation of Ulfelion
Goz, Iz'd Yar's half-Azgod/half-Ascapundi general
Gray Ess, the Western Sea
Grazmesnil, eldest earthbound dragon
Gugnir, Sarc's twisted spear
Haunted Vale, the Starfall Valley

Hel, plane of Tiamat's imprisonment
Henlee, the Black Dwarf
Hyllae, Valley of the Twin Gods, the Holy Vale
Iblis, Emperor of Kör
Icing Flow, a glacier river
Igwain, Galor's unicorn stallion
Ilacus, Apieron's son, middle child
Ilycrium, land of the Sea Kings
Ingold, Gilead's Pegasus
Isander, Paladin of Wisdom
Iskhtmanur, Master of the March—the Army of Brass
Isolde, warrior-priestess
Iz'd Yar, Kör's great marshal
Jamello, Rudolph Mellor
Jillia, Apieron's youngest daughter
King Dryas of the Malave
Klea, a noble of Ilycrium, leader of the battalion of women
Kör, empire ruled by Azgod
Körguz, capital of Kör
Khôsh, servants of the Gate
Lampus at Hyllae, Temple of Wisdom
Leitus, Xephard's great sword
Liflyne peoples, winged elves
Llund, Hel's East Fort
Lylwelvyn, river en route to Sky Gate
Malave, Greenwolde of Ilycrium's wood elves
Malvoisen the Ghaddur, brother to Bolechim
Matog, the Duskbridge
Melónie, wife of Apieron
Mgesh, steppes riders of Kör
Mogush, slave city of Panj
Nogaret, king's vicar at Bishop's Gate

Ohm Runemaker
Orrustudale, the battle valley
Ozur, greatest land of the Mgesh
Panj, land of the Khôsh, servants of the Gate
Pilaster, Grand Faquir, Kör's Magnus
Pleven Deep, the Dragon Rift
Prebanks, the Saad Isles
Quas, celestial beings
Rel, dwarven general in Saemid
Renault, chevalier of Ilycrium and First Knight
Rhoccuus, shaman of Mgesh
Rudolph Mellor, also known as Jamello, and Edshu the Jongleur
Sadôk, demon apes
Sadszog, creature of the Abyss
Saemid, Henlee's secret redoubt
Sandos, wrestling champion at Lampus
Sarc, Liflyne elf druid
Seamus, Gault's bodyguard
Seod, Western hillmen of Ilycrium
Setie, Apieron's eldest child
Shabla, underchief of Ascupundi
Shaxpur of Tyrfang, Azgod officer
Sisteros, Commandant of Kör's Royal Marines
Skegga, overlord of Ascupundi
Sky Gate, on Heimhill
Snake of Kör, military legion of approximately six thousand soldiers
Starfall Valley, the Haunted Vale
Strumfyr, also called Farstriker, Tallux's mighty bow
Sujita, Apieron's youngest, Little Jilly
Sut, Tallux's warhound
Sval, river north of the Gorgonj

Sway, Ilycrium's capital city
Swaymeet, royal palace at Sway
Swaywynde, Sway's harbor river
Tallux, half-elvin scout
Tannhauser, Eric's captain of Northrons
Tartarus, the Hel of Tiamat's imprisonment
Telnus, Ranger of Windhover
Templars, guardians of the Vale
Teucer, officer of Ilyicrium
The Far Darter, the Healer, brother to Wisdom
Thir, a Drudge
Thyrmgjol above the Nostrand, Shore of Corpses
Tiamat the Beast, Mother of Dragons
Tizil, imp of darkness
Trakhner, General of Ilycrium
Turpin the Fallen, High cleric of Sky
Tyrfang, Iblis's palace in Körguz
Uglich, chieftain of Seod
Ulfelion, Prestidigator of Hel
Uxellodoum, fastness of Western dwarves
Varkold, coastal northland
Vergessen, centaur chief in Foslegen
Vigfus, spaedam come to the Waelstow
Vilmar, Second in Command of Kör's Marines
Vodrab the Foul, Makis of Kör's march
Vur, fabled herdsmen of Ilycrium
Waelstow, the battle gathering
Waelwolf, Eirec's sword
Wgend race, Ilycrium's ruling caste
White Throat, the Vigfil Stair to Kör
Wiglaf, infantry sergeant
Windhover in Foslegen

Windstrong, Tallux's steed
Wisdom, Goddess of the Vale
Wodensteel
Wulfstane of Wicklow, Apieron's neighbor
Wyrnde, great swamp below Foslegen
X'fel the Accursed, the Dog Star
Xephard Brighthelm, Wisdom's perfect warrior
Xistus Farsinger
Yggdrasil, the World Tree

Printed in the United States
By Bookmasters